men in black

men in black

a novel by

Scott Spencer

ALFRED A. KNOPF   New York   1995

THIS IS A BORZOI BOOK
PUBLISHED BY ALFRED A. KNOPF, INC.

Copyright © 1995 by Scott Spencer

Library of Congress Cataloging-in-Publication Data
Spencer, Scott.
Men in black : a novel / by Scott Spencer.
p.   cm.
ISBN 0-679-43452-6
I. Title.
PS3569.P455M46   1995
813'.54—dc20   95-2669
CIP

Manufactured in the United States of America

First Edition

5/95   B+T   12.67

for Celeste

men in black

chapter one

i am an early riser. Daylight and a sense of all that I have left undone pull me from sleep, and once I have parted the dark curtain there is no going back. Sometimes I patrol the house, in some vague way protecting my loved ones. Sometimes I watch the children sleep. But more often, perhaps, than I should, I roll next to my wife, Olivia, and court her sleeping body.

This morning, I had awakened from dreams of sex, and with full prior knowledge I would not be winning any popularity contests with this gesture, I nevertheless turned toward Olivia and pulled her close. She wore a cotton nightgown, ankle length; she took care to keep herself warm, even wore socks to bed. That used to drive me crazy, but now I sort of liked it; there was something a little wonderful about making love to a woman who was wearing kelly-green mid-calf socks.

Olivia's nightgown had responded to the static electricity of our flannel sheets and hiked itself up during the night. Her loins presented themselves to me, scalding. I kissed her forehead, stroked her hair. Tenderness was in a sense a disguise for lust, but I felt it, too; it was a lie I meant.

"Olivia?" I whispered.

"What time is it?"

"I dreamed about you, all night."

She opened one porcelain-blue, bloodshot eye. Her hair was in her face; a few strands of it had gotten stuck into the moisture at the corner of her wide, pale mouth. She had dark brown hair, thick, Jewish, like my mother's, though that was the only physical similarity between the two women. Olivia was tall, ivory, barely breasted, while my mother had been short, full, gnarled—put a black dress on her and she would have looked like one of those Sicilian widows on Mulberry Street.

"I want to sleep," Olivia said, her voice an untuned cello.

A few months ago, Olivia had calculated that in our sixteen years of marriage, I had deprived her of an average of two hours of sleep a night, totaling 11,688 hours since the first night of our honeymoon in Mexico, which came to 1,461 full nights of sleep. "You've deprived me of about four years of sleep," she'd said, "and that doesn't even count when we were dating."

" 'Dating'? We never dated. I hate that word."

Because Olivia and I wanted a bit of erotic privacy (or at least I did), our son, Michael, who had always been a little sexually curious about us, now slept as far from our bedroom as our old Colonial house would accommodate. A warm breeze rattled the thick, glazed windows and I walked down the second-floor corridor, going from east to west, past our daughter's room, who slept deeply, innocently, and who could not be kept too far from us because, even at nine, she still sometimes awakened in the middle of the night and came looking for us. Then I went down a half-set of stairs that led to a dead-end landing, once a maid's room and now our son's.

The early light touched the glass of the wall sconces; the glass rims of the shades shone red. *My* lamps, *my* sunlight, mine, mine, I thought. After a lifetime of renting, I was amazed to own anything.

The walls recently had been decorated with family photographs (it had been Olivia's response to Michael's withdrawing from us): snapshots from birthday parties, mementos of family vacations, all standard nuclear-family memorabilia, though several mornings ago I had noticed something askew in several of them—my gaze was on Olivia, and Michael's was, too, while Olivia herself and little Amanda looked at whoever was taking the picture.

I opened Michael's bedroom door slowly, trying to keep the old hinges silent. His room's one window faced west, where only a neighbor's silty pond reflected the sunrise, and so Michael was still swathed in darkness. I stood there, barely breathing, letting my eyes adjust to the darkness. His room had been sliding into disorder for weeks, perhaps months. Clothes were strewn over the floor, where they commingled with candy wrappers, cellophane ripped from CD packages, and pennies, bottle caps, broken pencils, and those nihilistic, somehow arty comic books which he collected and never allowed me to criticize. "You do your kind of book and they do theirs," he'd say, but he clearly believed that the creators of X-Men and Lobo were operating with some greater integrity than his father. (He also believed these comic books were, or would be, worth a fortune, while my own work, clearly, couldn't even keep us in New York City, where Michael still longed to live.)

He was not terribly interested in what I wrote, read, or listened to on the stereo. That was fine with me—he could find his own culture. And he had never seemed like a child who took after me in very many ways: my feelings ran toward the sentimental, whereas Michael was empirical; I tried to get along with people, but he was a frustrated leader, a leader without followers, who had quit more games than he had won. When he was very young, we used to be able to share the first light together. On holiday by the ocean, we lay on the black cool sand and watched the stars gradually fade from the sky. At home in New York, we walked to a nearby bakery and ate the freshly baked croissants, the insides still warm, like pudding in our mouths. But when he got to be about ten he began sleeping late. On school days we had to rouse him out of bed, and on weekends he was a corpse.

Even in poky little Leyden, population four thousand, he slept with a pillow over his head—a nocturnal behavior learned in Manhattan, where he had to sleep through a constant cacophony. This morning the pillow had shifted and tottered and I could see his face pressed into the weave of his white bed linens. His mouth and nose were pushed to one side, as if his face were putty. He slept with one knee raised and the fingers of his hand wrapped around the slats of his pine headboard like the grip of a prisoner around the bars of his cell. He slept in his clothes, and often would not change them for days: he kept his aroma close to him to lessen anxiety, to create a wall behind which he remained private, like a ghetto kid walking through a hostile middle-class neighborhood with a boom box howling on his shoulder.

Michael's grievances against me, though painful to me, who longed to be liked, had generally been predictable, manageable—he faulted my temper, my unfairness, strictness, quack quack quack. But since our move to Leyden, he had come to romanticize his life back in New York, misremembering it in ways that accused me of plucking him from Paradise. Michael's rendition of life in the city included only the highlights, stitched together in a way that made it appear that the Pearl Jam concert, Eddie Rosenberg's birthday party at the Hard Rock Cafe, Carol Tang's appearing at our door one evening because her parents weren't home and she'd lost her keys, and a steam pipe exploding beneath Perry Street, which reduced us to candlelight for three days, had all occurred in one blissful burst, one event after the other, with no longueurs between.

I crept closer to him. He was still small enough for my hand to fit over the top of his head like a yarmulke. "Want to make a slop omelette?" I asked, not altogether softly. But he slumbered on, great oceanic waves of unconsciousness rolling over him.

Those slop omelettes came from better times than these. When Michael was six and Amanda was still in her crib, we cooked together on the weekends, preparing breakfast in bed for the love of our lives, Olivia. Michael would stand on his Woody Woodpecker stool next to the stove in our cramped and sunless Perry Street kitchen. A slop omelette might contain cheese or salami, olives or green peppers; it might, when Michael called the shots, even have a gumdrop or two. As he grew older, his techniques became more sophisticated, if not his taste. He learned how to pour a stripe of Hershey's syrup down the spine of the finished omelette and then stick the whole thing beneath the broiler for a moment or two, and he also developed the theory that if you put any citrus fruit into the eggs it would cut down on the cholesterol by fifty percent.

And then, one day when he was about thirteen, we presented Olivia with her Saturday breakfast in bed and we sat perched on either side of her while she ate. Michael talked to her about something he had seen on TV—he liked the old shows, the dumb comedies thirty years old, which seemed interesting and ironic to him, relics of the past—and then he happened to notice that my hand rested in the no-man's-land of burgundy blanket between the spread of his mother's legs. His face colored; his eyes turned to ice. He felt the casualness and the constancy of my access to Olivia as a door slamming in his face. It was not the last time we made breakfast together, but soon after that the ritual began to falter and fade, which was somehow a more painful demise—I kept thinking those slop omelettes might kick in again.

I left him there, asleep. Looking back on it now, I cannot help but wonder what might have changed if I'd simply torn the covers off of him, lifted him in my arms with the strength

I still had, and—and? And what? I was filled with the mere preludes to solutions. I had a dozen ways of saying "Now listen here . . . ," but I had nothing after that.

I walked down the corridor, past the faintly unreal family photos, and down the steps. Like most old houses, this one whispered to me whenever I was alone: "You could spend fifty thousand dollars fixing me up and no one would ever know."

I went to the kitchen. It still smelled of last night's fish-and-broccoli dinner—having such a large kitchen had made us a bit lax about cleaning up, just as having an extra room had decreased our will to patch up little marital disputes. I took the teakettle off of the electric stove and shook it to see if any water was left in it. Having my own house, heating it myself, assuming responsibility for its repair and upkeep, drawing water out of my own well, had revealed in me unexpected compulsions toward frugality (which I could more or less disguise as ecological awareness). The kettle was empty, and I held it beneath the tap and listened as the water thundered in. I turned up the thermostat to a bearable sixty-two and then sat at the table and stared out the window.

Now that we lived in the country and the sky (rather than that dome of smoke and light that capped Manhattan) seemed a part of our life, I often looked up at it—for signs of weather, to try and remember the names of the different kinds of clouds, to watch the migrations of the birds, and to see if alien spacecraft might be in the area. This last, admittedly foolish, preoccupation was a product of (yet another) book I had recently published, under a pseudonym. The book was called *Visitors from Above*, and it was a basic, standard primer on UFOlogy, with one added feature, encouraged by my publisher: near the end, the book stoops to prophecy, boldly predicting that by the end of the millennium the earth will be visited by dozens and perhaps even hundreds of beings from Deep Space. I wrote the book because I couldn't make a living writing what I would like to and I didn't have the financial cushion to even dare. The meager advance they gave me for *Visitors from Above* was the bird in the hand, and the novel I would have liked to attempt and which, if it succeeded, might bring me a decent wage and a little respect, was mere faint twittering in a very thorny bush. And though writing *Visitors* did not convert me to the UFO religion, it did leave me with a fantasy of escape. Wouldn't it be something if a silver obelisk descended through the trees beyond my kitchen window, the rays of its landing lights pouring down like organ music through the early-morning fog? I had a wife and two children sleeping upstairs—and now, suddenly, the teakettle began to scream—but there were times when my life felt so hollow, so insubstantial that being abducted and whisked to the edge of the galaxy seemed every bit as good an idea as going through a second forty years as the man I was.

I lifted the kettle off the stove and its whistle faded within it, like the sound of a siren getting further and further away.

No spacemen took me away. The morning passed and by noon Amanda was at dance class, Olivia was out scouting attics and barns in her new capacity as a buyer for a New York antiques dealer, and I had driven Michael the five miles into town for his weekly appointment with his therapist, Bruce Pennyman. Pennyman did not inspire confidence, at least not mine; but the town's senior shrink, an old snob called Bronson Cavanaugh, who wore tweeds and had the demeanor of one of those drawing-room psychologists in an Agatha Christie mystery, was reputed to be pill happy. Half his young patients ended up on antidepressants, and quite a few ended up in the formerly grand river houses that were now private psychiatric hospitals. Pennyman might not be state-of-the-art when it came to psychotherapy, but his not being a medical doctor meant he could not give Michael drugs, and he was also unlikely to refer Michael to a hospital. All I wanted was for Michael to grow up, get to college.

I parked the car in the lot behind the bank and walked with Michael toward Pennyman's office. We had been wordless in the car—he had his mother's dexterity with silences, could texture them, make them spin like tops.

"I'm going to run a few errands while you talk to Pennyman," I said to Michael. The sun seemed to tilt forward like a face over a crib.

"Talking to Pennyman," he said, shaking his head. "Some conversation."

"It's not supposed to be like an everyday conversation."

"What do you know about it? Have you ever seen a psychiatrist?"

"No. Not yet."

"Well, you should." He looked at me for the first time all day. I was surprised by the lack of anger in his expression. He seemed to be scrutinizing me.

We were walking through Leyden's complex of ball fields—baseball diamonds with their generous backstops, football fields with H's in the end zone, soccer fields with their goals shaped like immense oxygen masks, all of it orbited by a cinder jogging track like one of the rings of grit around Saturn.

Today, the baseball diamond was full of activity. It was the Father 'N Son Baseball Tournament, sponsored by the Leyden Farmers and Merchants Bank, which also supplied donuts and little cartons of milk for the town's teens, who the board of directors must have imagined were still connected to the simple things of life. I knew these were kids with condoms and Camaros, boys with mousse in their hair and hormonal treachery in their hearts. Still, here they were, Saturday morning, suited up in jeans and T-shirts, challenging on the manly battlefield of sports the accountants, cops, contractors, plumbers, and IBM technicians who were their fathers. How had they all remembered that today was the day of the game? In our house, PTA meetings, dentist appointments, school concerts all tended to disappear behind the fog of our collective forgetfulness, an amnesia that included only the practical matters of life, and nothing emotional: grudges, for example, were written in stone; slights were matters of legend.

"We should be in this game," I said, gesturing toward the field.

"What about therapy?"

"What better therapy in the world is there than a clutch hit with men on base?"

"Right."

"I mean it," I said, as if this were a tenet of personal belief that went deep in me, though it had just struck me a moment ago.

"I don't get clutch hits with men on base," said Michael. "I strike out."

"Not necessarily."

"If I'm even chosen."

"There weren't that many games in the city," I said.

"There's not that many games here, either, Dad." He had long before turned the word "Dad" into a piece of verbal irony, the punch line in some sad running joke.

It had rained that night, and the ground as we crossed the park was still mucky; the mud slurped at our heels. Facing the park was Broadway, a two-lane blacktop with a bright center line, with the playing fields on one side and a row of Federal-style brick buildings on the other. The historical correctness of Leyden wasn't the result of preservationist instinct but of economic doldrums. No business in town could afford new construction, and so they made do with these pleasing antiques.

Michael could not bear to look at this street, which had as

much relation to his Broadway, the real Broadway, as Athens, Georgia, has to the home of the Parthenon. I hadn't anticipated how much Michael would contrive to miss New York.

"Look at this place," he said to me. "What are we doing here?" Michael had his hands dug into the pockets of his overly large Army fatigue jacket, which he had bought at a surplus store last year on the real Broadway. He said it had once belonged to a soldier killed in Vietnam. I'd never stopped to decide if that was true or something he said to tweak the remains of my student radicalism.

"What would you be doing if we were still in New York?"

"Being in New York."

"Anything else?"

"I don't know. Hanging with my friends."

I let it stand, though in fact the only friend he had at the time of our move was Oliver Green, a fat boy in skintight pants and a coconut-oiled pompadour, with whom Michael haunted the used-comic-book stores and watched TV. Michael might remember it otherwise, but the truth was he had been bored silly with and by Oliver. There were times when they were so idle they made cakes and cookies together; I had even found them one Saturday afternoon napping in our living room, with Oliver sacked out on the sofa and Michael snoring lightly in our armchair, with his hands folded in his lap.

"You've always hated my friends," Michael said.

"That's not true."

"It's not like your friends are so great. You think they're so special because they write for some magazine or work in an art gallery. Well, I don't think they're so great."

"Any friend of yours is a friend of mine, Michael," I managed to say.

"Remember that woman Nadia?" he said to me, as we stopped and waited for a break in the traffic on Broadway.

A truck was passing, hauling a prefabricated house wrapped

in clear plastic. The noise was such that I couldn't discern if he was mentioning Nadia with any particular emphasis. His eyes avoided mine.

"What about her?"

"I remember when she came to our house. She was trying so hard to be friendly. It was embarrassing."

"I thought you liked her."

"Well, I didn't."

"Well, there you have it. I don't think she'll be visiting again."

"Yeah," said Michael, looking at me, smiling. "Probably not."

I felt a shimmer of danger, but then it passed—no: what passed was my consciousness of it. I looked up through the overhang of maple branches to see if Pennyman's second-floor window was visible from where we stood. I didn't want him looking at us.

"Did you see where they're doing *Macbeth* over at the college?" I said. "Maybe we should check it out? You always liked Shakespeare. Even as a little kid—you never had any trouble with the language. You understood it better than most adults, actually."

Michael looked at me, an expression that was not quite his own on his handsome, sallow face. It had been printed over his features by the television set, burned into his pliant young flesh like a laser tattoo. The expression on Michael's face was that sitcom look that meant "Are you nuts or something, Dad?"

But why did that sour, trumped-up, secondhand grimace, with its failed irony, its lack of respect, its third-rate derisiveness, make me want to gather my son in my arms? I longed for Michael's touch; it was almost like yearning for the embrace of a lover. In fact, I did not know how to love without touching; I was a failure at all the world's principal religions for precisely this reason. My version of fatherhood was tactile. I was a head patter, a hair ruffler, a lap puller-onto, a good-night kisser. Amanda still put up with me, but Michael had been dodging my touch for years, and now I was emotionally inarticulate, dumbstruck. I was caught between the language of being father to a boy and father to a man. I was like poor Kerensky, who came to America after the Bolsheviks booted him out of Moscow and who never learned to speak decent English and who eventually forgot his Russian and died unable to speak to anyone.

"How come you bring me here and Mom doesn't?" he asked, as we stood before the door to Pennyman's building. I looked through the window; the steep staircase rose before us like an object in a dream.

"No particular reason. You know she works on Saturdays."

"Why does she have to?"

"Work?"

"She hates what she does."

"I think she finds it quite interesting. Anyhow, we all have to make compromises to pay the bills. That's civilization and its discontents."

"If she was my wife, I wouldn't want her to do something she didn't want to."

"You are free to discuss that with Pennyman," I said, smiling—though why I thought Michael would find that amusing is now unclear to me.

"I know things about you," he said.

"Really?" I opened the door for him, made an After You gesture, a deep bow, a sweep of the arm. When there's nothing else to serve, there's always a little leftover ham.

"Did you hear what I said?" Michael said, stepping over the threshold, the wood brown and fat from a century of repaintings.

"Yes. You know things about me." What sort of things? Yet I was putting it together. The claim that he would be a better husband to Olivia than I was, the mention of Nadia . . .

We walked up the narrow staircase. It was so steep I held the banister, but then I let go, scolding myself. Gestures like that speed the aging process, like getting a suitcase with those little wheels.

"Ah, there you are," said Bruce Pennyman, emerging from the water closet at the top of the stairs. He closed the door behind him and rubbed his hands together. We heard the roar of the toilet, penned like a porcelain beast inside the small bathroom.

It struck me every time how large Pennyman was. He'd been an athlete in college, but somewhere along the way had gone sensitive. He had a large anarcho-syndicalist mustache, a bit of a paunch; his eyes glittered with intellectual insecurity.

"We're not late, are we?" I asked.

"No, no, not at all," said Pennyman. He barely glanced at me; it was part of the method. He wanted to make certain no kid ever felt the shrink and the parents were in cahoots. "Come on in, Mike."

He gestured Michael into the inner office. Maybe, I thought, as Pennyman closed the door, maybe Michael had not been born to be happy. Maybe the melancholia, the silences, maybe that's just who he is, and it cannot be any more easily repaired than having small bones, large eyes.

I stood in the waiting room and remembered the tone in Michael's voice when he said, "I know things about you." It was a mix of sorrow and satisfaction, with a certain smugness, too: power. I was not a man without secrets, by any means, secrets I was very committed to keeping. But then my attention drifted toward the window and the playing field beyond. The fathers were up in the Father 'N Son game. A stocky dad took a vicious cut at the ball, hit nothing, spun, and fell down.

I looked at the fish tank in the waiting room, blue and yellow tropical fish, almost lacking in dimension. They didn't disturb the torpid waters of the aquarium as they flitted beneath the pinkish fluorescent light; first they were here, then there, as if they were just pictures of fish randomly projected onto the water.

I left Pennyman's office. It was April, the first good weather since this Saturday ritual began, and it occurred to me I might take a nice stroll—"perhaps" fall by the local bookstore to see if anyone had bought my latest.

When I opened the door it was raining dandelion fuzz. The wind raked through every dandelion in town. The dandelion seed was everywhere and it was all at once. The dandelions seemed to explode in every yard, every driveway, vacant lot, garden, and sidewalk fissure in Leyden. If it had been cold it would have seemed like a snowstorm.

I walked down Broadway, through the curtain of seed. The great diffuse orgasm gave me a sense of solace, just as I took comfort in my own persistent desire, the feeling it gave me of being an animal, alive.

Little Christmas lights were still braided through the crowns on the maple trees; soon the leaves would cover the wires. I passed the crafts shop where the town's aging sewing-machine jockeys still shopped, the hardware store where they were closing out on red-enamel Swedish wood-burning stoves, and I waved through the glass to whatever shopkeeper made eye contact with me. I liked strolling through my dinky adopted home. I liked its manageability, and I really liked being recognized. Olivia said I had developed a Blanche DuBois complex, but taken down a few notches: rather than depending on the kindness of strangers, I was merely looking forward to the acknowledgment of passersby.

I was forty years old and had no idea what I was doing with my life, except fulfilling responsibilities—and the prospect of a life of obligation cultivated in me a bloom of boredom that not only leached its nutrients from the deepest layers of self but also shared a root system with rage. Yet it was not rage I felt as I walked through Leyden that afternoon. I was suddenly drunk with sadness, a sadness that had me practically stumbling as I passed young mothers pushing their amazed babies around in strollers, and the ten-year-olds on their garish bikes, and most especially the teenagers who hadn't gotten themselves roped into the Father 'N Son softball game, maladjusted and randy, bound together in tight precoital packs, the town's poor kids, living in shacks, trailers, dressed in hip-hop clothes, with studs in their ears, hoops in their noses, styling gel in their tiaras of hair.

How I loved them, how I momentarily loved them. I wanted to hold them, like a dying man who feels the world like silk running through his fingers. Spring engendered in me a feeling of bliss followed by a dark twist of dread; my heart was a seesaw with an angel on one end and a clown on the other.

I turned off Broadway and headed toward Oak, pelted by the feathery hail of dandelion spore. Molly's Books, my destination, was on one of the side streets that sloped toward the railroad tracks. Molly Taylor had once fondly hoped that people would buy a book or two from her before taking the two-hour train ride to New York, but the little magazine kiosk in the station more than satisfied the commuters' cultural yearnings, and Molly was always on the brink of Chapter 11.

Molly's Books was in a clapboard house built around 1920. It had a nice circular porch, which Molly used as her secondhand-book section. Inside, the light was bright but soft—Molly was seeing Len Ackerman, an electrician, and he'd fixed her up with pinkish track lighting.

Molly was at her post near the cash register, sitting on a three-legged stool, her knees drawn up beneath her long Liberty print skirt, the tops of her green leather boots balanced on the stool's wooden rung. She was reading something called *The Goddess Handbook* and looked up when my entrance rang the little bells above her door.

"Author, author," she said, smiling. Her red hair was in ringlets, and she had a cold, which put ringlets of red around each nostril.

When I first moved to Leyden, Molly had briefly considered me a sexual prospect, and my response was to pretend to a certain stupidity. This feigned lack of perception had somehow embedded itself in me, and I usually felt a little dense around Molly.

"Look around you!" Molly said. "Saturday afternoon and where is everybody? What a town." She shook her head; her hair swung back and forth. I wasn't sure if I'd ever actually touched her. Maybe her flirtatiousness was a mere hallucination on my part; maybe my libido was a lonely child conjuring imaginary friends.

"Did you see what's going on out there?" I said. "It's raining dandelion fuzz."

"And that's what makes this such a special place."

"Now you sound like Michael. He's so depressed. You know, I think life is essentially bipolar—you're manic when you're young, then you're depressed. Now he'll have to be manic when he's older and risk having a heart attack."

"He'll get used to it. Your wife's happy here, yes?"

"I suppose. She likes the birds, that kind of thing. The gallery she was running closed. It was time to leave. She likes her job with the antiques people. She has that bright red Subaru and a wad of twenties in her purse, like a gangster."

"I often wonder how it works—marriage."

"It doesn't," I said. "Turning love into marriage is like having the Unicorn Tapestry and using it as a tablecloth."

"But that sounds wonderful. That sounds exactly how a unicorn tapestry ought to be used."

"Maybe. So, how's *Visitors from Above* doing?"

"I hope Olivia gives you stern scoldings about wasting your talent on these crazy books of yours."

"Not really. We have to live, you know." I felt the color rising in my face. A spinner of Famous Author postcards was on the counter near the cash register. I looked at the faces of Mailer, Updike, Hemingway, Frost. All of my idols had become thorns in my side. "Anyhow, I haven't written a novel in years. Now, I'm just a hired gun, a hired cap gun, a pop gun—"

"Sam—"

"A flop gun."

"Sam, stop. Please." She fished a Marlboro Light from her purse. She lit up, exhaled a long lilac plume of smoke. "Are you familiar with the *Protocols of the Elders of Zion?*" she asked.

"Why? Is it selling?"

"Then you are."

"I may have told you my father was anti-Semitic, but not to that extent. We didn't read the *Protocols*, nor did we have *Mein Kampf* in the house."

"Let me tell you something about the *Protocols*, Sam. Millions of copies have been sold. And they still sell. Have you ever read them?"

"Why would I?"

"Henry Ford used to give them out with the weekly paychecks, during the old days at Ford."

"Wasn't there."

"A copy of the *Protocols* was found with the tsarina's body, in her country house, where she and her family were killed by the Red Army. Someone had sent her the book; it was probably unread—she barely read, you know. But being found with her body fueled the fires of Jew hatred and increased the book's reputation."

"What is it? It's a bunch of bearded, humpbacked rabbis

dressed in black, huddled together in some cemetery, discussing how to dominate Europe—right?"

"Something like that. But the point is—where did this so-called document come from?"

"God?"

"I'm serious, Sam. It came from a novel, written by a postal worker, who churned out books and was more or less paid by the word—he just wrote whatever popped into his head and wrote it quick because he always needed money."

"Is that what you think I do?"

"Listen to me. People believed it. It was written down. It became a fact."

"That certainly didn't happen to me with *Traveling with Your Pet.*"

"People are buying this one, though. I sold three on Tuesday, two on Wednesday, five on Thursday—"

"Are you serious, Molly?" I actually felt a bit faint.

"—and nine on Friday."

The book was, at its most responsible, a rehash of half-truths about extraterrestrials lifted from popular science magazines, weekly tabloids, and the "controversial" testimony of a few embattled professors from third-tier colleges. Yet even with these typical instant-book materials (just add exclamation points and mix) I still needed to make things up, at first to add a little drama and then for padding, since the deal with my publisher was for eighty thousand words and my first draft had hobbled in with a little over sixty thousand.

Just then, the sleigh bells over the door jangled and a woman in her sixties walked in with the aid of a stout black cane. She was large and vague; she looked as if she spent a great deal of time in bed, though unable to sleep.

"Hello, Pamela," Molly fairly sang. "I was worried that maybe you'd forgotten us."

"Well, to tell you the truth, Molly," Pamela said, as if to

gently but frankly share some extremely upsetting news, "my foot's been acting up."

"Oh, Pamela, I am so sorry to hear that."

I'd had no idea that Molly needed to pander to her customers like that; it made me feel very close to her, and I forgave her for her little lecture about the *Protocols*.

"We've gotten in a new shipment of mysteries," Molly said.

"Well, dear, what I came in for is that *Mysteries from Beyond*." She opened a greenish piece of paper torn from a stenographer's pad. "By John Retcliffe."

"Oh, you mean *Visitors from Above!*" said Molly. "Well, that's a popular item, I must say."

With a brief wink in my direction, she lifted the drawbridge contraption at the corner of the counter and beckoned Pamela to follow her down the store's center aisle, past the novels, past the gift books, and on to the section hopefully designated Hardcover Non-Fiction, though the bindings themselves were just pasteboard and the texts often as not a mere tissue of lies.

I walked toward Pennyman's office. Every so often, a spit of dandelion fuzz landed on my chest, my eyelashes, stuck to the corner of my mouth. Though the air was cold, there was a sense of summer—freedom, desire, boundless dreams.

But was it the air, or thoughts of my book and its little surge of sales? How I longed to stop worrying about money, to wheel a cart down the aisle of a supermarket without a calculator tapping in the middle of my skull. I wanted the fun of money, the comfort, and I wanted to never again have to write a book because the mortgage needed me to. I wanted to find out if what I once called my "voice" could ever be summoned again in the service of serious writing. And with money, I could move my family back to New York. Michael would like that.

Near Pennyman's, I noticed a boy called Greg Pitcher strolling down Market Street with a couple of other teenagers who'd been playing in the Father 'N Son game. Greg, fatherless, with a sad, hot-tempered mother whose own life was irregular, had been Michael's first friend in Leyden, and Michael had felt encouraged, even blessed by Greg's attentions. Greg had actually lived with us for a week. He was large, muscular, golden, and Michael fell in love with him the way teenagers often do, which meant he wanted to be Greg: he wore, for a while, Gregish clothes (blazers, loafers, pale yellow shirts), he started shaking hands with the people he met and addressing his elders as "sir." For a while, Greg's friendship gave Michael a kind of social pedigree, but unfortunately he wasn't able to parlay it into a wider social success.

"Hello, Mr. Holland," Greg said, making a long, graceful stride away from his friends and extending his powerful hand in my direction.

"Hello, Greg," I said—I felt shy, a little low on the pecking order around Greg. Michael's lack of status among the local teens was forcing me to relive my own.

"We missed you at the game, you and Mike," Greg said.

"The Mike-man," one of Greg's friends mumbled, giving me the sinking feeling that my kid might be the butt of some running joke.

"Yeah, well, so much to do, so little time," I said, hoping to convey that Michael had better things to do than to whack a softball around in a blizzard of dandelion fuzz.

"Yeah, well, maybe next time," said Greg.

"You ought to give Michael a call," I found myself saying. "I'm sure he'd like to see you."

"I just saw him," Greg said, a slight quiver of defensiveness in his voice. "In school, yesterday."

"Right." I nodded, giving myself a chance to switch over

into a better mode of behavior. Michael surely did not want his father matchmaking for him; I was only devaluing him in the eyes of these kids.

"Say hey for me anyhow," Greg said, smiling, reassured I would not press my kid's case any farther.

"I will." I squeezed my hand into a fist because I was not comfortable, not proud of what I was about to do. "And I'll tell him you'll give him a call." There. Done.

I climbed the steps to Pennyman's office. Michael was just coming out of the inner office, moving unsteadily, blinking like someone emerging from a theater, bouncing into the bright belly of the day.

He wore a sweatshirt bearing the name of his old high school back in New York. He looked frail, miserable, dispossessed. And my soul demanded of my intelligence that it come up with a plan, a word, a gesture that would break the spell under which Michael had fallen, and once again my intelligence came back with its tattered net empty.

"Perfect timing," I said.

Michael glared at me; his moods were all he had.

Pennyman followed behind Michael, looming.

"Hello, Sam," he said. "I wonder if I could have a word with you. I've already asked Michael and he said it's okay. Right, Mike?"

Michael made a gesture of assent so minimal that it held within it the grounds for its own denial.

I followed Pennyman in, but before the door closed I turned to Michael and said, "I ran into Greg. He says he's going to give you a call." Michael looked back at me with utter dismay.

I sat in an old rose-colored chair and Pennyman sat at his desk. The windows were halved by venetian blinds; the bookshelves held scholarly books and examples of Eskimo art—scrimshaw polar bears, stone seals, Mongolian profiles hewn from jade. Pennyman slid a sheet of computer paper toward me. *L'addition, s'il vous plaît.* I glanced at it and noted with a deep unhappy jolt that we now owed him six hundred dollars.

"How's Michael making out?" I folded the bill in two, slipped it into my breast pocket.

"I'd like to start seeing him twice a week, Sam."

"Great."

"I would have suggested it before, but I didn't have any after-school openings. However, my Tuesday at four-thirty has terminated." He patted his black appointment book.

"I'll have to talk it over with Olivia," I said, but even as I said it I was thinking, No fucking way. Why did any of this have to be happening? Frustration bred fatigue. I felt some neuronal replica of myself curling up inside, closing its eyes.

"Of course," said Pennyman. "I understand these things are stressful."

"How does he seem to be getting along?" I asked. "To you?"

"How does he seem to be getting along to you?" Pennyman volleyed back, like an old tennis player bunting the ball back over the net.

I wanted to say: Look, pal, this shrink technique of turning the question around went out with the waterbed.

"I'm not sure," I said. "He seems melancholic. He's doing well in school, academically. But he keeps talking about how he misses New York, his friends, his life there. But the thing is, he wasn't really happy there, either." I sighed, as if I'd been holding my breath. "It's so awful."

"His unhappiness?"

"Yes." I looked at Pennyman. The tone of voice he used to say "His unhappiness" surprised, disarmed me. He sounded tender, real. A sudden tide of emotion scalded my face. "I love him. Of course."

"Of course."

"But I feel as if I've failed him, terribly."

"Sam, Michael wants you to know something." He let that sink in, and then continued. "He knows you are involved with another woman."

"I am?" For an instant, I actually believed in my own innocence.

"He found a letter to you, from a woman, a New York City woman, apparently a professional contact."

I just sat there. I could hear the white-noise machine Pennyman ran in the waiting room, a little black plastic blower shaped like a hair dryer.

"Oh, Christ," I said. I pressed my forehead.

"He has wanted to show this letter to Olivia," Pennyman said. "As you know, they have a special closeness. But I worry about the letter. In most households, a letter like this could have a devastating impact. Such an upheaval would have a very bad effect on Mike at this particular point of his treatment."

"His treatment? What about his life?"

"And his life," said Pennyman, not really conceding anything.

"What should I do?"

"I don't know. I have no degrees in advice."

"How very droll, Bruce."

"I'm sorry, Sam. I feel what this must mean to you."

"Is he going to blackmail me or something?" I was starting to unravel now, saying whatever occurred to me. That little border guard on the line between thought and speech had apparently passed out from the shock of Pennyman's news. "I can't let Michael become the dictator of my marriage. He can't have all this power."

"I suppose you could tell Olivia yourself, before Mike does."

He looked at his watch and shrugged apologetically.

Another patient would be on the way, and Pennyman was careful about his clients not crossing paths. It was a small town.

He walked me to the door. Coins and keys jingled faintly in his pockets.

Sudden sunlight exploded in the solitary window. A bit of dandelion fuzz rested on the outside of the air conditioner.

And then when Pennyman opened the door leading to the waiting room we were both silent. We looked, left and right. There were four empty green vinyl chairs, a copy of *Newsweek* dropped onto the mustard-colored carpet. Michael was gone.

chapter two

spent an hour searching around town for Michael, and then I checked the entrances to the thruway and the parkway, to see if he was on his way to New York. Finally, I drove home, wondering if he was already there and, if he was, whether he'd given Olivia the letter Nadia Tannenbaum had sent me. I wanted Michael to be there, but a stain of self-interest spread over my feelings, obscuring everything delicate in their design. There was a kind of undeniable convenience in having a chance to tell Olivia myself—but tell her what? I feared her reaction, her retribution; more than any other thing I feared her unhappiness. No matter how I told the story of my half-year affair with Nadia, no matter how sorry I was, Olivia would still rage, she would still weep, and she might even leave me.

Our house was two miles away from the center of town, on Red Schoolhouse Road. The red schoolhouse itself was gone; the road had been paved, widened, a double yellow line painted down the entirety of its three miles of curves. This was not the chicest spot in our little river town. Our flight from New York was a couple years too late to get in on the bargain prices. We had no view of the Hudson, no rolling fields, no caretaker's cottage, no princely privacy. Our nearest neighbor had a stone elf on his lawn and an aboveground swimming pool with a water slide—perfect for those sunset parties when the Whitmores "boogied" with their computer-programmer pals and got hammered on Canadian beer. They liked to drink Labatt's, and the private joke of their set was "Gimme another Labattomy!" On the other side of our house was an old farmhouse, slowly caving in like a mouth without teeth, lived in by two obese, suspicious brothers, who floated bottles on their pond and shot their necks off; the bottom of the pond was a foot thick in broken glass.

I pulled my dusty Dodge into the driveway and sat there for a moment, surveying my property. (I must have sensed my moments of repose were numbered.) The house was a beauty, a hundred and fifty years old. Its Protestant provenance impressed my tradition-loving, status-hungry, anti-Semitic father, he who married my Jewish mother and tormented her for his failure to become a working actor, while she fled from him, first into melancholia, then into catatonia, and finally into death. "Fine house, Sam, really first-rate, I'd live here myself," he said, after surveying it, carefully, walking around the place like some martinet, with a walking stick, wearing a tweed hacking jacket, an Irish woolen sweater, green rubber boots. It wasn't even that fine a house. It sat on a six-acre lot, three of them lawn, three of them marshy, a singles bar for raucous red-winged blackbirds. Yet it was not only the first house I had ever owned, it was the first house I had ever even *lived* in. I pushed the mower up and down the lawn, chanting "Mine, mine." I carried a picture of the house in my wallet, along with snapshots of Olivia, Michael, and Amanda.

I climbed out of my car and walked toward the house. Smoke poured out of the chimney. Ordinarily, Olivia making a fire was a good sign—a few logs in the hearth, a soulful wet kiss, a heightened sense of humor, that sort of thing—but today it wasn't what I wanted to see. I was hoping Olivia was not at home—after all, wasn't it Saturday? Weren't there auctions to attend, yard sales to scour, brittle-boned widows to fleece?

I mounted the stone steps to the front porch, and before I touched the door Olivia opened it for me. She peered questioningly at me. Had she had a premonition that her son was not entirely safe? Was she suddenly one of those Psychic Moms who wake with a gasp in the middle of the night at the very moment their soldier son falls dead on some besieged beach on the other side of the world, a woman in some pseudonymous quickie about ESP which I had not yet been reduced to writing?

Nervously, I kissed her on the cheek. She had such nice bones, lovely perfume, a little tug of glamour in every gesture.

"I'm sorry about this morning," she said, pulling me into the house. "I know how excited you feel when the sun comes up. Do you still feel that way?" She offered so much of herself through sex, it still made her blush.

"Is Michael here?" I asked her.

"No, that's why we have a little time," she said, still caught up in her erotic agenda. She wanted to make us close. Maybe she'd been standing at the window, watching the dandelion rain.

"He's not here?" I moved away from her, closed the door behind me. The opportunity for our being able to fall into each other was already past.

"No, and neither is Amanda. She's got a play date at Elektra's house. She may even spend the night."

"Elektra is a creepy little brat," I said, and then realized, from the way Olivia was looking at me, that I sounded insane. Elektra, in fact, was a mousy little born-again kid in a gray jumper.

"Sam!" said Olivia, with mock admonishment. In fact, she liked that semi-Tourette aspect of my conversation—she came from a household in which words were carefully measured, and every now and then my verbal recklessness tickled her.

I put my hands up in a gesture of surrender that was meant to be a little funny, and as I did the phone rang. We had a telephone right near the front door, on a little oak table, above which was a beveled mirror that held in its wavy surface the reflection of our pineapple-patterned wallpaper. (It was Michael who first noticed we had furnished our house as if it was the set for "Father Knows Best.")

I grabbed the phone immediately. "Hello?" I heard the anxiety in my voice and cleared my throat.

"Sam! It's Graham."

Graham Davis was my literary agent; he had never before called me on a weekend.

"Graham, I can't talk to you right now," I said. "Can I call you back later?"

"Oh."

"Soon."

"Well, actually, I'll ring *you* later, if it's all the same." Graham claimed he was continually hounded by crank calls—breathers, hang-ups—and he was selective about to whom he gave his home number.

"Okay, fine," I said. I hung up and looked at Olivia, who regarded me with some amazement.

"That was Graham Davis?"

"Yes."

"You just brushed him off."

"What of it?"

"It's odd. I mean, really, it's good. You always seem so anxious to hear from him. You complain about how long it takes him to return your calls." She smiled, as if I were some desperate little schmuck who finally discovered his own personal dignity.

"Look, Olivia," I said, "Michael should be here and I'm worried."

"Sam," she said. She had long before adopted the policy of discounting much of what I said. She liked to take about thirty percent off, except during quarrels, when I was marked down by half.

"I had a conference with Pennyman and when I came out Michael was gone."

"So? Maybe he just went out."

"No. I don't think so."

"Did you look for him?"

"Yes. He could be anywhere."

"He's probably in town."

"He hates town. In a world filled with things Michael hates, town is particularly loathsome. What if he's taken off again. Oh, Christ! I should never have moved him out here."

"You didn't. It was a family decision—and I think a good one. Your taking responsibility like that is just arrogance."

"Then I'm sorry." I wouldn't have minded a bit of marital discord. It would have made me feel a little less miserable for having recently spent six months in and out of Nadia Tannenbaum's bed. I readied for the battle like a certain kind of soldier, looking to it for protection from vaster anxieties.

"Let's just give it a little time, all right?" said Olivia. She came from a family that, unlike mine, did not take everything irregular as the harbinger of total catastrophe. Her childhood was a series of close calls. Pets mysteriously took sick and the next day were back on their paws again, tails flicking. Fevers spiked and vanished, wrists were broken but it could have been worse. Olivia's parents were academics, but their vacations were vigorous (hiking the Appalachian trail, biking through Scotland, a pilgrimage to Mexico to see the spot where Leon Trotsky was murdered) and their sabbaticals were downright dangerous (a Land Rover trip across Africa, six months in the Andes). Olivia had learned equanimity, she believed in Gaia, the name J. E. Lovelock gave to the entirety of creation, which he postulated was in a constant state of self-repair, and which would ensure that life on the planet continued, no matter what.

I went out again to look for Michael. Up and down the streets of our town. Nothing. I wanted to go into my office and try and figure out which of Nadia's letters he had, but, as yet, I did not dare.

When I returned home, we still had the house to ourselves, and we spread out as far from each other as we could get. After years of living in each other's pockets inside that walk-up on Perry Street, the relative spaciousness of a real house was quite a luxury—but, perhaps, a costly one: we could now spend hours, even days, virtually ignoring each other.

Olivia, who was still taking Michael's not being home as an *absence*, while I was more and more convinced it was a *disappearance*, went upstairs to a room where she kept track of her wheelings and dealings in the antiques trade. I poured myself a Scotch and water and sat in the small room on the north end of the house, in which the previous owners had installed the husband's dying father, and which was now my office. "This is where the magic happens!" I liked to say to city friends who came to see us, throwing open the door with a flourish and waving my hand toward the low-ceilinged, ten-by-ten room with a schoolboy desk, a swivel chair, an old IBM typewriter, and metal file cabinets.

Over the months, Olivia had bequeathed me the occasional antique, and by now my office was looking more like a study—the schoolboy desk was replaced by a wormy Colonial tavern table, the green wall-to-wall carpeting had been torn up and replaced by a chic threadbare Oriental carpet, an old Shaker butter churn stood in the corner, useless and decorative. Next to my writing table were a couple of tiers of lawyer's bookcases, the kind with the lift-up glass fronts, which held my birthday present from Olivia a few months before—leatherbound copies of my first two novels, the ones I still sentimentally thought of as my Real Books.

I picked up *Stops Along the Way*, the novel I wrote right before meeting Olivia, in which I gleefully cannibalized my own New York childhood, describing the damp, evil-smelling apartment I was raised in on the outskirts of Greenwich Village, and my sister Connie's wild, ultimately self-punishing sexuality, and my brother Allen's doggedness, planning his every step just so, in a lockstep toward dentistry, a pot belly, and a wife and five kids. Connie was called Denise, Allen was called Barry, and my father, Gil, was called Heinrich, a.k.a. Henry. All I did was move everybody up a letter; I didn't care who made the connections. I wanted them all to see themselves. I burned with the possibility that my novel would create a kind of Truth that would sear them, and me, too. And so I presented my father and his job at the United Nations and his night life as a failed actor, a man longing to impersonate others, to play a role, to be given a part, but denied at every turn, the song he longed to sing cut right out of his throat by an indifferent world—a world that saw him for exactly what he was: charmless.

But the real focus of the novel was my mother, Adele, whom I moved a letter back and called Zora. I described as a young man what I could not prevent as a boy: her long punishment for her husband's misery and her self-effacement that became self-erasure. Her soft voice getting softer, her body, face, eyes—all becoming softer and softer, until she became, as Mayakovsky would have it, a cloud in a housedress. We watched it happen; we looked away. Gil felt blocked from the stage by a conspiracy of crass, conventional Jews, and Mother was Jewish. He held it against her, terribly. And everything about her: her thick dark hair, her taste for herring, Rodgers and Hammerstein songs, her affection for him—he detested her adoration, her loyalty. It struck him as weak-minded.

"Opposition is true friendship," Gil used to say, though now that he was in effect a gigolo, he had probably changed mottoes.

I loved *Stops Along the Way*; it moved me, made me proud, and, really, the world had not treated it badly. It did not jog the planet from its customary orbit; there were no ads for it plastered on the sides of the Fifth Avenue bus. But it had been well reviewed, welcomed; it had evaded the death ray of silent indifference that kills most first novels. But it didn't make a dime. I had worked on it for three years and it scared me to think that, financially speaking, I would have had more to show for it had I been selling my plasma on a bimonthly basis. It was through *Stops* that I met Olivia, which I knew even then was a greater reward—if what I was really looking for was Fate's pat on the head—than a check in any amount; but she got pregnant so quickly that the reality of having to make a living became even more acute, which is to say oppressive.

I wrote a couple of quickies after that. The first was *An Intelligent Woman's Guide to Pro Football*, which furnished our third-floor walk-up on Perry. Then I wrote *Crystal Death*, about the health hazards posed by table salt, and that helped pay for Michael's birth and layette.

I often think about the ejaculation that started all of this. I am certain which one it was. We had been at a party, downstairs in our building, in the apartment of Ira Schuster, who had been such a sweet friend to us and who looked so virtuous in his gray suits and blue shirts, with his prematurely graying beard and dark eyes that registered the regular setbacks he suffered as a lawyer in the public defender's office. Ira not only drank to frightening excess but caused others to drink as well. They're called "enablers" nowadays, but back then we just thought of Ira as a good host; everybody got hammered and danced sweatily to old Edwin Starr records. Afterwards, Olivia and I stumbled up to our apartment, kissing and pawing at each other as we ascended, and by the time we let ourselves in Olivia had unbuttoned my shirt and her kisses were so warm and enormous, I could feel myself tumbling through them and into her: I felt she could swallow me body and soul, and I wanted her to. We undressed, we tore the blankets off the bed, because even though it was winter we were sweltering. The foreplay was over. We both wanted me inside of her; it seemed like an emergency. There was nothing fancy about it. I knew even as that ribbon of protein was pumping out of me that Olivia would get pregnant.

Often, I would rehearse suggesting to Olivia that we, as the phrase goes, terminate the pregnancy. We could not afford a child. I wanted her to myself. I despised fathers and I dreaded becoming one. But I said nothing of the kind. We took the infant Michael home from the hospital and sex and sleep were never the same. Michael howled like a pack of wolves in the wilds of his own colic. Olivia and I began quarreling: in those days, acrimony was the only exercise we gave our hearts; bickering took us through the paces that had once been led by love.

And then our families descended upon us. Olivia's parents, Sy and Lillian Wexler, flew in from Chicago, and brought so many baby presents they had to take separate cabs from Kennedy. Olivia's sister, Elizabeth, who had been interested in me for a moment and through whom I had first met Olivia, had moved out of New York shortly after Olivia and I were married but came in from Ohio, where she worked in the admissions office of an experimental college and where her job was to make people admit things, or so Olivia used to joke, in those prebaby days when a sense of humor was as free as the air. Next to arrive was Olivia's brother, Stuart, from whom she hadn't heard in two years, since he had moved to Houston to manage a hotel and had gotten involved with a Messianic Jewish cult. He deemed our union a mongrel marriage, but nevertheless news of Michael's birth sent him hightailing to Manhattan—all those Old Testament tales of who begat whom had made him a soft touch for procreation.

Our apartment was bursting with learned, argumentative Wexlers. Sy and Lillian were still tenured at the University of Chicago; they hung out with a lot of brilliant ex-socialist intellectuals, and their analyses of everything from Allende to the politics of nineteenth-century utopian Zionism were delivered with bite and sarcasm. Even the La Leche League was subjected to the rigors of the Wexlerian intellectual style—a style built on the assumption that the world was full of vanity, stupidity, and darkness, and that even those who would want to do good were lured into destructiveness by their own incomplete thinking.

When the Wexlers were exhausted, the Hollands came to relieve them of their adoration duties. My brother, Allen, came in from Massachusetts, looking as sleek and prosperous as a big, happy otter. Making a fortune filling teeth, he brought Michael a gag present of two pounds of white chocolate. He had already fathered a child, and he was pompous with his sense of having survived numerous domestic trials. When he held Michael, he slipped on a surgeon's mask, and when he gave me an (unasked-for) lesson in diaper changing, he quickly put on a pair of rubber gloves. Connie, for her part, was tearful, leaning over Michael's bassinet, weeping freely, the way people do when they are completely alone. She was between marriages, infertile, in her own mind doomed. At thirty, she looked fifty. She wore tight clothes despite getting heavy; she had puppet lines around her mouth; her eyes looked wounded, offended; her hair was colored the yellow of an old man's teeth. "Hello, mister" she said to Michael, through a vibrato of melancholy, like some poor old broad in a piano bar, "welcome to the good times."

There was a brief interval of time—a half-day, or it may have been just an hour—when Connie, Allen, and I felt pleased to be with each other, enjoyed the camaraderie of veterans from a distant war. But then Gil arrived, unfresh from a fact-finding mission in Panama City—he had by now been promoted to a rather responsible position in the UN Office of Economic Development, though he knew nothing of economics, cared little about industrialization or demographics, and, in fact, more or less despised Third World peoples. He was haggard, hollow-eyed, unshaven, gassy from the Panamanian cuisine. He came to us straight from the airport, blew in right past Connie, whom he hadn't seen in at least two years, nodded at Allen, whom he had seen a few months before at a conference at MIT, slapped me on the back, kissed Olivia, and then rubbed his hands together and said, "Bring me my grandson."

Having a child might not have been so unsettling if only other people in our circle of friends had children, too. But this was before my generation's procreative panic, and every writer, editor, sculptor, lawyer, tennis instructor, architect, music teacher, reporter, computer programmer, and Buddhist we knew was childless. I wrote, and made enough to keep at it full-time. Olivia at that time was putting together a folk art catalog for the Manhattan Museum. She wore beautiful dresses; we ate out whenever we chose to. Life was dinner parties, gossip, worries about careers and money, plans for holidays, sneering remarks about the President. It had all seemed (if not perfect, then at least) fine. It was what I had wanted all along: an apartment in the Village, a wife who loved me and believed in me and who, in those early days, was avid for me, mad. I had art, I had love, I had the name of an importer who sold wines from the *petits châteaux* for half of what they fetched at Sherry-Lehmann.

But now all I had was a child. He loomed over everything, casting his shadow. Life, at least our life, was too fragile to survive the onslaught of Michael's needs—his cries, his rashes, his sleeplessness, his abhorrence of having his diapers changed, his little stuffed nose, the narrow nostrils plugged with green, his eyes glittering with panic as he tried to howl and breathe through his mouth at the same time.

Our apartment looked like a dive within weeks. We were too tired to clean, too annoyed to even pick up after ourselves. And now we were dominated by his *things*. The mobile of rubber rabbits vaporized our books, the aqua-and-yellow rattle disintegrated our KLH stereo components, the Snoopy pacifier turned our wine to vinegar, and the bassinet curled the Brassaï prints right off the wall. And then came the diaper pail, white and plastic. For all its environmental awareness, it obliterated our Pakistani prayer rug, rusted my Olivetti, canceled my subscription to *The New York Review of Books*, it opened the window and scattered Olivia's folk art notes, and then extinguished every candle, candelabrum, candlestick, and, of course, every candlelight dinner.

Now, fifteen years later, the evening lay before us, unsettling in its emptiness, challenging us to turn all this free time into a romantic renaissance. I poured another Scotch and, as I made my way back into my study, I listened for any signs of movement, like a thief in my own house.

The coast was clear, and I slowly closed the door, actually (and utterly) fearful that Olivia might hear the click of the lock's mechanism fitting into the housing of the frame and, like some creature in a horror story, come whooshing down the stairs.

I opened the bottom drawer of my desk and carefully lifted out the manila folders in which I stored the various reviews my books had received. The folders holding the reviews for the books written under my own name were plumped up by other reviews and articles that held even passing references to me, such as: "Steadfastly refusing to discuss the reprint, movie, or foreign rights deals that have surrounded his latest book like so much plush velvet, ———— chose to steer the conversation back to his favorite writers, a crew that includes writers as wildly divergent as Cervantes, Charlotte Brontë, and Sam Holland," and (one of Olivia's favorites) "Not since Sam Holland's *A Natural and Unnatural History of My Wife* has a writer so passionately misunderstood what makes his spouse tick."

Beneath the folders of my real reviews was another, this one holding notices garnered by the various books I wrote under pseudonyms. (To call these the products of my "false self" would be, I think, merely fanciful, a little sprinkle of existential pixie dust on the rather plain business of staying alive.) These for the most part came from magazines that catered to the specific market to which the book itself was pitched. And the reviews were, as a group, glowing—yet what an eerie glow: the luminescence of swamp gas spreading its methane blush against a hot black sky.

At the bottom of that drawer was an old oversized envelope, in which Graham had, more than a year ago, sent back a proposal I had worked up to do a book called *Patricide*. "As your agent," the note had said, "I must concentrate on such a book's lack of commercial appeal. But as someone who would like you to think of him as a friend, I must also say that the half-joking, half-hellfire tone of the whole thing made me rather uneasy." The old proposal and Graham's note were still in the envelope, but now there were several other sheets of paper as well, and these were the few letters that Nadia Tannenbaum had sent to me during the course of our affair and in its immediate aftermath, letters that constituted her reviews of Sam Holland as Lover, letters that I was too sentimental, too vain, and, it now seemed, too fucking stupid to have thrown away.

I hadn't thrown them away because, in some sad, weakened way, I wasn't finished with them. I read them when I missed her. I read them when Olivia sneaked off to bed and turned off the light without even saying good night to me. I read them when I thought about friends with whom I had started off as a young man and how they had gone on to write books that were reasonable, respectable, friends who had secured teaching positions or quirky little jobs at foundations, or were writing scripts and chasing after actresses on that aptly named Sunset Strip, where the change from day to night becomes something lewd and commercial. I read them when I felt life was a race I was losing—losing to others, to time, gravity. I read them often.

> *Dear Sam,*
> *I feel like Lazarus, raised from the dead. What an idiot I've become! I'm already an hour late for work and here I am in my apartment, twirling around, singing with the radio. I never expected to feel happy, not ever again. And now you've given me a happiness that so far exceeds any happiness I have ever felt—I mean it blows every laugh, sigh, and orgasm right out of the water. . . .*

I did not know how to throw something like that out. And the others were of the same genre—the once-lonely woman catapulted into the sensory tumult of life by some tomcatting husband, lured by passion deeper and deeper into a hopeless love.

I quickly looked through the letters because I knew it was time to rid myself of the mimetic device through which I could dependably plunge myself into those days, those weeks, those shuddering, sweaty beds, those long dinners and silent walks—all of it impossible, wrong, finished.

Nadia, though young, was a widow—a fact that I very much wanted to believe saved our liaison from the stereotypical older man–younger woman scenario. She had married her college sweetheart, a rich boy from Napa Valley, but he had drowned while hang-gliding on their honeymoon in Bali.

Nadia carried her tragedy like a single perfect rose. She was willowy, dark, with straight black hair as thick as a broom, and deep, secretive eyes. She was full-breasted, narrow-waisted; there was something a little too perfect in her beauty—it was a beauty that, had it not been for her wound, might have become merely pretty, like those doodles school-girls make on their notebooks while they daydream in class. (Actually, I made those doodles, too, which may explain all of my subsequent difficulties in life.)

As a young widow, Nadia lived in a group apartment in San Francisco. She had an affair with a Chinese baker; she tried to become a nature photographer, spending long, euca-lyptus-scented days in Muir Woods, waiting to be moved. But the waiting saddened her, as did the technology of making a photograph—the chemicals, even the click of the shutter were depressing. Everything saddened her. She missed Leo. He had died perfect in her mind.

Then she had an accident. She was in a cab that lost its brakes on a downhill plunge on Geary Street and banged demolition-derby-style into a dozen parked cars before coming to a stop. Her back was viciously wrenched. Her old Chinese boyfriend introduced her to an acupuncturist, but it did no good. From there she made the rounds from chiropractors to physical therapists, massage gurus, aroma therapists, faith healers—this was San Francisco, after all—and finally gave in and sought some conventional Occidental treatment in the person of an elderly German doctor named Frieda Manheim, who gave her massive doses of muscle relaxants that made poor Nadia so rapturously depressed she tried to kill her-self. Pills.

News of Nadia's condition reached Leo's family and they were decent about it. Recalling Nadia's ambition to become a photographer, they put her together with Leo's Aunt Lorraine, who owned a stock-photo service in New York, one of those places with a library of a million or more images, which they leased out to advertising agencies, chambers of commerce, magazines, textbook publishers, and the like.

Nadia was put to work cataloging a recent acquisition of European photos from the twenties and thirties, bought from a Connecticut collector who had stored the old photos with shocking carelessness. The name of Aunt Lorraine's company was International Image, Inc., known in the trade as III, or Triple I. Their offices were on East Twentieth Street, just eight blocks from my publisher's office, and after I wrote *Visitors from Above*, my editor sent me to Triple I to find suitable and affordable pictures for an eight-page photo insert.

Their offices were well lit, immaculate, but the walls of fireproof metal files lining the walls made the place seem like a morgue—open a drawer and find where the waterfalls are buried, open another for six hundred and ten renditions of the Eiffel Tower. My publishers often produced topical books on the cheap, and they had a long-standing (that is, whole-sale) relationship with III.

When I went over to begin searching out pictures of flying saucers, I was helped by Aunt Lorraine, Lorraine Wasserman, stout and smartly dressed, with a frank, calculating air, a small mouth, stylish shoes, a whiff of Dentyne in her smile. I sat in her office and explained to her the sort of pictures I was looking for. I was particularly interested in finding some illustration of a MIB—that is, a Man in Black, one of those supposed intergalactic disinformation specialists who are said to pay ominous, unannounced visits to those who have spotted extraterrestrials and to threaten them with . . . I don't know . . . evaporation, atomization, some kind of spacey punishment. Of course, there were no actual photos of the MIBs, just crude drawings that made police composite drawings look like portraits by Sargent. But I thought we might fake up a MIB, perhaps by using some other picture of a moody figure wearing a dark suit.

"Men in black, men in black," mused Lorraine, twiddling her Mont Blanc pen and then, suddenly, staring at her fingernails, as if someone had mischievously painted them red while she slept. "You want priests? We got thousands of priests, but mostly they're either praying or playing with children, and the feeling I'm getting is something a little spookier. Maybe an exorcist kind of thing?"

Just then, Nadia came into Lorraine's office. I noticed her, utterly. There was no intention behind it, just a fierce and total attentiveness.

"I found something," she said, her natural reticence for the moment overcome by the tremendous excitement of just having found a little-known Brassaï photograph, of considerable artistic and monetary value. When Olivia found a little treasure in her antiques-rustling gig, she usually got a high color in her face, as if she had just raced up several flights of stairs and then quickly downed a cup of scalding tea. But Nadia's Mediterranean skin remained opaque, as cool as terra cotta. The tone of her voice wasn't one of celebration but self-justification, as if she had proved her own value, or at least her lack of complete valuelessness, to Lorraine.

Lorraine frowned, indelicately. The charitable impulse that had motivated her hiring Nadia had by now run its course. "Not now, Nadia," she said.

"Sounds like a musical—a little twenties revival," I said, feeling obligated to cover Lorraine's bad behavior. *"Not Now, Nadia!"* I said again, moving my hands in some lax approximation of a chorus girl's gestures.

Nadia smiled. It was the smile of someone who appreciated my effort to smooth over the situation with a little humor, someone who would be able to forgive me—for being less charming than I appeared, for being selfish, for lacking some essential energy I needed to catapult me out of the deep glassy groove into which my life had settled, and to forgive me as well, and most importantly, for the large sin that lay at the center of me, a sin that dominated me and which I could not, nor would ever be able to, name.

The next morning I awoke, wild with yearning and guilt, after spending the night in a dingy, beige midtown hotel, thinking of Nadia. (This is, I confess, an inexact use of the word "think": I pictured her, speculated upon her, imagined, and ravished her.) I read for an hour and then showered with fanatical care. The telephone on my night table rang, and I answered it with my hair slicked back, a skimpy towel wrapped around my middle.

It was Olivia, just calling to say hello. It was not her usual behavior; she generally liked our brief separations—"little mental-health breaks," she called them—and she wasn't fond of the telephone. But we had parted on bad terms—even the very next day, I couldn't remember why—and she was showing me a kind of mercy by ringing my room.

"I miss you," she said.

"You do?"

"Please, Sam, don't milk it. Anyhow, Amanda's right here."

"Oh. Sorry."

"She wants to say hello."

Mandy got on the phone. She sounded shrill and uncertain, as if I were very far away and she had no idea when I might return. Remorse over my night of psychic unfaithfulness barked like temple dogs within me as I pictured Amanda and Olivia in our humble, cheerful country kitchen. I told Amanda I loved her, reminded her to pay attention in school, have fun, et cetera, and then asked if I could speak to Michael—why have but two arrows pierce my scheming heart when there was a third in the quiver? Mandy didn't answer, just passed the phone back to her mother.

"What's up?" asked Olivia. My petulance a few moments before had turned her off.

"I was just asking Mandy to put Michael on."

Silence.

"How long have you been living here, Sam?" she asked, at last. "Michael goes to school at seven-thirty."

"Oh, right."

" 'Oh, right.' That's it?"

"What do you want? I forgot."

"You forgot. This is what I *do*. This is my *life*. When you forget, or pretend to forget, it's just a way of saying you think my life is crap."

"Oh, Christ, Olivia, do we really have to do this? Remember when we used to say our family seal should read, 'In Each Other's Arms or at Each Other's Throats'? Well, it isn't charming anymore."

"It was never charming, Sam. You're the one who can't bear normal life. You're the one who is addicted to crisis."

And so forth. It was just a low-level skirmish, no big deal; marriage is full of them. But as I kept up my end of the match, I realized I was experiencing a certain lifting of my spirits. Olivia was making it easy to justify my night of dreaming of Nadia and whatever was about to happen later this morning. I welcomed this unpleasantness; I could use it like a blade to cut the cord that tethered me to Olivia and home.

When I arrived at III, Aunt Lorraine was waiting for me. One of her employees had found some fascinating Air Force photos of strange airborne objects, recently declassified, and she wanted to give them to me personally.

"I really appreciate your getting into this yourself," I said. "But I hate to take up any more of your time. Why don't I work with that woman named Nadia? I think that would be a lot easier."

Don't look away, I told myself. Just keep your gaze right in her face.

"Are you sure?" she asked, smiling. She had a faraway look in her small violet eyes, as if she were already thinking of all the long-ignored little tasks she could see to in this sudden space of open time I had granted her.

"If I need your help, I'll be sure to find you," I said. I liked the way that sounded: smooth, confident, worldly. This love affair, not even beginning to begin, was already doing me a world of good.

Most of my memories of flirtation and courtship were from my adolescence, when courtship was fraught with anxiety, awkward silences, mistimed lunges in which my lips ended up on the nubby upholstery of a hastily vacated sofa cushion. But I was older now; I was married. It was like playing poker when you don't mind losing a few hundred bucks—the cards just seem to come to you.

I worked that day with Nadia. I allowed my hand to brush hers as we passed old photographs back and forth. I rolled up my shirtsleeves and let her see my slender, muscular forearms, the very best part of my otherwise fading physique. I talked casually about my wife, took out wallet-sized snaps of Michael and Mandy, though I didn't show the one of Olivia, because it made her look so pretty and I didn't want to frighten Nadia off.

After the first morning's work, I took her to lunch. I made her laugh. I talked about how I had moved out of New York for the kids' sake (leaving out how I couldn't afford to live here any longer) and then the shock of finding how much my kids hated living in the country. I knew how to tell this story so it wasn't so pathetic. I could make it funny; I'd been telling it to city friends for a year, and it had evolved into a satire on the hopelessness of good intentions, a kind of post-yuppie Mr. Blandings. Yet with Nadia I made the move to Leyden what I dared not make of it with older, savvier friends. I tried to turn it into an opportunity. There were stories in that river town, ghosts of old Dutch settlers; there were eccentrics, unsolved murders, natural wonders that made the heart leap. She believed me; she believed I could write about these things. She saw something in me, something of value. And then, even though we had begun to run out of conversation while we waited for our camomile tea, I asked her if she wanted to have a drink after work and she answered with a shrug and said okay, and her gesture was so casual and her "okay" so soft that it made me think she would have said yes to anything.

I did not rush things. My sense of deliberation was not merely tactical. I was mortally afraid of committing adultery. I was afraid of detection. I was afraid of falling in love, of her falling in love with me. I did not want anyone to be hurt; especially right there, in the beginning, the idea of anyone suffering pain because of my errant emotions made me want to slit my wrists.

Yet I did not want the flirtation to end. In a way, I needed to flirt with Nadia much more than I needed to go to bed with her. I craved her attentiveness, that sensitivity to nuance and gesture you get when things are just beginning, when the ear ransacks every word for a hidden meaning.

At the end of the week, I invited Nadia to Leyden. "A country weekend," I said to her. "It'll do you a world of good." (I worried about her, ostensibly; I was older, compassionate.) And then I added, "Olivia and I promise not to quarrel while you're around." I faulted myself for saying that: it was so obvious, so coarse—I had been expertly flicking little smooth pebbles into the pool, and that last lob was a brick.

We took the train up together from Penn Station. The tracks ran along the river, and the water was a mirror full of clouds. I sat Nadia near the window; she rested her long, narrow feet on top of her black canvas bag. A sack of woe, I thought, in a moment of prescience. I pointed out sights along the river: a nesting place for swans, a ruined castle once owned by a munitions king, the Vanderbilt house. I was chattering away, trying to transform myself from suitor to tutor. I loved talking to her.

"What is it like to be married for such a long time?" she asked me, as the train neared Leyden.

"Tricky," I said. "You can so clearly see through each other that you in all decency must stop looking, and then when you stop looking the person changes, and *then* you're living with a stranger."

"My parents were always so happy together," she said. "My dad ate only fruit and took about fifty vitamins every day, just so he could be vigorous for Mom. They made love all the time. The foil wraps from his condoms were everywhere. Sometimes he'd just put his spoon down in the middle of dinner and look at her. And Mom would make this funny fake scream and say 'Oh no!' Now, half the girls I know, they can't even get their boyfriends to touch them."

"I'm from the past," I said. "The deep past. And we men from the deep past would never dream of turning a woman down."

"Because she might be the last one?" Nadia asked, smiling.

"No, because it might hurt her feelings."

Olivia met us at the station. Nadia sat in the backseat and Olivia conversed with her, glancing continually at Nadia through the rearview mirror, as we made our way home. I saw in Olivia's eyes that she was studying Nadia. Olivia had, or knew of, no reason to distrust me, but I hadn't quite realized how beautiful and profoundly sexual Nadia was, until she was in the car with Olivia and me. As soon as we arrived at the house, Olivia recruited Nadia to accompany her to an estate auction in an old house along the river, a peeling Victorian that had been the home of a woman called Bonnie Beaumont.

"That sounds like the name of a young, beautiful woman, with her blond hair braided up in a French twist," I said. "Or she runs a chic little shop at Lexington and Eighty-first."

Olivia looked at me strangely. Calm down, her eyes said. "Bonnie Beaumont died at the age of ninety-three," said Olivia. "Her chic days were behind her, if they ever existed. But she had some good rugs." She turned to Nadia, who was listening to us, with her back against the kitchen counter, her thin arms folded over her breasts. "I work for a guy who runs a string of antique stores called Past Perfect. I can spend up to five thousand dollars without calling for his okay."

Olivia and Nadia got home in the late afternoon; I was frantically trying to prepare a brilliant dinner. I wouldn't let either of them come into the kitchen.

"The Texans were there in their goddamned pickup trucks," Olivia said, throwing herself heavily into a wingback chair. "They bid up everything. They don't have the slightest idea of what anything is worth. They just know what they want. It distorts the market."

"You got your rugs, though," I said.

"I paid too much." Olivia looked queasy, as if realizing everything in her life was a little bit off.

Nadia sat holding a cup of tea with both hands. She looked sleepy, melancholy; she was dressed in a loose-fitting sweater, checked wool pants. In fact, she looked rather dowdy, which managed to excite me—I took it as a disguise behind which she hid the rich, radiant fact of her desire.

"It was so sad, seeing everything she owned being sold," said Nadia.

"She doesn't need it any longer," said Olivia. "And she died without a will, just debts."

Nadia took to the children. They responded to her youth. She rode bicycles with them; together they discovered an old hemlock in our three acres of woods, a gnarly old tree perfect for Amanda to climb—I had never climbed a tree in my life. They raked leaves, played chess; she braided Amanda's hair.

"She's sweet, isn't she," said Olivia, as we lay stone still in bed that night.

"Who?" I asked, acutely aware of Nadia's presence in the guest room down the hall.

"Oh, please, Sam."

"You mean Nadia? I'm sorry, I was drifting."

"I'll bet you were."

I looked at Olivia through the corner of my eye. She was propped up on one elbow; her satin pajama top hung far from her body; moonlight caressed the breasts that had fed my children. She was jealous, and my heart reached out for her, as if waking from a long hibernation. Could this have been the point of bringing Nadia home? Had what I been seeking been this edge of worry in my wife's voice?

"She's okay," I said. "Her life has accrued more tragedy than her character can bear. She staggers beneath its weight."

"Why don't you say things like that about me?"

"Because they're not true about you. She's a widow, for Christ's sake."

"Yes. And so terribly needy."

"What's wrong, Olivia?" That was the trouble with living outside the truth: you had to pretend to such stupidity to maintain your position.

"Why did you bring her here? And why are you having *insights* about her?"

"Shh. She'll hear you. Anyhow, I thought you were enjoying her. The kids are."

"They love her, we all love her. But she's *in* love with you. How old is she, Sam? Twenty-two, twenty-four? I'm sorry I can't be twenty-four, Sam. I'm sorry I can't pretend to know nothing about men, or life, or you."

"I think she's older than that, Olivia. I think she's quite close to thirty. That's not so much younger than you."

A silence. Then Olivia grabbed her pillow and the top

blanket and said, "I think you must be so unhappy that it's driven you insane."

It was not really inspiration but mere instinct that made me grab for her before she was out of reach. I pulled her back onto the bed. I kissed her mouth, her cheeks, her eyes. She wanted me to. She returned my kisses with hunger, avidity; to be kissed that way by a wife of so many years was like making time run backward. When we made love, she cried out with pleasure in a way she hadn't allowed herself to do since Michael was old enough to be curious about sex. She might have been summoning it forth because she knew Nadia would hear, but the element of premeditation, that little twist of artifice, only made it sweeter.

That was on Saturday; the next Wednesday, I made love to Nadia. She had sublet an apartment on West Twelfth Street, not far from where Olivia and I used to live and, in fact, in a building where an old friend of ours still lived. Nadia had a studio apartment, just one room, with bare floors, cinder-block-and-pine-plank bookshelves, Hindu and Buddhist art on the walls, a window with a back view of the brownstones across the way.

"I never thought I'd be living like this," Nadia said, as she handed me a brandy poured into a teacup. We had worked late, seen a movie at a nearby multiplex. "I thought I'd be married, teaching somewhere, have a baby or two."

"Teaching? Teaching what?"

"I don't know. Poetry. Meditation. Whatever."

"I think you'd be a wonderful teacher," I said.

"You think so?"

"Yes."

"I think *you* could learn something from me," she said.

"What?"

"How to care about yourself, and not ever, ever dislike yourself."

After a long silence, I finally managed to ask, "How long did you and Leo live together before you married?"

"For a while. Then we had a big fight. He used to speak to me so disrespectfully in front of his friends, like he wanted to make sure they understood that he didn't take me very seriously. He was a real motherfucker when it came to things like that. He always had these plans. He wanted to design furniture, or do landscape architecture. But he never did anything, not really. And he took it out on me, his frustration."

"So what happened after the big fight?"

"I was going to go to New Mexico to study with the Hopi Indians. I was putting my name and number on the ride board at the Co-op when he came and got me and talked me out of it."

"Study what with the Hopi Indians?"

"How to live."

She abandoned the safety of the rocking chair and sat herself next to me on the sofa. My heart began to race, and I thought: I would not be here if I were a success.

"I came to New York because I didn't know anyone here," Nadia said. "I wanted to disappear."

"I thought you knew people here."

"And then I met you."

She took my hand, turned it over as if to read my palm, and then with great ceremony—was this a Hopi thing?—bent her head and planted a solemn kiss on the crisscrossed lines of my fate. The kiss was dry but somehow grew moister, which was a little confusing until I realized she had parted her lips and now pressed the tip of her tongue against my hand. No, I wouldn't be here if I were writing the book I had meant to write. I would never have even met her if I hadn't been sent to find pictures for my spaceman book, and I never would have needed her if I had been living the life I wanted. My life had shrunk, it was smaller than Nadia's apartment, and I wanted to punch a window into the wall, to breathe, to see how other people were conducting their lives.

"If I don't make love with you tonight, I think I'll die of unhappiness," I heard myself say.

I was full of desire to be with her, but, in fact, that first night Nadia was a mild and meandering lover. Sex was a seance in which the object was to bring forth her pleasure from the spirit world. She received me on her side, with her head propped up on one hand, like a Persian on a sofa. She moved away from my thrusts, as if afraid of pain. She kept her eyes open; I could not tell what she was looking at. Somewhere along the way it struck me that I was having one of the very worst sexual experiences of my entire life.

Nadia was immense inside, oceanic. She touched me lightly on the back of my head. I felt myself wilting. I thought of Moses throwing his staff onto the ground and having it turn into a slithering snake. I began counting my thrusts, timing them to the beat of the Marvelettes singing "Don't Mess with Bill." My sharpest experience was the nagging guilt, the sense of irreparable wrongdoing. While I tried to make love to Nadia, I ministered to this guilt by telling myself I was hurting no one. I even dredged up the times in which Olivia had said in anger that I should find another lover—those early-morning encounters really brought out the worst in her. Still, the guilt banged away inside me, like a shutter in an upper room.

And then, suddenly, darkly, mysteriously, the guilt disappeared, the shutter stopped banging, it fell from the house and was lost in the bloomless forsythia, the house was quiet, the universe was hushed, and I became exquisitely aware of this stranger, this struggling soul, this fragrant woman beside me, and it was then, as if she knew that my thoughts had finally fastened upon her, that something caught hold in Nadia, too. She gripped me tightly with her free hand and pushed me onto my back, holding me so I wouldn't dislodge from her, and now she was astride me, animated, her once-dreamy eyes flecked with madness. A minute later she had an orgasm and roared in my face with such intensity that it was all I could do to keep from laughing.

"Why are you smiling?" she asked, looking at me through the net of damp, dark hair that hung over her face.

"I don't know. You're awfully nice. You really are."

"Did you come yet?"

"No big deal." It was her house; I wanted to be a polite guest.

She touched my cheek apologetically and got off of me and onto her back. Her pubic hair was abundant, luxuriant, and combined with the darkness and prominence of her nipples made her look somehow anthropological, an idol made for sex rituals. She guided me into her, gripped me tightly; the night shook in its hinges; and when I embraced her, I further surprised myself by whispering, "That was wonderful."

She asked me to spend the night, but I didn't dare, and I went back to the sterile safety of my hotel on Fortieth Street. I thought Olivia might have called, but there was no message from her. As I fell asleep that night, I vowed I would never sleep with Nadia again. I slept soundly, dreamlessly, satisfied, but woke at dawn and was downtown at her apartment twenty minutes later.

A week later, a letter from Nadia came to the house. She'd read my first novel and wanted me to know how wonderful she thought it was. "It was so sad, and so funny; I heard your voice in it, too, which was sort of neat."

"Poor girl," said Olivia, reading over my shoulder.

"Why?" I was startled; I hadn't heard Olivia come up behind me. "There *are* funny parts and sad parts. What's your problem? That she said 'neat'?"

Olivia frowned briefly. She had efficient gestures and expressions; she could flick them like levers in a voting booth.

"I read that book, too, Sam. I loved it, and you." Then she looked more closely at me and an expression of wonder lingered over her face. "Are you trying to relive those days? Find some girl to fall in love with you all over again, just the way you've already been fallen in love with by me? The object of life is to move forward."

"Toward what? Failure? John Retcliffe books? Death?"

"Leave her alone, Sam."

"Oh, come on. Do you ever have me wrong! I don't see how you can live with someone for so many years and get him so wrong."

I watched her as she left the room. Her words cauterized my feelings about my new mistress, and it seemed just a matter of time before they disappeared.

Yet the cooling of my feelings mixed with the heat of Nadia's produced a dense emotional fog and, sooner rather than later, I wandered into that fog and stayed with her for six months.

I had already told Nadia we should stop seeing each other, had even managed to stay still and unresponsive as she wept against my chest and said she knew it would happen, and that of course it was what we must do. But then Olivia, in the spirit in which she calculated how many years of sleep my early-morning amorousness had cost her, figured out how much birth control she had pumped through her body—in the form of gels, foams, pills.

"I'm not going to do this anymore," she said. "I'm too old to pour that stuff in me."

"You want to use condoms?"

"No. They irritate me, and they're not even safe."

"So what are we going to do? Have oral sex for the rest of our lives?"

"Haven't we had *enough* sex?" Olivia said.

"Have you?"

"I want you to have a vasectomy," she said.

"Fine," I said, feeling aggrieved, martyred—yet the snip might be just the limited, symbolic punishment I needed to get back into the marriage.

The next day, Nadia called me at home, blue, lonesome, just wanting to hear the voice of the one person on the planet who knew what she was going through.

"So what's going on with you?" she asked.

"The usual. I'm getting a vasectomy."

"You are? Why?" She sounded truly alarmed.

"Olivia—"

"Don't you know how dangerous they are?"

"They're not at all dangerous."

"There's a huge increase in testicular and prostate cancer among men who've had them. I was just reading about it in the *Times*."

I was silent. I had the distinct yet dizzying sense she was saving my life.

"I'm coming into the city."

"So."

"I want to see you."

"We can't."

"Yes, we can. You're saving my life."

I craved her. More than that, much more, I fell in love with her. The sexual awkwardness took care of itself; in fact, our night life became sleek. The rituals of betrayal became somewhat commonplace. The exertions of leading a double life agreed with an aspect of my soul that preferred tumult to knowledge: being two things is like being nothing in particular. Like a born-to-lose gambler, I liked to spread my bets.

Our ending was unremarkable. She grew tired of being my mistress. I was exhausted by my own lies. She told me someone had come to work, a man, unmarried, of the proper age, who seemed to like her. A few days later, she said he had asked her to dinner and I said she should go with him and she struck me hard across the face. I held the hand that struck me and kissed its fingertips.

"You never planned for things to work out between us," she said.

"I never said they would. Did I?"

She sent me away; she didn't call and neither did I. Every once in a while, she sent a note. It was as if we had met traveling and promised to stay in touch.

I held these letters in my hand and looked through them. I must throw them away, I thought. I listened for Olivia. I paged through the letters, wondering which one Michael had seen. Nadia's final letter had been ferocious. All of the others had been written in her plump, schoolgirlish hand; this last communication was scrawled in a cramped, collapsing script.

> *You made me love you. No, no, you fucked me, you just fucked me. I have never been treated so shabbily in my life. I have heard about men like you but this is the first time I have been defiled by someone so callous. And I loved you, Sam. I still love you. I gave you my heart. Do you think that was easy? I gave you my one and only heart, my precious God-given body and you used my cunt as your toilet. Oh, I hate you, how I hate you, and your precious wife and those children and their oh so very uninteresting little problems. . . .*

And this was the letter that was missing—the one that Michael, wherever he was, had in his pocket.

At around eight that evening, I went down to fix myself another drink. Olivia came down. Her denim-blue eyes were red. At first I thought she'd strained them repairing a quilt, but then I looked a little closer and realized she'd been crying.

"Okay, now I'm really worried," she said.

The telephone rang and I bounded out of my chair, sloshing my drink. Naturally, we both thought it must be Michael, or someone with news of Michael, but in fact it was Graham Davis calling back. He was calling from a bar or a party. I heard music, laughter in the background—it made me long for Manhattan.

"Oh good, I've got you," said Graham. Telephone calls were a pivotal part of his life, and he discussed their placement and completion in exceedingly dramatic terms. "Now see here, I've only got a few moments, but there's something you have to know."

"What is it, Graham?"

"I ran into Ezra Poindexter at the Vertical fitness center this morning. He's as thin as a whippet, but with all these *muscles*, for God's sake."

"Thanks for the information."

"Ah yes, I didn't think you'd get through the weekend without knowing how fit your publisher is looking these days."

You could never throw Graham off track with a sarcastic remark; he was always prepared for mockery. He was unserious about everything except money, about which he was reverential.

"What is it really, Graham? This is sort of—" I looked at Olivia and shrugged apologetically.

"It's about *Visitors from Beyond*, Sam."

"*Above.*"

"Sorry?"

"*Visitors from Above.*"

"Oh, isn't that what I said? Well, no matter. The point is it's selling, Sam, and selling like mad. Ezra's going back to press on it. They're running off—I hope you're seated, Sam, and that your serving tray is in an upright position—they're running off a second printing of fifty thousand copies. What was the first printing, anyhow?"

"I don't know." Yet I did. It was seventy-five hundred copies; I just hated to say so.

"I can check when I get to the office. I think it was something in the seventy-five-hundred range. But who cares? It's flying out of the stores. Sam, I sense some very serious money here."

I went silent. I felt as if I'd just bitten into a rare delicacy and didn't know whether to savor it or spit it out.

"You must come in first thing Monday," Graham said. "We'll meet at my office and then we're going to meet Ezra and discuss how to maximize this whole thing. Oh, thank you, love, that's brilliant."

"What?"

"Sorry. Someone just handed me a drink the size of a fire plug. Okay, Sam, I better ring off. If I'm not in my office Monday promise you'll check the hospitals for me. Cheerio!"

I hung up, wondering if Graham said "Cheerio!" back home in London or if it was merely part of his stateside persona.

Olivia was staring at me.

"I think we're about to get rich," I said to her.

"I think we have to start looking for Michael," she said, not quite simultaneously, yet a little before I had finished what I was saying, and so I wasn't sure if she had heard me or not.

chapter three

 called the police. They took Michael's name and description, and then Olivia and I left the house, walking into the cold, damp darkness of the night. A long cloud swam like a crocodile across the face of the moon. A few scattered stars shone here and there, like illuminated houses in a sparsely populated valley.

We had no idea where to begin. We drove to what Michael called "beautiful downtown Leyden," that oppressive Lionel-like line of Federal storefronts, closed from five on, with all that sexless merchandise suffocating behind the plate-glass windows.

We drove in a silence that seemed designed to make me miserable. We saw a few kids Michael's age around a Mobil station/convenience store: black jackets and Marlboro Lights, their pants belted a half-foot below the waist, making them look like dwarves. A few blocks away, we saw a knot of teenagers hanging around a boarded-up bowling alley. "They're on a vigil, waiting for the fifties to return," I said to Olivia. Silence. In the park, where the father-son softball game had been played, a couple of dogs chased each other from street lamp to street lamp, darting in and out of the circles of light.

"Small-town Saturday night," I said. At this point, I didn't expect a reply, but talking relieved a little of the pressure in my head. I turned onto one of the residential streets, past the ample houses that faced us like Dutch merchants, stolid, expressionless.

"Where is he, Sam? I can't bear this."

I reached for her left hand, but it was in her lap, clutching the right. We were aimless now, just driving around. If we had been looking for a dog, we could have rolled down the windows and called its name, whistled; yet somehow searching for our son made us not more demonstrative but more circumspect.

"We need some kind of plan," I said, but I had no more than that to offer.

We were on Parsonage Street. One of the streetlights sent its crime-stopping cadmium glow into the car like a fleeting inspiration, and then we were in darkness again, with only the acid-green lights on the dashboard.

"You said you saw Greg Pitcher today," said Olivia. "Where's he staying these days?"

"At the Connellys'." And just as I said that, we passed the Connelly house. It seemed, in the quiet anxiety of the moment, something of a miracle. I pulled the car next to the curb in front of the Connellys' historically correct black-and-white colonial, its large porch filled with bicycles.

I turned off the engine and looked at the house. The second story was dark; only one window was lit on the first.

"It doesn't look like much is going on in there," I said. "Don't you sort of despise Russ Connelly?"

"What do you have against him? Oh God, Sam, please, not now." But the truth was she was glad for a few more moments in the car, a few moments to imagine that Michael was in there.

"He walks around his appliance store with a walkie-talkie clipped to his belt. Come on. I mean, is that necessary? He has only one employee. And his wife—she gives the Japanese a bad name. There's fifteen percent unemployment around here and she's got seven different jobs. She teaches skiing, she's a caterer—"

"All right, Sam. I had no idea you made such a study of them."

I could feel some internal movement within Olivia, a move in my direction. I reached again for her hand and this time I connected. She laced her fingers around mine.

"They're the perfect family," I said. "They belong on a cereal box. Russ is full of hero talk. Have you ever heard him? 'Dare to be great.' "

"You're not going to start in on how heroism is a form of fascism."

"Olivia. The man has a snooze alarm on his clock radio. How can you be a hero with a snooze alarm?"

She leaned her head against my shoulder. I put my arm around her. We only had this moment and we wanted to make it last.

"All right," she said, "we better go."

Though the spring was slow in coming, the Connelly landscaping design, dominated by early-blooming bulbs which only they could obtain, was already in full flower. The magnolia was sweet in the night air, ringed by narcissi, their heads bowed in devotion. A gaudy chorus line of tiger-striped tulips blew in the breeze, their tops illuminated by the living-room lights.

I rang the doorbell, and somewhere in that interstice between the ding and the dong I realized we were making a terrible mistake. We were humiliating ourselves in the Connellys' eyes and, more importantly, in our own. But before I could translate that thought into a suitable action— say, leaping off the porch, catapulting over the hedge—Russ Connelly, all six-and-a-quarter feet of him, dressed in wide-wale corduroy trousers and a tight taupe turtleneck, threw open the door and grinned at us with his apocalyptic high spirits.

"It's the Hollands! Whatever brings you here on a night like this?"

I moved back a step and made something of a show of looking up at the sky, as if wondering if perhaps Russ had noticed something about the weather we might have missed. I was just trying to amuse Olivia.

"We're looking for Michael," Olivia said.

Russ's smile was replaced by a show of concern. He was a master of the cardinal emotions—happiness, sadness, rage—and he hit each of them dead center, like an Army bugler. "Come in, come in," he said. "Sharon!" he called over his shoulder. "Visitors!"

The Connelly living room was patriotic-casual. Currier and Ives prints, a framed Declaration of Independence repro, beanbag chairs, a tweedy old sofa festooned with big floral pillows probably sewn by Sharon one rainy Saturday afternoon. A fire burned in the brick hearth; the Connellys owned a wood lot just outside the village and through careful arboreal management were okay on logs for the next hundred years. Above the hearth hung a painting by Louis Tiffany, the Connellys' prize possession. I could sense Olivia appraising it with her keen, practical eye. Though the painting itself wasn't remarkable—a man, a cart, a horse, a serpentine smudge of river, all dutifully rendered—the fact that Tiffany had gone on to greatness in stained glass and that the world's most famous jewelry store bore his name made the painting valuable.

Sharon Connelly was sprawled out on the carpet in front of the fireplace, where she and sixteen-year-old Cliff Connelly were categorizing old baseball cards, in preparation for a Baseball Card Swap-a-Thon at a nearby Holiday Inn. Sharon was slight, girlish, with bad teeth, the legacy of her deprived childhood in Japan. Her dark hair was pulled back into a ponytail; her eyes glittered feverishly. She always seemed exhausted, propelled by black tea and diet pills. Whenever I

met her she seemed uneasy, as if she had recently said something mean about me.

"Look, Russ," she said, "we just found the Elston Howard
rookie card." She held it tightly, waved it back and forth. "It's
worth two hundred dollars."

"The Hollands are looking for Michael," said Russ.

"Michael?" Sharon's voice was high, evasive, as if she'd
been accused of something. "He's not here."

"Well," I said, "we're just checking. It's probably nothing,
we're just being ridiculous, I suppose. . . ."

"Ridiculous?" said Russ. He had small, lusterless eyes, and
when he squinted they all but disappeared. "I don't understand. Is he missing or not?"

"I don't know if he's missing. He's not home, that's all."

"That's all? I'd say that was quite a lot."

"We thought maybe someone here would have seen him,"
said Olivia. "Is Greg Pitcher still staying with you?"

"Greg is not here!" said Sharon, with an air of innocence
and desperation. "He goes out. All the time. It is not our
place to ask where he goes."

"You know where I'd look?" said Russ, bringing his hands
together with a meaty slap. "The mall."

"Greg is the original mall rat," said Cliff, looking up from
his cards on the carpet. He was on the swim team: short hair,
a lean body, his eyes stained red by the chlorine of a thousand
pools.

"The Windsor Mall?" asked Olivia.

"He might have gone there with Michael," I said to her. I
heard the enthusiasm in my voice. I sounded as if we had
already spotted him, and I thought to myself: Calm down.

Russ escorted us to the door. He was glad to be rid of us;
our tale of woe, the chaos we dragged in our wake, didn't go
with the domestic regularity he had established in his own
house. They were playing the music of family life; there were

easy harmonies and the *click-click* of a metronome—and Olivia and I were coughing compulsively, wrecking the recital.

"We haven't seen much of Michael lately," Russ was saying. "Maybe he *is* with Greg."

"I certainly hope so." I felt an almost absurd levitation of spirit—just the thought of being out of that house, into the night air, on with the search. I think I must have believed that the act of looking for Michael was a sacred ceremony at the end of which he would be magically restored to us.

We scurried from the Connelly house, as if involved not in leave-taking but escape. We slid into our car, full of merriment. We were shaking with suppressed laughter—we often felt closer, luckier to have each other, after leaving others. But when the doors shut and the pitiful few watts of overhead lighting were extinguished, our shared ripple of hateful glee had expended itself and we were plunged into a sudden, devastating exhaustion. If not for the fear that Russ might be peeking out his window, I would have rested my forehead on the steering wheel.

"Let's go, Sam," said Olivia, in a murmur. She used my name so gently, so naturally, it actually gave me a chill.

The Windsor Mall was eight miles from Leyden. It was a mall like all the rest—a Sears, a Kmart, a J.C. Penney, a Gap, Kaybee Toys, a couple of banks. It was the place I would want to conjure while gasping my last mortal breaths, so as to not feel all that bad about dying.

It was nearly ten o'clock when we walked in. We spotted no other adults in the mall. Even the other parents were teenagers—pale youngsters pushing collapsible strollers in which toddlers slept with scowls on their faces. The clerks in the stores were teenagers, for the most part girls with ruinous makeup habits to support. The stores were relatively empty. The mass of teenagers—there must have been about five hundred of them—prowled the faux-marble corridors of the mall, the boys in packs, the girls in less threatening clusters of three and four. The occasional boy-girl couples were on their own, holding hands or staggering around with their arms slung over each other's shoulders, as if helping each other limp out of a war zone. Yet their faces were proud, like those of people who have just bought their first piece of real estate.

Olivia's eyes combed through the faces, dividing the mall into quadrants. I was circumspect. Like a white man in Zaire, I felt suddenly bereft of my status as a member of the majority.

Olivia must have seen it in my face. "You're the only guy here with a collar on his shirt," she said.

"But the girls dress like you. Or are you dressing like them?"

Suddenly Olivia rose onto her toes and touched the fingers of her left hand against the bottom of her chin. "Wait! Isn't that him?"

I followed her eyes into the crowd.

"Michael? I don't see him."

"No—Greg, Greg Pitcher. Over there, near the Fashion Barn."

The Fashion Barn had a red neon sign, the letters shaped like logs, and there below it, more or less out of the restless flow of teen traffic, was a moody-looking, dark-complexioned girl in a floral print dress. Her arm was around a tall, bewildered-looking boy in jeans, who if he didn't go home soon and get some rest would be milking his father's cows in his sleep tomorrow morning.

"That's not Greg," I said. "It doesn't even look like him."

"It doesn't? Are you sure?"

"That kid is the president of the local 4-H Club, for Christ's sake. Greg was living in our house. Can't you remember what he looks like? Like an athlete with drinking and alimony problems."

Olivia presented a blank face. Her soul could leave her body like someone slipping out of the house for a smoke.

"Let's surprise everyone," she said, "and not turn on each other during this crisis."

In a fit of penance, I took her in my arms and stroked the back of her head, the enduring silkiness of her long hair, the abrupt Nefertiti-like curve of the back of her skull.

The mall closed at eleven. We stood by the exits—Olivia near the Cineplex, myself near Penney's—and watched the teenagers leave, and when that was over and the lights in the stores were going off, one at a time, right down the line, like dominoes falling, we met back at the car, and it was difficult to speak, or even make eye contact. We were in the throes of an emergency which remained maddeningly dim.

Olivia took the wheel and we got into line with the hundreds of cars leaving the Windsor Mall.

"I think we should go home," I said. "For all we know, Michael's there."

"I called. There's no answer."

"Oh."

"Exactly. 'Oh.' "

"What's that for?"

"Sam, you have to tell me something. I'm not blaming, but I have to know. Did anything happen between you and Michael today that might have caused this? Something, anything—an argument, a comment, some caustic remark, a misunderstanding?"

If life was a story written by God, then this was the moment in which I could fearfully light the flickering flame of my confession. Olivia looked at me through the corner of her eye, awaiting an explanation. There might never be a better, or even another, time for me to tell her about Nadia, about my feelings of ridiculousness and remorse. Olivia had set the scene for me, relieving me of the most terrible part—that moment in which you say, in effect, "Darling, there's something I must tell you. . . ." I considered the moment, tried quickly to imagine what the rest of my life would be like once I uttered the words "Michael may be upset because he found a letter. . . ." In front of us, teenaged drivers sailed past the flashing red traffic light and out onto the state highway, bordered on one side by hills and on the other by a desultory commercial strip—one-hour lube joints, Roy Rogers, Penn Auto Glass. It amazed me: the power of words, the corrosive power of a lie, how I could say one thing and ruin my life and say another and ruin it in a different—though possibly, in the short term at least, more tolerable—way.

I took a deep breath. The moon had risen out of range of the clouds, a cantaloupe-colored hole in the sky.

"It was just like any other day," I said.

In Leyden, the town's occasional crimes were easily handled by the nearby branch of the state police, which was headquartered in a small, low-slung brick building a couple miles out of town, on Route 100. There were four blue-and-tan patrol cars parked in front, a desultory, unkempt air in the gravel parking lot—scraps of tissue such as come with hot dogs, a dying rhododendron packed with last autumn's leaves.

When we pulled in, Olivia shut the motor off but then just sat there, with her hands on the steering wheel. She breathed deeply, trying to calm herself.

"I don't want to cry in there," she said.

"Don't worry, you won't." I meant it to sound encouraging, but I detected something hard in the remark. I was so compromised, my words were turning to salt. "Anyhow," I said quickly, "maybe we're heading into good news."

"Do you think so? I don't. I don't have the feeling we're anywhere near good news."

She pulled the key out of the ignition and dropped it into

her purse. She went to open the door but I stopped her, taking her arm. She turned toward me, the whites of her eyes alive in the darkness of the car.

"I love you, Olivia."

She settled back in the seat. I was immediately and ravishingly sorry I'd said it. It had come from nowhere; an emotional hiccup.

"I love you, too," she said, softly.

It broke my heart. I looked away from her, toward the police headquarters. The windows were lit, but somehow none of that light left the building. It was as if the glass had been painted to look as if the lights were on.

I had never asked the police for help. I didn't even ask them for directions. My only contact with cops had been as a potential defendant—the campus police wading into the University of Wisconsin administration building to remove anti-war students during a Vietnam War protest, highway cops zapping me with their radar guns, street cops on Second Avenue eying everyone in line for the Albert King show at the Fillmore East, hoping for a quickie drug bust.

But now I had to hand myself over to them, willingly, imploringly. I was turning my life in a new direction, and things would never be the same. I would always be, among other things, a man who'd come to the police and said, "My son is missing!"

"Name?" asked the cop behind the desk. A young guy, he wore his blue shirt open-necked; a tangle of dark fur grew in the hollow beneath his Adam's apple.

"We called a couple of hours ago," said Olivia. "About our son?"

"Holland," I said. "Michael Holland." I felt the requirements of the drama into which I'd been cast. I was there as the steady male, the one who can dispassionately handle matters of fact. Olivia would play the woman with emotions.

"Have you heard anything yet?" she asked.

"Not yet, ma'am," said the young officer. His nametag announced him as Sergeant Rick McGrath. A good name for a ball player. Good old semireliable Rick McGrath, with his brilliant plays in the outfield and his weakness for the off-speed pitch. As good-field, no-hit McGrath delivered this disappointing news, he tightened his jaw, looked away, as if to shield his ego from jeers and catcalls after popping up with men in scoring positions.

"Can you tell us what's been done so far?" asked Olivia.

"All of our personnel have been alerted and a description of your son has been circulated."

Olivia colored. She looked at me, but I wasn't sure what she expected me to do just now.

"Isn't that just saying you've mentioned it to people?" she said.

"No, ma'am."

Again, Olivia looked to me. Your turn, I said to myself.

"How many officers are specifically assigned to look for Michael?" I asked. There. When in doubt, revert to statistics.

"Well, no one, at this point in time, sir."

I saw the cop was trying to be nice, had been taught to respect his elders. "Your son's only been out for a few hours."

" 'Out'? Is that the new way of putting it? What about 'missing'?" I looked at Olivia; her gaze had softened, she stood a little closer to me—in fact, she was reaching for me, to touch my elbow.

Just then, the door to the station opened and two more officers came in.

"Were you out checking that break-in on River Road?" McGrath asked, speaking to them through the space between Olivia and me, and adding to his inquiry a certain tone that let us know that now he was devoting himself to real police business.

. . .

At home that night, we tried to sleep, while anxiety hummed in the force field between our bodies.

"Olivia?" I whispered.

She was on her back, her eyes not so much closed as unexpressed, like a Roman statue on which the sculptor has merely indicated the shape and location of the eye but nothing more. A gnarled twig of moonlight trembled on her bare arm; the vanilla blanket gently rose and fell with her Methodical breaths. Truly, Stanislavsky had nothing to teach Olivia about what had become her premier role: the woman too tired to talk to her husband.

Where in the fuck is that kid? I asked myself. For all the effort we had put in that night, I was left feeling we might only have managed to obscure the path that could lead us to Michael, that we had kicked up dust, trampled clues, somehow driven him further away.

I closed my eyes and saw Michael's face before me. It was too unnerving to have the boy appear unbidden. I turned in my bed, looked at the shadow of our budding maple, a slender, trembling thing, a piece of filigree placed upon the bedroom wall by an aged hand.

There is something dangerous in this boy, I thought, and the complaint hit me with the force of revelation. I thought back to the preceding spring when I brought Michael over to the schoolyard to play a little ball. I wanted to make some unspoken point about the casual pleasure of country life— Michael might be giving up the greasy, cumin-drenched smells of souvlaki, but in return he was getting a bit of batting practice with Dad. We walked behind the school, where there was a baseball diamond with a backstop. I pitched slow to Michael; he seemed perfectly content to whack them over my head and send me chasing. Not once did Michael ask me to pitch a little faster, and I was happy to let him succeed. I shagged his hits through the white and cinnamon-colored clover of the outfield and tossed high pop-ups to myself during the trudge back to the mound. Finally, Michael asked me if I wanted to take a couple hits. It had been at least fifteen years since I had swung at a baseball, but once I had enjoyed it and hadn't been bad at it, so I agreed, and Michael handed the bat to me and I handed Michael his glove and we changed places.

The first pitch Michael threw hit me square in the head, and I could never explain why but I was certain it had been deliberate. The pain had a kinetic power; it bored its way down from my skull to my bowels. The world looked as if it were a quick sketch—Michael was a few shaky lines, the grass a mere suggestion of green, no one had filled in the sky. But then reality returned and the pain jumped up a couple of notches and I threw the bat down.

"Goddammit, Michael!" I said.

"Sorry," Michael said, in a tone so casual, as if he had stepped on my foot, not at all appropriate to having brought his father to the cusp of concussion.

In all likelihood, the casualness of his apology was meant to provoke me. I picked the bat up again, threw it down again, kicked it, and then stalked out toward the mound. Instinctively, Michael turned and ran. I set out after him, moving almost as fleetly as Michael. I knew I was losing this contest but took a certain brutish satisfaction from it anyhow because I knew I was frightening him. Phrases like "wring his neck" and "kick his ass" droned within me. Michael zigged, I zagged; Michael streaked and I lunged. We circled the school building, and when we reached the parking lot Michael went toward the Dodge. He flung his hands onto the hood, as if he could not be harmed while touching it. I caught up to him, accepted the fact that the chase was over.

"That hurt," I said, my voice unstable with exhaustion.

"I *said* I was sorry," Michael said. His tone was mild, unrepentant. What is happening to us?, I had thought, my heart suddenly breaking in two.

In fact, Michael had a long history of hitting me, breaking

my things, adding a measure of misery to my daily life. As an infant, he liked to flail in my arms, and often his little pink fingers with their razor-sharp, obdurate cuticles would make contact with the side of my nostrils, the corner of my eyes. When he learned how to control himself a little better, he graduated to grabbing the tip of my nose, as if to pull it off. He scattered my papers, jammed and bent the keys to my typewriter, and on and on and on. I accepted the existence of a certain oedipal rivalry between father and son; I could conjure memories of those feelings in myself, that little boy whom my father so liberally bounced around through the fifties. But to this inevitable Freudian fandango I also added a certain specific culpability of my own: that is to say, Michael destroyed my silk ties and dropped my cat's-eye cuff links down the drain because he felt on some fundamental level that I was not a fit father.

And that was what broke my heart all through Michael's childhood—my own inescapable inadequacy. Now, next to my supposedly sleeping wife, with the poised and intimate spring night lurking like the bird of death outside every window of our house, I, for the fifty thousandth time, berated myself for being so congenitally unequal to the tasks of fatherhood, beginning with Olivia's pregnancy and continuing with the undulating implacability of a Möbius strip to this very insomniac instant.

"We're going to have a child," she'd said.

"Oh, great," I had replied. I eventually got back on track, but the race was lost; I was like a horse who spooks in the starting gate, and it would have taken a miracle to win the race, or to place, or even show.

When Olivia announced her pregnancy, I had been at the kitchen table, typing my second novel. We were living on Olivia's *Rolling Stone* salary and the remains of my advance.

"Aren't you excited?" she asked.

"Excited?" I turned off my Olivetti; the red indicator light stayed on for an extra moment and then faded to black. "We've only been married two months. You don't even know what you want to do when you grow up."

She smiled at me; it was important to her that she remember this day in a certain way. "Aren't you happy?" she asked, giving me another chance.

"I don't know."

"Sam, you know Dr. Mead always told me if we wanted to get pregnant I'd probably have to take fertility pills. I only get my period three or four times a year. This is a miracle, Sam. I really think it is."

"I never thought Dr. Mead was much of a doctor," I said.

Yet I did get caught up in the whole miracle-of-life angle of Olivia's pregnancy. I read the popular books on the subject, like *So You're Having a Baby!*, written by a fellow calling himself (certainly pseudonymously) Lawrence Kindheart, author of *So You've Got Cancer!* and *So You're Going to Declare Bankruptcy!* I made lists of names, boys and girls; shopped for baby furniture on Orchard Street. Olivia eschewed any of those tests available to pregnant women—no peeks behind the curtain for her, no shaking of the wrapped present for some telltale rattle within. What if it's a terribly deformed . . . well, you know, I asked her, as delicately as I could, since I thought we should avail ourselves of the entire array of tests—amniocentesis, sonograms, whatever. But she insisted she was far too young to worry about things like that, and she said it in a way that fairly implied that my concern was perhaps a form of projection, that I had turned our unborn child into some kind of translucent Quasimodo because that's how I felt about the poor thing. I love this little guy, I had insisted, and fell to my knees before her, wrapping my arms around her ample waist, resting my suddenly tear-slicked cheek against her bountiful belly, and the strange thing about these declarations is that they become resonantly true as you make them—function follows form and you say what you think you ought to be feeling and then, lo and behold, you are feeling it.

Not only did Olivia avoid any sneak previews of this progeny, but she chose to have the child delivered by a midwife, a woman named Gloria Wurtzel, with tight auburn curls, pop eyes, and a rotting tooth somewhere in the back of her mouth. "Sometimes God makes people look that way to warn others about them," I said to Olivia, but she was blind to Wurtzel's defects. She told me that in the Middle Ages the so-called witches who were burnt at the stake were in many cases midwives, whose familiarity with the mysteries of birth was construed as a kind of sorcery. Makes sense to me, I thought; but really there was nothing more to say. Olivia wanted Wurtzel, so Wurtzel it was. I was somewhat mollified to learn that at least Nurse Wurtzel made her deliveries at a real hospital, so if any medical intervention was necessary it would be available.

And it *was* necessary, at least in my opinion. When we arrived at the hospital, with a portable Sony and a few tapes of favorite music—Albert King, Samuel Barber, Billie Holiday—and a bottle of Moët, Olivia was brought to the midwife's birthing room, where she stayed in useless and excruciating labor for eight hours, until she was finally transferred to a more conventional labor room, where such things as fetal monitors and an intravenous drip of some labor-inducing drug were added to the program. She was suffering so much. There was nothing like natural childbirth to make you despise the natural world.

We had taken our Lamaze classes. I had attended them faithfully and had looked around the little gray-and-boysenberry classroom in the Ethical Culture Center, at the other prospective fathers, most of them, like me, trying to play catch-up ball with their utterly absorbed wives. What are we doing here, gentlemen? I had wanted to say. Do we really think we can escape the spells of our own fathers by becoming fathers ourselves? Well, of course we were there to learn ways to lessen our lovers' pain when the child within began kicking and twisting its way toward the light—breathe, darling, puff puff puff—but at least for Olivia and me it all turned out to be a waste. Olivia was in far too much pain to follow the rules of rhythmic breathing, and when she could it did no good anyhow. She held my hand and wept silently. I looked at her pale, sweaty, stricken, appalled, and overworked face, and then at the oscilloscope upon which our baby's heartbeat was recorded, and then at the IV bottle of Pitocin, which was meant to induce her contractions, and then, finally, at Nurse Wurtzel, who continually jabbed her fingers into Olivia and scolded her for not dilating.

"Let's get a doctor in here," I said to the midwife. She pursed her lips, furrowed her brow, and shook her head no. "We've been here for fifteen hours," I went on. "She's dilated four centimeters. I think—"

"I know what you're about to say," said Wurtzel, now adding mind reading to her medieval bag of tricks, "but I can't interrupt Olivia's labor. She came here for natural childbirth."

"No," I said, "*you* came here for natural childbirth. *We* came here for a baby, and I want that baby, and I want it now. You understand me? Get that fucking baby out of my wife."

"Sam, Sam," said Olivia, feebly, her voice of reason making its way to me through a gauntlet of pain. Her lips were white, cracked. She patted my hand: more than a little humiliating, that.

Wurtzel extended her fingers into Olivia and manually stretched the recalcitrant cervix. Olivia shrieked with pain.

"What are you doing?" I bellowed.

"It's all right, Sam," said the midwife; like many people uncertain of their status, she spoke in a superior tone.

"I want her to have a Cesarean, right now. I want a doctor in here and I want her taken out of your hands—"

"Sam," said Wurtzel.

"Look here, this natural childbirth is all you've got. Without it, you're selling frozen yogurt. You understand me? Why do you have that peculiar expression?"

"Stay with Olivia, Sam—she's pushing, and I don't want her pushing."

"Don't push, Olivia," I said. "Breathe."

"Okay, okay, we're getting some action, folks," said Wurtzel, evidently going through a bit of a personality transformation once the child's head poked through, which was why she must have gone into this line of work to begin with, for these very necessary personality transformations. "We've got a baby coming through. Come on, Olivia—you've been wanting to push, now's your chance. . . ."

And so forth and so on, all of that cheerleading and self-help lingo and gentle scolding and passionate rooting; but it would only be in retrospect that I could be arch about it—at the time I was as crazed as Wurtzel, practically shouting my encouragement into Olivia's ashen face. In all the excitement, I didn't notice Wurtzel had taken a pair of surgical shears to Olivia and widened her for the baby's premiere. There was so much wetness, so much pain, redness, and chaos. I heard in my own voice a certain desperate quality; I was screaming and cheering like some loser on the rail of the clubhouse turn. Olivia held on to me, she squeezed my hand. She lifted herself off the bed as she made the effort to push the baby out, and she pressed her forehead into mine. The optimist who had told us these breathing techniques would greatly reduce the woman's discomfort during birth had also warned that at a certain point in the labor it is not uncommon for the woman to turn savagely against the man, but this too did not turn out to be true. She clung to me as if I was her best friend as well as her husband and lover. I had never been so happy in all my life.

"It's a boy!" cried Wurtzel. She sounded jubilant, triumphant, and greatly relieved, as if—and this only occurred to me for a split second—this were the first time she had ever pulled one of these deliveries off successfully.

I kissed Olivia. I placed her soaking, boneless hand upon her stomach, which even now was deflating. Wurtzel wrapped the boy in a blanket and handed him to Olivia, and in a frenzy of joy I kissed Wurtzel hard on the mouth.

Michael was not an easy child. He seemed to miss the floaty darkness of the uterus, and we kept the apartment as dark as possible. He seemed also to dislike gravity—his face contorted all day long as if he were in a rocket ship going through G-force. Born with a full, minky head of hair, he soon lost it all save a few long, silky strands, and his naked scalp grew little scabs. He loathed having his diapers changed; cold pee and slimy shit were better than the intrusion of my hands. It had been agreed upon that this was my job, since Olivia had to do all the feeding. I warmed my hands near the electric heater, smoothed baby oil on them, tiptoed, smiled, cooed; but still Michael howled, arched his back, hovered above the changing table as if he were being given shock therapy.

Michael slept in two-hour segments, a revolutionary howling in the hills of his own colic. Olivia and I walked him, but he was inconsolable. We rocked him back and forth, devised little dances that might jiggle him to sleep. "Go to sleep, go to sleep, you fucking asshole," I would sing in a lilting whisper, as I held my miserable, squirming child in my arms.

Eventually, inevitably, Michael would fall to sleep, and I would place him into the crib with almost psychopathic gentleness. And looking down at my son's troubled face and his angry little body, I would suddenly love the boy with a kind of punchy rapture. He was so small, so tender; the will to protect him was so fierce that it must have somehow been there to govern an errant desire to do away with him once and for all. "My little guy," I would whisper. "Son."

And now, beside me in my bed, Olivia truly was asleep. Her breaths were deep and slow. I slid next to her, held her warm body close. Some shrink I once interviewed for one of the men's magazines told me that touching your wife while she sleeps is a return to taboo; it is our mother's haunches we caress in the deep, timeless darkness of the boudoir. It amazed me that whatever a man does, there is always another man willing to charge money to tell him he is doing the wrong thing.

I fell asleep for half an hour and then reawakened, my heart pumping stones. I thought of the first words of the *Inferno*: "Midway in our life's journey, I went astray from the straight road and awoke to find myself in a dark wood."

chapter four

earlier that day, while Sam talked to Michael's shrink, Michael sat in Pennyman's waiting room and reread Nadia's letter. It aroused him, sickened him. He folded it up, stood, and slipped the single page into his back pocket. He stretched; his fingers almost touched the soundproofed ceiling. He forced himself to sit down again, picked up a copy of *Newsweek*, an old one with a picture of several pregnant teenagers on the cover. Nice to have been a part of that, he thought, and then, repelled by his own lonely lust, feeling that it connected him to the repulsive reality of his own father, he threw the magazine onto the carpet and stood up again. He had a strange and powerful urge to plunge his hand into the fish tank and squeeze the life out of those iridescent slivers of slime.

Michael left Pennyman's office, not yet realizing that he could not face his father, or his mother, or any part of his life until he decided what to do with that letter in his pocket. He was already running, but he didn't know it. He waited for Sam for a few minutes in front of the Leyden Craft Shop, next door to Pennyman's building, but the sight of those skeins of yarn bunched up like toxic figure-eights made him physically ill: everything irritating about the move to Leyden seemed to be captured by those packets of copper, yellow, and pink. Who in their right mind would ever make or wear something those colors?

And so he drifted down Broadway and then, when he was on the corner of Broadway and Route 100, with the Smoke Shop on one side of him and the George Washington Inn on the other, Michael, with the casualness of someone flipping a coin, stuck out his thumb.

The first car that appeared stopped. "And so it was ordained by fate," Michael intoned to himself as he ran toward it, a Honda Accord the color of shit.

Michael opened the Accord's door and peered in. The driver was wiry, with a freckled face, dark glasses. He looked like a pilot for a small regional airline, whereas he was in fact a salesman flogging stainless-steel juicers. He had boxes of them in the backseat, along with a tan sports jacket on a wooden hanger, its sleeves stuffed with pink tissue paper.

"What's up, champ?" the salesman said, delivering the line with gusto, believing in the indelibility of first impressions.

Michael slipped into the car, relieved to be entering someone else's life. The car smelled of the air freshener that came off the little cardboard pine tree that dangled from the rearview mirror. Crosby, Stills and Nash were on the cassette deck. Michael hated oldies.

"Where to, champ?"

The salesman patted his own hair and frowned. The scented pine tree swung back and forth as he negotiated a curve. They were picking up speed. He noticed that Michael was staring at the cassette player.

"You like the sounds?"

"Not really," said Michael.

"You want to listen to something else? I've got tunes for every mood. Jazz, rock, torch songs—I even have show tunes. I sing along with them when I'm starting to nod out." He gestured toward the glove compartment.

"It's your car, you can listen to whatever. Anyhow, thanks for stopping for me."

"Out there for a while, huh."

"Negative, sir."

The salesman squinted at Michael, a little uneasy with that last remark.

"You haven't told me where you're going," he said.

"Correct," said Michael. It was a form of reply he had picked up in Leyden High: to the point, crypto-military. It spread gloom in his house when he used it. The salesman looked at him and then, slowly, smiled. Michael sensed the guy was already regretting having stopped.

"So. Where are you going?"

"This way is fine. The way you're driving."

Now the bud of the salesman's regret was opening quickly; it was almost in full flower: time-lapse photography.

"Are you in some kind of trouble, champ?"

"No."

"You are, aren't you?"

Crosby, Stills and Nash were singing about how life used to be so hard and then they bought a house in the country and a fucking pussycat and that made everything great.

"Actually," Michael said, "since you offered, I guess I wouldn't mind turning the music off."

He pressed the Eject button on the cassette player and the radio kicked in, tuned to a station the car had passed through hours ago, now reduced to a storm of static. Michael touched the Power button and the car was silent. Michael listened to the hiss of the tires over the two-lane blacktop. They were already well out of town.

"You sure you're not in trouble?" the salesman asked, in a level, almost friendly voice, as if sounding sincere would elicit sincerity in others.

"What if I am? Isn't everybody in some kind of trouble?"

"I'm not in trouble," said the driver.

"Then neither am I."

"I think you're kind of a wiseass, is that it, champ?"

"Sorry. My father's screwing somebody and I don't know what to do about it."

"What makes you think you gotta do anything?"

"I just think it. I don't know why I think half the things I do."

"You want to know what I think? I think you and I aren't going to be able to do business." He was already slowing the car down, steering it to the side of the road, up on a shoulder of pebbles and pine needles. "Take a hike, champ." The salesman drummed his fingers on the steering wheel. His nails were manicured, lightly coated with clear polish. His gold ring had a dark red stone at the center.

"Oh, come on," said Michael. He stalled for time, but he knew he was out. He could feel the salesman's desire to hurt him; it was like a dog whose growl was so deep you couldn't hear it, but your bones buzzed.

"I'm not going to debate it with you, champ. This is my car and what I say goes." He reached for the passenger-side door, brushing against Michael. Michael sensed the guy's tense, hard body beneath the bright white shirt. The door flew open so quickly it bounced on its spring hinges and almost closed again.

"Thank you ever so much for the ride," Michael said, getting out, carefully, insanely carefully, closing the door behind him. He stepped back as the car peeled out, the tires spitting pebbles and dirt. Michael cupped his hands over his mouth and shouted after the car, "I forgot to tell you to go fuck yourself!"

He waited there until the car disappeared and then there was silence, except for the wind blowing through the treetops.

He walked along the highway, bereft of plans, with no idea where he was going. It struck him: until this moment he had always been on his way somewhere—to school, to bed, to dinner or the movies. Even the hours of excruciating boredom were crossed by the shadow of some looming obligation. As a young child, he had once despaired that all of the continents, even every island, had already been discovered, and wherever you would go someone else had been there first. But now, at last, he had found a place to call his own, an emptiness that was his and his alone, a private preserve of nothingness.

Suddenly, he didn't want to risk being seen. Maybe his parents were already looking for him; maybe a friend of theirs might coincidentally drive by. He got off the highway at the first dirt road. The mouth of the road was wide and dusty, but it immediately narrowed, darkened, as it wound through the dense, budding woods that grew on either side of it.

Michael walked south on Paige Road. Spokes of soft, lint-drenched sunlight fanned through the trees. Here and there, dandelion spores rotated slowly in the breeze. The sky was dark, the electric, almost pathological blue of airport landing lights.

He heard a sound, looked up. The treetops moved slowly, in a kind of visual stutter, pictures in a flip book propelled by a faltering thumb. Michael reached into his Army fatigue jacket and pulled out a lone Marlboro. In the other pocket was a book of matches Sam had brought home from Shun Lee West in New York. He lit up and stepped off the road. He didn't know exactly where he was, or how close to the nearest house. He only smoked in private; it just wasn't something he wanted to do in plain sight, any more than he'd want to urinate or pick his nose or read *Penthouse* in front of others. He inhaled voluptuously and stood there in the budding brambles along the roadside. He looked into the woods. The spokes of sunlight seemed further away. He scrambled up a slight incline and now he was in the first row of saplings. Deeper in, the trees were gnarled, thick. There was no pathway, but the trees lured him in, farther and farther. They exerted a kind of irresistible green magnetism.

chapter five

e were homeless. Though we still had a roof over
our heads, several changes of clothes, food, heat,
bank accounts, toilets, a TV, Michael's disappearance rendered it all useless. The things of life are not pleasures
so much as protection from pain, and once they can no longer
stop or even mitigate your misery it is as if they have disappeared. Our beds turned to stone; the food rotted in the
refrigerator, or the frying pan, or in our very mouths; and
the roof was lifted off as if by a storm—though we could hear
the rain beating against it, it also fell directly upon us, soaking us, freezing us, as we staggered from room to room, wondering where in the entire world he could be.

Amanda came home Sunday morning around eleven. We
had hoped she would stay with Elektra for the whole day, but
Elektra and her mother were fervently religious and they
spent Sunday in church. We would have liked to protect
Mandy from the truth about Michael, but we were ravaged,
and we knew we had to tell her he was Out There Somewhere
and that we were looking for him.

"The important thing, sweetie," I said, "is that you don't
worry. Okay?" I was sitting at the kitchen table, with
Amanda half on my knee. She had slept in her clothes; her
hair held a faint whiff of incense. I tapped my knuckle on her

chin and smiled. Olivia, I noticed from the corner of my eye, was frowning at me. Was I saying the wrong thing? Or the right thing in the wrong way? Was I appearing too nonchalant, or acting like a liar? What? It was all I could do to restrain myself from looking at Olivia and saying, "Do you have a problem?"

Amanda was beautiful, like Olivia, like Olivia's sister, Elizabeth, like their mother. Tall, bony, dark-haired, coal-eyed, with a full, red mouth and a long neck, she even had a copper-colored birthmark the size of a ladybug beneath her right ear, just like the rest of them. She seemed to belong to them in some immense and fateful way. I could imagine all of them, years from now, shopping together, traveling to Scotland, drinking tea laced with whiskey by the fireplace, sharing their secrets. They seemed like an unbroken chain, a chain of women, and I was just something that had happened, someone who had come in and out of their lives.

As the immensity of Michael's absence settled into Amanda, she began to cry. And as she wept, she managed to say many of the things Olivia and I had been thinking but would not say.

"What if someone takes him?" she said. "What if they kill him?"

"He just needs a little time out," I said.

"But you must never do this," added Olivia.

"I *know*. But what if?"

"What if what, sweetie?" I said. I heard my voice; it sounded so reasonable, that baritonal calm.

"What if someone hurts him? What if he's crying for help and we can't even hear him?"

By now, Olivia had walked around the table and scooped Amanda off my lap and held her close. In some way too vague to mention (then) but real enough to sting, I felt she was rescuing her from me.

By noon, I was aching with sleeplessness; my undreamed

dreams seemed to have turned to flu. Waiting was intoler-able—we had to do something—so we got into the car, this time with Amanda, whom we could not decently leave on her own, no matter how we wanted to shield her from our predic-ament, and began again to look for Michael. It was hopeless, and we knew it. For every road we turned down, we passed ten without turning. If he was running from us, he would be able to spot our car well before we spotted him, and he might hide. If he had found a place to sleep, then he was hidden from us. If he had left Leyden, gone to New York, or hitch-hiked in whatever direction the first driver was heading, then we certainly had no chance of finding him. If he was injured, a hospital might call. If he was dead, we would hear from the police, once the body was recovered.

I did not believe he was dead; but the possibility of it, or, really, the impossibility of completely ruling it out, assaulted me. I felt his absence as a kind of wanton violence against me. I felt what he was doing was unforgivable. Yet I had been a runner, too. Many times, growing up, I had shot out of the house and stayed at a friend's apartment, or slept on the sub-way, or just walked the streets, catching catnaps on park benches, or with my head down on the counter of a Chock Full o'Nuts. (Nabokov was right and Tolstoy wrong: all *un*-happy families are alike.) I had survived these times on my own and had not even been aware of any particular danger.

"Go on Maple Street," said Amanda, pointing to a block of modest, stocky frame houses.

"Why? Do you see him?"

"No, just . . . I don't know."

"Does Michael have a friend on this street?" Olivia asked, as I made the turn.

"I just have a feeling," said Amanda.

My heart swelled with extravagant, idiotic hope. "A feel-ing?" said Olivia; and though I did not want to see her expression, I could tell from the sound of her voice that she, too, was lending particular credence to our daughter's pointing us in a direction, any direction. It was our first lead. And even as I went from one end of Maple to the other, and then turned around and patrolled it a second time, though there was nothing we could have failed to see the first time, even then it seemed as if we might actually find him.

"Then how about . . . whatchamacallit? Where the school is?" said Amanda.

"Livingston?" said Olivia.

"Yeah. Livingston. Let's go to Livingston and look for him."

"Are you just saying whatever pops into your mind, or is this based on something?" I asked.

My daughter looked at me, visibly hurt by my tone. Add it to the list: ambivalent, unfaithful, verbally abusive.

When we finally arrived back home, Michael's voice was waiting for us on our PhoneMate answering machine. "The beep's a little long. Are you clearing your old messages? Anyhow, it's me." (A pause, background sounds of wind, a passing truck—he was obviously calling from a phone booth.) "I'm okay. Sorry for . . . well, you know. Things aren't right for me and I'm just going to figure stuff out. I need a little time. I'm okay. I'm completely safe. Okay? So don't worry. I'll make up the schoolwork when I get back. I realize I'll be grounded or punished in some other way, but that's cool." (Another truck went by, downshifting. I wondered if some computer analysis of the noise could determine exactly where a road was graded in a way that would cause a truck to downshift in close proximity to a phone booth.) "Maybe I'll call later so you can realize I'm saying this stuff on my own and there's no one putting a gun to my head or something."

We played the message over and over, with Mandy standing to one side, wondering, isolated, afraid. And then, while we played it for the fifth or sixth time, the phone rang and I grabbed it quickly, not wanting to give Michael a chance for second thoughts.

However, it was my agent, Graham Davis, on the line.

"It's me again," he announced, like a kid, expecting his voice to be instantly recognized.

"Hello, Graham," I said, with a roll of the eyes toward Olivia. She sighed, put her arm around Amanda, led her out of the room—as if I were about to embark on something obscene.

"This is an awkward time," I said. "I've got family problems."

"Oh," said Graham. "I'm sorry."

There was a long silence, and finally he waited me out and I asked, "Well, what was it you wanted?"

"It's not what I want, Sam. It's what Ezra Pointy-Head Poindexter wants. It's all this incredible mania about *Visitors from Above*. They got orders for fifteen thousand copies."

I sat down on the steps leading to the bedrooms.

"This is just yesterday, Sam. Not grand total—one-day sales."

Amanda and Olivia emerged from the kitchen and walked around me, mounting the stairs with delicate, almost inaudible steps. Where are you going? I asked with my eyes. "Bath," Olivia mouthed. I nodded, but something felt wrong. Like anyone with a guilty conscience, I was beginning to refer everything to myself and my shitty little secrets; I could not help thinking that this midday bathing was somehow associated, even if only unconsciously, with a feeling of there being something unclean in *me*.

"That's great, Graham," I said. "That's a lot of books."

"Understatement. It's fucking marvelous, is what it is. May I tell you something in absolute confidence, and please even under pain of death not to repeat it?"

"I may crack before they actually kill me, but I'll try not to."

"I've never represented a book that's sold fifteen thousand copies in a single day, not in my entire career." He said this as if he were a dying man confessing he had never known love.

"It's not been such a long career, Graham. You're younger than I am."

"I mean, fucking hell, even at that somewhat reduced royalty we took—which I think was the right way to go, by the way, and I hope you're not annoyed, but, you know, given past performances and all that—but even at five percent royalty, we made $14,212.50 yesterday."

"Good."

"Good?"

"Great, fantastic, wow."

"I must say, I thought you'd be more pleased. Those family problems must be grim."

"Yes, I guess so. But I am happy about the money. It's the stupidest book I've ever written, but at least now I'll be able—"

"Oh, don't say that. I think it's extremely professional and much if it is fascinating. I was just looking through it before ringing you."

Right, I thought, and probably for the first time, too.

I felt something crashing within me, like a chair banging down in the next room. Michael.

"Anyhow," Graham was saying, "the thing is, Ezra feels we have to respond to this sudden flurry of sales. He says we need a plan, and of course he's dead right. I've been telling him this for weeks."

"God, Graham," I said, "maybe this is it. Maybe this book can actually make some money, some real fucking money, and I can put this whole nightmare behind me and do what I meant to do."

"What you meant to do?" asked Graham, forgetting for the moment that I still considered myself a real writer.

"Write novels—write things that are real."

"Yes," he said, back on track, "exactly. That's the whole point, isn't it? I understand how you feel, I truly do. That's why I've been telling Ezra Pointy-Head Poindexter we need a plan of action. That's why we need you."

"Me?"

"In Ezra's office, eleven tomorrow morning."

"Do I really need to be there? I don't think I can."

"Please, Sam. Don't give me a nervous breakdown. It would be an unmitigated disaster if you weren't there. Ezra's talking about putting tens of thousands of dollars behind your book, and you need to be there."

"You need John Retcliffe, not me."

"Listen, Sam, for the next few weeks you *are* John Retcliffe. Come on, it won't be so bad."

"I can't."

"You have to. We'll get you in and out of there quickly. I promise."

"Graham . . ."

He knew I was getting ready to say yes, just the way I said his name; it was like "Be gentle with me."

"Sam," he said, "if you fail to capitalize on this opportunity, you'll hate yourself for the rest of your life. How many chances like this are going to come along? If this thing continues to grow, you could be set financially for years, maybe for the rest of your life. Meet me in my office and we'll walk over together."

I heard the water thundering into the tub upstairs, thought of my wife and daughter in the bathroom as it slowly filled with steam.

"Okay," I said. "I'll be there, but I have to make it quick."

I hung up but continued to sit on the steps with the telephone on my lap. I expected Michael to call. Perhaps the planets had just lined up in my favor, as the universe turned in a circle like a vast combination lock. He would call, say he was on his way home; I would be free to go. But the phone remained a silent weight on my legs, and finally I got up, put it back on its spindly little table, and proceeded to my study off the kitchen.

Was it just because I thought I might become rich, or was there some other reason that I chose that moment to finally do what I should have done months before? I gathered Nadia's letters into a bunch, resisted the impulse to read them a final time, to savor them. Tearing them to shreds as I left the house, I got into my car and drove to town, more or less looking for Michael as I went. Once in town, I deposited bits of Nadia's letters in various public trash barrels, so it would have taken a genius of paranoia and detection to ever piece them together again.

There, I said to myself, driving back to the old homestead on Red Schoolhouse Road. Done with it. I felt such a surge of happiness and accomplishment that I forgot for a moment that my son was still out there.

chapter six

monday morning Olivia drove Sam to the train station. It was raining and the wind blew; a cold mist joined heaven and earth. The Leyden train station was rudimentary: a little brick warming house where tickets and magazines were sold, and a covered staircase leading down to a wooden platform badly in need of paint, where every two or three hours a train came down from Albany or Niagara Falls on the way to Manhattan.

As Olivia pulled into the little parking lot, Sam rubbed a porthole into the steamy window and looked out.

"Is the train coming?" Olivia asked.

"Not yet. What if he took the train to New York?" Sam asked.

"I know. I called everyone we know there."

"So now they know, too." Sam closed his eyes, rubbed his forehead. "Fine. Who gives a shit?"

"Sam. It doesn't matter."

"I just wanted everyone to think we moved to the country and everything was great."

"It's hard to keep secrets when everything is falling apart."

"Right. That's the incentive for keeping your life running neatly. Look, I don't care what you tell our friends. Just—" He stopped, looked away.

She didn't really want to know what it was he didn't want her to say. She was tired of bearing the burden of his feelings. He kept on coming up with new ones anyhow, and they were so various and so strong they didn't seem altogether real to Olivia, whose character was more stoical. When she read about marriages in the magazines, it seemed she was the man and Sam was the woman: it was he who clamored for more and more communication, constant contact, reassurance, and she who often wanted privacy, silence, just to be left alone. Anyhow, when Sam wanted to say something, there was no need to coax it out of him; in fact, he would say it whether or not she wanted him to.

He turned toward her, his face a mask of utter vulnerability. "Just don't tell anyone I only have a medium-sized penis."

She began to laugh, and Sam, pleased to have amused her, laughed, too. He was delighted; he was vindicated. It sometimes seemed to her he would say anything for a reaction. And the more she resisted giving him his reaction, the more thrilled he was to achieve it.

"I wish you weren't going," Olivia said, turning off the windshield wipers. Rain sheeted the window like melting silver.

"I'll be back. Tonight."

"Just the look on Amanda's face when we dropped her at school . . . Too much is going on."

"I know. But there's not an awful lot I can do here anyhow. I just keep driving around."

"He's out there. Somewhere."

"At least we know he's all right."

"Do we?"

"He's calling. He'll call again."

Sam had the impatience of the one who is leaving and she was stuck with the slightly shaming recalcitrance of the one who stays behind.

The train appeared, waving its plume of smoke, its whistle howling through the early-morning gloom.

Sam reached in the backseat and grabbed his briefcase, a birthday present from Olivia ten years ago. She was so convinced he would sense its extravagant expense and return it that she paid an extra fifty bucks and had his initials burned into the leather. Today, it was filled with a little umbrella, a copy of Cioran's *The Temptation to Exist*, which Sam began three years ago and forgot to finish, a copy of *Newsweek*, in case the existentialism didn't hold his attention, and a roll of antacid tablets.

"I'll call you," he said, kissing her. His breath smelled of toothpaste and coffee.

"You *are* coming home tonight, aren't you?"

"Of course. But I'll tell you which train. Help Amanda with her spelling words, okay? She needs the whole week to get them right."

With this final gesture toward fatherhood, he bounded out of the Subaru. He wore gray slacks, a slightly linty blazer. Olivia momentarily wished she was one of those women who take good care of people. She watched him go, with his briefcase slapping him like a saddle bag against a pony. It was so strange, so unexpectedly moving to now and again spy the surviving boy within him. When, sixteen years ago, she surprised him with the news of her pregnancy, she told Sam (trying to make it up to him, unfortunately) that now he would always have someone to play with—he had already exhausted her appetite for board games and long walks, his antic jokes were as frightening as they were funny, and his early-morning high spirits were appalling. But it had not worked out like that. The children were not proper playmates for Sam; they were more like her. Victory left them cold, defeat insulted them, and the rules to games seemed arbitrary, exhausting. If she and Sam ever shared an old age, he would certainly add this to his litany of complaints, this failure on her part to give him amusing kids. He had no one to play catch with, no reason to join a gym, no excuse to visit the sporting goods shops for high-tech Frisbees, dart boards, tents. Once, trying to whip the family into enthusiasm for a dog, Sam placed an empty economy-sized mayonnaise jar on the table, asking them to drop their spare change in, with the plan being the adoption of a dog from the Humane Society, paying for its neutering, shots, upkeep. But only Sam dropped his quarters in; the others forgot, weren't really that keen about a dog in the first place. No: actually, Amanda tried to help, too—with pennies she had painted with red nail polish so Lincoln looked like Lenin. Sam was so discouraged by his family's lackluster response to his scheme that he emptied the jar into an old Yankees cap and bought himself an atlas. "You used Mandy's pennies," Olivia had scolded him, regretting it as she did but holding her shaky ground nonetheless.

She waited in the parking lot until the train pulled away. She listened to the car's guttural idle. Her hands gripped the steering wheel. Her heart beat in a strange way that was at once annoying and frightening; the beat did not seem to come from its center but from the side.

Olivia steered the car out of the parking lot and headed back toward town. Daffodils pushed their way toward the huge slate sky. One of the town's few surviving farms had its Holsteins out to pasture; the newborn calves watched their mothers chew fresh shoots of grass. Olivia stared at the cows, the blue enamel silos, the old fences in need of repair, a long giant willow spreading its hazy yellow branches over a pond. Lost in reverie for a moment, she gasped, suddenly realizing she wasn't looking at the road. She yanked the car to the right as a school bus shot past. It was filled with boys from the Cardinal Morgan School, neurologically impaired welfare kids, with their faces pressed against the smudged windows, calling out to her.

She pulled to the side of the road, suddenly needing to catch her breath. Even in duress, her life was tinged by the miasma of déjà vu. She was one of those people whose life had assumed the qualities, shape, and dimensions she had always more or less expected. There was something endlessly unsurprising about her life. She had once tried to explain this to Sam. "Nothing really surprises me," she said. "A weather report or a knock-knock joke surprises me more than my own life." He had looked at her balefully, as if this might mean she did not adore him. He could not understand that this was not about him.

She drove to Leyden High School. Classes began at 7:45, and she and Sam had been posted there earlier in the morning, watching the students come in. Now she just wanted to make sure Michael wasn't lurking outside. The building was squat, red brick. A banner hung outside the main entrance: JUST CAN'T HIDE THAT LEYDEN HIGH PRIDE. The banality was crushing; she felt generally bad about sending her children to these hopelessly tacky schools, to memorize faded facts with kids named Sean and Tara, almost all of whom actively hated school and planned never to read a book in their adult lives. But what choices were there?

Olivia herself had gone to the University of Chicago Lab School, steeped in Western Civ in the company of suicidal little geniuses with dark circles under their eyes. It hadn't worked out for her. The intensity of the students, the superior attitudes of the teachers—she felt like a lightweight, a very ordinary mind who was there because her parents were U of C faculty. Furthermore, the Lab School curriculum was so advanced that her first two years at college at Skidmore were like a series of review courses, and by the time challenging material was presented, in her junior year, she had lost the habits of study. Suddenly, she was a C student, and then, in the midst of a consuming love affair, she was a D student, and then she quickly dropped out of school before she visited any more disgrace upon herself. She went to New York to live with her sister, Elizabeth, who helped Olivia save face by getting her into an intern program at *Rolling Stone*.

Her own education had left her feeling skeptical and a little annoyed at those parents who approached their children's schooling with such vigor and anxiety. She was content to let Michael find his own way through the public schools—and it was just as well, since they were never able to afford a private one. As for Amanda, she might end up needing a little extra help, though Olivia suspected that what appeared as slowness was mostly shyness, idiosyncrasy, and distraction—Mandy had an artist's temperament. She would do fine; her time would come. What formed you was not school and grades and letters of recommendation but some alchemy of character, luck, health, and timing.

She waited in the school's parking lot, looking at the building, the soccer field, the scrubby fringe of woods to the west of the school. She thought, for a moment, she saw something—a person, a deer—but when she rubbed the steam from the window to get a better look all there was was emptiness, and rain, and mist rising slowly from the wet ground.

A Ford Explorer pulled next to her. It was a rugged, practical-looking vehicle, full of horsepower, with deeply grooved, wide wheels, a search light attached to the side, and a sticker on its wide chrome bumper that said HUGS NOT DRUGS. At the wheel was Russ Connelly, in a suit and tie, and next to him was Greg Pitcher, wolfing down the last few bites of a donut. He drank something from a cup, put it back in the Explorer's cup holder, and then grabbed his books and hopped out.

"Greg," Olivia called out, quickly rolling down her window.

Greg stopped but did not turn around. When he finally faced her, his expression was guarded, put-upon.

"Have you seen Michael?" Olivia asked.

"No!" said Greg, his voice cracking with anger. "What am I supposed to be around here? I don't know anything about it, okay? I don't even know Michael."

"What's going on?" asked Russ from his truck. He threw the door open and jumped out, but once out in the raw weather he stopped, looked around, as if he were just becoming aware of the rain.

"You stayed at our house, Greg," Olivia was saying. "Of course you know Michael."

"I don't know where he is."

"I'm not accusing you of anything. We're just worried, that's all. We're extremely frightened." It was a mistake to say that; she felt the sting of tears in her eyes, felt her insides shaking like the bough of a tree.

But Greg seemed not to have noticed at all how upset she was, or he noticed and didn't care.

"I said I don't know," he said, as if she were a complete idiot.

"All right, buddy, that's it," said Russ, who was by now next to Greg and gripped the boy's arm. "I have had just about enough of your selfish us-against-them attitude."

Greg tried to yank his arm away, but Russ's grip was strong. Olivia sensed the frequent terrors of the Connelly household, with Russ's self-righteous anger lurking beneath his cheerful exterior. Finally, he was the type of man who awakened teenagers in the middle of the night and marched them down to the kitchen and silently pointed at the uncapped jar of Skippy left on the counter top. Watching Greg trying to wrest his arm from Russ, Olivia's stomach slowly turned; yet she could say nothing to interfere. It was not her business. And what if Greg actually knew something?

"I don't know where he is," Greg said. The fear was leaving his face. It was as if he were losing the last of his innocence before their eyes, standing in that parking lot, in the rain. The fear drained away, and taking its place were fury and contempt.

"You don't know," said Russ, sarcastically. "You don't know anything anymore. You don't know if you have any homework, you don't know where the chainsaw is. You don't know whose turn it is to feed the snakes. And today you oversleep and I have to drive you to school." Greg turned quickly on his heel and walked toward the school, hefting his book bag, keeping his head down. Russ turned to Olivia and shrugged. "You want to know what?" he said. "I think he's telling the truth."

"I didn't mean to make you think he was hiding something."

"Why not? He lies all the time—they all do." Russ grinned. "It's the hormones." When Olivia failed to respond, he pushed the matter a bit further. "We've all got them, you know. Men too."

There was something intrusive and faintly distasteful about Russ talking about hormones. Yet as vulgar as he was, there was something in him, as in nearly every man, that frightened Olivia. She hated this fear, but it would not go away, she could not break it. It was pliable; it wrapped itself around every relationship she had with a man. Their bodies, their neediness, their rage.

"I better be going," Olivia said.

"If there's anything we can do," said Russ. "I realize you haven't had long to establish yourself in Leyden, so feel free to call on Sharon and me. Okay?"

He reached for her, touched her wrist, smiled. She wanted to pull away, but she stayed there, transfixed by a frightening glimpse of some inner Russ, as tender and repellent as that rim of red children show each other when they yank back their eyelids.

The police knew nothing more about Michael. They had called the youth shelters in a fifty-mile radius, informed police in neighboring townships. What had she expected—bloodhounds fanning out through the forests, helicopters dragging their searchlights up and down the riverbanks? Instinctually, she withheld the fact that Michael had called home; with that bit of information, the police might stop paying attention to them altogether.

Olivia sat at the kitchen table, paying household bills and waiting for another call from Michael. The silence was oppressive; the paperwork, too. She could not bear paying bills, though the chore had fallen to her. Sam used to do it, but now she protected him from those fits of despair. "What am I doing with my life?" he'd ask, waving a sheaf of invoices from MasterCard, the fuel company, New York Telephone. "Look at me! I can't even support my family!" He didn't blame the credit company for its usurious interest rates, he didn't blame Gateway Oil for price gouging; he only blamed himself for not somehow managing to drill into that rich vein out there in the cultural mountains where the gold freely flowed.

She longed to call her mother, but it was only ten o'clock in Leyden, seven in the morning in Santa Barbara. The ocean was inky; cool fog still wreathed the jacaranda. America's Riviera, the place actually made Olivia physically ill. The town seemed so pleased with itself, so appallingly unfazed by its own wealth. She had never seen so many frozen-yogurt shops in her life; everyone in town was fixated on putting friendly bacteria into their lower intestines. They were health know-it-alls, they knew the best foods, the best waters; they seemed perfectly content to outlive the poor. "The earth belongs to the Santa Barbarians," Sy Wexler proclaimed; but what was she to make of the implied irony of this if he chose to make his life among them, eating free-range chicken on their patios, joining their clubs, even taking tennis lessons from their slow-witted nephews?

Maybe Lillian, her mother, would be up early. Like Sam, she used to wake with the birds; it was part of being virtuous. Lillian used to paraphrase Wallace Stevens—something about life being two dreams, and what kind of fool would choose the dream obscured by sleep? (For most of her adolescence, Olivia slept with a goose-down pillow over her head, protecting the sanctity of her own dream theater.) Back in Chicago, before retirement, Lillian fought off creeping arthritis by swimming in the pool in Ida Noyes Hall every morning for an hour, after which she had a second breakfast with her friend Abigail Dobkin, who taught dance at a nearby Jewish community center and who shared with the Wexlers a youthful Trotskyism. Sy used to rise early, too. He liked to do Canadian Air Force exercises in his striped pajamas and leather slippers, run hot tap water over a couple of spoonfuls of instant coffee at the bottom of an unwashed cup, and then meticulously correct student papers until his morning class on the Russian Revolution, come home, drink some Manischewitz borscht out of the bottle, and correct more papers until his afternoon class on the Revolution Betrayed. Olivia used to secretly admire her parents' vigor, and the separateness of their days seemed romantic to her—they were bachelors by day, happily reunited each night.

Now, however, retired to Santa Barbara, they were inseparable, and it didn't seem like intimacy but fusion. They shopped together, walked hand in hand on the beach, attended lectures at the university, and whispered to each other while all around them young students assiduously took notes. They slept close, curled into each other like little groundhogs until ten or eleven o'clock and chose their slacks and tropical shirts from the same large cedar closet. It didn't matter who wore what; they were both the same size, virtually the same sex.

Yet Olivia must not call her mother, regardless of the hour. Relations were cordial, but not as close as they might have been. The impediment between them was Sam: it was her mother's unstated but unwavering belief that Olivia stole Sam from Elizabeth, Olivia's older sister, with whom she lived after dropping out of Skidmore.

Elizabeth had flourished in the academic boot camp of the Wexler home and had gone on to Radcliffe and a year of graduate studies at the Sorbonne. While well enough connected to get Olivia a job at *Rolling Stone*, she herself worked, for less money, at a short-lived but tony literary quarterly called *Cradle*, which published well-known writers such as Tennessee Williams and Doris Lessing along with newcomers like Sam. *Cradle* was owned by a man named Val Gryce, the dissolute heir of a fading New York fortune made originally in pelts and then squandered on Broadway. Gryce was a man of sharp, rapid-fire wit, except with Elizabeth, with whom he was in love, despite being thirty years her senior.

Sam's story ran in the last issue of *Cradle*—Gryce was killed in a fire in the residential hotel he called home up on Broadway near Columbia, and the magazine folded. Sam's piece was an excerpt from his first novel, which at that point he had entitled *My Holocaust*. Elizabeth had read the excerpt aloud to Olivia one night, her usually unperturbable alto cracking with emotion. "This guy is so tender and brave," Elizabeth said, holding Sam's manuscript to her breast. "Val is making me have a party and we're inviting our authors. Maybe Sam Holland will come. He's so great."

"I don't know how you stand writers," Olivia said. "I want to meet musicians or baseball players or even criminals—

people who *do* something rather than just talk about it all the time."

Elizabeth's party was on a sultry summer evening; their two-room apartment on West Eighty-eighth Street smelled as if the paint were cooking right off the walls. As it happened, both Sy and Lillian were in town to see Max Schachtman, one of Leon Trotsky's former secretaries and a man whose splinter group had once been the Wexlers' ideological home. Schachtman and his wife, Yetta, were holding court in their Chelsea apartment, with Max propped up in his bed, his large, lethal belly slowly shrinking beneath a single dingy sheet. He was dying, and former comrades from all over the country were coming to say goodbye. Sy was still with the Schachtmans, but Lillian had come back to Elizabeth's to help with the party, though she was no help at all. She could only make curt, old-fashioned suggestions—she wanted a silver cup filled with cigarettes, she said they needed rye and sweet vermouth, she warned them about playing the stereo too loudly—and was too tired and sad to lift a finger, except to now and then brush away a tear that rolled down her stoically expressionless face.

"Try and cheer up a little, Mama," Elizabeth said, as she ran the carpet sweeper under Lillian's grudgingly raised legs. "I'm sorry about Mr. Schachtman, but I've got people coming over any minute."

"The man defined an entire generation of anticommunist radicalism," said Lillian. "Everyone from Howe to Draper sat at his feet. His analyses of the new class in Russia is still twenty years ahead of its time, and all you're worried about is a party?"

"He's not even dead yet, Mom," answered Olivia.

"Who knows?" said Lillian, her voice heavy and humid with sarcasm. "Pick up the phone. Maybe he is."

The humidity was not only in Lillian's voice. It was everywhere. The leaves on the sycamore out beyond Elizabeth's window hung as if defeated by the August heat. Fish fried a week ago still scented the air; every aroma was as clear and dreadful as skid marks on a country road. The ice melted in the ice buckets and the new ones came out of the freezer as insubstantial as spun sugar. The guests arrived flush faced; more than a few seemed snappish, and Val Gryce, who had encouraged Elizabeth to host this soiree, was in foul temper. Tennessee Williams was nowhere in sight, nor was Doris Lessing, or any of the other well-known writers who had appeared in *Cradle*. However, the younger writers were at the party, and even as they sweated through their clothes they managed to go through the drinks and crudités like a swarm of literate locusts.

Sam arrived late. Of all the novice writers present, he seemed the only one who had to work a job that paid wages; he sold men's furnishings at Altman's and, by night, doctored theses for NYU graduate students. It was the summer of '75. He arrived in a white shirt, baggy khaki slacks. His hair was slicked back. After Altman's he had stopped to take an aikido class at a dojo on Fourteenth Street. Olivia watched him as he entered the apartment. Elizabeth made a signal: There he is. What do you think? Sam poured himself what was left from a bottle of Mâcon Villages and then stuck the dead soldier into the bucket of ice water, neck first. Carrying his plastic cup of straw-colored wine, he walked directly over to Olivia.

"All my life," he said, "I've been seeing you getting in and out of taxicabs, coming from dance class, or a concert, sometimes with snowflakes in your hair, or a bag of plums in your hand, and I've always wondered where you were going."

"Me?" she said.

And in the years to come it would seem not only an intelligent question but a prescient one as well. Sam fell in love as soon as he saw her, but what became less and less clear was: with whom? The composite, desirable, unattainable multitudes of women who he decided were represented by Olivia?

Or his own luck, his rising fortunes, his face which he saw reflected back in Olivia's placid, unformed oval?

Lillian saw what was happening, and she abandoned her self-appointed task of cheering up Gryce and concentrated on Sam. She talked to him about Max Schachtman, the theory of bureaucratic collectivism; Sam, to her surprise, knew what she was talking about. Someone at the dojo was an old Schachtmanite. (But then, Olivia was to learn, Sam knew a little about a lot of things. There were very few conversations he could not get through, though this gift for gab was finally a hindrance, like a trust fund that gives you just enough money to sap your ambition.) As they spoke, Lillian kept her hand on Sam's shoulder, guiding him toward Elizabeth, who had been cornered by a large, extravagantly freckled nun who was writing an essay about Flannery O'Connor. Yet even as Sam talked about the Independent Socialist League and expressed his regret over Mr. Schachtman's illness, and even as he allowed himself to be steered toward Elizabeth, he continually scoured the room for Olivia.

Sam, in courtship, was a heat-seeking missile. He had had early success with a technique based on frankness and persistence, and that was now his permanent style. When he left the party, he pointed at Olivia and called out, "I'm going to phone you and make a dinner plan. Okay?" The remaining guests stared at Olivia until she nodded yes, as subtly as possible.

"I liked that Sam Holland of yours," said Lillian, as she and the girls cleaned up the party's debris, emptying ashtrays, plunging Pottery Barn tumblers into the hot suds, opening the windows as wide as possible and waving the galaxies of gray-violet smoke out with wet dishtowels.

"Of *mine*?" said Elizabeth, with a high, fluttery laugh.

"Wasn't he the one you said you were interested in?" asked Lillian, in a voice that sounded so innocent, but she looked at Olivia with alligator eyes as she said it.

Sam called that very night, right after Sy picked Lillian up and they cabbed it over to the Mayflower Hotel. As quietly as possible, Olivia held him at bay, but still, somehow, at the end of the call, she agreed to meet him at the Riviera on Sheridan Square the next night.

"He *was* supposed to be for me," Elizabeth said later that night, but even this was delivered in a not-quite-direct tone. It made it possible for Olivia not to respond, and in the silence she realized something about herself. Sam had moved some great wheel that had been stuck in the goo of her natural dreamy ambivalence and pessimism, and now that it was moving there was no stopping it, no wanting to. She could feel her internal landscape changing.

"Oh well," Elizabeth was saying, "that's what I get for having a younger sister."

Elizabeth had always criticized Olivia for her life's lack of direction. And until this moment, as Elizabeth finished the last of her eighth glass of water for the day and silently belched into her knuckle, and Olivia sat on the sofabed and felt its springs through the stingy mattress and the cold of the metal frame on the backs of her legs, somehow Olivia had always accepted the characterization. It was her fault; she was not as clever as Elizabeth, not as serious. But suddenly all that was changed. Elizabeth might have construed that Sam was for her, but nature would have it otherwise, and here Olivia was on the side of nature. Something was within her that drew Sam toward *her*. There was a rightness to it, a sense of fate— though even at twenty, Olivia realized that everyone falling in love feels the hand of fate.

Elizabeth forgave Olivia for falling in love with Sam and letting him fall in love with her, but Lillian cooled to Olivia after that. It was a remarkable blow to Olivia's sense of her place in the world. The politics of the Wexler family were such that none of the children felt the complete ease in confiding in each other that they felt in opening their hearts to

Lillian, and now, with Lillian angry with her, Olivia lost not only the approval of her mother but the person in whom she would naturally want to confide that loss as well. When Michael was born and the Wexlers were crammed into Sam and Olivia's apartment, Lillian cuddled and bathed the baby while maintaining a little wedge of aloofness between her and Olivia. She even managed to give Olivia a sponge bath and feed her consommé and read an issue of *The New Yorker* to her and still keep that quarantine around their old easy intimacy.

For quite a while, Olivia noted this development without feeling so awfully bad. She had her own life, and the love she felt for Sam sometimes made her feel lucky she had enough left over to give to her child. She adored them both; she accepted the richness of her life with a calm gratitude, as if it were an inheritance. She knew it was old-fashioned and probably a little nuts, but Sam thought she was his muse, and it was flattering. No, it was more than that: his adoration of her and his need of her went to the center of her being; it filled her and erased her, over and over and over, until she could not imagine herself without it. Even when the pressures of poverty and parenting began to take their toll, Sam sometimes crawled across the floor and kissed her feet; her sexual nature entranced him, the sounds she made, her taste and smell. He would sometimes just come up to her and touch her arm and breathe a sigh of relief, as if he had for a moment been afraid she was a figment of his imagination. He told her everything that ever happened to him; he wanted to hear about every moment of her life. He was insatiable; he would have driven a woman like Elizabeth mad. He would have driven a great many women mad. He showered her with presents, brought coffee to her bedside, wrote poems to her which he would read aloud over a bottle of wine and then throw away because they were not good enough to keep. When a child would awaken her in the middle of the night, she would have to extricate her hand from Sam's.

"I'm so in love with him," she told her mother, on a visit to Chicago, after her parents had decided to move out to Santa Barbara and the children were invited to ransack the family house on Dorchester for keepsakes, photographs old toys, baby clothes. Olivia was pregnant with Amanda at the time, and Lillian was kind, solicitous, aware of every possible discomfort Olivia might be feeling. But still the hedge of reserve was there, and Olivia quite consciously began to push at it with declarations of her love for Sam. Could Lillian, upon hearing the truth of Olivia's feelings, possibly believe that Elizabeth would have been happier with Sam? Wouldn't Lillian come to understand that Sam had gone to the daughter for whom he would do the most good?

"For a while, I thought I loved him so much because he showed me such affection," Olivia said, sipping a glass of ale, with her feet propped up on the immemorial ottoman, while Lillian maintained a metronomic rhythm of busyness, dusting the top of a Daniel Bell book, and then the top of a Durkheim anthology, and placing them in a packing crate. "But now I see that is just the beginning of it, my feelings." She cringed inwardly. How could something that had such searing internal clarity come out so muddled? She forced herself to go on with it. "It's that Sam lets me love *him*. I think that's so rare, don't you?" Lillian looked up at her—skeptically? Olivia kept her eyes on the window, at the budding maple dancing back and forth in the brisk Chicago wind. "All the love I ever wanted to give any man but couldn't, I now can give to Sam. He welcomes it, and so I feel welcomed."

"You've been feeling unwelcome?" Lillian asked, a little sharply.

"Maybe what I mean is underutilized."

"Your father always loved you. In fact, I'd say he adored you."

"I know, Mom."

"He *is* a person of enormous dignity. There could conceivably have been some confusion because of *that*." She shrugged and went back to packing the books she'd been using in her course work for the past twenty years.

"You know what your Sam once said to me?" Lillian asked, a note of humor in her voice—though this was not necessarily a good sign.

"Am I going to like this?" asked Olivia.

"He said that sociology was the American academic establishment's answer to Marxism. Is he a Marxist?"

Olivia shook her head no.

"I didn't think so," said Lillian, and went back to her books.

Olivia took a long drink of the ale. She had been raised on unrefrigerated beverages—it was one of her parents' European affectations—but on her own she had become used to the icy American taste, and the tepid ale tasted like spoiled bread.

"It's hard for me to keep track of myself, sometimes," Olivia said. Her voice was steady; she realized now what she had been wanting to say. "I think about Sam so many hours of the day—what he's doing, how he might be feeling, the way he touched me the night before. I still get excited when I hear his footsteps coming up the stairs."

"That's because you're there, waiting for him."

"I know. I haven't made much of my life."

"I don't mean to say that."

"I realize that I've given my life over to love, and now to children. That never works out."

"Well, perhaps it will for you, Olivia."

Olivia put her glass down and folded her hands over her belly. She felt a stirring—the first. The child inside of her was alive, moving now for its own mysterious reasons. It gave her the courage she needed.

"You've never really forgiven me for marrying Sam, have you, Mom?"

"Oh, I wouldn't say that."

"It wasn't as if he and Beth were lovers. They weren't even going out. It's just been so crazy. And I miss you. We were always so close. Really. What have I done?"

Lillian draped her dust rag on the side of the packing crate and turned toward Olivia. Suddenly she looked alarmingly keen. Lines appeared above her upper lips as if the skin had been scored by the teeth of a comb. "I always believed that women should support one another. God knows, I'm not a radical feminist, but I do maintain that simple courtesy and compassion ought to be the rule among women—especially sisters."

"I do, too."

Lillian had sadly shaken her head. "You're my daughter, no matter what, if you want to talk about the bottom line." It was a consolation prize. The resignation and finality of it shocked Olivia. She would come to wonder if the misery of that moment permeated her amniotic sac and marked poor Mandy forever.

At eleven the phone rang. Michael. She knew from the sound of him that he was inside.

"Hello," was all he said.

"Where are you?"

"Mom. It's okay." As if he were being patient with her.

"Is it? Where are you calling from?" She heard her own voice, shrill, helpless; she was becoming one of those people. She took a deep breath, looked out the kitchen window. An upside-down chickadee was prying out the last sunflower seed from the Hollands' Lucite bird feeder. It was typical of them, thought Olivia, to lure the local birds with promises of ready food and then to let the feeder go empty for weeks at a time.

"Everything's fine," Michael said.

"Michael, nothing is fine."

"How's Dad? How's Amanda? You two ought to get off her case. She's a great little kid. She's just different, that's all. But in a good way. You two think that everything has to be a certain way or else it's all wrong, and then you get so freaked out and everything. But it doesn't have to be just one way. What if Mandy never learns to read? So what? You know what I mean?"

He was, Olivia decided, drunk. Or high.

"You don't sound well, Michael."

"I feel great. Can I tell you something?"

"Yes."

"I met some people."

"What people?"

"People."

"Where do they live? Are they your age?" She had no idea where her questions came from.

"Some of them."

"Are you safe?"

"Are *you*?"

"Yes, of course I am."

"Yeah, well, whatever. I better hang up. I just don't want you to worry."

"But I am worried. We all are. You have to come home."

"Where's Dad?"

"In the city. He had an important meeting."

She was going to explain this further, but she didn't want it to seem she was making excuses. Sam was doing what had to be done—even though nothing on earth could have made Olivia leave Leyden with Michael on the loose.

"Amanda in school?"

"Come home."

"I'm okay, Mom. I promise you I'm safe. And I will come home."

"When?"

"I don't know." There was a silence, and then he said, softly, in a voice she knew could only tell the truth, "When I can."

"You can right now," she said, inwardly realizing that for some reason he couldn't.

"No."

"What's stopping you?"

"Everything."

"Michael . . ."

"I have to hang."

"Michael . . ."

"Don't ask me any more questions, Mom. If I wanted questions, I wouldn't be out here. Don't you see? I'm here because I can't answer your questions."

She sighed. Irritation rose up in her, like a swarm of bees. The boy was so fucking dramatic, but he came to it honestly: Sam's emotions often ran toward the grandiose.

"Michael . . ."

"Bye, Mom. Sorry. Take care of yourself."

As soon as the connection was broken, Olivia called the police. It made her feel as if she were betraying Michael, and when the dispatcher answered the phone Olivia was so rattled she couldn't remember the name of the cop they had spoken to Saturday night and Sunday.

"This is Olivia Wexler," she said. "I have a missing son?" Silence. The dispatcher patiently waited for her to say more. She pictured him there, a Drake's Cake resting on its own cellophane next to a styrofoam cup of coffee.

"Is there someone I can speak to about this?" she asked. "I have some new information."

"Is your son home now?"

"No. But he called. And I have a theory."

"A theory?"

"I think I know where he is."

"Where, Mrs. Wexler?"

Another conversation going nowhere. She had nothing specific to tell, no address, no phone number, no hot tip, and so she would be ignored. Her intuition that Michael was living in an abandoned house was meaningless to the police; her sense that Michael wanted to come home but would now create circumstances that would make an easy return impossible would be not only meaningless but completely ignored. The sum total of everything she knew about Michael meant less to the police than would one number from a license plate.

She placed the phone back into its cradle and looked at the blur of paperwork on her table. She rubbed her fingertips into her closed eyes. It felt remarkably good. It felt wonderful. She couldn't stop. She felt the brightening jelly of her eyes beneath the silky sheath of their lids. The pleasure of it was sublime, and when she stopped and looked out toward the bright window the air exploded with circles, crescents; the world was oil on water. And when it clicked back into its customary intransigence she felt a surge of desire go through her; a flaming arrow of sex shot across the inner darkness. She did not want to be kissed or held; she did not want her nipples caressed, she wanted no tongue in the ear, no words of love: she wanted to be entered, filled, fucked. The brutality of this need startled her, and then, quickly, it was gone.

The phone rang, and though she was normally shy, even phobic, about the phone, she picked it up before it was through its first ring.

"Hello?"

"Olivia? This is Sharon. Russ's wife?"

Olivia noted the centuries of female oppression in that form of identification, and then said, "What's up?" She had a curt phone manner, partly out of annoyance with the instrument and partly in reaction to Sam's telephone effusiveness—he always sounded so pleased when someone called.

"Russ saw you at the school today."

"Yes, I know."

"You must be so worried, Olivia."

"Michael called. Just a few minutes ago."

"Oh!"

Of course, Sharon didn't know what this call meant, and Olivia had no impulse to make it clear. The chickadee was back at the bird feeder, this time with five others from its flock. It was able to communicate where it had gotten the sunflower seed, but not that there were none left. The birds fluttered around the empty Lucite cylinder.

"You must be so relieved," said Sharon. "I'm very happy for you, Olivia." Sharon's conversation was slow, a little stilted; she hovered over every syllable she spoke, holding her accent at bay.

Yet Olivia believed her, suddenly, rapturously, overpoweringly believed her. The simple goodwill of "I'm very happy for you" made Olivia swoon; she lowered her head, breathed heavily through her mouth.

"This has been a nightmare," Olivia said. "It should happen to Hitler, as my father says."

"I was wondering if you wanted to come over," said Sharon.

"I can't now. Sam's in New York." That didn't quite make sense, but no matter. "But thanks."

"It's a business thing," said Sharon. She said it with a slight flirtatiousness, as if doing business would be like drinking wine in the middle of the day, or going to one of those clubs where middle-aged women slip dollar bills into the Lycra jockstraps of male dancers.

"What kind of business thing?" asked Olivia. She wondered if Sharon was being kind, getting her out of the house, away from her troubles.

"Your business. You buy antiques, don't you?"

As soon as Sharon said this, Olivia knew it was about the Tiffany painting hanging over the Connelly fireplace.

"Yes, I do. Is there something you want to sell?"

"We think so. But it would be so helpful if you could take a look at it."

"Is it portable?" Twenty questions. Is it animal, vegetable, mineral, bigger than a bread basket?

"I guess so."

"That would be better. I feel I need to stay near the telephone."

"Oh, of course. I'm sorry. It's just that Russ and I are nervous, with so much going on."

"So much going on?"

"There's been many robberies. They don't put it in the newspaper, but Russ has good friends on the police force. That's why Russ wants to sell the painting." Sharon paused, and then was somehow compelled to add, "It's not that we're desperate for the money or anything. It just seems a little foolish to have something so valuable in the house, with all that's happening."

"How valuable do you think it is?"

"Well, that's what we wanted to get from you, Olivia. If you're not too busy."

"If you'd like to bring it over, that will be fine," said Olivia.

"Thank you. I'll come right now. I'm just taking some zucchini bread out of the oven. Do you like zucchini bread?"

Do I like zucchini bread? thought Olivia. How the hell should I know?

"It's very dietetic," said Sharon. "I use almost no sugar and only one egg."

"Okay, then. Thanks." She tried to think of what else to

say. She struggled for the next phrase, as if she were in France. "I'll make some coffee."

When she hung up the phone, Olivia sat silently, motionless at the kitchen table. She thought about the painting, closed her eyes to remember it better. It was mostly sky and water, with the brownish plane of the river's distant shore cutting the canvas in half. In the bottom of the painting, a farmer stood in his one-horse cart, slightly obscured by the gathering blue darkness. The cuffs of his undershirt were the same bright white as his horse's-rear socks. The reins were slack in the farmer's hands; his head was bowed in reverie. That was the sweetest part, that bowed head.

At last, Olivia picked up the pen with which she had been writing checks. It was a stubby, maroon-colored ballpoint, bearing the name of the Wyndham Hotel. Wasn't that one of the places Sam stayed when he was in New York? She no longer paid attention, not really. She turned the pen around in her hand and looked at it, mildly, emptily curious.

chapter seven

i t felt so good to be in the city. Steam poured out of open deconstruction holes in Madison Avenue; taxis blared with murderous rage; a Sikh and a Chinese engaged in a shouting match while they unloaded boxes in front of a stationery store.

I strained to keep pace with Graham, whose gait was driven by the pistons of urban anxiety. For all the meandering, meaningless chatter we indulged in while at his office off Union Square, once we were on the street and making our way toward Ezra's office, Graham's manner was suddenly grim.

We hurried past a Blarney Stone, with its special darkness inside—not the darkness of romance but the stale, beery darkness of "Give me a little fucking privacy, okay?"—and in a moment of fearful prescience I imagined myself in there, hour after hour, day after day, after my life fell apart, after I was exposed as the fraud who wrote *Visitors from Above* and after Olivia found out about Nadia and left me. I imagined myself in that bar, other bars, any bar, drinking to forget and remembering everything I lost.

"Come on, Sam. It won't do to be late for this."

My publishing company was called Wilkes and Green, after Stephen Wilkes and Aaron Green, two brainy, enterprising New Yorkers who began the firm in 1922. They held on to the company until the early 1960s, when it was sold to another, larger publishing company, who in turn sold it to a Seattle-based radio-and-television outfit, who in turn sold it to a group of Belgian investors, who diddled with it for less than a year before off-loading it onto the Japanese, who now, according to publishing rumors, were talking to a few select Americans about taking the venerable old company off their hands. That the company still bore the name of its founders was cold comfort to Ezra Poindexter, who, though nominally publisher of Wilkes and Green, routinely expected each day at the firm's fussy offices to be his last.

Graham and I were ferried up to the fifth floor by an elderly attendant in a loose-fitting uniform. The man held on to the control lever as if he had had recent experiences of passengers trying to wrest control of his car.

My happiness about being in New York was beginning to fade, and without that giddy sense of being outrageously stimulated, my real feelings began to reassert themselves: I was, after all, a man with a missing son, a man whose marriage hung by a thread, and a man about to see his publisher about a book that he was too embarrassed by to put his real name on. I had never been in this building in a decent frame of mind; always something was wrong—working on a project that was abominable, coming to an appointment that had previously been canceled and rescheduled three or four times, feeling bad about money.

I jiggled my leg, reached into my pocket and jiggled my change.

"You know how I judge it?" Graham said. "It's based on whether he sends his secretary out to reception or if he comes to fetch us himself."

"I'd prefer it if we were meeting him for lunch."

"God, writers and lunch! Everyone complains about editors and agents, but it's the writers who insist on the lunches."

The elevator stopped with a lurch and then the operator goosed it up a few inches until we were parallel with the fifth floor. With a soft grunt, he opened the heavy door.

Graham told the receptionist, a beautiful Caribbean woman who read the *Iliad* while seated at a polished Sheraton desk, that Mr. Davis and Mr. Holland were here to see Mr. Poindexter. She asked Graham to take a seat and he joined me on the green leather sofa, where I was paging through an issue of *Publishers Weekly*. A picture of a book called *Loving an Addicted Gambler* was on the cover. The author's name was Ed Bathrick, and I wondered if this was a real name, a real author, or yet another fraud like me.

"It's better this way," Graham said. "Meeting at the office instead of lunch."

"It is? I didn't have breakfast—I don't think I had dinner last night, either."

"Lunch is for relationships," Graham said. "Well, we've all worked out our bloody relationships, so it's utterly unnecessary. We're meeting here because there's business to be done, and that's a much better sign."

"What kind of business? If the book is selling as well as you—"

"Graham! Sam!"

"*Hello*, Ezra," said Graham, springing to his feet. He was accustomed to doing business primarily with women, and he brought a kind of italicized courtliness to the job. He took Ezra's hand, and for a moment it looked as if he might even kiss him on the cheek.

I got up. My agent's quickness to rise slowed my own movements. I gripped Ezra's hand in an excessively manly handshake and said, "Howdy."

It looked to me as if Ezra had arrived at work not from his home but from the overheated apartment of a model he picked up at a club the night before. His expensive clothes were rumpled, slightly dirty; his long blond hair could have used a wash. He was one of those men who at forty looks thirty but who will perhaps in a few days look fifty. His porcelain complexion held valiantly on to the blush of youth, and his vivid blue eyes showed the merriment and cunning of a man with a great many unpaid bills.

We followed Ezra through the wide, wooden corridors of Wilkes and Green until we came to his large corner office, with its immense, dusty casement windows looking out over Madison Avenue. Ezra's office had its own cozy little reception area, with a few comfortable chairs, floor lamps, and a table displaying a few choice Wilkes and Green books. On the way through this anteroom, I noticed that *Visitors from Above* had been placed on this display table, along with an anthology of Brazilian short fiction, the memoirs of an FBI agent drummed out of the service because his wife was bisexual, a book by a young German philosopher named J. Kufner called *The History of Sadness*, and a first novel by an author so young and attractive that his picture was on the front of the dust jacket.

When I looked up again Graham and Ezra had already entered Ezra's office. There were others waiting for me as well: a stocky, ruddy woman in a long skirt; a graying man in a rather inflexible-looking blue suit, who was stealthily slipping a Life Saver into his mouth; and a gaunt, edgy woman with pewter hair and purple lipstick, whose self-presentation was all determination—she seemed one of those women with a sexist father, living a life of furious, sorrowful determination to prove him wrong.

The ruddy, matronly woman was named Marie something-or-other, and she was the head of publicity. The middle-aged man concerned with the freshness of his breath was Ken something-or-other, the director of sales. And the truculent woman was Heather Kay, a media consultant. During the meeting she spoke authoritatively, even curtly, her voice frosted with condescension; yet from time to time she blushed, deeply, from cheekbone to the tips of her ears, as if behind everything she said was only emptiness. She was full of conclusions but did not have a very orderly idea of how she had reached them. Nevertheless, the meeting primarily belonged to her; she worked for a public relations company that had contacts with radio and TV stations all over the country.

After Ezra talked in general about how well *Visitors from Above* was doing, Marie said that though none of the more traditional reviewers had noticed the book, there were mentions in all four of the major weekly tabloids, and she was busy lining up reviews in a few magazines. Heather Kay stared at Marie, and Marie's voice, which was cultured and vaguely southern, wobbled a bit beneath the scrutiny—her efforts suddenly seemed small-time and beside the point. Then Ken spoke, in a flat, genial midwestern accent, with those rubberized lower-middle-class vowels the Wexlers used to like to make fun of. Ken once worked as a salesman for a sunglasses company. When the company folded, Ken was without a job and a little too old to be considered by most companies. He was rescued by the book business, and now he was deeply grateful and fiercely loyal to Wilkes and Green.

"We're getting great sell-through," he said. "No problem with stock remaining on the shelves. The only problem is getting the books out of the warehouse fast enough." He smiled, satisfied: this was the kind or problem he could live with.

"Have you gone into a third printing yet?" Graham asked Ezra.

"We're planning to," Ezra said.

"How many?" asked Graham.

"Thirty thousand more."

"Well, that's the whole problem right there. It's too bloody conservative."

Ken nodded at Ezra, agreeing with Graham.

An enormous grief opened within me like a black umbrella. Why couldn't something like this happen to a book with my real name on it? My name, *my* name—I had had no idea it meant so much to me. Once, Olivia had speculated that I wrote under a pseudonym because my father's surname hung on me like a millstone. Possibly, I'd thought, yet with faint conviction; psychological theorizing was strictly tennis without a net. But now I was certain that whatever I thought of my own father and the ancestral Hollands who comprised his genetic past, I nevertheless wished my own name were on a book that was going into its third printing, a book that could summon a director of promotion, a sales manager, and a media consultant into my publisher's office—was it too late to put Sam Holland's name on *Visitors from Above?* Or perhaps I could change my own name to John Retcliffe. Why not? Who in the world of arts and letters would wonder what had become of Sam Holland?

"Sometimes that's exactly what you want to do when some beautiful girl wants to go to bed with you," Ezra was saying. He raked his long, graceful fingers through his fine hair, perhaps recalling a moment of tenderness from the night before. "She may want everything right now, but if you play it cool maybe you'll have a more lasting relationship. Am I on to something here? Those returns can kill you. You know the old saying, 'Gone today, here tomorrow.'

"Ezra," said Heather Kay, holding up her hands as if he were an irrational man who needed to be calmed down. "Let me just say that if you let me do . . . what I do, with the media, then you're—" She stopped suddenly, and the look of keenness left her wide hazel eyes, to be replaced by a startled, self-doubting expression. She seemed either to have forgotten what she had set out to say or to have taken a quick look ahead at it and found something wrong with it.

"I'm?" prompted Ezra.

Graham smiled at me, confident I had seen the same panicky expression in Heather's eyes and not only evaluated but enjoyed it in the same way. Olivia used to tell me that Graham despised women, and though at the time I had found the judgment irritating and false, it seemed suddenly true.

A blush darkened Heather's face. She crossed her legs tightly, tucking the toe of her right foot behind the heel of her left. "I just don't think you'll have trouble selling copies of the book, that's all I mean to say." She shrugged and reached behind her for her briefcase. She took a sheet of computer paper from a long gray envelope, upon which was a list of cities and dates and the call letters of various radio and television stations. "This is what I was able to line up in just twenty-four hours," she said. "There's a lot of wanna-see-wanna-hear about John Retcliffe, and the whole extraterrestrial topic seems to have struck a chord. Besides, you know how the media obsesses about and competes with itself. Everyone wants to get in on what Jerry Hopper has done. They worship and despise him. You know how that is."

"Who the hell is Jerry Hopper?" I asked. All of my contacts with publishing people were dominated by chitchat about people I'd never heard of, and I was sick of it. I had always accepted this as part of the mean mercantile justice of being unsuccessful, but now I felt I had won the right to complain a bit—or John Retcliffe had.

"Jerry Hopper?!" exclaimed Heather.

I looked at her blankly, feeling a bit of prissy pride that I had no idea whom she was talking about—I still had a few remaining moments to feel above crass commercialism.

"He's a radio guy," said Ken, rather gently.

"He *is* radio, right now, in New York," said Heather. "Drive time, morning and afternoon."

"Drive time?"

"During the commutes, when most people are in their cars," said Heather, with a certain warmness. Ah: so she liked it when she knew the answer. I felt my heart turning in my chest, to get a better look at her.

"People in New York don't have cars," I said. "They're in the subway, or on the bus, or maybe in a taxi, in which case they're listening to something in Turkish."

"I keep getting Russians," said Graham, very cheerfully, trying to counteract whatever unpleasantness I might be generating.

"If you want to know why our . . . book is selling," said Heather, "then the answer is Jerry Hopper. It was his mentioning it on his program that began the upsurge in sales. Maybe, living out on the farm, you don't realize how influential the media has become."

"I don't live in an Amish community," I said. "Every other house has a goddamned satellite dish in front of it, the place is cabled up the kazoo."

"You two," said Ezra, grinning, wagging a long finger at us. "Behave!"

"Look, let's stay on track here, okay?" Heather said. "There's two areas of concern—radio, which Sam could possibly handle, and television, which is a problem, since we are dealing with an author who wishes to protect his anonymity."

Protect my anonymity? I never thought of it quite like that. My anonymity was always my extra helping of humble pie.

"I've worked with an author who had to keep his identity secret, and when we had him on TV, local and national, they rigged up this kind of electronic blockage of his face and disguised his voice, too. But this guy was a government witness for those Mafia trials last year."

"Andy the Candyman," said Ezra, nodding.

"Yes."

"*I Am a Killer,*" remembered Graham.

"Right," said Heather.

"How did that book end up doing?" asked Graham, idly.

"Very nicely," said Heather. "It was on the best-seller lists."

"People can't get enough of that shit," said Ezra.

"I don't suppose you know who represents him," Graham asked.

"What do you mean, 'represents him'?" said Ezra, his voice a blend of amusement and annoyance. "Like he's going to write *Andy the Candyman, Part Two*?"

"You never know," said Graham. "Remember that . . ." and he launched into an anecdote about a weightlifter who was held captive for three weeks by a movie star and her sisters and then wrote a book about it, which was a huge success.

I sank into myself, wondering why, even in the midst of my first success, I could not inspire people to keep the subject on me. I fully realized how childish and petulant this was, but I couldn't bear these digressions. I remembered Michael's eighth birthday party, thrown at a lucky time in my boy's usually solitary life, a time when he seemed to have enough friends to keep a small party going. In the middle of it, Michael had burst into a torrent of tears. "No one's paying attention to *me*," he said. "Everyone's acting like this is just any other day." I had stroked Michael's soft sable cap of hair while he bawled against my belly. I had actually been frightened by the kid's reaction, his lack of familiarity with how the world worked. Yet here I was in Ezra's office, feeling neglected, slighted because mine was not the only book they were talking about. And the book was not even mine, not really. I reminded myself to keep repeating that essential fact of the matter: it was not really mine.

"Something's just struck me," said Marie. "About Carol Mahoney, at the *Times*, I mean. One of her weirder quirks is she really believes in reincarnation."

"What does this have to do with anything?" I said.

"I was just thinking how nice it would be to have the *Times* review your book, and maybe I could use the reincarnation angle to pique Carol's interest."

"But there's nothing about reincarnation in my book."

"Oh," said Marie, not particularly distressed. "I thought there was."

"And God willing, the reincarnation angle won't be in my next book, either."

"You know what, Sam?" said Ezra. "Let's not talk about your next book right now." He put his index fingers on either side of his skull. "Focus," he said. "Now, Heather, when does Jerry Hopper want John Retcliffe on his program?"

"He seems flexible, Ezra."

"How about this afternoon, then?"

"This afternoon?"

"Yes."

"Ezra, these things are usually done quite a bit in advance."

"Who cares how things are usually done? Call him and tell him we've got John Retcliffe here, that he's passing through town and he can go on the show today."

"Are we talking about me here?" I managed to ask.

"Don't worry, Sam," said Graham. "This will be fine." He darted a look at Ezra.

"I thought," said Heather, "we were going to consider hiring someone else for the tour."

She reached into her briefcase and pulled out several black-and-white photographs. The top one showed a mild middle-aged man with his hair neatly combed, wearing a turtleneck sweater, his eyes friendly and eager behind horn-rimmed glasses. She handed the pictures to Ezra.

To my great surprise, I found myself standing up. A consciousness of having made a great mistake descended upon me. How could I come here with everything in Leyden in such turmoil?

"I need to call home," I said. My ratio of head to body weight had changed. My body was lead and my skull was just frozen wind.

Ezra gestured toward the phone on his desk. "Or would you like some privacy?"

"Yes," I said softly. My heart did not so much beat as bubble; a percolating column of blood raced up and down my chest cavity.

"The office next door is empty," Ezra said. "Feel free."

The office next to Ezra's was small, with one window looking out onto Twenty-eighth Street. There was space only for a small bookshelf, a chair, and a desk, upon which were a bottle of Evian water and a paperback edition of *Warrant for Genocide* by Norman A. Cohn. I dialed my number and sat in the chair, turning it to face the window as I listened to the phone in my haunted house a hundred miles north ring once, twice, a third time. Usually I had to signal Olivia it was me, or she wouldn't answer the phone. I had assumed it would be different today.

"Hello?" Olivia's voice was high and tight.

"Thank God you're there."

"Oh."

"Any word?"

"Yes, he called."

"Thank God. Where is he?"

"Don't get too excited. He's somewhere, he's alive. But that's all I know."

"Shit."

Silence. Olivia breathed on the other end of the line.

"What did he sound like? Did he say anything?"

"Did he say anything? What do you mean? About you?"

I shook my head, offended for a moment by what Olivia implied, but then realizing that, yes, it had been exactly what I'd meant. About me. Did he say, "Mom, I have a letter in my pocket from a woman who says Dad used her cunt like a toilet"?

"Did he sound okay, that's all."

"He sounded as if he was fine. He didn't sound hungry, or cold, or even tired. He's living indoors. Now all we have to find out is where."

"Yeah," I said. And then there was more silence.

Finally, Olivia said, not with any great kindness, "How is your business meeting going?"

"Not that well," I said, realizing I was stepping into a trap by discussing it right now, by not saying "Who cares?," by not saying "What's important is Michael," by not saying "I'm coming home right now, we must be together." But I needed to talk. "They want me to go on 'The Jerry Hopper Show.' "

"Who's that?"

"They want me to go on today, with no preparation, just bang, cold."

"Who's Jerry Hopper, Sam?"

"The hottest guy in radio."

I sighed, as if disappointed by her question. A petty, combative sound came out of me and I felt a strong pull of remorse: I was scrounging for advantage, at a time like this. Five minutes ago, I hadn't known who Hopper was either. I closed my eyes, touched my forehead.

"Sorry, Sam, I don't keep these people straight. You know I don't."

"No, it's okay. He mentioned the book the other day on his show and thousands of people ran out and bought it."

"Are you going to do it?"

"I don't know. They want me to."

"As you? Or James Retcliffe?"

"James?" My voice rose in annoyance. "It's John, *John* Retcliffe, Olivia. Come on." I could not, at that moment, at gunpoint, have said for certain if I was pretending to be wounded or actually feeling it.

"I don't want to keep the phone occupied, Sam."

"We've got call waiting. No one can get a busy signal once

you have call waiting." I paused, waiting for my sanity to return, but it got worse. "You do remember that we have that feature on our telephone, don't you?"

Olivia answered by hanging up.

I held the phone to my ear, listening to the drone of the dial tone. When I'd heard enough, I slammed it down and stared out the window. Dirty beige beads of rain spotted the glass; across the way, in a dark glass tower, a woman worked at a computer terminal, her face greenish from its glow. The world was dying. I picked the phone up and dialed my number again.

Olivia didn't answer. I couldn't believe she would let it ring. What if I was the police, or Michael, or someone with a lead, a message? Could she really be so angry with me that she would take a chance like that? I let it ring. Somewhere around the sixth or seventh ring I began to count. When I got to the twelfth ring I hung up, waited a moment, and then dialed again. Clever, no? Well, this time she picked up on the first ring.

"Hello?" Her voice was uncertain, defeated.

"Hi," I said.

She was silent.

"I love you, Olivia." I was a little surprised by the declaration; I felt moved, flushed, as if someone had just said it to me.

"I know you do," she said. It's what my children said when I kissed them good night in their beds and told them that I loved them. It sometimes made me feel slighted, as if I had been making an overture that was being rebuffed. Yet there was nothing noncommittal or evasive about it; they had just been lifting their faces toward me like flowers to the sun. Fool of fools, how could I have let my life go by without knowing I was loved?

"You're my one true friend," I murmured into the phone. "You're all that's real. I think you'd be amazed if I could ever really express how much I love you." I laughed happily; my own ardor soothed me.

"We've got to stick together, Sam, at least until this is over."

"What do you mean?"

"Until Michael comes back."

"I know, but . . . Look, we'll stick together until Michael comes back, which will probably be today—I know that kid, he's going to miss the comforts of home—and then we'll stick together after he comes back, too."

"Are you going to go on that radio program?"

"Think I should?"

"What do Graham and Ezra say?"

"They think I should. I can still catch the seven o'clock train."

"Would it be all right if you got a cab at the station, then? I don't want to take Amanda out that late."

"I better get back in. They have a sheaf of photographs, guys who they want to put on the road as John Retcliffe, to go on TV talk shows. The levels of unreality are so exhausting. They're going to hire an actor to pretend to be someone who doesn't even exist. But we'll make some money. Won't that be nice?"

"I've got to go, Sam."

"But won't it be nice?"

"Yes. It'll be fantastic. It'll solve all of our problems."

After we said goodbye, I sat in there for a few moments, not wanting to go into Ezra's office with my conversation with Olivia like egg on my face. Idly, I picked up the Cohn book and flipped through it. It was about the *Protocols of the Elders of Zion*; it seemed strange, and somehow darkly serendipitous, to find a book about the *Protocols* so soon after talking about them in the bookstore with Molly Taylor. The pages blurred by, propelled by my thumb. What was I looking for? Pictures? Did I think that perhaps Professor Cohn had

cobbled his treatise together in much the manner that I constructed *Visitors* and that he had used a stock-photo house
and met a Nadia of his own? Whatever it was I was seeking,
what flew from one of the book's passing pages was the very
pseudonym I was using: John Retcliffe.

Or did it? Was it just the mania of that name and the book
that created the illusion of seeing it? The name John Retcliffe
was my telltale heart, beating behind the bricks of my own
crime against the printed word. Now I would see it everywhere, hear it, read it.

I thumbed back, to see if I could find the name again. I
was certain that the postal clerk who Molly said wrote the
Protocols as part of a hack novel for which he got paid by the
page was in fact John Retcliffe, or at least wrote under that
name. I looked for the word "John," for "Retcliffe," for
"postal," even for "clerk." I looked for the word "pseudonym." But every page was opaque; the words huddled
together, keeping their black backs toward me. I tried to slow
my gaze, but I was too nervous to do anything but scan; in
fact, the more unsuccessful I was in finding "John Retcliffe"
again, the more I suspected I had only imagined seeing it in
the first place. Finally, I looked in the back of the book to see
if there was an index. There was. But that's as far as I took it.
If John Retcliffe was the New Grub Street scribbler whose
ravings had spawned the *Protocols*, I didn't want to learn it,
not today.

When I walked back into Ezra's office, Graham held up a
photograph of an actor in his forties, the psychiatrist in a
soap opera a few years before, now unemployed, with silver
hair, polar eyes, a high forehead. "What do you think?" Graham asked me. "Does this bozo say 'John Retcliffe' to you?"

They bought me lunch after all. Ezra, Heather, Graham, and
I ate at Positano, where I noted the largeness of the bill and

how easily the money flowed now that I was a cash cow. And then, after finishing off the wine, Heather Kay and I got into a cab and made our way to the studio of Mr. Jerry Hopper, who now, I had been convinced, not only held my future in his hands but actively wanted to see me succeed, as if I had become his personal project. Feeling a little tipsy, I found myself wanting to sit close to Heather in the taxi, and so sat as far from her as I could. As we headed north on Eighth Avenue, past the porn theaters with their Tom and Jerry film titles slapped up on the marquees—*Box Lunch*, *When Harry Wet Sally*—Heather took her briefcase off her lap and tossed it casually onto the large stretch of seat between us.

Jerry Hopper broadcasted his program out of a suite of studios on Fifty-seventh Street, not far from Carnegie Hall and directly across the street from the gloomily ornate apartment house where my father was currently ensconced with Isabella Padilla.

"That's where The Dad lives," I said to Heather Kay, as she gestured me into Hopper's building. I stopped in front of the revolving doors and pointed across the street.

"I never knew my father," Heather said, and I felt something stirring within me. Until Olivia, my romantic career had been a string of fatherless girls.

Up on the fifteenth floor of its glass-and-steel building, Hopper's studio was airless. Every piece of furniture, every watt of track lighting, every inch of industrial-gray carpeting spoke of closeout sales and brothers-in-law in the business. Stuffing oozed from the wounds of the old sofas; trash cans overflowed with cellophane, computer paper, Pepsi cans, Big Red gum wrappers.

The staff were in their twenties. The men wore slacks, ties; their jackets were left on the backs of their swivel chairs. The women were a dainty lot, with big hairdos and long-skirted suits that seemed to have been spirited out of Mom's closet. Phones rang; video display screens shuddered with the transit of numbers; sheaves of paper were whisked from one desk to another.

From speakers perched in every corner of the room came the sound of Hopper's show, which he was at this moment broadcasting from a smoky, caffeine-soaked warren at the very back of the fifteenth floor. "Well, I see by the old cock . . . I mean clock on the wall that it's time to switch over to Henry Merron at the news desk. News desk. *News* desk. I've got to get me one of those. A *news* desk."

"SHUT UP!" screamed a woman, as if from the bottom of a copper well. Her voice curdled, echoed. Yet Hopper seemed not to mind at all. It took me a moment to realize this scream was just a sound effect that he could summon at the press of a button.

"I want to have sex while sitting at a news desk," he said.

"FILTH!" screamed the woman.

"I want to order takeout from Sammy's Famous Rumanian Restaurant and have sex while I eat my lunch at the news desk."

"YOU MAKE ME SICK!"

No one in the office seemed to be paying the slightest attention to Hopper's sexual fantasies or the screaming woman he was supposedly offending. I looked at Heather, who smiled, shrugged.

"This is a nightmare," I said.

She put her finger over her pursed lips.

A woman with a sun-lamp tan and hair whipped up into a tsunami came over and said "Hi," very loudly, with absurd emphasis and excitement, as if finding us on the sofa was the capper on an already wild and fantastic day, but at the same time she was *doing* excitement, imitating and satirizing it. She was one of the Spoof People.

The woman extended her hand toward me, holding her arm stiffly. "Welcome to 'The Jerry Hopper Show,' Mr. Retcliffe. I know Jerry wants to get you on as soon as possible. Can you just sit tight for another minute and I'll tell him you're here." As she spoke to me, her eyes glided away from me and settled on Heather. "Heather?" she said.

"Hi, Risa," said Heather.

"What happened to your hair? I love it."

"I broke up with Bruno and then I got myself scalped so I wouldn't take him back," said Heather.

The recorded voice of the woman scolding Hopper for his sex fantasies was reaching new heights of scorn and vehemence. Phrases like "abusive" and "patriarchal pig" echoed through the studio, but still no one noticed.

Risa disappeared into the back of the studio and soon came out with Jerry Hopper. Hopper in the flesh was all flesh indeed. He must have weighed three hundred pounds and wore black velvet bib overalls and a flowing red silk shirt. His hair was long, greasy, and unkempt. He had a hard, ruddy face, as broad as an anvil. Each of his short, thick fingers was adorned with a ring. Smiling as he rolled toward me, he stopped suddenly in his tracks, slapped his belly with both hands, and then threw his arms open wide.

"Welcome to Planet WWBV, Mr. Retcliffe."

He stood there, poised and immobile, like a little mad dictator on a balcony waiting for the roar of the crowd below. Risa gestured for me to follow her.

"Do they know my real name?" I mumbled to Heather.

"Just follow Jerry's lead," she said.

"Do you know how many books I read in the course of a year?" Jerry asked, looking over his shoulder.

"Not really."

"Try five hundred," he said.

"That's a lot of books."

"Well, not *read* read," said Risa. I sensed their relationship: Hopper huge and imprecise, Risa underpaid and pedantic.

"And maybe," continued Hopper, "two and a half of them

stick in my mind for a day." He patted his stomach, implying that when he said he devoured a book, he wasn't kidding.

"Well, you read so quickly, Jerry," said Risa, giving me a look that seemed to say "Whatta guy!"

"But your book—man, your book blew my fucking mind." We were only a few feet from the broadcasting booth; Hopper stopped, raised his abrupt, fleshy arms, and howled at the cream-colored perforations in the acoustic ceiling tiles. "Mr. Spaceman, take me AWAY!!"

I followed Jerry through a black glass door over which there was a small red light bulb. Inside the broadcasting booth there was a long table, six microphones on flexible stems, and a wall of clocks, showing the time in New York, Chicago, Aspen, Los Angeles, Maui, Bora Bora, Siberia, and Liverpool. A litter of styrofoam coffee cups and Hi-Fiber bars. The only other person in the booth was a strung-out-looking guy in a tank top and white jeans, Hopper's engineer. Beyond the studio was another room, separated by an opaque glass panel, where five unseen employees took calls from listeners and routed them to Jerry's speakerphone.

"I know what you're thinking," Hopper said to me.

"Really?"

"You're thinking, This is where this guy makes eight hundred and fifty thousand dollars a year?"

"Something like that."

"Well, sit right down, Mr. John Retcliffe, and by the time I'm through with you, you'll be making as much as me-o." He gestured toward an imitation leather chair.

"Two rules, okay? Don't touch nothing, and don't talk when I'm talking. Other than that, just do your thing—be as natural as you want, go crazy, you know. As nuts as you go, I got people out there twice as crazy."

The engineer counted off five with his long, nicotine-stained fingers and then pointed at Hopper.

"Mmmmm," Hopper moaned into the microphone. "Oh God . . . yeah, there . . . no, a little lower—wait, there. Ahhh . . . What? Oh." He cleared his throat. "Well, that was . . . I don't know who the hell that was—I don't know who I am, either. In fact, let's start a contest: anyone who can tell me who I am gets to come over to my house and give me a bath. Send your answers in on a three-by-five postcard, addressed to Who Is Jerry Hopper? care of this station. Okay? And don't think I don't love you more than your mother does, because I got a stomach that just can't be turned." He pointed at me and raised an eyebrow, tilted his hand back and forth. He seemed to be asking me if I was comfortable and I nodded yes.

"Well, guess who I found for you? And don't think it was easy." As Hopper spoke, he opened a drawer beneath the overhang of his belly and pulled out a copy of *Visitors from Above*. He glanced at the name on the dust jacket. "John Retcliffe, who those of you not brain damaged will remember is the author of Jerry Hopper's favorite book—*Visitors from Above*." He glanced at the engineer, who pressed a button, summoning up a sound effect of high winds howling and then a deep, sinister laugh.

I retreated into the cave of myself while Hopper went on to talk about "my" book. I looked at my hands: soft, uncallused hands; the Khmer Rouge would have had no difficulty identifying me as a cultural worker and adding my head to the mountain of skulls. What if I had been able to wield a hammer; what if the idea of tough physical work had not been essentially horrifying to me—then might I have escaped the crisscross of decisions and defeats that had brought me to this painful point in time? There were writers who kept themselves going by renovating SoHo apartments. It seemed so plaid-shirt honorable, such a good, long-necked-Coors kind of life. And there were writers who earned a living by teaching others to write; but I didn't have the advanced degree or the reputation to attract academic offers. What was I supposed to do?

"It's all here," Hopper was saying. "The Air Force coverups of UFO sightings, the scary Men in Black, testimony from people as early as, geez, I don't know, the Middle Ages? He's talked to pilots, religious leaders, top astronomers. . . ."

I talked to no one, I reminded myself. I sat in the library, I sat at my desk; it was more like typing than writing. I kept pressing the spell-check button on my word processor, not because I was worried about the spelling but because it also counted the words and I was on a three-thousand-word-a-day schedule. I read similar books, I watched movies, I never went further out of my way than a couple of trips to III to help choose the pictures for the midsection of the book, and even that relatively honest bit of labor was finally compromised by my taking home my research assistant, parading her in front of my family, for God's sake, I must have been insane, and then fucking her for six months, falling in love with her, driving a stake through the congested heart of my life.

"Tell me, John Retcliffe," Hopper was suddenly asking, "tell me a little something about yourself."

I looked at him, blinked dumbly. I felt as if I had just awakened from a coma.

Hopper poked me in the shoulder with no excess of gentleness.

It had been promised to me during lunch that there were certain ground rules already in place. An amalgam of frankness and dissembling had informed Hopper that Mr. Retcliffe had a degree of anonymity he wished to preserve. Hopper may or may not have known that Retcliffe was a fiction and I was a phony, but it was not something he wanted to know too thoroughly for fear of becoming an accomplice. To have entered a world in which information was denuded of truth made me breathless; it was like being on the crest of the

Himalayas—normal life was somewhere down there beneath the clouds.

"I'm a New Yorker, Jerry," I heard myself saying. "Married, a couple of great kids."

Hopper smiled at me; the gesture was so warm it was almost impossible to believe it was not real.

"Well, that's just so peachy-keen," he said, winking at me, preparing me for the spritzing to come. "I mean, really unique, man—you know what I mean. Families, right?" He glanced at his engineer, who flicked a button that created a bloodcurdling scream of rage.

I laughed out of surprise and nervousness, a weird bark of a laugh.

"Oh, good, an author with a sense of humor," Hopper said.

"Thank you, Jerry," I found myself saying. "It's always been very important to me to keep a sense of humor about . . . things." I had no idea why I said this, or what it meant. It was not me who was speaking but the context in which I had been placed. Yet what made this reflex even more frightening was the nod and smile from Hopper. We were joined now, off in a world that was completely unreal, but which half the people listening to us found more real than their own lives.

"Well, John, let me ask you what I ask all my best-selling authors. How does it feel?"

"If you mean, Jerry, how does it feel to have people reading my work—"

"No," said Hopper, the basket of his voice suddenly filled with the weight of his sarcasm, which was not really sarcasm but Jerry *doing* sarcasm, "I mean, how does it feel to be sitting next to me with my hand on your knee?"

I laughed, or John laughed, whoever. The soullessness of this encounter was stunning. "It feels fine, Jerry. Naturally, you want people to read what you've written. But I must say, this best-seller thing, I don't really know. My publisher seems to think some people are buying the book, you know, you're always a little bit in the dark—"

Hopper's hand chopped at his neck, scuba language for running out of oxygen.

"—as an author," I managed, and then fell silent, feeling a scald of shame on my cheeks.

"Okay, we're taking calls, and according to my galley slaves we've already got quite a few." Suddenly his voice grew confidential; he leaned toward me, and it was as if this were meant for me alone to hear. "This is a drive-time show, where most decent people are stuck in their cars coming home from work. So most of our callers are kind of special, you know— either rich enough to have phones in the car or welfare chiselers, lolling around the house while the rest of us bust our butts to keep them in tonic water." The engineer cued up a tumultuous ovation.

Hopper flicked a button in front of him and the booth filled with the whooshy, staticky sound of someone calling long distance. "Hello?" the voice said. It was a woman, elderly, with a Yiddish accent. "Jerry? Is that you?"

"Yeah, it's me. Is that you?"

The woman was confused for a moment. "I listen to your show every day, Jerry."

"I know who this is," Hopper said. "This is Lawrence Taylor, isn't it?"

"Who?"

"Lawrence Taylor, former New York Giants defensive back. It's you, L.T., isn't it?"

"Well, as a matter of fact," the woman said, trying to get into the spirit, "my name happens to begin with L. Lillian. Lillian Bergman."

"Oh, L.T., please, don't give me this old-Jewish-lady bit. It's crazy, it's tasteless, and for all I know it may be against the law. Just give us your questions, L.T., and let's get on with it."

"Well, my question is for Mr. Retcliffe. And it is this: What do your children think of your book?"

Hopper rolled his eyes and pantomimed the word "wow."

"Well, of course my family has been very supportive," I said. "It's been difficult for them sometimes, having their father associated with a forbidden area of research and investigation, but the great reception the book's been having has given them a lot of support."

I paused for a moment, to give Lillian Bergman a chance to reply, but suddenly a switch was thrown and another caller's voice was in the studio.

"Hi, this is Frank from Woodside. Have there been any threats—you know, from the government or anyone else?"

I pointed at myself and mimed "Me?" to Hopper. Hopper gestured for me to speak. What a team!

"I'd rather not go into that right now," I said.

"Good choice, John," said Hopper. " 'Cause I love you more than your mama do."

My mother? I felt the offense of that remark, like a trail of slime left behind by a slug, a little gooey skid mark where something vile has crawled. But Hopper meant John Retcliffe's mother, in a farm twenty miles from Spokane, in a condo on Maui, taking off a few pounds at the Canyon Ranch, a gift from John on the crest of his unexpected success.

Another caller was on the line, his voice spectral, tense, obsessed. "This is Roy Scattergood," the voice said. "I live in Baltimore, near the airport—"

"That's fascinating, Roy," Hopper said, tilting back in his chair, plucking at the crotch of his velvet overalls to rearrange his genitals.

Roy's breathing came through the speakers. I heard within that amplified column of air the unmistakable rattle of fear, as distinct as a penny sucked up through a vacuum cleaner.

"You still with us, Roy?" asked Hopper.

"Remember the plane that blew up five days ago?"

"We're talking about UFOs and Men in Black here, Roy," said Hopper.

"Yeah, well, I heard this—this—this BOOM, but you see, I *knew* it was going to happen."

"What are you trying to tell us here, Roy?" Hopper said, with an edge of citizenship in his voice.

"It was in the book, Mr. Retcliffe's book. It's . . . all there."

Hopper looked at me accusingly.

"There's nothing at all about plane disasters in my book," I said. "There's sightings by both commercial and military pilots, but nothing like what happened last week. Authorities believe a bomb was on that plane."

"I know why you have to say it like that," the caller said.

"I say it like that because that's how it is."

"I understand," Roy mumbled.

I looked at Hopper, wondering why he didn't summon the next call. But Hopper had an instinct; he was letting it play out.

"The first word in your book is 'On,' " Roy said.

"Yeah?"

"And the second paragraph, first word, that's 'Tuesday.' "

"Uh-huh," I mugged in Hopper's direction, who shrugged, lifted up his hands, as if to say "Welcome to my world."

"Well, when you read down the page like that, just reading the first words of each paragraph?" The tone of his voice changed; he was reading now, and the words were delivered in a measured, defensive tone, as if he were standing next to his desk in school. " 'On Tuesday it falls flames Mary land heavens death.' It's a prophecy, isn't it, Mr. Retcliffe? Your whole book is a book of prophecy. So are you a good witch or a bad witch? Are you going to tell us what happens next?"

. . .

Cutting through the gas-jet-blue New York twilight, dodging the traffic on Fifty-seventh Street, I dashed from Hopper's building to my father's stately brown apartment house. It was a measure of how unsure I was of the wisdom of the visit that even as I hurried toward him I was hoping he wasn't at home. I hadn't seen him in nearly a year. Did I want to crow in front of him that I, or some fractured version of myself, had just been on "The Jerry Hopper Show"? (I had already made the transition from never having heard of Hopper to thinking he was a cultural icon of the utmost importance.)

I felt as if I were entering a Baltic courthouse. The lobby was brooding, ornate; the ceiling rococo, a mixture of green and glinting gold. The doorman was hulking, hairless. He looked at me intently when I announced myself. And then he took out a tattered soft-covered notebook and peered hopelessly at the pages, looking for my father's number. At last he pointed to something with his blunt forefinger and slowly dialed the number, all the while shaking his perfectly round, oversized bald head.

The last time I saw my father he had recently returned from Bogotá with his current love and meal ticket, Isabella Padilla. Olivia and I, in the midst of some raging, unrememberable spat, met them at a chic Italian restaurant in the theater district. Gil and Isabella came late; their eyes swept through the restaurant until they saw us nattering tensely at a back table. Isabella had been morose since returning from Colombia, where her family's vast land holdings were being liquidated. "Strangers walking around our beautiful house, trampling the wildflowers, crossing bridges my great-grandfather made with his own hands." She inhaled cigarette smoke dramatically, exhaled through her angrily flared nostrils, and then waved the smoke away, her bracelets clattering.

The elevator stopped on the seventh floor and the door opened slowly. (It was part of the faded elegance of Dad's apartment house to have a poky elevator, one that clanged its old chains like Marley's Ghost, leaving those sleekly automated lifts to the nouveaux riches in their boxy high-rises.) He, the man, the monster, was waiting for me right at the elevator, his eyes glittering with . . . I had no idea why they glittered. Was he fighting back tears? Was he just plain happy? Was it something he ate?

"Sam, for God's sake! What brings you here?" He was dressed in a first-rate gray suit, with chalk stripes, beneath which he wore a dark blue shirt with a white collar. The top two buttons of his shirt were undone and a corsage of gray chest hair bloomed beneath his dimpled chin. He was sleek, powerful, and suntanned; though English and Dutch, he looked this evening like a rich Greek shipping tycoon.

"I was just across the street," I said.

"Really? At the Tea Room? Working on some kind of deal?"

He was generally avid for details about my career, and my dependably gloomy reports seemed to satisfy him. But today I took him by surprise.

"I was on the radio," I said.

"The radio?" he said, losing twenty percent of his tan.

He tried to orient himself to this. It was premature to react; after all, maybe it was nothing—maybe I was on some tiny channel, maybe I had abandoned any hope of writing and now I was announcing the weather reports.

Since Gil stopped being poor, it was often difficult to reconcile his appearance with my memories of him. In memory, Gil was gaunt, pale, with a ruthless demeanor; a hacking cough; thick, angry eyebrows beneath which stared furious, frightened eyes. In memory, his fingernails were not coated with clear polish but chewed down past his fingertips—the fingertips themselves used to protrude, pink and unprotected, like the sensitive tendrils of an extraterrestrial. He used to sit on the edge of the sofa, listening to symphonies on WQXR, pointing his fingers, closing his fists, waving his hands, as if he were creating the music himself, though I always suspected that what he really was doing was proving to whoever was looking that he knew the music so well he could pretend to conduct it. In those days, when he was most real, before the money and before the tan and before the Savile Row tailors, before muting his anger beneath the goose down of affluence, in those old days on Commerce Street, when we lived above Mrs. Hennessy and her two obese daughters and below two dashing gay men who made their money hustling backgammon and who played, endlessly, Erik Satie on their piano, in those days Gil was a bohemian, dressed in wrinkled gabardines and T-shirts that showed his ropy, angry arms. He paced our four small contiguous rooms that were laid out one after the other like an art-school lesson in foreshortening, holding his copy of *Soliloquies of the Modern Stage*, from which he memorized passionate passages from Ibsen, O'Neill, Max Frisch.

For Gil, his job at the UN, where he drew maps, charts, and graphs for the Office of Economic Development, was most painful for what it was *not*. It was not his name in the paper or on a dressing-room door. It was not an expression of the secret self. It was not having his drunkenness become the stuff of anecdotes. It was not fame, wealth, pleasure, or transcendence. It was not having his favor curried; it was not having his every word and gesture hung upon and ransacked for clues to his mood. It was not gaiety, it was not passion, it was not excess, it was not Paris, it was not Park Avenue, it was not cocktails, canapés, tinkling chapel bells, honorary degrees, Jamaican holidays, custom-tailored shirts.

And for all this and more someone had to pay. I paid, Allen paid, Connie paid; but our mother paid most of all.

"My life is a nightmare," Gil would bellow in Adele's

frightened, unhappy face, and when she tried to console him he used her frail attempts to prove her incompetence. Here he was, bleeding to death, and no one was doing a damn thing. He had suffered a wound that could only be stanched by a tourniquet of success.

"Don't you understand?" he'd say to her. "Is this too difficult a concept? I am an actor. I need a part. I'm not a painter—I don't need a beret and a brush—or a writer. What I do, I can't do on my own. I need a stage, a director. I need to be chosen. And no one ever chooses me. Okay? Got it?"

"I chose you," Mom would say. "And I would again, over and over."

"What is that? From a song?"

The last time we had been a family, Adele was in a plain pine box and Connie, Allen, Gil and I were at her graveside—as a concession to her parents, Brooklyn Jews who lost their daughter first to Barnard and then to Gil, the funeral had been officiated by a rabbi. When the sparse band of mourners dispersed, Gil and we children wandered around the hilly, sun-struck cemetery, as if to console ourselves that there were plenty of other dead people. Connie by now was married to an ex-drug-dealing bean-sprout entrepreneur in Tampa, and Allen had set up his dental surgery practice in Waltham, Massachusetts. I was a senior at the University of Wisconsin.

"I'm leaving New York," Gil announced. We were lingering, for some reason, in front of a broad, brutal pink marble tombstone, beneath which rested the dust of a stranger. "I'll be doing a little traveling. I've never been to Europe. Did you know that? Never. I've managed to do almost none of the things I wanted." His voice was level, factual. And I thought: Free at last, great God Almighty, he's free at last.

Now, nineteen years later, I followed Gil from the elevator to the open door of Isabella's apartment. Strange country,

America: where else can you spend a life as an actor too manifestly without charm to ever land a role and then find yourself in a two-thousand-dollar suit, part of some subtropical jet set?

He ushered me in. The apartment was so close to how I had imagined it that I wondered if I perhaps had visited it before. The long entrance foyer was dark salmon, with little wall sconces lighting the way, their beige silk shades scorched by flame-shaped bulbs. Audubon prints in aqua linen mats and framed in gilded wood. A plush Oriental runner. I followed behind Gil. In his sober suit, with his silvery hair and his shapely, disciplined body, he looked like an expensive mortician.

The living room's windows, double-glazed against noise, looked out onto Fifty-seventh Street. A fireplace with a white marble mantel. Walls painted pale green with white trim. A chintz-covered sofa, a glass-topped coffee table, upon which was a glass of orange juice and a copy of Condé Nast Traveler. He gestured me into an easy chair and he sat lightly on the sofa—he moved around as if to leave as little evidence of himself as possible.

"So. You're on the radio. What for?"

"It's just bullshit. I wrote a book. Under an assumed name. And now I'm promoting it."

"Really?"

"It's nothing. It's less than nothing, really. To achieve the level of nothing would be a great advance."

"Oh. I see. Modesty. The great luxury of success. I would have loved to have been modest myself, but in my case modesty was unnecessary and so impossible. Oh, when I think of those years and years wanting to break into the theater!" He smiled, shook his head, as if the rage of failure had become, for him, a piece of nostalgia. "Well, that was then." He glanced longingly at his half-finished glass of orange juice. He wanted to drink from it, but to do so would mean he'd have to offer me something to drink, and he didn't want to bother with that just now.

"So. You're getting a lot of publicity?" he asked. "The royal treatment?"

"Not even close."

"You don't have to make less of it for my sake, Sam. I'm not the frustrated ogre you tried to write about. I have a good life."

"It's just a book for money, written under a pseudonym. No one expected it to catch on, but it has. Now they're trying to decide if they should send me on a book tour, or hire some-one else to be me."

"Someone to pretend to be you?"

"I don't want to go on TV and pretend to be John Retcliffe. Someone might recognize me. And anyhow, it would be like saying that I don't ever expect to have a chance to go on TV and promote a book as Sam Holland. The whole point of doing these fucking quickie books is so I can have the time and space to do my own work."

"They're thinking of hiring an actor?" Gil said, his wolfen eyes narrowing.

"Yes—somebody much more distinguished and handsome than me."

"And who decides who this lucky person will be?"

Perhaps I was expecting Gil to encouragingly contradict me, to say something on the order of "Why, son, you're a fine figure of a man yourself, your voice is pleasant, your eyes honest, your wit quick." But the absence of this paternal reassurance made me feel like a perfect fool for having expected it. What in my life with Gil would have led me to believe he could cheer me on? He was forever a drowning man, trying not only to dunk those who would rescue him but anyone in the general vicinity as well. The strategy of his self-rescue was to fill the ocean with corpses, to build up a silt of bodies upon which he might stand with his head out of the water at last.

"I'm not sure who decides," I said. "My publisher? Me? There's this attractive young woman with pewter hair who seems to be running things."

"God bless the attractive young women with pewter hair," said Gil, leaning back, folding his hands on his hard little belly. "But I think *you* should be able to decide who's going to go around the world claiming to be you."

"Around the world? I think it's just a few stops—you know, the major markets, that sort of thing."

"And this is a book about . . . ?"

"I was afraid you were going to ask me that." I cringed, letting him rejoice in my bad feeling. "Extraterrestrials."

"Really?"

"Really. UFOs, Men in Black."

"I know about the Men in Black."

"You do?"

"Yes, they visit you after you've had contact with an extraterrestrial. They are sallow of complexion and they always dress counter to the season. In summer they wear heavy wool suits; in the middle of winter you're most likely going to see them in a light linen. They always travel in pairs. There's a sense of nausea that overtakes many after the Men in Black have gone. It's as if they've been inside you." He paused, te-peed his fingers, nodding sagely. "But winter or summer, whatever these Men in Black say, no one who encounters one is ever quite the same again. They can convince you that what you have seen, you haven't seen it. They are in a galaxy-wide program of disinformation, and no one really knows where they come from."

"Where did you get all this from?"

"I don't know. Maybe *I'm* a Man in Black." He laughed. "The point is—this is how I'd do it, if I was—what did you say your name was, on the book?"

"John Retcliffe," I mumbled. My bones were starting to ache.

"Well, that's the kind of way I'd present my ideas if I were to become John Retcliffe. Very informally. I think that's key. I don't want to come off as if I was trying to convince anyone of anything, not like some shyster salesman, you know?"

"Where's Isabella, anyhow?" I asked.

His face fell. His hands separated, came to rest on either side of him on the sofa. "She's with her sister and her sister's doctor, at Petrossian." He glanced listlessly at his watch. "I was supposed to be over there an hour ago. As usual, I'm late."

"I am, too. I'm going to miss my train." I stood up; the blood left my head as if through a trap door. I staggered a little.

"Don't call me, I'll call you?" asked Gil, a lifetime of rejections suspended like fish beneath the ice of his eyes.

"Dad, I'm not casting the role. Anyhow, do you really want to trot around America pretending to be John Retcliffe?"

"It sounds as if it would be an enormous amount of fun."

"Most authors lose their minds on these things. It's grinding hard work."

"That's where the lovely ladies with the pewter hair come in. Anyhow, it's not so difficult when you're pretending to be someone else. It's being yourself that causes the wear and tear in a person. John Retcliffe." He pronounced the name majestically. "I'd be playing a role and it would be easy."

"It's a bad idea, Dad."

"Will you at least promise to think about it?"

"Oh, there's no question that I'll be thinking about it."

He walked me to the door, patting my back. A nerve was ticking on the side of his face. He stood at the door and watched me go toward the elevator.

"Come more often," he said.

"Till the next time," I said, with a ridiculous mock salute.

"Sam," he called, when the elevator doors opened and I was about to get on.

I turned to face him again.

"How's Olivia? The children?"

"Fine," I said, and then let the doors close.

I missed the train I had planned on by four minutes, and then spent two hours in a smoky purple-and-gray bar in Penn Station, drinking with cops and transit workers. I called Olivia, drunk, and told her I'd be arriving late.

On the train, I sat next to the window, my head drunkenly resting against the black glass. A hundred feet away, the river moved through the darkness.

I could not bring myself to think of Michael. I could not bring myself to imagine what the look on his face must have been when he read that letter from Nadia. "You used my cunt as your toilet"? How could she have been so poisonous? My God! I loved her, once; I had. I used to count the hours before I could see her again. There were times when I would deliberately not wash after being with her, when I kept her smell on my fingertips, the deep, sonorous scent of her. Why this deliberate act of sabotage? Those words, those words: clumps of letters that could stop a life, ruin a family, change history.

I couldn't think of Michael and I couldn't think of Nadia, and I had stopped thinking of Gil after the second drink at the bar in Penn Station. I couldn't think of Olivia, because I had betrayed her and she let me go off to New York to be John Retcliffe partly as a way of telling me that I was irrelevant to the tasks that faced us.

The club car, with its dollhouse bottles of vodka and gin, was three cars back. Too far, too unstable to walk. Just as well.

I thought of my mother, I thought of Adele. Freud wrote

that no man who is secure in the love of his mother can ever be a failure. Well, I had been busy proving that theory wrong. She loved me, she loved the lot of us; but we, or at least I, joined Gil in his campaign against her. I was drawn to Dad, drawn to the power of his scorn, to the maleness of his rage. I lacked the courage to fight for the lost cause that was Adele's life. I found, find, will always find what I did unforgivable. I shifted alliances. With the taste of her breast still in my mouth, I turned my eyes toward my father, saw his sneer, and imitated it.

And, yes, how much easier to love her now. But where was that love she had so profoundly needed and deserved when it might have done her some good? Gil put his eyes in my head and I saw her as he had: walking slowly from room to room, plucking at the twisted belt of her bathrobe but never getting it to lie flat, stumbling over the treacherous, invisible stones of self-doubt that Gil himself had strewn in her path.

She loved me. She smoothed the hair away from my forehead and planted deep maternal kisses on my brow, and I sunk deeper away from her, disappointed that it was only her, only her, not my father, whom I longed for as if he were some unattainable god, a man of such high standards that his approval would have been a benediction.

She was a quiet woman, dark, with deep, watchful eyes. Raised by a kosher butcher deep in Brooklyn—Midwood High, six months in the Young People's Socialist League, summers in arts-and-crafts camps around Lake Mohonk. She loved the theater, Arthur Miller, musicals. Gil was the great sexual adventure of her life: a tall gentile with blazing eyes. He snapped his fingers at waiters, sent the wine back. He called cabbies "Driver," creating a fiction that somewhere in his past rolled dove-gray chauffeured limousines. He was not a socialist; he was a Social Darwinist. Survival of the fittest. Destroy the weak as a way of strengthening the pack. That sort of shit. He cut her off from all those Hiroshima Day observances. He was above it, above compassion, above suffering. He read to her from *The Fountainhead*. He invited her into the dugout of the winning team, and then he benched her.

I had written this once, in my first novel. But I wanted to try it again, get it right. The first time through, I had let myself off the hook. Now I wanted to write the truth, about how I collaborated with the enemy.

And I wanted to write about the love I felt but could never bring forth. The incoherence of feeling that filled me like that dandelion rain. I wanted to write about soaping my children's hair with Wella Balsam shampoo and watching my fingers disappear into the lather. I wanted to write about friends, snow, January, forgiveness.

The train rocked back and forth. A station flipped over into the darkness like a playing card.

Across the aisle sat a woman, sharing her seat with two stuffed Macy's shopping bags. She wore a black satin jacket and tight jeans. She was too old for her clothes, and she had the expression of someone for whom the promise of youth had not been kept, someone who once believed in rock and roll and now was embarrassed by her own reality.

"Hello," she said.

"Hello." I cleared my throat.

"Are you okay?"

"Sure. Why?"

She shrugged. She wore a great deal of mascara. Something in her eyes made me touch the side of my face, and I discovered it was slick with tears. Oh my goodness, I thought. I'm all alone on a train and I'm crying. I must be losing my mind.

chapter eight

It all happened so fast, like a fall. Michael stumbled into the woods; a gigantic blue heron flapped above the tree line, a winged dinosaur, and Michael followed it with his eyes, his pounding, frantic heart. The woods were damp, ten degrees colder than the plowed and leveled world surrounding. Like a church, a Spanish church, a haunted church, an MTV church. The flaming tips of the budding wild apple trees were the candles; the twisted hemlocks were the fourteen stations; the wind was the heavenly choir. He wandered in and in and in, kicking off vines and brambles that grabbed at his legs like the hands of lost souls who lived beneath the soft, leaf-slick rot and renewal of the forest floor.

He let himself get lost. I want to get lost. He wanted to see what happened. Sam used to talk about a guy in an old song called Long Tall Shorty, who wondered where the lights went when the lights went out. Soon, Michael had no idea where the road was. A turn here, a rise there, a detour around a grassy stream. The heron passed again, enormous, pterodactyl, indifferent to Michael below.

An hour or two later: smoke. Just the scent of it, wild, errant, yet a sign of civilization. By now, Michael's shoes were wet. His knee ached from a quick but wrenching slide down a wet, mossy ledge. He was thirsty. Not scared, not really. Concerned. He had to take a dump. Alone, nevertheless he did not want to drop his pants. Does the Pope shit in the woods? Sam's joke: Michael remembered Nadia laughing at it, her little Persian hand covering her mouth.

Eventually—darkness was coming in now, bits of the sunset visible through breaks in the trees, stretched out across the west like a twisted bloody sheet—Michael found the source of that smoky smell. The hideaway, the hut, the lean-to, the shack. He waited in the bushes, afraid to approach it. (By now he was becoming afraid.) In a blink of an eye it was night. The shack had rectangles of satin nailed over the windows, except for one that was still glass and where the reflection of the rising moon swam like a creature beneath the ice. A faint glow of what Michael correctly guessed was a kerosene lamp came from the inside. A bright stainless-steel stovepipe ran up the side of the house, and white smoke poured out of its spout like milk from a pitcher.

Softly, boldly, Michael crept close to the house and looked through the window. Inside, a thin, sneaky-looking guy in his forties stood in the middle of the room, holding his body at an odd angle and flapping his arms, while a couple of teenagers, a boy and a girl, watched, laughing. There were candybar wrappers on the plank floor; there were clothes, blankets, sleeping bags, and comic books everywhere. The teenaged boy dissolved into a fit of laughter, rolling closer to the girl, who then moved away from him. Michael wanted to be in that house with a sudden and devastating paroxysm of longing—it was as if desire were an exotic poison that accelerated his pulse, closed his throat.

He was looking into the secret hiding place and home sweet home of Walter Fraleigh, who two years before had disappeared from Leyden—people assumed he had gone out

west to find his wife, Cindy, who was believed to have run off
with Fraleigh's partner in the swimming-pool business, Jimmy
Rugerio.

Michael had been with Fraleigh three or four or maybe it
was five nights when Fraleigh, swigging on a bottle of
Smirnoff vodka and cracking the swollen knuckles of his otherwise delicate hands, convened his little band of outsiders,
after a day of supervising them while they dug an enormous
pit in the spring-softened earth, which Fraleigh hoped to use
as a repository for his growing cache of stolen goods.

"I feel so close to you guys tonight, I want to tell you
something." The kerosene lamp put a golden glow on his
impish face. Even after two years in the woods, there was
something dandyish about him. The law of survival of the
fittest, which some men go to the woods to re-enact, would be
no friend to a Walter Fraleigh. He had the lithe, jittery build
of a third-rate jockey on the take, a jailhouse snitch. He
looked around the cabin. He smiled. His teeth glinted
between his mustache and goatee like a hacksaw in the grass.

And this was the story he told to Michael, and to Carmen
and Johnnie, who had been living with him for nearly a year,
and with whom he had had uncountable adventures, but of
whom, he had quickly confided to Michael, he was getting
tired.

"I knew Cindy was fucking my partner and supposedly
best friend, Jimmy Rugerio. The only question was what was
I going to do about it." He sucked in some vodka through his
whiskers with a sharp, sibilant slurp. "Michael. Move the
lamp more to the center, okay? Carmen's face is in shadows
and it weirds me fucking out."

Michael picked the lamp up by its wire handle. The tall
glass chimney radiated heat onto his knuckles. Outside, the
tree frogs were peeping off and on like little transistors. He
placed the lamp in the dead center of their circle. Its light

spread over Carmen's serene, beautiful face. He could barely look at her, she was so beautiful.

"I used to think about it all the time. I mean, I stayed up nights. Cindy always came home, sometimes half-crocked, and she'd just plop into our bed and be out like a light. She was what you'd have to call a real fucking whore. She lost all respect for her own body and so did I." He went silent for a moment and then repeated himself, but slowly, with a kind of obvious drama that made Michael suspicious. "And so did I."

"Your wife was screwing this guy?" asked Johnnie. He was a pale, puffy guy of about nineteen. He had a tattoo of an eagle on his meaty forearm and little stud earrings that said EAT ME. His dark hair was buzz-cut, shorter than a Marine's; it grew in whorls, and when Michael stared it started to look exactly like a fingerprint.

"That's right, Johnnie," said Fraleigh, shaking his head. He winked at Michael. He had decided that he and Michael were intellectual equals, wise men in a world of fools. Somewhere along the way, Fraleigh had developed a habit for reading and learning, and it seemed to have turned him against his own nature, like one of those yappy little apartment house dogs who can't go out to take a leak without a sweater and booties on. When Michael had first told him that his father was a writer, Fraleigh's eyes widened, his jaw literally dropped. "The life of the mind," he'd said, sighing, wringing his hands, cracking his knuckles.

"Getting rid of my lying, thieving partner wasn't the hard part," Fraleigh was saying. "I had enough shit on him to put him in jail for twenty years. He was kiting checks, robbing the business, robbing me. I had it all figured out and I had him dead to rights. I mean, BOOM!—I just dropped that motherfucker." Fraleigh tapped the side of his head, indicating that his weapon had been the intellect.

"So Jimmy Rugerio—he's out of there. He knows if I don't

slit his throat for fucking Cindy then I am sure as hell going to have him arrested for taking fourteen thousand dollars out of our swimming-pool business. Next, I gotta deal with Cindy."

Carmen stretched nervously. Her white knit sweater rode up, exposing a band of brown flesh. She checked through the corner of her eye to see if Michael was watching.

"So one day, I don't know, Jimmy's been gone about a week. I know for a fact he's gone out to San Diego, where his sister lives and her husband's brother is in the swimming-pool business, which of course is a million times better out there anyhow. Jimmy always makes out. But the point is Cindy. Cindy has no fucking idea where Jimmy is—did he go out for a Slurpy or fall off the edge of the world? Not that she seems particularly upset or anything. Cindy has this way. She's like her mother. But never mind, I'm getting off track.

"I'm waiting for her to crack, just say something. Like 'Where's Jimmy these days?' Or even go out looking for him. Every day she goes to work, driving the school bus, coming home for lunch and a nap, going out again until dinner. She don't give away a thing. She even has me fooled, if you want to know. Not really. I waited a week and two days. One night I rolled next to her in our bed. We had a waterbed, so she could always hear me coming."

Fraleigh smiled, as if this were an awfully pleasant memory. Michael's heart beat in his stomach. The big chunks of wood were popping in the rusted potbelly stove.

Every night it had ended something like this, sitting on the floor with the stove pumping out heat like organ music and Fraleigh talking until they one at a time fell asleep. It was bedtime stories. He talked about the houses they had robbed and the ones they were going to hit next. Or all kinds of high-flying poetic musings about life in these woods and how they, his band of outsiders, were the last real Americans. The next night he told them the story of the book he had just read, *Stranger in a Strange Land*, told it like a child, with exhausting, undifferentiated detail and a hundred self-interruptions, like "Oh yeah, I forgot the part when. . . ." They slept curled like dogs, and when they awakened—Michael shy, nervous, Johnnie and Carmen politely distant from each other, as if some huge fight had been resolved with an uneasy truce— Fraleigh was right there, making coffee on the potbelly stove top, humming happily, his yellow hair dark from a dunk in the stream and combed straight back so that his pink scalp showed through.

But tonight's tale would not put them to sleep. Each of them knew from the story's beginnings that it was going to end in killing. (The life in the forest made the idea of killing easier to take: in the few days that Michael had been there, they had already killed two ducks, a raccoon, and a rabbit. Johnnie had gutted them, shoved sticks through them, turned them slowly over the fire. They were delicious. "I love springtime!" Fraleigh had said, wiping the grease from his beard.)

"So I rolled over to her. We had this signal. I put my hand on her hip and shook her back and forth. But her skin was cold and she moved away from me. Not sleepyish, but like she's totally pissed off. Like I did something wrong. It made me . . ." He paused, let them wonder. "It made me crazy.

"I kicked her out of bed and she landed, *bang*, flat on her back, and when she tries to get up I push her down again, but this time her head cracks against the floor and she's wild. Cindy had real spirit, I'll give her that. She was not someone you could just push around. She's cussing me out, calling me a little faggot. Real sweet stuff. She could really be a little darling. 'Thank you so much,' I said to her. 'That does wonders for my self-esteem.' And *bang*, I push her down again. But this time she doesn't go down so easily, so I just sweep her legs out from under her. So now she falls like a ton of bricks."

Michael took a quick inward breath. He felt Carmen looking at him. What was he supposed to show here? Interest?
Fear? Revulsion?

"Now she's not acting so angry. Her expression is kind of
blank, and it's like her eyes are suddenly filled with milk. Oh
Jesus, kids, I shouldn't even be telling you this. But you have
to know. What we're doing out there. . . . going into houses,
taking what we need . . . living the life . . . we just all have
to be real straight with each other. In truth we find our
strength." He gestured with his hands, like a priest patting the
heads of adoring little children.

"She made a sound." Fraleigh expelled his breath, tried it
again, shrugged: he wasn't doing it justice, that last sound
Cindy made. "I knew right away she was in trouble. Her
brother is an epileptic; I guess she was wired up crazy, too,
without anyone knowing about it. But a couple cracks on the
head and she's dead? Come on. That don't figure." He rubbed
the back of his neck.

"I just left her there, right in the bedroom, in the dark. I
went into the living room and watched TV. Isn't that just like
me?" He laughed and talked through his laughter. "I mean,
they were selling food dryers, hits of the sixties, Dial a Psychic, and there's me kicking back in my La-Z-Boy, with Cindy
dead in the next room.

"Next morning, I wrapped her in a shower curtain and
shoved her into the trunk of my Celica. Cindy in the Celica."
He rocked his head back and forth, as if it were a song. "It
was hard getting her in. The Japs design those Toyotas for
killing a very different-sized woman. But I managed. Gently.
Then I called these people who I was supposed to be cleaning
their pool—that was how bad business was, because I promised myself I'd never clean a fucking pool, but now I was and
glad for the work."

"Wait a minute," said Johnnie. "You killed your wife?"
His voice was stunned, but that wasn't so unusual.

"Shut up, Johnnie," said Carmen.

"I was just asking," said Johnnie, looking down at his hands, which were laced in his lap, the fingers rising up and down like the undulations of sea plants.

"Isn't he a fucking trip?" Fraleigh asked, jerking his thumb at Johnnie but grinning at Michael.

"Tell us what happened to Cindy," said Carmen. Her voice was deep, shredded, as if she were always on the mend from laryngitis.

"Worried?" Fraleigh asked her.

"Should I be?"

"I drove her out to Pennsylvania, filled her up with stones, and dumped her in a river."

"Yeah, right," said Johnnie.

"I was going to take her apart with my chainsaw. I laid her out in the woods. Took off all her clothes. It was cold out. Her pussy hair puffed up and turned like silver from the frost, and there I was with my Stihl saw smoking in my hands and the chain going around and around. But forget it, I couldn't do it. I got my limits. So I just put her in in one piece. Why? Do you think that was a mistake?"

"Are you shitting us?" said Johnnie.

"Now *that* was the middle of nowhere. A forest preserve. There were picnic tables, but even the squirrels were asleep. Lucky for me, the river was still moving. There was a corny little bridge, one of those fairy-tale jobbies, you know, 'Let's tiptoe through the tulips, la-la-la, everything is beautiful.' I dragged Cindy to the middle of the bridge and gave her a sailor's burial. Her father was in the Navy, in World War II. And what a sonofabitch piece of shit he is! Boils on his back and so much hair on his big fat paws it looks like he's wearing gloves. You know the type?"

"You actually killed her?" said Johnnie.

"What if I did? You're a thief."

"That's different."

"Is it? 'Thou shalt not steal.' "

"It's different. And you know it."

Fraleigh took a long swallow of vodka, closed his eyes as it warmed him, dried the corners of his mouth with his knuckle.

"The Bible says, 'Thou shalt not kill' and 'Thou shalt not steal.' It doesn't say, 'Thou shalt really really not kill because killing is worse than stealing.' It's all on the same level—same thing. Same fucking thing, Johnnie boy. And *you* know it."

Fear entered Michael's skull, just the way he entered that flimsily locked river house the night before, and now fear pushed Michael's mind around as if his brain were a thing on wheels. He could not complete a thought. Knowing Fraleigh's crime made them all a part of it, unless they now were to turn him in, which was out of the question.

"If this is bullshit, Walter . . ." said Carmen. She stretched her legs before her with deliberate languor, then poked a finger under the elastic cuff of the black leggings she wore beneath her girlish skirt.

It was what she was wearing two days later when she stood with Michael on a rocky rise in the woods, overlooking an old, well-cared-for farmhouse. There was a smell of rain in the air. A couple, a man and woman in their forties, were loading up their Lexus with a few things they wanted to bring back to the city. They were vibrant, fit; they had, like some childless couples, managed to avoid growing old.

"Who are they?" Michael asked.

"The Caldwells. They own these woods. They got about two or three hundred acres, but they just stay in the little grassy mowed part." Carmen carried a thick white bath towel, stolen from the Martin house a couple days ago. It was rolled tightly and she tucked it under her arm.

"What are we doing?"

"Waiting for them to leave. What's today?"

"I think Monday."

"Yeah. They should be gone. Is it a holiday?"

"I don't think so."

"When they leave for the city we can go into their house. I want to take a real shower, and we can watch TV. What shows do you like?"

"I don't know. Whatever."

He looked at his watch. It was nearly noon. The news would be on and maybe they'd be on it. The last house they robbed, it went sort of crazy. Michael put himself in charge, telling Fraleigh what was worth real money. No one wanted silverware anymore, silver wasn't worth shit, and it weighed a ton. Textiles, take the hooked rugs, the faded-aqua needlepoint samplers; take the *paintings*. Fraleigh didn't mind a kid telling him what to steal, that didn't bother him at all; but it made Johnnie jealous, and when Johnnie got jealous Johnnie got rough. There was considerable breakage. Glass figurines—ballerinas, puppies—then a painted glass lampshade, a huge smoky mirror that hung over the white marble mantelpiece. Scuff marks on the woodwork. Fraleigh just let him. He understood. It was either this or something worse. They're only things, was how Fraleigh saw it. Funny philosophy for a thief.

Down below, the Caldwells were kissing. It was a very big deal of a kiss, as if they knew they were being watched, or had always hoped to be. Everybody wanted to be a star, even a childless banker weekending in the boonies with his childless photographer wife. Sam used to say that publicity has taken the place of grace. Now His eye wasn't on the sparrow, but a camcorder lens was.

Fuck you, Sam, get out of my head.

Carmen pointed at the Caldwells as Mr. pressed Mrs. down onto the hood of their black car. She threw her arms back, offered herself up.

The rain was starting to come in big, fat, lazy drops. It stirred the trees around them, made Michael look up.

"They better not start having sex," said Carmen.

"But I like to watch," said Michael, in a deliberately drooly, creepy voice, but when he heard it he wondered all of a sudden if maybe this was his real voice, at last.

"I want them to go back to New York so I can go into their house and take my shower." She was always at one with her feelings. She wanted this, she wanted that; there was never any maybe about her.

The phone rang within the Caldwell house. The sound carried up, light, tinkling, cheerful birdsong. Mr. Caldwell abandoned the project of romancing his wife and ran back to the house to answer the phone. She remained there on the car, lifted her feet off the ground, raised her legs. She was doing exercises while she waited for another take of their love scene. Too rich to worry about the rain. He came out a minute later, full of gestures. She slid off the car while he locked the back door to the house and put the key in an empty planter, and a few moments later they were gone.

Michael and Carmen waited for the Caldwells to be safely gone, assumed they would not double back for some forgotten item.

"Let's go," Carmen said. She was in charge. She reached out for him, and Michael took her hand. He had a momentary impulse to pull her close. What would that feel like? he wondered. His lust was monstrous. Would his erection be sheer blue steel, a special-effects hard-on, fabulous and humiliating?

"Kiss me, you fool," she said, clasping her hands, batting her lashes. Carmen waited for a moment to see if Michael's face contorted in a confession of desire, and then stepped back, laughed. In the past couple days, there had been more and more jokes between them, all of them having to do with what it would be like to sleep in the same bed, to kiss, to have sex.

At first these jokes shocked Michael, but the tension they

released was a relief, and soon he could not stop himself from making them. Last night he sneezed, and when Carmen said "God bless you" he grabbed his crotch and said "Bless this." Part of the rules of this ritual was that they would both have to laugh, no matter how bad the joke was.

Yet even the jokes could not stave off the intimacy growing between them. Carmen told Michael she was starting to hurt between her legs and then further amazed him by telling him the source of her discomfort was a recurring yeast infection and then, seeing the confusion on his face, explained what that meant in calm, semimedical terms. She breathed directly into his face and asked him if her breath smelled okay.

For the first time ever, Michael felt a countervailing weight to his desire—a sense of his own desirability. Routinely, almost compulsively, visions of his ungainliness and flat-out ugliness were the inevitable Pong off the Ping of yearning. He had a dim memory, fished from the murk of psychotherapy, that once Olivia subtly moved away from him when he prolonged a certain kiss on a certain night (bedtime, thunder), a memory of her fingers pressing firmly against his chest and her face receding from that part of the darkness tinged by streetlights and into that part of the room where the existence of anything at all was a matter of faith. For most of childhood and all of adolescence he had felt as if he were repulsive, and so he could not take jokes; the rough-and-tumble of life with other kids made him ache with unhappiness. He had developed habits of the heart that were fruitless, destructive: he perfected poetic fixations that would implode from lack of air, passions that went unnoticed by others, unacted upon by himself, and he was used to gnawing through these secret connections to rid himself of them, like a fox chewing off its own leg to spring free of a trap.

On the way down to the house, staggering through the brambles that became thicker and greener day by day, both Michael and Carmen had a sense that Fraleigh was somewhere close behind them. Neither mentioned anything, but from time to time they stopped and looked back. Trees, mist, the smell of the wet earth, the sound of raindrops hitting against the leaves.

The Caldwell house was only a couple of hundred feet off the dirt road that wound through their property. It was like those old white houses with black shutters that Olivia picked on when she went hunting for antiques.

Next to the house was a small garage where they had left their Saab. There were new garden tools; cross-country skis rested across the beams. Thick spider webs trembled in the corners of the shed's greenish windows. The car was old, with nearly one hundred thousand miles on it. The Caldwells kept the key under the mat around the clutch and the brake.

Michael and Carmen went inside the house, through the kitchen door in the back. They took off their shoes; Carmen's red socks were torn at the toe.

It no longer felt particularly strange to Michael to be sneaking around someone else's house. Short on friends and shorter still on that outgoing quality that allowed one to make friends, Michael had always been curious about how other people lived, and now he was finding out. The things people kept in their pantry—the red-and-gold can of Portuguese olives, the tin of sugar cookies with ice skaters on the lid, the chutney, the bitters, the honey mustard, cookbooks, manila folders crammed with recipes clipped from *The New York Times*, even a breast pump—were now a matter of experience rather than conjecture. He had helped to rob only three houses, but his mind was already full of new knowledge of refrigerators, Jenn-Air ranges, hooked rugs, magazine racks holding medical journals, family albums embossed with elaborate coats of arms, sconces and portraits on the walls, human smells, perfume, rot, dead flowers, squirrel shit, the contents of bedside tables (bifocals, lubricants, sleep mask).

Walking with Carmen through the Caldwells' kitchen,

thinking of the bedroom upstairs, and for some reason not only noticing but staring at a solitary pale-green coffee cup on the wooden counter, Michael was suddenly beset by the impulse to call home and reassure his parents that he was still okay. He hadn't contacted them in a while, and it seemed somehow smart to remind them (in case he ever wanted to move back) that he was only missing, not dead. He didn't want to spend the rest of his life hearing how they didn't know if he was dead or alive.

"What are you thinking about?" Carmen asked. "You look scared."

"I'm not scared at all. I was just—" He stopped for a moment, hoping to think of something to say.

"Did you hear him last night?"

"Fraleigh? No."

"He was saying things in his sleep. I wanted to get close so I could hear, but maybe he'd wake up and grab me."

They wandered through the dining room, with its long cherry table and lyre-backed chairs, its salmon-colored walls, brilliant white woodwork, and worn carpeting. Next, they came to the library, where the television set was. Carmen knew exactly where they kept the remote control.

They sat on the sofa and Carmen raced through the stations, past a soap opera, "The Price Is Right," a household-hints show. She stopped at a talk show with a panel of very thin men sitting with their heavy wives and talking about the love they have for each other and the trouble they have in the world because people cannot accept a thin person loving a fat one. First to speak was an immense woman with short curly red hair and the face of someone who used to laugh a lot but no longer does. "Look, I've got health problems, financial, employment, you name it. . . ."

"Can you imagine even kissing her?" said Michael, without really giving the matter much thought. He just wanted Carmen to listen to him and not the set.

"When you love someone you just love them."

"I guess."

"It doesn't matter what. Maybe they have a great job and lots of money or maybe they don't. Maybe they're Catholic and you're not. Maybe they live out in the woods and rob houses at night."

Michael laughed. A feeling of warmth spread through him, as if something hot had spilled inside him.

"I'm serious. When you fall in love with someone, all that stuff is just little stuff. You hold on with both hands, until they saw off your arms. And then you hope someone comes along who'll fall in love with a girl who's got no arms."

The show broke for a commercial. An ocean liner cut its way through glassy, sun-struck waters while a woman sang about the pleasures of being on a cruise, and how your friends will envy your freedom and all the fancy foods you'll be eating.

"Is that how you were when you were in love?" Michael asked.

He could actually feel himself moving toward her, inwardly. It was as if every stray feeling, every romantic and erotic impulse, every dream, every thought of being with a woman—all his disparate moments of desire, beginning with the smell of his mother's skin and going forward in time to include the first girl he had held hands with, the first girl he had ever kissed, the strangers in skin magazines whose wide-openness he had studied beneath the tent of his blankets—all of those moments and images of love were suddenly airborne and in formation.

Carmen shrugged. "Almost."

"Who did you love like that?"

"My first boyfriend."

"Your first boyfriend?" He forced a laugh. "How many have you had?"

"Two. But Thomas was just to get back at my mother

because she made me break up with Julius." As she spoke, she took Michael's hand and pretended to count his fingers.

Michael's heart was a maniac in a locked room. He looked at their hands together, the difference in their colors. He had a moment of absolute certainty that their lives were joined and would remain so. His heart, his imagination, were taking possession of her. He could see them in a restaurant together, wearing beautiful clothes and eating by candlelight.

"I have to tell you something," he said.

"What?" She furrowed her brow, withdrew her hand, as if expecting him to say something critical of her.

With a casualness that surprised him, he took her hand again. It was a gesture more unmistakable than a kiss. It said: You are mine.

"My father is going out on my mother."

"Yeah? Well, *my* father—"

"No, wait. Okay?"

"Sorry."

"My father met this woman. He even brought her to our house. She was okay. Actually, I sort of liked her. Then they broke up or something. Maybe they just had a fight. Anyhow, she sent him this really pissed-off letter, and really intense, too. Can I tell you what she said?"

"Go ahead."

"It's sort of disgusting."

"I think I can stand it, Michael."

He breathed in the air into which she had just said his name.

"She said he used her box like a toilet."

" 'Her box'?"

Michael shrugged. "Her cunt."

"Where do you get 'box'?"

"A friend of mine used to call it that."

"You know the Eskimos? They got a hundred different names for snow."

"Really?"

"Men are like that, for the place down there." She pointed to her lap and smiled.

She sat back on the sofa and moved her head to the side, so she could see the TV screen better. One of the skinny men was remembering what it was like when his wife was trying to lose weight, what a trial their life had been. And a woman in the audience was shouting back at him, "But you should have encouraged her, for God's sake! This is her *life* you are talking about."

"I don't know what to do," said Michael. "I don't want to be a part of his secrets, but I don't want to tell her, either. She'll hate me. Everyone will."

Carmen switched the TV set off with the remote control and turned her full attention on Michael. He could feel her filling him. He had often wondered what it must feel like to be fucked, and this might be it: another human being was inside of him.

"Maybe she already knows. Maybe she knows and doesn't want to do anything about it. Women know what a man feels."

They were silent. The rain beat against the roof. Michael felt he had been suddenly led to a moment he wasn't prepared for. But now he stood before it, like a man before a vast, locked bronze door, compelled by fate to knock.

"Why do you stay here?" he asked her, his voice small.

"I don't have anywhere else to go."

"But where are you from?"

"What difference does it make? The Bronx, Tremont Avenue. Then my mother and her boyfriend and me moved up to Newburgh. He started to mess around with me, and when I told her she told social services I was crazy and they tried to put me in a hospital."

"Are you with Johnnie?"

"Please."

He shrugged.

"Fraleigh?"

"What do you think I am? Because I'm not white or something?"

"I feel that you're the nicest person I ever knew," he said.

"Then you ought to get out a little more," answered Carmen.

"If I could get Fraleigh to listen to me . . ."

"He don't listen to anyone. You should know that."

"About robbing the houses. What to take."

"He took your advice last time. That was weird. He sort of looks up to you. Johnnie to him is an idiot and I'm just a girl. But he respects you."

"He's been breaking into places for a year."

"Longer. I've been with him almost a year and he was doing it way before then."

"But what does he have to show for it?"

"He just does it. He says a real thief doesn't do it for the profit. A real thief isn't afraid to have everything and he isn't afraid to have nothing."

"We could make a lot of money. We're in the places anyhow. You can't just go in and use the bathroom and eat their food and take a bunch of junk. You have to know what's what, and you have to know where to sell it. Even if you're stealing the best things and you don't know where to sell it—what's it worth then? You know?"

"Who's he going to sell it to? The Easter Bunny?"

"I know people. In New York. We could make money. A lot of money."

Michael's insides throbbed with the audacity of what he proposed. Complex plans of deeply criminal cunning seemed suddenly his second nature. He took a deep breath, let his eyes lock fiercely onto Carmen's, until she demurely averted her gaze.

"I better take my shower and then we have to go."

He took her arm in his hand.

"We'd have all this money. And we could go wherever we wanted."

"Who? Me and you?" Her voice rose, as if she was a little offended by the presumption.

"Yes."

She was silent for what seemed like a long time.

Finally, she said, "Let me think about it."

chapter nine

money was in the wind. The check was really and truly in the mail, and one hoped the mailman was bonded, because it was going to be a biggie. Somewhere, everywhere, sales of *Visitors* were being totaled up, cash registers were making like sleigh bells, fresh copies of my stale book were being forklifted onto trucks.

I bought a baby-blue solar-powered calculator and diddled around with fantasy numbers. Forty thousand bucks, sixty thousand; six percent interest, eight percent. I was whistling in the dark, I was a bearded babe in toyland. With Michael gone and the TV unoccupied, I looked in on the Financial News Network, to get a sense of where interest rates were on those long-range T-bills I had once heard someone mention.

This money, unarrived but already mine, was a set of keys to allow me entrance into the rooms I had long wanted to stroll through—the rooms in which you order from a chic little typewritten menu without making a little mental running total of the tab, the room in which you bought your wife a pair of ruby earrings because they were wrenched from the earth to live next to her raven hair, and the room in which you sat at your typewriter with a fresh stack of high-rag-content paper and a goose-necked lamp and wrote something so true and so necessary that for a while you could imagine you were doing God's work.

In the beginning, it was written, there was the Word, and the Word was God, and from now on I would honor the Word and tell the truth, the whole truth, and nothing but the truth, so help me.

Except.

Except I would, by necessity, continue to maintain the lies I had already told and which were so firmly and intractably in place.

By necessity. Necessity must be taken into account, necessity must be given its due. I was not an angel. All I could do was leap winglessly into the air; but there was gravity, too, stronger than my ability to leap.

By day, while Amanda was in school, Olivia and I continued our disorganized, desultory search for Michael. We went back to the high school. We loitered there, drove around the nearby neighborhoods—newer, pastel, humble one-story houses with a hint of domestic violence beneath their aluminum siding. I drove into neighboring towns, villages of roughly the same population as Leyden, with similar stores, but shuffled and dealt out in different order, so that they seemed strange, eerily distinctive. I went back to the state cops, but now that they knew that Michael had called the house they had lost interest in us. It seemed no longer in their jurisdiction. It was a family matter—that was becoming a chilling phrase. One of the older cops suggested I contact the truant officer.

"A truant officer?" Olivia said to me. She was sitting at the kitchen table, with her back to the window. Behind her was a curtain of rain.

"What can I tell you?"

"I don't know, Sam. What *can* you tell me?"

She wrapped her hands around her coffee cup with

the dark-orange Chinese hummingbirds on it, for warmth, but the coffee was cold and she glanced at the cup with annoyance.

That cup failing to give her warmth is me, I thought.

"Ever since this thing began," she said, "I've had this feeling."

She looked at me. She wore a red turtleneck sweater that drained the color from her face.

I may have been looking for trouble to think I was the hummingbird coffee cup, but I was certainly spot-on in believing that Olivia was sure I knew more about Michael's disappearance than I was saying. Yet what good would it have done for me to tell her about Nadia and the letter? If there were laws of karma, I was breaking them—but that was fine with me. This was not a Bengali crisis; this was a *fin-de-siècle* American crisis, and I doubted karmic law was one of my most pressing problems. What if I made a clean breast of it? Would it bring Michael home one second sooner? I was living a lie, but it was *my* lie, and indulging my compulsion to confess would only make matters worse. Then we would be at each other's throats. Then Olivia would have no one to trust, no one with whom to go through this agonizing experience.

"What do you mean, you 'have this feeling'?" I asked, content to sound thick.

"There's something you're not telling me. What happened that day. You left with him—you went to Pennyman."

I looked at my watch. "Amanda will be home any second."

"I just can't believe something didn't happen, either on the way to the office, or while he was with Dr. Pennyman."

"He's not a doctor," I said, because it was my turn to speak.

"What happened, Sam? Did you have a fight with him? Did you say anything?"

"Did I *say* anything? Of course I said something." I was lunging at any possible opportunity to sound guiltless. "I talked, he listened, or pretended to. As to what happened with Pennyman—" I shrugged, pushing out my lower lip like a Montmartre pimp—"you'll have to ask him." I almost gasped; I couldn't believe how stupid I was, saying that. Pennyman, I suddenly remembered, knew enough to kill me and send Olivia up for murder.

"I called Pennyman," said Olivia.

"You did?" My heart was a hive full of bees. I went to the window and pretended to look out for Mandy's school bus. I was afraid the blood would show in my otherwise composed face.

"He wasn't in, or wasn't picking up. I left a message."

"Mandy's here!" I fairly sang, as if her arrival from school were an annual rather than daily occurrence.

I hustled out to the front hall and pulled an umbrella out of a length of cobalt-blue stovepipe we used as an umbrella stand. I was going to give sweet little Mandy the royal treatment.

Holding the rather-skimpier-than-I-had-expected umbrella, with its purple-and-puce waltzing hippos, I rushed out of the house to escort her in, like a Fifth Avenue doorman a week before Christmas. But then I stopped. The umbrella was too small to keep us both dry, and those hippos were an embarrassment. The school bus's doors opened with a pneumatic wheeze. Surely, Mandy wouldn't want her friends to see her father sporting such a loser's umbrella—why not just show up with a watch cap pulled over my ears and my pants unzippered? I ducked back into the house, shoved the little umbrella back into the porcelain stovepipe, and touched the handle of one and then another and then still another of our umbrellas, momentarily paralyzed, as if this were the choice of weapons in a duel.

"Just a second, sweetie!" I called out the front door, as

Amanda got off the bus and began running toward the house, her backpack held over her head.

I chose my umbrella—an old Tory number I found in the back of a taxi years before—and raced to fetch my daughter, who waited for me, with a puzzled, hopeful smile, while her friends' faces slid away into the rain.

Yet she was pleased. The gallantry of my gesture amused and reassured her. She liked me bringing her in, and she smiled happily as I undid the snaps on her slicker and ran my hand over her damp, shining hair. She had Olivia's hair, thick, water repellent, with that wonderful scalpy aroma. She held me in her gaze as I fussed over her. I could never, even if I were an emotional genius, give her the love she deserved.

"Are you chilly?" I asked her.

"Dad," she said, "I walked from the bus to the house." She used comic intonation and it was funny, but it pained me, too, because the delivery was from a show, I could tell that.

I stayed with Amanda, away from Olivia. We watched "Duck Tales." I somehow believed that those Disney ducks were less destructive than the newer cartoon characters. After the cartoons, Amanda showed me her math quiz. She'd gotten a 100, and her math teacher was considering putting her in an advanced class. Good news, but I overreacted. "Dad, you're squashing me," she said, as I hugged her to me, saying over and over how proud I was, as if she had been given early admittance to MIT. What difference did it make that she could barely read? Maybe tonight we'd hunker down for a little Financial News Network action.

She told me she had a test on the state capitals coming up.

"Then let's study and get you another A," I said, with a great, toothy, lopsided, imbecilic grin.

We went over the capitals. She knew very few of them. I supplied her with the answers. Olivia came in, watched us for a while, though I didn't raise my eyes to look at her.

"I'm going to make linguine with clam sauce," Olivia announced, hoping to remind Amanda that this was still a home, a place where people were nourished, enjoyed themselves; but her voice sounded flat, resigned.

"Okay, honey," I said to Amanda, listening to Olivia leave. "Let's go over the ones we've been studying."

"This isn't studying, Dad. This is just hanging out. I really like hanging out with you."

"Don't worry. It's studying." I felt myself blush, a great red tide. Happiness rushed into me, announcing its general absence from my life. "All right. Capital of Maine. Quick!"

She looked at the ceiling. She had a long, graceful neck, full lips, luxurious lashes, skin so soft and pure it could make you gasp. In some people, physical beauty is the unearned asset that makes life simpler, but I often feared Mandy's beauty would mainly bring her trouble.

She took a deep breath and folded her hands tightly on her lap.

"Augusta?" she said, softly.

"That's right," I said, with relief, just so glad something had turned out right.

Once again, we ate without Michael. The table, set for three, looked wounded, a war veteran sitting upright in his cranky bed with only one leg beneath the standard-issue blanket. The linguine steamed in its light-blue bowl, a tablespoon and fork jabbed haphazardly on either side of the gray, clammy mound. There was no salad, no vegetable, not even bread—just this, as if all Olivia had wanted was to have achieved the fact of having prepared a dinner.

"I'll bet you Michael comes home tomorrow," Amanda said brightly.

"We'll see," I said. "It would be great."

"Do you think he will, Mom?"

"I don't know," said Olivia softly. "I hope so."

Oh, lighten up, I thought to myself. If she wants to pretend, let's all pretend with her.

"Is this how you made it last time?" Amanda asked. After several forkfuls, she was suddenly skeptical of the linguine. She frowned at her bowl, started wagging her knees.

That night, I put Amanda to bed while Olivia went out to look for Michael. This making of the rounds virtually defined the concept of Useless Action, but finally it was easier on the nervous system than just waiting for something to happen.

I read to Amanda from a book called *The Itsy-Bitsy Dinosaur*, written and illustrated by an old friend of ours from New York City days, Peter Conn, a cherub-faced guy with the eyes of a dissolute choirboy and a shock of golden curls. He liked to say he spelled his name "Conn, like in Connecticut—but without the etiquette." Peter used to write poetry—dense, opaque verse, full of classical references and sexual perversity. He self-published a book called *Anal Rape Etudes*. Then his girlfriend got pregnant, became his wife, and Peter switched to children's books, often a one-way ticket to Palookaville. But Peter clicked with kid lit. *Itsy-Bitsy*, his fourth book, sold over one hundred thousand copies, and Peter was a made man.

"Why don't you read the next page?" I said to Amanda. She lay perfectly flat in her bed, the blanket drawn up to her chin, her head centered on her pillow, and her dark hair fanning out on either side.

"I like it when you read," she said. Her hands gripped the edge of the blanket tightly, as if in terror.

"If you don't practice, you can't make your reading better."

"But I'm an excellent reader, Dad."

I nodded, feeling, as usual, out of my depth. Had Amanda been put on some regime of enhanced self-esteem? I didn't want to interfere with the magic of her believing she was good, though it did strike me that, from an educational stand-point, it might be a bit easier to raise self-esteem than actual reading scores.

I handed her the book and pointed to the rectangle of text floating above the illustrator's rendition of a brontosaurus riding the escalator at Barneys. I hadn't chosen this page by accident. There were no difficult words—nothing hyphenated, no long words except for "brontosaurus," which I had already read to her twenty times.

" 'Up up up went the moving stairs,' " read Amanda. She looked up from the book, at me, for praise. What did she want, a brass band? It was a *sentence*, for Christ's sake. Yet I smiled at her, and in a way I *was* proud.

" 'When she get—' "

" 'Got,' " I said.

" '—got to the top, she saw the old lady. She went up to the old lady and said, "Hello, how are you? My name is Charlotte Brontë." ' "

I laughed, and Amanda looked at me, startled, thinking she had made an embarrassing mistake.

"That was a joke," I said.

"It was?"

"Well, supposed to be. Do you remember Peter?"

"I think so. He was nice."

"Did you think so? Anyhow, Charlotte Brontë—"

As I tried to parse Peter's joke, Mandy slipped the book back into my hands, and I was by then resigned to reading the rest of it. She watched my face for signs of impending pedagogy but then trusted that she wouldn't be required to read any further and settled into a sweet alpha-rich reverie.

I finished the book, turned off the light. Mandy's tan-and-blue room, with its meticulously hung National Geographic posters, its spotless surfaces, the clothes for tomorrow folded neatly on the chair at the foot of her bed—all of it, with its order and its desire for order, vanished into the darkness: with a flick of a switch, I had made her world disappear. I leaned over her bed and kissed her forehead, her eyebrow.

"I love you, Mandy."

"I love you too, Sam."

"Sam?"

"I'm just kidding, Dad."

I stood up, waited. I wished there were more I could say. Should I kiss her again, repeat that I loved her?

"Good luck on that capitals test," I said.

She pretended to be already sleeping.

When I went downstairs, Olivia was back from her nightly rounds. She was in the kitchen, with an extremely large glass of Scotch before her, resting her head on her arm.

"Are you asleep?" I whispered.

"No," she said, muffled, into her sweater.

"I was reading Mandy one of Peter Conn's books." I waited, went on. "We should call him, have him up."

"Them," said Olivia.

"Right. Have them up. Remember that weekend we took with them in Bridgehampton? That was so much fun."

Olivia lifted her head and faced me. Her eyes were drenched but holding on to every tear.

"It seems like a long time ago," she said. "But I liked being at the beach. I liked seeing all those ambitious people with their clothes off, the big media kings with their skimpy little Speedo suits."

"Remember his girlfriend?"

"Wife. Ginny."

"Her cooking."

"The amazing versatility of eggplant."

"She had no pubic hair," I said.

"Get over it, Sam. She shaved. And paraded around so everyone would notice."

"John Ruskin was married before he learned that women, unlike statues—"

"I know, I know," said Olivia. "That John Ruskin pubic hair story has been told too many times. But Sam . . . ?"

"What?"

"I have to ask you a question. And please tell me the absolute truth."

"All right." I braced myself.

"This afternoon, when you went out looking for Michael?"

"Yes?"

"Did you stop at the bookstore to see how your book is selling?"

It seemed such a reasonable question, and so much less incriminating than what I had feared, that I answered without thinking. "Yes. I did. But Molly's still waiting for her new order. I should call Ezra and complain, actually."

"You really did that?" said Olivia, fiercely. "You checked to see how your stupid book is selling?"

This time I was not quite so fast to answer. I stood immobile, and then, finally, I nodded my head.

She took a long, somewhat melodramatic drink of her Scotch. "I feel like I'm going to fucking lose my mind," she said, getting up, walking out of the kitchen.

"That stupid book is paying the bills, my darling," I said, as she left the room. She didn't answer, and I hoped she hadn't even heard me.

I got my orders from Heather, via fax, a list of places, dates. My first stop was Boston, where I was to attend the New England Independent Booksellers convention, which was held this year in a hotel surrounded by cheap steak houses, Chinese restaurants, pawnshops, and porn theaters.

It was not an event to which most publishers gave high priority; in fact, I (or John Retcliffe) was the only author present whose book was being nationally distributed. For the most part, the publishers here were two- and three-person operations, with offices in their homes, in places like Concord, Portsmouth, and White River Junction, pleasant, slightly vain Protestants, smugly removed from the mercantile hurly-burly of big-time publishing, and the books themselves listed toward the sincere—books about living with cancer, lots of books about boating, living on islands, histories of small places.

Each publisher had a small kiosk in the hotel's Grand Ballroom. A publisher with a bit of capital or an artistic niece might tack up posters on the walls, but most of them stood in their little booths as if they were rug merchants in a forgotten souk, one in which the date palms had turned to drooping brocaded drapery and the sand to parquet.

The Wilkes and Green table was completely filled with *Visitors*, and my job was to stand there with Heather (who was looking pretty, kind of weekend-in-the-country-ish) and W&G's New England sales rep, a tall, mournful guy in his forties named Morris Springer, who was remarkably saturnine for a salesman—he seemed more a bankruptcy lawyer and utterly lacked the energetic winking high spirits and likability that most drummers relied upon.

The purpose of the fair was to sell books to New England bookstore owners, and since I was clearly holding the hot hand in this room, most of them made their way to the W&G booth. With Heather smiling on one side of me, and Morris Springer sighing on the other, I shook so many hands that I felt as if I were running for alderman in some lonely, bookish precinct, a place where half my constituents wore Ben Franklin specs and the other half wore orthopedic shoes.

I would have thought that for Heather this regional Gutenbergian hoedown would have been small potatoes, but she was grinning and pressing the flesh as if her career, her very life depended on the successful promotion of my book. (I liked that.) I would have also guessed that spending time on the road would be annoying to her; I imagined her life back in Manhattan as intensely social, complicated, full of sexual intrigue. But ever since my successful showing on Jerry Hopper and Ezra designating me the official traveling John Retcliffe, Heather's attitude toward me had become warmly collegial. She stood close to me, smiled adoringly while I chatted up the customers, touched my hand now and then. My sexual compass, plunged into the magnetic field of this trip, was spinning like a helicopter blade. The slightest kindness, even eye contact, was immediately alchemized into the fool's gold of erotic fantasy.

Next booth to us was a Boston publisher called Crescent Press, which published commentaries on the Koran, denunciations of U.S. Mideast policies, a lavishly illustrated biography of the singer Cat Stevens, and, probably most profitably of all, little puce cones of incense, which they kept burning on small hammered-copper plates. The couple running the Crescent Press table were two Americans, one a towering, lantern-jawed Yankee, who kept his blond hair concealed beneath an Arafat-style swath of red-and-white cloth, and the other a stocky young woman in a powder-blue caftan, which she might have purchased in Tehran, or perhaps on Rodeo Drive—there was a kind of Liz-Taylor-at-home aspect to her.

"I want to ask them to stop burning that horrible incense," Heather said to me. "But they look so nuts, I'm afraid of them."

"Do you want me to?"

"Would you hate me if I said yes?" she said, with exaggerated demureness.

"Absolutely not," I said, rolling right along with her.

The Crescent Press might be in opposition to all things American and Occidental, but for the day, at least, they were amiable, passing out catalogs and free samples of their incense.

"Hello, neighbor," the man with the PLO textiles said to me.

"Isn't this something else?" said the woman at his side. Her costume included a veil, which she presumably wore when she went outside, but which here in the ballroom she yanked down under her chin.

I spent a moment pretending interest in their wares. It all looked like one of those folding tables set up on Manhattan street corners, usually manned by ascetic-looking blacks. They were even selling the *Protocols of the Elders of Zion*, this one with a cover that showed a Star of David formed out of dollar and pound signs.

"I was wondering what we could do about that incense," I said. "It's been going since ten this morning and it's getting a bit thick."

"This is clarifying incense," the man said. He sounded like what the rich call "wellborn." I imagined him as a professor of Islamic studies who hadn't gotten tenure—departmental problems, sex with a student—and then went off the deep end.

"Well, the thing is—I don't know, maybe it's the atmosphere in here, but for *us* it's not having much of a clarifying influence."

"We do three hundred thousand dollars annually in this incense," the woman said. She had a ragged, weary voice, as if she had been berating a roomful of imbeciles the night before.

"Maybe if you got a fan or something," I suggested. "But the way it is now, there's a cloud of the stuff." I gestured toward the Wilkes and Green booth, smiled.

"A fan?" asked the lanky convert. He looked as if I had suggested he buy a vibrator.

"We have as much right to be here as anyone else," said the woman. Each of her fingers bore a plain gold ring and each of them was too tight. "I realize you people are pushing this big best-seller, but that doesn't make you the boss of the whole place."

" 'The boss of the whole place'? What are you talking about? We're not bothering anyone."

"That's right," said the man, with a smile in which snobbery and madness danced cheek to cheek. "All you're doing is making a peaceful little *settlement*."

"What is that?" I asked. "Some sort of reference to the West Bank?"

"You can take it any way you choose."

"Yes, well, I notice you've got copies of the *Protocols of the Elders of Zion* here. It's about time someone brought that back into print, right?"

"It's never been out of print," said the woman. Her chubby fingers played with the edge of her veil; she seemed tempted to pull it over her mouth and nose again.

"It's hate literature," I said.

"The slave owners said the Emancipation Proclamation was hate literature," the man said.

There was a time when by now I would have been red-faced, trembling, when the enzymes of disagreement would have had my heart pounding. But my weirdly secondhand success and the money it was going to bring were a drug, smoothing me out. Of all the forms of stupidity in the world, I had always been made most livid by Jew baiting, not because it was worse than other forms of bigotry, or even because it was potentially directed against my own person, but because it inevitably recalled my own father's moronic displays of pique and brutality against my mother and forced me to remember, as well, my own passive response to the long sadness of my childhood.

"What's your name?" I asked.

"Ibraham," he said, clasping his hands behind his back.

"Malla," said the woman, with a certain puzzling stoicism.

"Well, Ibe, Malla, what can I say? I'm sure this new translation of *Ali Baba and the Fifty Thieves* is first-rate—you know, I always was under the impression that there were but forty, but what the hell. And, I'm a supporter of the First Amendment, even when it comes to nutty garbage like the *Protocols*. Really, if you knew me better, you'd realize how fervently I believe in the right to publish whatever you want. But this incense—the incense isn't really a First Amendment thing. You want to call the American Civil Liberties Union? I don't think you're going to find too many lawyers interested in handling incense cases."

"How about restraint of trade?" said Ibraham.

"I don't think so, Ibraham."

"Are you a *lawyer*?" said Malla. She pronounced the word in such a way that it seemed code, a way of saying "Jew."

"No, I'm not a lawyer. And I'm not on some Lawrence and Lucille of Arabia trip, either. But I'll tell you what I am. I'm unstable."

"Are you threatening us?" asked Ibraham.

I stroked my chin, squinted. "I think I might be." I hadn't had a physical fight in thirty years. I retired as undefeated champion of the fourth grade, and by the fifth I was on to sarcasm.

Just then, Heather did one of the finest things a woman can do for a man—she came over and got me out of having to fight.

"There's someone here to see you, Johnnie," she said to me, tugging at the cuff of my blazer.

Really? I almost said, but I didn't want to press my luck. I gave Ibraham one of those "Boy, did you just come close" looks and then said to Malla, "Lose the incense." I turned quickly, before they had a chance to reply, which would mean that I would have to say something more, and I followed Heather back to the Wilkes and Green booth.

"Was someone really here to see me?" I asked her, safe in our bookish turf. "Or was that just feminine chivalry?"

She gave me a peculiar look. Relations between men and women were filled with unexpected boundaries, unintentional encroachments, like the life of the suddenly balkanized independent states in the former Soviet Union.

"Why would I lie to you?" she said.

"But I don't see anyone," I said, gesturing. After just one radio interview, I could feel the artificiality already overtaking me, the canned, exaggerated mimicry of doing rather than being, the coarse necessities of projection.

"He sent a note. They won't let him in without credentials. He says he's your brother."

"My brother?" My voice was incredulous, as if I had no such relative.

"He's been out there for a while," Heather said, passing me the note. It was a folded square of hotel stationery, with my name—Sam Holland, that is—penciled on the front of it. Beneath my name was "Green Publishers."

"Obviously, the name was a bit of confusion," said Heather. "And 'Green Publishers.' It went to the Greenpeace booth, and then there's this outfit out of Vermont calls themselves Stephen Green."

I must have been showing distress, because she smiled rather sweatily at me as I opened the note.

"They won't let me in because I can't prove I'm in the book biz," the note said, beginning with his usual abruptness. "I'll wait for you in the lobby until four o'clock. Allen (The Alien)."

Was this a joke based on the subject matter of my book? I certainly didn't remember us, or anyone, calling him The Alien back in childhood.

"What's the big deal with security?" I said to Heather. "We're a bunch of booksellers, for Christ's sake."

"Stephen King's supposed to be here," she said. "Later."

Did I detect a little wistfulness?

"Stephen King? I'm selling more than Stephen King, aren't I?"

Morris, the sales rep, looked up from his paperwork.

"Not really," said Heather. "But it's good. Keep your confidence up."

I hadn't seen my brother (or sister) in two years. We didn't keep in touch, disgracefully. In fact, the problem was we felt disgraced around each other. We shared memories like people who had witnessed a crime and walked away.

I found him in the lobby, ashing his cigarette into a potted palm. He took up the entirety of a maroon club chair. The bulk of his massive legs hiked up his trousers, revealing his skimpy socks, his bone-white shins. He had loosened his tie, undone his vest; his face was brutalized by fat, the very bones of him seemed to have been pulled apart trying to accommodate what the years had added to their burden. He dragged on his cigarette, looked at the tip, and then ground it out in the palm's pebbly soil. He looked like a gangster between indictments.

"Allen," I said, taking a deep breath, walking toward him. "How did you know I was here?"

He pushed himself out of his chair, brushed his lapels on the assumption they were dusted with ash.

"Sammy, look at you. You putting on weight?"

"Actually, no. I'm down a few pounds."

"Yeah? I always thought of you as such a skinny kid." He waited for me to get closer and then he grabbed me and pressed me close in a sudden but somehow tender embrace. "I heard about Michael, Sam. I'm just sick about it."

"How did you find out?"

"Pop told me."

"How did he find out?"

"I don't know. He called your house and got Olivia. She told him, I guess."

"Do you want to know *why* he called my house? He wants to be *me*, on my book tour."

"What difference does it make? Come on, Natalie and the kids are dying to see you."

I had only a couple of hours to spend with them. Heather had me booked for a late-night radio show; Allen was supposed to drop me off at the studio on Commonwealth Avenue around nine.

In the meantime, I sank into the familiar but eager solicitude of his family. Natalie was dark, petite, but with severely cut hair, extreme makeup, the look of someone who spends too much time at the so-called beauty parlor—like with hospitals, the more time you spend in those places, the worse you look. Every time she looked at me, all she saw was a man with a missing son, and her eyes filled. My nieces and nephews—chubby, quick-witted Tara, moody Eliot, garlicky Marty, bespectacled, abundant, musical Daphne, and smiling, evasive, brainy Ken—sat with their parents in the enormous, freshly painted family room, with the giant Sony snugly enclosed in a Mediterranean-style cabinet, and the gray draperies, with their subtle glitter of metallic threads, tightly shut over the picture window, and they all listened with astonishing attentiveness as I more or less told the story of how I had come to write *Visitors from Above* and its weird unexpected success.

The presence of my brother's children, their coziness, surprised me, made me jealous. My children had never had much use for adult conversation. The only friends of ours they could tolerate were the real arrested-development cases, who showed active interest in model trains, Legos, Sega Genesis. But Allen's kids seemed to hang on every word. Perhaps what they saw in me was the embodiment of domestic dread: the man who had lost his son. Perhaps those stares were not really ones of fascination but of morbidity. I was the smoking wreck on the side of the highway, and they were just rubber-necking.

"So what does Olivia think of this success of yours?" asked Allen.

"I don't think she has any idea what to make of it. She's gotten used to me being a certain way—desperate, applying for grants, not getting them. You know."

"Connie says she always knew you'd make it."

"So Connie knows all about this, too?"

"Sure."

"And about Michael, too?"

"Was it supposed to be a secret?"

"Not really. I just had no idea everyone was in such close contact. How long has this been going on?"

"Sam. We're a *family*."

"From a census taker's point of view."

"Allen's always been such a family man," said Natalie. I chose to understand this as a statement of some small bitterness. Natalie, after all, had been trained as a special-ed teacher and ended up housebound, raising child after child.

"I don't understand something, Uncle Sam," said Marty, fourteen years old, earnest, literal. "Do you *believe* in people from outer space?"

"I think it's mathematically unlikely that we are completely alone," I said, with scant conviction. The Retcliffe within scowled, wanting more.

Natalie served a dietetic dinner: pineapple chunks,

romaine lettuce, green beans, Poland Spring water. Allen had several servings. I helped Natalie clear, and in the kitchen she confided in me. "I'm worried about Allen's health, Sam."

"His weight?"

She looked slightly offended. "No. His weight is fine. He's large boned. I'm worried about his smoking. He was supposed to quit, but I know he's sneaking them. I smell the smoke on his clothes."

"I heard that smoking was actually pretty good for you," I said.

"You did?"

"I read it in a booklet printed up by the International Tobacco Institute." I had no idea what the reasoning behind this ridiculous joke was. Was I trying to ingratiate myself? Or was this some sort of self-satire, a reference to the lies written by hacks?

"You know, Allen loves you, Sam," said Natalie, running the dishwasher. "We want to see more of you. Our children should be friends."

"When Michael comes back and my tour is complete," I said over the watery roar.

Natalie and the kids saw me to the door a while later. Allen was in his Audi, warming the engine, despite the arguments this caused within his household. It was the old engine-care-versus-energy-conservation controversy. Marty fetched the copy of *Visitors from Above* I'd brought over, in lieu of a bottle of Côtes du Rhône.

"Will you sign this for us?" he asked.

I held the book, accepted the Patriots souvenir pen.

"Which name do you want me to sign?" I asked him.

He blushed, but he knew what he wanted. "John Retcliffe, I guess." He tapped his manly finger on the dust jacket.

Allen and I were silent in the car until he was well away

from his house. The night air left streaks of itself on the windshield.

"Getting rich?" he asked me, with a furtive glance. It reminded me of the way he used to come late into the bedroom we once shared back in that tragic land called Childhood and peel off his black sweater with all that white fuzzy flesh beneath and say, "Gettin' any?" He was sixteen; I was eight.

"Probably not by your standards," I said, fending him off and then experiencing an almost crushing depression: so much time was spent fending people off, or lying to them, or trying to get them to like you. If you added it all up, it would come to a figure far vaster than Olivia's calculation of how much sleep my early-morning randiness had robbed from her. And this man, this relatively nonhostile hulk beside me, was, after all, my one and only brother. Where was that woozy oneness of brothers in the dark?

"I was pretty worried when you moved out of New York," said Allen. We were driving past a synagogue with an immense bronze *art moderne* menorah on its lawn.

"Really?"

"Yeah, with me here in the greater Boston area, and Connie out in Flint—"

"Connie lives in Santa Fe," I said.

"At the time of your move, she was still in Flint."

"Oh. Right."

"It just meant that Pop would be all alone in New York."

I looked out the window, counted to five, skipping three and four. "May I ask a question?" I said.

"What?"

"Who the fuck is 'Pop'?"

"Pop? Dad."

"Oh. Him. Since when do you call him Pop?"

"I always have."

"You never called him Pop. That is the most ridiculous thing I've ever heard."

"Well, I do now. I don't even see what point you're trying to make. Pop, Dad, what's the difference?"

"Just trying to hold on to a little reality."

"I was worried, him being all alone."

"He killed our mother."

"He what?"

"He hounded her to death, death by disparagement."

"I'm in a time machine," Allen sang. "I'm with someone very, very young."

For some reason, I laughed. Maybe there was something about a brother; I couldn't imagine taking this kind of shit from anybody else.

"So you were worried about 'Pop.' "

"Don't get me wrong," said Allen. "I wasn't losing sleep. It was more Connie than me."

"He was so fucking horrible to her. He batted her around, and made her feel like a slut, for Christ's sake."

"The world according to Sam," said Allen.

"You remember it differently?"

"Well, the important thing is Connie and Pop have gotten close over the years."

"When has all this taken place?"

"Over the years, that's all, over the years. Am I taking you back to the hotel, or do you need to go to the radio station?"

"Radio station."

Allen drummed his fingers on the steering wheel. I tried for a moment to imagine those fingers probing the inside of a patient's mouth, scraping at tartar, probing a gum—lately, periodontal woes had become his specialty. With my own dentist, I had always felt a revenge was being taken—these were boys who never got invited to parties in high school, and now they could spend the rest of their lives torturing all the hotshots who had snubbed them in adolescence. But Allen had been a big, cheerful boy, a jock, though capable of turning himself into a bit of a beatnik as well, if he had his eye on some girl in leotards. All I could locate in my memories of him that would suggest his profession was that he was the first person I knew who flossed—in fact, Allen had been fanatical about his teeth, their soundness, whiteness, his breath.

"Why did you become a dentist?" I asked him, as he steered the car onto a four-lane highway leading back downtown.

"I'm not a dentist. I'm an oral surgeon."

"All right. Why did you—"

"The money."

"Really? End of story?"

"Fucking A, end of story. Why did you write *Visitors from Wherever*?"

"Yeah, but that's not all I write. It was a question of supporting other, less commercial projects."

"Naturally. Who doesn't think that? I've got a lot of projects to support too. I've got the mortgage project, the private-school projects, and the lovely-wife-who-wants-to-go-back-to-school-and-get-a-master's-in-psychology project. Anyhow, who doesn't want a little spending money? For vacations. I guess you heard all about Bar Harbor."

"No."

He glanced at me; the light from a passing car leaped on and off his face, like a bird that had landed on the wrong branch.

"We took a house on Bar Harbor last summer." He paused, waiting for me to ask a question, and then supplied the rest. "Me, Natalie, the kids, Connie, and Pop. Or Dad, whatever you want to call him."

"All of you went on vacation together?"

"You were invited."

"Really? Some kind of telepathic invitation?"

"We all wanted you to be there. It was you who didn't want to."

"Strange. I mean, since this is the first I've ever heard of it."

"You should have been there, Sammy. Pop's become quite a sailor. I mean, he really knows his way around a boat. He taught the kids how to sail. And Connie, you should see her. She just jumps into the ocean. You know how cold it is, the water. It's like getting hit in the shin with a five iron. But Connie never flinched. She's got this real physical self-discipline."

"How long has all this been going on?"

"What do you mean?"

"You and Connie, you and Connie and Gil. I feel like the family has re-formed without me."

"Families are families," he said.

"That's true, Allen. I never quite saw it like that. Thank you."

Allen laughed. Older than me, larger, the first to know everything, there was little I could say that would offend him. I was not a contender, not a threat. I was just his little brother.

"Things okay with you and Olivia?" he asked me, as he passed a mud-spattered Subaru, driven by a college girl. Allen looked at the girl before speeding in front of her, as if she was supposed to eat her heart out at the sight of him. He loved beauty in women. The first time he'd met Olivia he took me aside and put me in a hammerlock. "You fuck," he said, "you little sneaky-assed fuck. How'd you get a girl like that?"

"It's never easy between Olivia and me," I said. Hinting at the tumultuousness of our relationship was a little like boasting; it was like saying we had a passionate marriage, full of all-nighters, jealousy, operatic tantrums, exquisite reconciliations—a marriage of twenty-year-olds rather than a nearly twenty-year-old marriage.

"You still fucking her?" asked old Al.

"I had forgotten this whole sensitive, perceptive aspect of your personality," I said.

"Well, are you? I may not be Carl Goddamned Jung or anything, but I know that when the fucking goes, the marriage is over."

"Our intimacy is fierce," I said. Headlights photographed my eyes. There was an expression in them—Michael used to say I looked maximally annoyed, and glad of it. Michael! What could I do to make him come home? And what could I do to purge my heart of everything that was secretly afraid of what would happen when he got back?

"You know what your problem is?" said Allen.

"Yes," I said. "I actually do."

"Your problem is you were the baby in the family and still won't grow up." There was something sour in his voice—my flaunting the semifictitious passions of my life with Olivia had gotten to him. Whatever had once been between Allen and Natalie was probably long gone. His immensity, her unhappiness, the children, the way time, even in the best of circumstances, can erode the erotic, until the libido is so smoothed down it becomes just like a wall of glass—I was certain all of this had befallen my brother and his wife. They were down to the occasional poke, and even those were corrupted by their singularity: sex, if it is not regular, becomes a little ludicrous; your sexuality becomes a special guest star on some long-running sitcom, your very sex organ becomes some old, safe, vaguely revered has-been, trotted out in a tux on Oscar night to receive his Lifetime Achievement Award.

"What would I have to do to grow up?" I asked.

"This crazy book you've written—"

"Which is making a fortune."

"A fortune? You don't even know what a fortune is. I don't fucking make a fucking fortune, and I make more than you or your outer-space book. You're making what we call a *living*."

"That could be. It feels like a lot to me. If you've been at sea long enough and you're finally washed up onto some little island with two coconut palms, it feels like the world."

"And that book you wrote about Pop and Mom. You had no right to do that."

"It was a novel. Novels are about the words that make them."

"Everybody knew that was Pop. You made him seem like he was Hitler."

"Oh, that's ridiculous."

"You compared him to Hitler."

"The *narrator* said that he often wondered what would have happened if Hitler had gotten into art school. Where would the world be if Hitler had had his first choice of career, could have completed his MFA, or whatever they called it then, found a nice little gallery in Vienna to show his work? I think that's an interesting question."

"You can say what you want to, but it hurt Pop. And what about Connie? Did you have to tell her I went through the hamper looking for her undies?"

"What are you talking about?"

"In your book. The older brother."

"I'm getting the impression you don't do a lot of reading, Allen. I noticed at your house, too—the bookcases have a lot of empty spots, with statuettes and ceramics where there ought to be novels."

"Who has time to read?"

"Who has time to shop for ceramics?"

He flicked his finger against the tip of my nose, a form of abuse so steeped in memories that it barely hurt. We were at the correct Commonwealth Avenue address, a tall, narrow building whose bricks shimmered like oyster shells beneath the glow of the street lamps.

"Thanks for the lift, Allen. And thanks particularly for fetching me at the hotel."

"Thanks 'particularly'?" he said, with a trapper's grim smile.

"I know I'm a pretentious asshole." (I didn't really think that, but I thought I'd throw the old dog a bone.) "But I really appreciate the concern you've shown, Allen. About Michael, me, everything."

"How many little brothers do I have?" he asked, gathering me manfully in his humid bulk.

We broke the embrace; his eyes searched for me in the darkness of the car.

"What station are you going to be on?" he asked.

"I don't know."

"Well, I'll just have to put the old Blaupunkt on autosearch until I hear your voice."

I got out of the car and stood at the curbside. He pulled away quickly and didn't look back.

I was alone in the night in a city I did not know, and a wave of melancholy swept over me, a rich nectar of loneliness and yearning. This sadness was mine; it was all that was really and utterly mine. My family, my work, even my name were all under a cloud, matters of conjecture; but this melancholy was not a book I would one day write, it was not a network of relationships that I had to finesse: it was in my bones, my blood, it was me. I took a deep breath. The night air was cool, a little raw. The stars were distant, barely visible. Cars streamed by, trying to catch up to the shimmering puddles of light cast by the headlights.

I walked into the building and found Heather waiting for me in the lobby, pacing in the cool darkness, in and out of the columns of brightness shed by the overhead lights. Her heels clicked on the marble floor, but then they were silent and she faced me.

"There you are," she said.

"Am I late?"

"I just had no idea where you were."

"I was with my brother. Didn't you know that?"

"How am I supposed to know? People never really know where other people go."

"Like Long Tall Shorty."

"Who's that?"

"An old song. He wondered where the lights go when the lights go out."

She clattered across the lobby until she was right next to me. Her chest rose and fell beneath her tight hound's-tooth jacket. She was probably one of those people who can be so exhausting if you ever get close to them—someone with food allergies and sleep disorders, violent fits of temper, scary dreams, right-wing opinions.

"The last thing in the world I want is to be inappropriate," she said. "But when you were gone, I was worried about you."

How nice! Heather's entire self seemed to have been constructed against passion, and for her to feel anything toward me—married, harassed, compromised, unhandsome, sold-out me—seemed miraculous, mind over matter. When had it happened? At the book fair? Had it been my gallantry with the ersatz Islamics? Or had she—dream of dreams!—seen something in me of which I was unaware, some flicker of character, some animal reality, that had slipped through the maze of personality?

"Let's have dinner after this radio thing. All I ate was vegetables at my brother's house. After I con the rubes, I like to have a nice piece of red meat."

"This is not some dopey little 'radio thing,' Sam. This program goes out to 350,000 listeners, and Jay Nash can be very cutting."

"I'm not worried. I'm John Retcliffe, and Johnnie doesn't have a care in the world."

Heather smiled. I was putting her at ease.

"I heard from Ezra this afternoon. Are you okay with a little upsetting news?"

"Sure. I thrive on it. It's my primary source of stimulation."

"Don't let it interfere when you're with Jay, all right?"

"What's the news? Sales dropping off? Tour canceled?"

"Oh, God no. The books keep going and going. It'll soon be at that point when it sells just because it's selling. People will buy it without even knowing why."

"So? What could be bad?"

It's Michael, I thought to myself, suddenly, in panic.

"Ezra heard from a woman—" Heather stopped, smiled at me, as if I was a person of wild reputation, some clown in the gossip columns rather than a country husband with a little bit of shit on his shoes. "This woman. She works at one of those photo-research houses. She says she worked with you on the book and now she wants to go public about you, about how John Retcliffe is a made-up person and—I don't know. I hope she doesn't make any problems for us."

I was silent for a while and then indicated with a gesture that we should walk to the elevators. I pressed the call button and then turned to Heather. I made sure I looked relaxed; I even smiled.

"The price of success," I said.

chapter ten

heather and I went to Pittsburgh, Washington, Baltimore, and then I was in Philadelphia, staying in a downtown hotel. The stoop-shouldered, shaking bellman dropped my travel bag on the bed and then asked me if I wanted some ice. Wherever I went they seemed concerned about my ice situation. All over America, they were turning down my bed, putting little mints on my pillow, and encouraging me to use the minibar. Seven-fifty for a Rémy, four bucks for those Hawaiian potato chips that look like atrophied ears. What the hell! Ezra was paying my bills, and I exercised my new sense of freedom with massive midnight snacks.

I was one of the Hotel People, that legion of hucksters going from king-sized bed to junior suite, peddling their wares. I was hurrying to make a plane, I was cooling my heels in the Admirals Club, I was in the town car, I was checking my watch, and there were millions of me, selling software, protein powder, chlorinators, mutual funds. We were the flies buzzing around the rotting body politic.

That day I had been to the National Public Radio station, which was housed in a little white brick building off an intercity cloverleaf, one of those boxy structures that look like the billing offices for an insurance company. *Visitors from Above* was a little beneath the usual NPR fare, but the interviewer, Ian Lamb, had recently suffered a massive heart attack, during which he had had a near-death experience (white lights, voices, flotation, et cetera). He was suddenly spiritualized, and Heather, hearing of this from her network of public relations cronies, had used his new interest in the otherworldly to get me onto "Lamb's Literary Corner," which went out to 150 NPR affiliates.

I was fabulous.

I had two hours in my hotel after the NPR gig and before the rather important bookstore and radio appearances Heather had me scheduled for that evening. The book was selling so well that Heather was getting urgent calls from TV programs, but I held fast to my position that I would not go on television as Retcliffe. It made no sense whatsoever to Heather; she went pale with frustration. After a tense conversation in the hotel's coffee shop, I went back to my room. I called Olivia, got Amanda.

"Hi, Dad," she said, her voice throaty—a cold or some new kick of confidence?

"Hey, sweetie, how you doing? How's school?"

"I got a B-plus on my English test."

"That's great." I leaned back in my hotel bed. I crossed my ankles, looked down at my L.L. Bean gray suedes, the glimpse of bright red anarcho-syndicalist socks. I slipped my hand beneath my Brooks Brothers blue shirt, rubbed my half-Jewish, half-psychotic stomach. "What was it on?" I asked.

"What was what on?"

"The test."

"It was on *James and the Giant Peach*," she said. "Mrs. Cuttler read it out loud to us."

"Dahl," I said, and then winced: did I really need to prove I knew the author?

"I guess," she said. "I would have gotten an A, but Mrs. Cuttler was so mean."

"How was she mean, sweetie?"

"At the end of the writing part of the test ...?" She paused. I heard the creaking wheels of a room service cart out in the hall: visions of shrimp cocktail, those wonderful half-lemons in cheesecloth netting.

"Yes?" I said, my voice prodding.

"Where you're supposed to give your opinion of the book ...?"

More silence. The room service cart stopped; I heard the obsequious knock at the door next to mine. Heather. So that would make it mixed fruit, cottage cheese, and a seltzer with lime.

"So? What was your opinion?"

"I said I didn't like it, but Mrs. Cuttler said it's a great book and I was wrong. That's why I didn't get an A."

"I would have given you an A," I said. "An A-plus."

"We don't have A-plus, and anyhow you're my dad."

I felt relieved to hear her say this. At least on a conscious level, she thought I was on her side. I wanted to quit while I was ahead.

"Is Mommy there?"

"I'm right here," said Olivia.

It jarred me to realize she had been listening in on the extension. She was usually indifferent, even evasive about the phone. Was she monitoring my conversation with Amanda?

"Any word from Michael?" I asked Olivia.

"No."

"Christ."

"You know what I'm thinking about?" asked Olivia.

"Tell me."

"A private investigator. Sharon called today. She knows someone. She gave me his name."

Sharon? I had, for a moment, no idea what the word "Sharon" referred to, but I didn't let on, and then I realized

Olivia meant Sharon Connelly, that strawberry-preserving, baseball-card-collecting, cross-country-skiing dynamo.

"I don't know where to look for him," said Olivia. "And the police around here, they're only set up for pointing their little radar guns at speeders on the Taconic Parkway. We have to do something, Sam."

"I know."

"This is just going on."

"I know, Olivia, I know."

"We're acting like people in a dream. I ride my car around Leyden, I call his name. I call his friends. I'm becoming one of those women."

"I'll come home. I'll leave tomorrow."

"No. That's not going to do anything."

"I'll be back in a couple of days anyhow."

"I think we should hire this investigator. You're making all this money now."

"Hire him. It's a good idea."

"He's down in Poughkeepsie. I have an appointment to see him."

"Take notes."

It was something I often said; it had always meant, Share your experiences with me, I want to know the world through your eyes. But this time the little tag line took on an annoying aspect, as if I were suggesting she was forgetful, or that I needed to review her work, control it. Somehow it came out sounding like, Leave the final decision to me. Everything was changing. My life was moving away from me.

"How's everything going out there?" Olivia asked me.

"It's your basic Nightmare in B-flat."

"I'm sorry."

"No, it's okay. I think this stuff is hard to do when you're really the person you say you are."

"Maybe harder. Having it be so fake, it's probably better, for you."

"You think so?" My spirits found a little space below the point at which they'd settled and headed for that lower spot. "I'm an impostor. I walk into these studios, everybody's calling me by a name that isn't mine. I have to keep reminding myself: John Retcliffe, John Retcliffe. But who is this guy?"

"He's nobody."

"I realize that. But he's also me. I'm doing this radio thing tonight, 'The Will Fisher Show.' Tony Randall is going on it, too. I can't stand Tony Randall. Next time, I'm going to have a clause in my contract protecting me from any appearances with Tony Randall."

"Sam."

"What?"

"I don't have it right now for irony."

"This isn't irony, Olivia. This is madness."

"I don't have it for madness, either. I just want to find Michael. That's all. There is nothing else."

After we'd said our goodbyes, I stared at the ceiling, its white, porous emptiness neither soothing nor provocative, but just there through no design of its own, as I was. Its emptiness depressed me, but I tried to turn it to some advantage. I stared at its blankness and tried to go blank myself. Maybe a few minutes meditation, I thought.

On Perry Street some time between the births of Michael and Amanda, we acquired as neighbors an Uruguayan couple in their sixties. They had divorced ten years before but had begun living together again. She was a psychoanalyst and he had been teaching chemistry at NYU, though now he had jettisoned science in favor of Buddhism. His name was Jorge; he was small, white-haired, with cerulean blue eyes. I was feeling, perhaps optimistically, at the low ebb of my career—I was writing term papers for rich college students, cranking out essays on everything from Hawthorne to Yalta, at about a hundred bucks a throw. I was even beginning to worry about my grades—I was calling my clients at home to inquire what we got on our paper comparing *Portrait of a Lady* to *Letting Go*, and if I received less than an A, I would suffer crises of confidence that verged on the suicidal. In the meanwhile, I gave birth to one piteously deformed novel, abandoned another, and then wrote something I considered rather avant-garde and experimental, but which my former agent said was not only unsalable but lifeless and unreadable, an assessment that the dozen rejections only confirmed.

It was into this emotional weather that Jorge came, and when he offered to teach me the principles of Zen meditation I wondered if he was in fact an angel sent to save my life. We would sit in his small sky-blue apartment, with an ionizer cranking out negative charges and white noise, and Jorge would direct my attention to my breath, the feel of it as it went into my nostrils, its slight increase in warmth as I exhaled it, nothing more, nothing more, just my breath, my reality, my life in the moment, without plans, reflections, associations. I was at the time taking over-the-counter diet pills for extra energy—I couldn't afford cocaine—and late at night I was putting myself to sleep with jelly glasses of cheap red wine. Yet after a week sitting for a half-hour in the morning with Jorge, I suddenly felt focused, powerful; out went the Dexatrim and the Inglenook. I wrote my term papers with good-natured industry, seeing in them opportunities to master new subject areas rather than crucifixions on the cross of failure.

Unfortunately, a few months later, Jorge and his ex-wife could no longer maintain their new arrangement, and he moved out of our building and into a Buddhist retreat on 106th Street, a twenty-five-minute subway ride from my apartment, and my hunger for enlightenment was overwhelmed by Jorge's suddenly being inconvenient to me—I could never work in a visit to him. When he was just across the hall, what he was teaching me seemed not only valuable but necessary; on the Upper West Side, he seemed like the purveyor of some spiritual esoterica. I continued to practice on my own, but my half-hour sittings were regularly interrupted by peeks at my wristwatch, and soon they became ten-minute sittings, and soon after that they disappeared altogether. Now, in my Philadelphia hotel room, I tried to re-create Jorge's soulful drone. I instructed myself to breathe, to feel my breath, in, out, in and out. I descended through the topmost layer of consciousness as if through a kennel of frantic, barking dogs. My preoccupations were legion. (Jorge said the mind was a tree full of monkeys.) I wish I could say it was only Michael that blocked my way to simply Being. But there was the firm, ascetic feel of the bed, the tone of Olivia's voice, calculations of how much money I had made in the past week, a memory of my brother sweeping the crumbs from his shirt front, the color of the letters on the cover of the *Protocols of the Elders of Zion*; there was the thump of Nadia's hand against the bedboard as I made love with her, the knock of that bedboard against the wall, the salty taste of her skin when I kissed her after—had she perspired or shed tears? The sound of her coming, the feel of her drawing me deeper and deeper into her.

The telephone rang and I reached for it immediately, glad to be released from my failure at meditation.

It was Ezra, calling from New York.

"This has only happened to me once before," he said. "Your book has a goddamned life of its own. We've got the printers on overtime keeping up with the demand."

"That's great, Ezra."

"It's scary. How many books are there about UFOs? A thousand? Why has everyone decided this is the one?"

"The writing."

"Hey, who knows? The Men in Black. That's got people scared. They love those little Men in Black. And this prophecy thing? It's totally out of fucking control. I've got booksellers calling in from Seattle to Chapel Hill, telling me their customers are using the book to pick lottery numbers, horses. I can't figure it out. They're using page numbers, the first words of paragraphs; some of them are tearing the book up and throwing the pages in the air. It's a weird country out there, and it's getting weirder. As we speak."

"That's great, Ezra. I'm going to take the money and write a real book."

"Yes, well, we can talk about it later. But right now, we do have a little problem. I think Heather might have mentioned it to you. I just got another call from this woman who works at that photo house we used for illustrations. Sorry, Sam, but I'm going to assume you know who I'm talking about."

"No comment."

"Yes, well, none necessary." He laughed; I supposed it was meant to be a male-bonding chuckle. "She hasn't shown up at the office yet. I hope she was beautiful, anyhow."

"What do you mean by 'anyhow'?"

"She wants to cause you a lot of trouble."

"What does she want?"

"I have no idea. She can't sue us; we haven't done anything to her. All it can be is a flat-out extortion, but she hasn't had the guts to come right out and say it. All she does say is she knows John Retcliffe is a made-up name and that you, Sam Holland, wrote the book."

"So fucking what?"

"Well . . ."

"What difference does it make?"

"None, really, all in all. But I thought you wanted to keep your name clear of this. And from our corporate point of view, it looks bad, like we've been trying to pull a fast one on the public. And from my point of view, I don't want anything to stand in the way of the book's sales."

"What do you want me to do, Ezra? Silence her?"

"We're making grown-up money, Sam, and that means grown-up problems and grown-up solutions."

"*Murder*'s your idea of a grown-up solution?" I knew as soon as I said it that I sounded insane and Ezra had meant no such thing.

"My, my, don't we have a rich inner life! I had something a little less genre in mind."

"Sorry, Ezra. I'm not myself."

"And that's what we're paying you the big bucks for, too." He laughed his short, busy laugh, a laugh that announced the fact of his own amusement but expressed nothing further. "But seriously, I do think you need to talk to her."

"Do you really think talking to her is going to make a difference?"

"Sure. Why not?" He sighed audibly. "Is this relationship a lot more complicated than I think?"

"No, not really. It was just something that happened."

"She's making a lot of fuss for something that 'just happened.' "

"I know she is. She wrote me some terrible letters, too."

Ezra was the first person in whom I had confided Nadia's letters, and he was not even a friend. If ever I were to change publishers, I might never speak to him again; if he were to marry, I would probably not be invited to the wedding. Yet here I was cutting him in on a secret that until now I had willingly shared with no one.

"Oh, a letter writer," said Ezra, implying that he was familiar with the various subcategories of spurned lovers. "That's not wonderful news. They tend to have delusions of grandeur, legends in their own minds, rumors in their own rooms. There's a kind of obsession with public life and putting it on record with these letter writers, don't you think?"

"I have no idea, Ezra. I was never unfaithful to Olivia before."

"Really?"

"Really. Is that so terribly unhip?"

"Now come on, Sam, don't get testy with me. You're the
one who let the little head think for the big head."

"I'll bet you have a million of those little-head-big-head
sayings, Ezra."

"Now listen to me, Sam. If there's anything you can do to
calm this woman down, then I really wish you'd do it. I guess
sooner or later a girl like that is going to blow, but if we can
just string out these extraordinary sales for a few more weeks,
I can't tell you the difference it would make."

"I don't want to string out my sales, Ezra. You're being . . . Look: I would like to save my marriage."

"I'm just trying to respect your privacy, Sam. If you want
to talk about your marriage, then fine, let's do it."

I was silent, for a long time. I heard his breathing on the
other end, the soft fiberoptic rustle of the connection between
us: I had never felt closer to him than I did then. I would have
liked to have stayed like that even longer, guileless, without
excuses, without angles, no hustles to run, no hemorrhage of
lies to bandage with words.

"I'll take care of it," I said, when I could stay in that safe
haven of silence no longer.

Heather and I arrived at the studio where "The Will Fisher
Show" was broadcast. It was another of Heather's coups that
we'd been scheduled. Fisher's show was old-fashioned mod-
ernist radio, a late-night variety show patterned on programs
from the pre-TV age. Actors, authors, comics, singers, even
tap dancers came on, flogging themselves as assiduously as
they would have on any TV show.

I was directed to the greenroom, where there were soft
drinks, sandwiches, a coffee urn, and a large cut-glass bowl of
mint candies. The walls were not green but beige, and covered
with photos of moments from "The Will Fisher Show,"
securely nailed in, as if there were a chance of pilferage. The

pictures showed, among other things, how svelte Fisher had become since his show had broken out of its regional rut and become a national phenomenon. In an older photograph, a beefy, rumpled Fisher shared a laugh with a pugnacious Philadelphia Philly named Len Dykstra; in the more recent photos, Fisher draped his articulated body across a clear Lucite desk and chatted up the likes of Emilio Estevez, Gore Vidal, and Colin Powell, with his now successful style of italicized intimacy—like most media personalities, Fisher didn't have emotions but could explicitly imitate them, showing you what people would say if they happened to feel in a particular way, what an angry person might say, or an ingratiating person, a racist person, a paranoid person, reducing feeling and opinion to a collection of amusingly lifelike masks. Culture, psychology, politics: all of it was just a pile of costumes stuffed into a trunk and stored in the attic that was his brain.

After swilling down a jolt of coffee, I sat next to a woman whom I recognized from the previous Summer Olympics, a sprinter turned singer, whose single "Fast Track" was a hit. I couldn't remember her name, but the etiquette of these rooms was that we were all so famous it would be ludicrous to ask anyone to identify herself.

"Hi," I said, settling into the seat.

"Hi there," she said, in a way that would suffice if we'd never met before or had shared other greenrooms in other cities. She wore a leopard-spotted one-piece something-or-other, with her Olympic gold medal around her neck. Her fingernails were long and curved and orange; her toenails, though shorter, were the same color. I imagined she and Will would talk about that, before he played a number from her album.

Across the room sat Tony Randall, who was in town previewing a play. He wore gray slacks, a blue blazer. He studied *Hungarian for Travelers* and every once in a while said something aloud in Hungarian, repeating the phrase two or three times, enjoying the feel of it in his mouth. I remembered the catty things I'd said about Randall and felt ridiculous; it took seeing him in person to make me realize I didn't know anything about the guy.

The fourth person in the room was an unusually small man in a three-piece suit, whose feet barely touched the floor as he sat staring at me, his tiny hands folded in his lap. At first I thought he might be meditating, but there was an appraising flicker in his eyes. I shifted my weight and his gaze followed me. I seemed very much on his mind.

"Hello," I said.

He nodded at me.

I wondered who he was and what he was going to be doing on Fisher's program. Fisher himself had started in the business as a comedian (a long stint with a Canadian improvisational group, a season on "Saturday Night Live"), and he tended to choose his guests for their entertainment value. This compact, middle-aged man surely had nothing to do with show business; he looked like an inventor, a vegetarian, the uncle you used to love but who's gone quite mad from loneliness. Now and again, Fisher was not above inviting some overly earnest person onto his show, to explain, say, the ins and outs of saxophone repair or how to build your own food dryer, and Fisher would deadpan interest. It was petty, cruel humor, bear baiting without the bear, and I hoped the old gent wasn't in for that.

And I hoped I wasn't, either. Heather and I had discussed the possibility that Fisher might be having a bit of fun at my expense. After all, the subject of my book lent itself to mockery. His engineer might cue up the theme from "The Twilight Zone" when I came on.

The door to the greenroom opened and a young fellow dressed in Wall Street suspenders and yellow tie poked his head in. "John Retcliffe?"

I raised a finger.

"Follow me, please. Ivan Rudmanian?"

The small gent across the room stood up, straightened his clothes, and then lifted an enormous black leather briefcase, which looked large enough to house him. His tongue darted in and out of his mouth.

We followed the assistant out of the greenroom. Tony Randall looked up from his Hungarian lesson and said, "Good luck."

Ivan Rudmanian and I walked through the narrow, airless corridor. The walls here were painted silver and purple, the dream decor of some nerdy, dateless college boy. A couple of Teamsters sat chatting near an upended sofa wrapped in brown paper. Our guide introduced himself as Darryl and said that because Mr. Fisher had come late to the studio today we wouldn't have the customary preliminary time with him. "Don't worry, though," he said. "Mr. Fisher is very familiar with both your work."

"We're going on together?"

"You'll have to discuss that with Mr. Fisher."

"When do you suggest we have that conversation?" I said. "On the air?"

"I don't know, John. My job is to escort you from the greenroom to the sound stage."

"Then we *are* going on together."

"I'm sorry, John, I just do what I do."

I wasn't crazy about the show-biz familiarity of his calling me by my first name—even though it wasn't my actual first name.

"I know for a fact we are scheduled to speak with Mr. Fisher together," said Ivan Rudmanian. He had a deep, booming voice.

The "Will Fisher" set was done in I-won't-grow-up! modern: beer signs, basketball hoops, a fifties juke box, pinball machines, black shag carpeting. Fisher, his hair slicked back, drummed his fingers on his desk, which had been shaped and painted like the face of Jimi Hendrix. Fisher looked gaunt and a little spooked, like a man who has quickly lost fifty pounds, doctor's orders. He sat alone, somehow private, though there were a dozen technicians and an audience of two hundred, in front of whom he was in full view. (Heather told me that Fisher's was the only show on radio that broadcast in front of a studio audience. I had clutched my chest and pretended to have a heart attack.)

Darryl delivered us into the care of a large, lively woman, whose red face looked as if she had just scrubbed it with sea coral. Large amber beads the size of kumquats heaved on her chest.

"Will's going to announce you, and then I want you to walk out there as if you were strolling into your own living room," she said. Then she turned from me and looked at Rudmanian. "Hello, Ivan."

"Hello, Mary."

"You two know each other?" I inquired, as lightly as possible.

"Oh, yes," said Mary, leaving further details to my imagination.

When Will Fisher spoke, his voice, sweetened by electronic bass enhancers, boomed through the backstage area. Even Mary, who must have heard him a thousand times, seemed suddenly reverential.

He deftly set up our segment, pegging me as an internationally best-selling author and identifying Rudmanian as an expert on unexplained phenomena of all kinds—everything from telepathy to Bigfoot. With the old novelty number "Purple People Eater" coming through the speakers, Rudmanian strolled from the wings of the sound stage and Mary gave me a not-terribly-gentle shove at the small of my back and I was on the air, too.

The audience applauded generously, for the very existence of us—one of the privileges of being media-ized is that people cheer just because you're, well, you.

What happened after that? I have no idea, except that it "went well." I fit into the chair, and I was placed closer to Fisher than Ivan was. Fisher nodded amiably as I spoke, reassuring me that I was making complete sense. I had already boiled my standard presentation into three main points: (1) the powers that be don't want reasonable inquiry into UFOs; (2) the Men in Black are spreading disinformation everywhere, though it's still unclear if the MIBs are from outer space or our own government; and (3) sightings of extraterrestrials have been a constant since the beginnings of recorded history. I made my points as confidently as possible—indeed, as Retcliffe, I was generally chatty, glib, relaxed, even charming—but I was always uncomfortably conscious of Rudmanian on my left, sitting there, 110 pounds of shrieking refutation.

But my dread of Rudmanian, of Ivan, was ill-founded. When the little tape that fame had placed in my skull in place of my mind stopped playing and it was Ivan's turn to speak, he was not only supportive of Jivin' John Retcliffe but downright laudatory.

"Mr. Retcliffe has written a good book," Ivan boomed in his oversized baritone, "and a valuable book as well. I don't think any book written for the general reader has ever presented the case for sightings more cogently than Mr. Retcliffe's."

"Please," I said, resisting the impulse to pick adorable Ivan up and place him on my knee. "John."

"So at least we know they aren't cousins," said Will, leaning over his desk and smirking at the audience. They all liked that a great deal. Fisher's joke assumed the audience was aware of the backstaginess of life, which flattered them. Like stock traders looking for special information, America was becoming a nation of inside-dope addicts.

"We're nearing the end of the millennium," opined Ivan (God, he was good at this), "and we can expect sightings to become more frequent with every passing month."

"Why? Why with every passing month?" asked Fisher.

"There's always a lot of anxiety at the end of a century," I said. "With the end of a millennium that anxiety is increased tenfold."

Fisher looked at me rather blankly. I had somehow given the wrong answer. In fact, I quickly realized that my remark tended to trash the thesis of my book—these blips on the horizon were supposed to be real, not the concoction of stressed-out optic nerves.

"John's right, of course," said Ivan. "But he's also being very modest. As his own book makes remarkably clear, the year 2000 is a target date for extraterrestrials. There have been an increasing number of isolated landings, and as we get closer to the target date there will be more, and then sometime in the year 2000, there will not be a man, woman, or child on our planet who has not had direct contact with a visitor from above." He looked at me and smiled beneficently. "It's right there in your book, John."

The studio audience was aghast at this prediction, and doubtlessly the audience out there in the radio-electric night was, too. I myself was pretty stirred by it—I didn't exactly remember writing anything about an increase in space traffic by the year 2000. Was Ivan getting this from my book through deciphering unintentional anagrams, or reading the first words of every other paragraph? Who knew? What the hell? The books were selling, the audience was engaged, and Will seemed particularly pleased.

Next to the studio there was a bar called Siena, though there was nothing Italian in the decor, nothing Italian in the bar snacks they served. It was just a bar in America. Heather and I had already made a plan to have a drink there after the Fisher show, ostensibly to discuss further stops on my tour. However, I was so grateful for (and relieved by) Ivan's kind words on the show that I invited him to join us, though I suspected he would demur, or, at the least, confine himself to a Coke or a cup of coffee.

But he was delighted to accept our invitation and ordered a double-strength vodka gimlet. He tossed his drink down, dabbed his lips with a cocktail napkin, and then turned in his bar stool to face me directly.

"Let me ask you something quite directly," he said to me. "Are you a MIB?"

I glanced at Heather: Help!

"So, Ivan," said Heather. "How is it you've never written a book?"

"I have," said Ivan. "I have written several books." He would not let her run interference for me. I felt his intelligence bearing down on me, like a mob that meant me harm. "I myself have had contact with MIBs. They are usually taller than you, and usually they are very, very gaunt. But there are similarities as well. In the hands. The large feet."

"I don't think of John as having large feet," said Heather.

"And the lack of biography. MIBs have credentials but no biography. Credit cards but no credit rating, housing without mortgages, impressive educational degrees but no friends from school—well, I don't have to tell you."

I felt tense, vulnerable. As I shook my head no, I felt my brain moving around my skull, floating in fluid like a Sea Monkey.

"I wanted to find as much about you as I could before coming onto Will's show. Will is an old friend—"

"Ahhh," said Heather, as if a mystery had just been solved.

"Are you?" he asked again, and this time Ivan reached quickly for me and pressed his thumb against my wrist. He was feeling my pulse, to see if it raced when I answered.

"Stop it, Ivan," I said, trying to remain calm, lest he mistake the adrenaline rush of aggression for the guilty extraterrestrial conscience of a Man in Black.

"Are you?" he said, moving closer to me. He peered intently at my eyes—looking for color change? transistor overload?

"Are you out of your fucking mind?"

"Let him go, Ivan," said Heather. "You're hurting him."

Ivan's thumb dug into the veins behind the meaty hump of my palm. The pressure was just short of furious, yet it was curiously painless. He had perfected a bit of technique, doing these impromptu interrogations.

"Just answer me," he said, in a somewhat hypnotic voice.

"I mean it, Ivan," said Heather, giving him a shove. "We invited you for a drink, goddamnit, not for this kind of shit."

I looked over at Heather. Her elliptical nostrils were flared, her spiky hair looked moist, a she-wolf in the moonlight.

Ivan relaxed his stout, robotic thumb and I pulled my hand away, resisting the impulse to give it a little welcome-home rub.

"I'm sorry," he said. "But you must understand why the question is important."

"You want to know what I understand, Ivan?" said Heather. "You really want to know? I understand that you're a creep. Where do you come off grabbing him like that?"

"All right," I said, "let's forget it."

"The MIBs are everywhere," Ivan said sadly, shaking his head, checking his gimlet glass. There was still some in there.

"I'm wearing a black suit, but that's as far as it goes," I actually said.

"Listen, Ivan," said Heather, still seething. "If—"

The situation had settled sufficiently for me to interrupt Heather by taking her hand. I laced my fingers through hers, and she responded to my touch by squeezing my hand in such a way that it released in me a chain of erotic imaginings.

Ivan finished his drink, signaled for another. Then he turned his gaze on me and got down to the next order of business.

"John Retcliffe is not your real name, is it?" he said, very quietly. In fact, he was virtually whispering now, and his eyes took in the rest of the bar to make certain we were not being closely observed.

"Where did you get that?" snapped Heather.

I let go of her hand, but, as if to compensate, I moved my knee over a bit, so that it touched her leg. She responded with a slight reciprocal counterpressure.

"If it is a name you have given yourself," said Ivan, "then I would say it is a very strange one. Is it? Is it an assumed name, a pseudonym, a nom de plume, or what have you?"

"First you want to know if I'm a MIB, now you—"

"All right, fine. You don't have to tell me. But let me ask you another question. Are you familiar with the *Protocols of the Elders of Zion*?"

I looked at Heather, wondering if she recalled that this was the pamphlet being sold by the incense-burning zealots at the next booth at the book fair. Heather rose slightly from her seat and tugged at the hem of her skirt.

"So?" she said, moving her leg away, back again.

"John Retcliffe," said Ivan.

"Yes?" I said.

"That was the name of the writer, the original author of the *Protocols*. And if you have made this name up, I wonder why you have chosen the name of a fake who has done the world so much damage. His words justified the slaughter of the innocent. Why would you take such a name for yourself? What are you trying to tell us? And please don't tell me that this has all been some strange coincidence. I absolutely do not believe in coincidence."

In the taxi, Heather was noticeably silent. The driver was humming along with the radio, streetlights darted in and out of the darkness inside the car, and Heather sat as far from me as possible, staring at the closed and abandoned buildings between the studio and the hotel. I was not unaccustomed to these womanly lulls. In Olivia, they stymied and infuriated me; I felt her silences pressing on me like two tons of feathers.

But Heather's being quiet was fine with me; it did not occur to me that she might in some way be thinking of me.

"Everything all right?" I asked, out of friendliness.

She shook her head no, which surprised me. I expected an answer a little more evasive or noncommittal. And then she continued to stare out into the mobile night, which also surprised me, warmed me.

"When Ezra hired me, it was only for the first week," she said, turning toward me. We were stopped at a traffic light; city workers had dug up the street, a gaping hole in the road, bright lights, a rising funnel of steam.

"You mean I'm going to be on my own now?"

"Well, it's not what I wanted. I'm having so much fun, and, I don't know, I feel this has really worked out, very, very well."

"This is really a drag," I said. "Maybe I should talk to Ezra."

"Would you? It would mean more, coming from you." Her spirits quickened. Maybe my convincing Ezra to extend Heather's services was what she had wanted all along, and that was the reason behind those slightly prolonged glances, the hand holding.

"Sure."

Silence. The meter clicked. The driver scratched his scalp through the tangle of his curly gray hair.

Finally, Heather nodded. "You don't have to, you know."

"I want to."

"I want you to," she said. And then she moved closer to me and repeated it again, softly, and it was, suddenly, utterly sexual.

Desire went off in me like an alarm. I took her hand. The lights from a passing car illuminated the down on her face, her fingers laced through mine. I put my arm around her, held her to me—there was a little edge of paternalism in the gesture, as if I might be comforting her, one old crony to another.

She pressed her forehead against my chest; I smelled the perfume of her shampoo and the deeper, more real and beautiful aroma of her scalp.

"Your heart is pounding so hard," she said, looking up at me.

I thought she was lifting her face to be kissed, and so I kissed her. She parted her lips; I sensed the dark, drenched emptiness of her.

When we got to her room, she told me she hadn't been with anyone in six months.

"Should I stay here, then?" I asked.

"Yes."

We raided the minibar; we were like giants holding these Lilliputian liqueurs in our hands. I sat next to her on the bed. I didn't really want to kiss her again. I only wanted to hold her. I took her in my arms; she could have been anyone.

And I could have been anyone, too. We just wanted a bit of comfort. We wanted some specific example of the multitudes whose voices had been surrounding us on our journey. Clothed, we got into her bed, kicked our feet to loosen the stranglehold of the sheets and blankets. She turned her back to me, pressed herself against me. I wrapped my arms around her, feeling her collarbone, smelling her hair.

"This is so nice," said Heather.

"I really didn't want to be alone tonight," I said.

"I like you, Sam," she said, as if I'd asked her.

I thought of Michael, and then Olivia, Amanda. I had never before felt so glad not to be making love.

"Sam?" She said it in a whisper.

"Yes?"

"Would you pat my head?"

I petted her until she fell asleep.

chapter eleven

jack Phillips, the private investigator Olivia hired, turned out to be a man of uncommon good looks, an undercapitalized documentary filmmaker who financed his deadpan movies about gay cowboys, aging tap dancers, and cruise-ship entertainment directors with six months a year in the detective business. Phillips's office was in Poughkeepsie, on the second floor of an old wooden house in a crime-ridden neighborhood. His dusty bay windows looked out over porch stoops full of idle men, broken Colt 45 bottles, fistfights. Raised in Shaker Heights, Harvard-educated, Phillips felt safe and strangely calm in the chaotic neighborhood, and when he pointed out the garish pink clapboard house across the street to Olivia and said, "The most lucrative crack den in upstate New York," it was with a discernible sense of pleasure, almost pride. He wore an old, shapeless Brooks Brothers blazer, a threadbare white shirt, a rumpled red tie, and lusterless wing-tipped shoes, and he seemed to take pride in these things, too. He liked to wear the uniform of his class, but in a shabby, somewhat deconstructed fashion, like a rogue prince wearing his crown at a jaunty tilt.

"I don't really care about that," said Olivia. "I don't care about anything, actually. Just finding Michael."

"Of course, of course," he said, standing close to her. He

was parting the venetian blinds with his long, tapered fingers.
"Well, then, perhaps we better get down to cases."

Astonishing to realize how little there was to say about
someone who had disappeared, even her own son. What did
a person amount to, once removed from context? Hair,
height, weight, eyes, no scars, no tattoos—whatever faint pat-
tern of habits he had created was already obliterated like
sandpiper prints washed out by the next wave. He went from
home to school to home, and now that he was no longer
doing that he could be anywhere. Olivia recited the bare facts,
her voice cracked and dry; yet Phillips wrote everything down
eagerly, nodding his encouragement.

"Okay, got it," he said, when the meagerness of what she
had to offer turned to silence.

She lowered her eyes. Her hands were in her lap. "Do
you?" she asked.

He smiled at her, leaned back in his old-fashioned swivel
chair. The mechanism squeaked loudly. He tapped the trigger
end of his ballpoint pen against the edge of his desk.

"Well, it's a start." He smiled; if he sensed the depths of
her distress, he didn't let it cause him any undue concern.

Yet his attitude did not strike her as cavalier. It was as if he
were watching her go through emotional stages that were predictable to him, feelings he was trained to deal with. Would a
doctor gasp and throw up his hands when a patient described
the aches and pains of a fever? The trick was to do some
good, to *solve* problems, not empathize with them. If
she wanted breast-beating, she could always call Sam, and
if she lost track of where he was in his coast-to-
coast fool's errand, she could just sit tight and he would
call her.

"Are you going to find my son?" Olivia asked Phillips.

He held her in his gaze. He was confident around women;
his good looks, his charm, and a rather low libido meant he
always had as much feminine company as he desired. He was

the kind of man who came late to dinner, or got absorbed in something and forgot to arrive altogether. He was the kind of man who didn't ogle women, who didn't really need women. Olivia sensed his vagueness, his evasiveness, his laconic touch-me-not quality, his self-absorption, and it struck her that to be with a man like that, if only for a short while, would be a little bit of heaven, and a relief from the nearly nonstop ardency of her husband, whose boyish passion and unceasing appetite for physical contact had, after winning her heart, come to exhaust and annoy her.

"Can you start right away?" she asked Phillips.

"Yes, of course." He gestured toward his notebook, as if to remind her that he had already begun. "But I'll need to come to your house."

She raised her chin yet felt herself shrinking back.

"Nothing mystical about it, scout's honor," he said. "But it's always helpful to see the room of the missing person, to see his *stuff*."

"When?"

Phillips shrugged. "Now?"

He drove behind her from Poughkeepsie to Leyden. She searched for him in her rearview mirror, but most of the time she could not see him; he was always four or five cars behind, yet keeping pace. Perversely, she sped up, considered a quick turn off of Route 9 onto one of the smaller, left-behind roads, most of them with stodgy, unpronounceable Dutch names. When she came into Leyden, Olivia checked for Phillips in the rearview mirror and did not see him, and as she drove down Red Schoolhouse Road, past the familiar sights that had of late become hideous to her—the lawn jockeys, the swing sets, the clicking plastic propellers meant to frighten the birds from vegetable gardens, the newly seeded lawns, the neighbors' sleek black Labrador skulking around in his cumbersome electronic collar that gave him a shock whenever he approached the outer limits of the invisible fence—Olivia's stomach turned, as if she had been stood up, rejected. Where was he? Everyone was disappearing.

Yet as she pulled into the driveway, Phillips was behind her, like something forgotten and then suddenly remembered.

"I thought you got lost," she said, as they got out of their cars. Her voice was peevish.

"I was right behind you," said Phillips, with perfect neutrality.

She showed him the house. Room by room, as if she was selling it. He took it all in with a practical eye: the colors she had chosen, the objects, all of the things that were more than things because she had chosen them.

He picked up a carved Christian icon from Guam, showing some saint on horseback, with a primitive-looking dog at his side. "Fabulous," he said, and then put it back down on the old pine tavern table, in the exact spot. "I once did a movie about Santería. It was really neat, watching these people lose their minds." His smile was quick, untroubled. He patted the saint's head, gently, with the tip of his finger.

"I'm in the antiques business." She had almost said, "I somehow find myself in the antiques trade," but lost the nerve for the affectation. She was realizing that she wanted to make herself interesting.

Yet he did seem interested. "Really? Why would you do a thing like that? Do you have a store or something? Or do you just sell things out of the house?"

"I work for a chain of stores in the city. I'm what's called a picker."

"Picker," he said, smiling. "Sounds wild. Maybe I'll film you, one day, when all this is over."

Olivia smiled back. She was grateful for the casual confidence of that phrase: "when all this is over."

"Do you want to see Michael's room? We'd better get this over with, before my daughter comes home from school."

"Amanda," said Phillips, remembering.

He followed her up the stairs. She sensed his eyes were not on her—unlike Sam, who still gazed at her ass when she walked in front of him, put his hands on her hips, slipped his fingers into her back pockets. What a relief to be away from that. Nevertheless, it felt strange to be walking toward the house's intimate quarters with a strange man following her.

The first thing Phillips did when he entered Michael's room was go to the bookcase and check the spines of his books.

"He's not much of a reader, is he?" said Phillips, after a quick perusal. "These books seem like they're for a much younger kid."

"He used to love to read. But . . ." She shrugged. "It might have something to do with his father. Sam writes, and he puts such an emphasis—"

"What does your husband write?"

"Books."

"What kind of books?"

"I don't see what that has to do with anything," said Olivia. She protected the secret of Sam's writer-for-hire oeuvre as carefully as she had been taught to tell no one of her parents' adherence to the teachings of Max Schachtman—they feared reprisals from certain conservative elements in the university, and what made it worse was that they now shared their colleagues' low opinion of socialism, just as Sam would share in the scorn others would heap on books like *Traveling with Your Pet* and *Visitors from Above*.

"Maybe your husband wrote something that bugged Michael. I was once going to do a film about the children of writers—a lot of them have problems, especially those who feel their parents use them as subject matter. Or maybe he writes things with a lot of gore and violence. I don't know. A strong sexual content. Maybe Michael was offended by something in his father's writing."

Olivia watched as Phillips picked up a few of Michael's

music cassettes—maybe she would turn into one of those mothers who testified in front of Congress against the music industry, fixing the blame for her son's disappearance on a bunch of flaxen-haired strangers in leather pants. "He's indifferent to Sam's writing. I don't know that he's ever read a word of it."

Phillips nodded at her. His expression was deadpan, neutral, but intrusive.

"But relations between them are strained, yes?" he said.

"What makes you say that?"

"Your husband isn't here. I have a sense of marital discord. And teenage sons and their fathers—" He held out his hand and then wobbled it back and forth.

Three evenings later, Sharon dropped by for an unexpected visit. She had been teaching a class called Making Fishless Sushi at the Lutheran Home for the Aged. Russ didn't object to Sharon's myriad commercial enterprises, but in other ways he was an old-fashioned man and liked a fairly minute accounting of her time away from hearth and home. Since the day Olivia had appraised the Tiffany painting, Sharon had called several times, to see if anything had happened in the search for Michael, to see how Olivia was faring with Sam on the road.

Now, Sharon was harried; she quickly unwrapped her purple scarf and folded it with an uncanny precision. Her dark eyes glittered with excitement. Her voice was quick and high. She allowed Olivia to drag her into the kitchen for a cup of tea, but she had no patience for the boiling of water. Glancing at the kettle on the stove, Sharon shook her head quickly. "Maybe just a glass of water, okay, Olivia? Tap water would be fine."

"Sharon," Olivia said, admonishing her, "it'll take two minutes to boil."

"Russ goes crazy when I'm late. You may not see this, but he's very emotional."

"Most men are. That's why there are so many of them in prison."

Sharon brought the glass of water to her lips and drained it in one long swallow. She patted her mouth dry with her palm and then fixed Olivia with a conspiratorial smile.

"Now you have to tell me about Jack Phillips," she said.

"He hasn't found Michael. What else is there to say?"

"I think there is a lot more to say."

"He calls, I'll give him that. He keeps in very close touch."

"Jack?"

"Yes"

"Well? You see?" Sharon smiled broadly, a child's false grin.

Uh-oh, she's in love with him, thought Olivia.

"He calls to tell me what he's done, where he's gone. That sort of thing."

"He likes you," said Sharon, with a wave, as if shooing away the spots before her eyes.

"Oh, stop it. It's all completely businesslike."

"Of course it is. That's Jack's way. Everything businesslike, but in the meantime he has a big erection in his pants." Sharon sat forward, and with her elbows on the table, slumped her face into her hands. She seemed utterly dejected. She tried to pull herself out of it by smiling at Olivia and then pinging her fingernail against the empty water glass.

"Would you like some more water? Or anything else? Beer, Diet Coke? I have this strawberry-and-lime juice."

"Russ doesn't like Japanese women, or Japanese people in general."

"You're kidding me," said Olivia.

"No, I'm not. It's very common. That's why Russ likes war. To him, it's a bunch of guys going out and killing yellow people. Every time America goes to war it's against Asian people. World War II, Korea, Vietnam."

"Was Russ in Vietnam, Sharon?"

"No. He has a bad back. But if he had gone, he would have liked it—except for the danger. I know him very well. He would have brought home a yellow ear in his bag."

Olivia remembered Russ's appliance shop, with its oversized American flag snapping in the breeze, or, on still days, drooping there like a turkey wattle.

"Look who they dropped the atomic bomb on!" cried Sharon. "Not on the blacks, or the Arabs. On us!" Incongruously, she laughed; the relief of finally saying these things made her giddy. "Russ is always buying me perfume and so I asked him why. He didn't want to answer, but I asked him over and over, and that's the night he told me I have a smell. Like fish. I don't ever eat fish. I don't even like it, and I don't think it's healthy. There are no government inspectors for fish, the way they have for meat. But Russ says I smell like fish. Is it surprising that I liked Jack Phillips so much?"

"If you feel this way about Russ, why don't you leave him?"

"For who?"

"I don't know. For no one. And why did you hire a detective to follow him?"

"Japanese pride. To think of people laughing at me." She drew her forefinger over her throat. "And we have so much between us. Things. Our house, the truck and two cars, a motorcycle, a wood lot outside of town. And our collections—comic books, and the baseball cards are worth sixty thousand dollars. Can you imagine? The paintings. And Russ's business. If he wants to leave me, then I need time to protect myself. I know you must understand these things." She gestured somewhat expansively, and it took Olivia a moment to realize the wave was meant to encompass the objects in Olivia's house.

"There's nothing here worth very much."

"But everything is so pretty. And you know how much things are worth. This is your field."

"Yes, well, I don't know how I ever got into it. I'm not terribly interested."

"You're not?"

"Not really. In fact, I sort of hate it."

They were quiet for a moment. Olivia was almost conscious of the entire world and her place in it, the curtain that concealed the grand design was about to blow to one side; but then it didn't, and then it wasn't really a curtain any longer, it was a wall, and a moment after that the wall wasn't necessary, because there was no grand design to conceal.

"But weren't you relieved," she asked Sharon, "when Jack told you Russ wasn't seeing anyone?"

"Yes."

"You see? You still must care."

"I don't want to be humiliated. And I didn't want Jack to see me that way. He might figure if my husband went around behind my back, then there was something wrong with me, or my body, and then Jack would start to lose interest. Not that he was ever interested in the first place," she added with a laugh.

"I don't think Jack is terribly interested in women," said Olivia.

"What a mean thing to say!" cried Sharon happily. "But don't worry, he's very normal, and I think you are his type. The model type, with large eyes and long legs, very tall."

"I'm not tall," Olivia was going to say, but then decided not to, because she was quite a bit taller than Sharon. "I'm too old for love affairs," she said instead.

"He doesn't care about that. Jack is no spring chicken. He's nearly thirty-eight years old—his birthday's in July. And what is he doing with his life? He works as a detective because no one will give him money to make his movies."

"The people we knew in the city," said Olivia, "most had to work at various jobs to support their art."

"To support their art? I thought a man worked to support his family. Oh well, I feel sorry for Jack. He told me about the movies he wants to make. They are all crazy. And then what will happen when he turns forty?"

Impulsively, Olivia reached across the table and took Sharon's hand. Sharon looked at her frankly. It was one of those fleeting moments when all of the pretense of life is dispelled, but as usual it was not dispelled for long enough to discover what lay beyond it.

"I'm just so happy," Olivia said, feeling she needed to explain to Sharon why she was touching her, "not to be talking or thinking about Michael for five minutes."

That night, quite late, while she was in bed reading Wilson's life of Jesus and realizing that in her exhaustion not only had she read the same page three times but each time she understood less of it, the phone rang, and it was Olivia's intuition that despite the hour it was Jack Phillips on the other end of the line.

"I'm sorry to be calling so late," Phillips said.

Olivia drew her knees up, and the satin comforter slipped off the bed. She was wearing an old flannel nightgown, not exactly fresh from the laundry, and turquoise woolen socks. She hadn't shaved her legs in a while. With the men out of the house, she was reverting to certain bohemian, solitary habits from college—eating irregularly, masturbating, falling asleep with the reading light on, waking in the morning with the goose-necked lamp peering inquisitively down at her, its bulb as intense as an acetylene torch.

"Olivia?" said Phillips, moving tentatively into her silence. "Did I wake you?"

It seemed more than coincidence that Sharon's visit and Jack's call were only three hours apart. Were they working together? Maybe. Maybe Sharon was a romantic stalking-horse, the way things were done back in high school, when an intermediary was sent to test the emotional waters. Olivia used to do it for her shy sister: what would you say if Elizabeth asked you to her party?

"Any news?" she asked Phillips.

"Nothing worth reporting." A long pause. She heard the street noise from his apartment. It gave her a strange feeling.

"Damn," she said.

"It's frustrating as hell," he said.

"I'm sure it is." She noted the coldness in her voice and reached down to pick up the comforter.

"I just want you to know," he said, "I'm not going to let you down."

"I appreciate that, Jack."

"You believe me, don't you?"

"I believe you're doing everything you can."

"No. I'm sorry. That's not enough. You have to believe I'm not going to let you down, you have to believe in *me*."

Oh—of course: he was loaded. He was alone, with a drink in his hand, making calls he would regret in the morning. It made her want a drink, too. And the sense of the glass in his hand and the lonely sound the ice made when he brought the drink to his lips moved her closer to him. They were joined by a bridge of regret; they each regretted the night, this night, night itself. And now the possibility that he had urged Sharon to visit her and speak about him filled Olivia not only with pity but desire. Maybe everything that had happened to her— the mysterious, dispiriting drift of her marriage, the move to this rural nowhere, the gloomy afternoons warming her hands on mugs of Earl Grey tea and looking out of some frost-laced window at the nuthatches hanging upside down in the bare trees while the windows of the house displayed her cameos, her damask, her tarnished treasures and second-tier heirlooms, each piece with a story attached to it like the tag on the toe of a corpse—maybe, maybe it was all leading to this, this moment, to Sam's tour, Michael's disappearance, Amanda's sound sleep, and Jack Phillips's voice in her ear; maybe it was all one long gesture culminating in the sudden, startling resurrection of her desire.

"I've been to his school," Phillips was saying. "I've talked to everyone he knows. Normally, I can talk to these kids, I'm good at it. I can make them sing."

"No one really knows Michael."

"Right. That's the thing. But there was something . . ." He let his voice trail off, forced her to come after him.

"What? What thing?"

"The kids talk about a guy who lives in the woods. Did Michael ever mention anything like that to you?"

"What woods?"

"Somewhere, anywhere. In Windsor County. It's half forest here. Still."

"He never said anything about it. Why?"

"I don't know. One of the kids in high school said, 'Maybe he's with the Tree Man.' I knew who he was talking about. Every time something happens around here, if no one can explain it, they bring up this guy supposedly living out in the woods. Weekenders come up, a can of peas is missing, it's got to be the man in the woods."

"Is it just a story, or is there someone out there?"

"I don't know. I tend to think there *is* someone out there, and people make up stories about him."

"Do you think he's got Michael?"

"There's one thing. All the robberies that have been taking place this past year? Well, suddenly, they're not as stupid as they used to be. Suddenly, the thieves are taking things of real value—paintings, carvings, stuff worth serious dough. Suddenly, they know what they're doing."

"Michael?"

"Well, his disappearance *does* coincide with the rise in the quality of thievery. But you realize, I'm just speculating. It's a speculation based on a speculation. It's just talk."

"Just talk? Jack, I want to know what you're doing. I feel as if we're running out of time."

"I look and I look and I look."

"Christ."

"And then I look some more." A pause. "There's one more thing."

"Yes?"

"It's a little . . . I don't know."

"What is it?"

"This Pennyman—I went to see him."

"Did I give you his name?"

"He was reluctant to talk to me. I mean, give me a small break, the guy's not even a Ph.D. and he's acting as if his fucking confidentiality is a matter of law. Anyhow, he told me Michael was upset."

"Upset? Of course he was upset. That's why he was seeing Pennyman in the first place."

"I realize. But—I don't know. Maybe I can get more out of him later. But it seems Michael was worried about something specifically about you and your husband."

"Really? What?"

"I don't know. But it seemed as if Michael knew something, or heard something, and now he and your husband had to have some kind of reckoning."

"What are you basing this on?"

"Instinct—that's what you're paying me for." He laughed. "May I ask you a personal question?"

"What?"

"Are you in bed?"

"Yes. Why are you asking that?"

"I don't know. Your voice. I feel as if I were in bed *with* you."

Scalding blood rushed to her face. Where had such hot blood been stored?

"Are you crazy?"

"I don't know. A little. I thought I could come over."

She hung the phone up and quickly pulled her hand away from it, as if the receiver might jump back into her grip.

She rearranged herself beneath the covers. The cold spring night pressed against the black windows. Her alarm clock was set to go off at seven in the morning and it was already eleven. If she fell asleep this very instant it would give her just eight hours. From now on every tick of the clock took a piece out of tomorrow. Yet: desire. She felt it moving within her, not exactly racing, but stirring, moving in its deep slumber, like a bear disturbed in the depths of its hibernation.

Soon after, Olivia was out of bed, scowling at the clocks as she passed them on her frantic night rounds. She looked in on Amanda, who slept on her back, her face placid, hands folded around a lily of moonlight. Next, she went down the hall and looked in at Michael's room; its emptiness was sullen, banal. She closed the door on it hard.

Downstairs. She hated the look of everything. The faded Persian runners, with their Islamic reds and oranges; the cane chairs pressed against the wall, the kind of chairs that made you not want to sit down. She could not look at anything in the house. The tasteful pictures on the wall—the sepia portrait of Crazy Horse, the dazzling lithograph of the *Lusitania* torn from an old *Harper's*, a credible imitation of a Renaissance Assumption done by a woman named Abigail Waterson, a distant cousin of Emily Dickinson. The correctness oppressed her; everything was so *chosen*.

What if she were to call Jack and tell him yes, come over, come over now—hurry? She thought of him in her house, in her body. She thought of the juice of him going into her, and she felt a twist of revulsion and a bone-deep chill of fear.

She hated the fear within her, abhorred it as something unclean. It was a fear of men, all men; she knew this without being able to say it, felt its justification without being able to defend it. Her father's petulant silences, his suspicions of academic plots and counterplots. Her several boyfriends' beseeching need of her, the way they plucked at her clothes, crushed her. Even Sam, though gentle, was fixated on the idea that his life was real and safe only when he was in her arms, making love to her, and his need for her was now oppressive, like caring for a sick person. And Michael: it was the hardest thing to say. The look of him suckling blindly at her bloated breast, his little razor-sharp fingernails, with no earthly use except the infliction of pain, the incitement of hatred—yes, Michael clawed at her, and when he had sucked her dry, he arched his back to get a better look at her and yowled miserably, accusingly.

She stood in her house, trying to calm herself with deep breaths. There: breathe, just breathe.

This was not her life, not the life she was meant to have. Her real life was elsewhere, but she had no idea where. She was out of the orbit of her destiny, tumbling through space. A fantastic yet pathetic series of accidents, compromises, held horses, bitten tongues had led her into this jerkwater life, this dollhouse without dolls. Where was it written that she would be scouring the countryside for undervalued antiques (often settling for knickknacks)? What was she doing anyhow? What in the hell was going on? What could she have possibly been thinking when she linked her life to Sam's? She stood at the carved Victorian bookcase, filled with his (and ostensibly her) books, and swept them off the shelves with sudden violence, not even flinching when some of them struck her on their way to the floor.

Had she really been one of those girls who wanted to be an artist's wife? How could she have thought so little of herself? What was the deal supposed to be? To pitch in with the typing and wait with him on the edge of the loveseat while he stared at the telephone? Why hadn't someone taken her aside and whispered in her ear: "You know, you have to have a life, too"? Why hadn't she thought of it herself—really thought it, not just have it pass through her head? Her mother was ambitious; her mother's chain-smoking, argumentative friends, her sister had a good career; most of the women she liked and admired had made their way persuasively in the world. Why not her? What did she have to show for her years on earth? One child on the dark side of the moon, another pierced by moonlight on her bed, and a husband on the radio pretending to be someone else? But you see? You see? Even this cold-eyed total excluded her. She was outside the arc of her own accountancy. It was all about Michael, Amanda, and Sam. Surely, there were things in her life outside of her family.

She went into the kitchen, turned on the overhead lights. Too bright. She flicked the switch off and the room settled back into its moony ambiguity. Not quite enough light to see, so she opened the refrigerator and let the twenty-watt bulb inside push its dim glow through the bottle of skim milk standing before it.

All she wanted was enough light to find the Scotch; was that asking too much? It was in the pine cupboard above the sink. She opened it up. Standing in the first row were bottles of Gallo sherry and Astor Home gin, which Sam used to mix cut-price versions of a drink that Lester Young and Billie Holiday reportedly enjoyed—a Back and Forth, or an Up and Down, something like that. What a pretentious pain in the ass he could be sometimes, though her heart went out to him, too, in a way, that he would actually want to better himself through a drink. As stranded as she felt, she at least did not feel the emptiness that was his, day after day.

She parted the bottles and found the Dewar's, and behind that bottle was another.

Without the ice you could really taste it—the grain, the barrel, the nicotine on the fingers of the old men who bottled it. She poured another.

She drank quickly, less interested now in reverie than in results. Yes, it was about time to get a little result-oriented here. That word—"oriented." A vague, irritating memory of Sam pontificating upon it, how with the rise of the Pacific Rim everyone suddenly wanted to get oriented, something like that, nonsense, blather against the anxiety of a still mind. He should have stuck with that meditation teacher. He should have broken the habit of running words through his mind like worry beads, fingering them, darkening them with the oil of his own touch. She hadn't even bothered to inform him that "oriented" meant finding east, Mecca.

She was about to leave the kitchen but stopped herself at the threshold, doubled back for the bottle. No sense wearing out the floor going back and forth. Economy of movement had always appealed to her. Her sister once told her of a girl from college who'd stay statue-still during sex and then, just when you thought she was either dead or resentful, she would flick her hips once and have a short, breathy orgasm, *comme ça*.

Oddly enough, she remembered nothing more of the night when she finally awakened the next morning. She was in bed, but wearing her robe; the bottle of Scotch was on the night table, touching the phone, as if the two had formed a relationship. And Amanda was at her bedside, looking both stricken and curious.

"Mom?" she said, shaking Olivia's shoulder. The thing about drinking too much was that it dissolved the boundaries between soul and shit, and it all mixed together like food some furious infant has mashed upon his plate.

"Don't shake," said Olivia, shading her eyes, though it was barely light in the room. What was that sound? Rain?

Oh God, what if Michael was out there somewhere, in the rain?

"I missed the bus," said Amanda. "You didn't wake me up, or make breakfast, or anything."

"Sorry, sorry." Her legs ached; her mouth felt like the inside of a vacuum cleaner bag. A sharp smell in the air—pine tar, turpentine, something.

"Mom?" Amanda's voice wavered between concern and amusement. There was no question that seeing her mother sacked out so helplessly was an event of some kind.

"I'll drive you to school," Olivia whispered.

"It's already started. And you get in more trouble for being late than being absent."

Olivia sighed deeply. There was something way off in what Amanda was saying, but it was too complicated to refute right now.

"Mom?"

"What."

"What happened downstairs?"

Olivia was silent. She was having no thoughts of which she was aware, yet Amanda's question disturbed her. It was like the physical equivalent of déjà vu, a bodily sensation familiar yet elusive; she remembered herself doing *something* but could not say *what*.

"Did you write on the walls, Mom?"

"What?"

Amanda reached for Olivia's hand and plucked it off of the satin comforter. Amanda's hand was icy.

Olivia opened her eyes and looked at her right hand, as Amanda held it before her. The sides of her first three fingers were stained dark blue. At first, it meant nothing to her, then it began to, and then she was blank again.

"Everything's knocked over, Mom. Maybe we should, I don't know—call the police?"

"What time is it?"

"Mom, I'm serious. Where's Daddy? Maybe we should call Daddy."

"No, that's okay." Olivia was silent. There were thick black velvet curtains over the windows of consciousness; no breeze could stir them. If she did not speak—now!—then surely she would fall back to sleep. "What kind of writing on the walls, sweetie?" It was what Sam called her—never mind.

"Your name, with a face in the O."

"You're—" She stopped herself from saying the rest of it: "kidding me." "What else?"

"Swears, in paint. Mom, did you do that?"

"Is anything broken?"

"I don't know. I don't think so. The books are on the floor."

"Is that all?" She forced herself up on her elbows; her insides fell away, groceries out of a wet sack.

"The windows were open, and it was real cold when I came down. I closed them, so it's okay now. But that's why I thought someone might have snuck in, maybe some teenagers or something. Or Michael?"

"No, it was me."

They were silent, mother and daughter, it was one of those moments that neither of them would shake loose; for a long time it would be a line of demarcation: things happened either before the night the walls got painted or after.

"Graffiti," said Amanda.

"Yes, that's what it's called."

It had taken her daughter that long to remember the word she wanted. Something inside of her kept snatching away the words she needed, hiding them under things.

"You know what you should do?" said Olivia. She sat up, leaned against the bedboard. The wood felt cold straight through her nightgown and her robe. "You could go to your room, and read, or color, or do whatever you want to do. I'm going to go downstairs and straighten up a little, and then we can both go to town and have a lovely girls' breakfast at the Silver Spoon."

"Okay."

"Okay?"

Amanda nodded but did not move. Finally, she asked, "Why did you do all that, Mom?"

"You know how it is when you get real mad and lose your temper? Well, moms sometimes do, too. Just because you get old doesn't mean you don't sometimes lose your temper."

"But I never paint anything, and I don't break stuff or throw stuff around."

"You used to. We called them temper tantrums."

"Yeah, but I was two years old, Mom."

"Well, last night, I was two years old."

"Are you going to be two years old tonight?"

"No. I promise. It's just that, you know, I'm worried about Michael, and I really miss Daddy." She was a little surprised to hear herself saying this, but as soon as it was out she realized it was true—she missed Sam, she wished he were here at this very moment, to survey the damage she had done, to help her get through whatever was next.

As soon as Amanda left the room, the telephone rang. Something told Olivia she ought to just let it ring, but she picked it up anyhow.

"Hello," said the voice at the other end of the line. "This is Nadia Tannenbaum. Do you remember me? I was a guest at your home last year."

"Yes," said Olivia, her heart pounding. "I remember you."

"It's . . . it's very important that I speak to Sam, Mrs. Holland," said the voice at the other end of the line. "Is he there?" And then Nadia began to weep. "Never mind," she said, and tried to hang up, but was too upset and failed to break the connection. "Oh, shit," Olivia heard her say. "Can't I do anything right?" A few more fumbling noises and the line was dead.

chapter twelve

despite our cozy, fitful night together, and the haze of animal attraction that still hung over me, Heather was unperturbed when I told her that Ezra had called yesterday and summoned me back to Manhattan to deal with a woman who claimed to have secret knowledge of my identity.

"Let's just see what we can do to make the best of your time in New York. I'm still plotting out your West Coast tour," she said. "We've got you Los Angeles, San Diego, Santa Barbara, San Francisco, and then . . . well, I'm not quite sure. Wouldn't it be great if we could get right into Denver from San Francisco?"

"That would be heaven on earth," I sullenly replied.

Heather booked us on Amtrak back to New York. I went to my room and sat on the bed, with my arm draped around my bulky suitcase, the way you might comfortably embrace an old black Lab, and I thought about going to New York. I thought about Ezra, and the combination of insistence and irony he brought to my postromantic difficulties with Nadia. He was amused by the folly of it, but in the end it was his profits that were being endangered, and he surely expected me to bring Nadia in line. But how? Was I really supposed to offer her money? Or throw myself on her mercy? Maybe Ezra figured I could begin sleeping with her again and sort of string her along until my book was in paperback. (The thought of making love to Nadia again awakened a Bergsonian memory of her flesh, the hardness of her nipples, the urgent openness of her kisses, the slightly sweaty, acrid smell of our sex together, the ecstatic locker-room pungency. . . .)

I reached quickly for the phone. It had just occurred to me that I would be only two hours south of Leyden and that Olivia and I could see each other. Maybe I could convince her to come down to the city. We could have lunch at an Italian restaurant, make love in whatever hotel Ezra was putting me in. Or maybe I would have enough time to get on the train and go home to her, to sleep next to her in our bed, with her back pressed against my chest and my hand resting on her beautiful bony hip, and have breakfast in my own kitchen, drink my coffee out of my favorite Pottery Barn cup, and watch the afternoon light the color of wet pearls come in through the window over the sink. Home!

I heard my own voice on the answering machine. I waited for the tone and then called out to Olivia to pick up the phone. She didn't, and I dialed her again, this time letting the phone ring once, and then I hung up and dialed again. Again, my voice came on, reedy, stunned, eviscerated by its own lies. I waited for the tone, my stomach churning.

"Hey, it's me," I said. "It's nine-thirty, and I'm on my way to New York to meet with Ezra. I want to see you. What are the chances of your coming in to town and meeting me? We can eat somewhere great on my expense account, or whatever." I paused. For a moment I felt utterly lost, having no idea of what I would say next, or why I would say anything at all. "Hi to you too, Mandy, if you hear this. I miss you, sweetie." I paused again. "I'll call when I get to New York."

The landscape was dead between Philadelphia and New York: closed factories, haunted ethnic neighborhoods; even the scrap yards had fallen on hard times. A steady spring rain was falling, but what was the use? There was nothing out there that could grow. Everything that would happen here had already happened. The rain fell on abandoned cars, rotting fences, empty lots so choked with trash that even the ironweed had given up.

I read the *Philadelphia Inquirer*, where once I had been given an enthusiastic notice by a reviewer who soon after that was canned for selling the books the publishers sent him to a used-book store down in Baltimore. It was that long drive to Baltimore that always struck me as the saddest part of the story.

After the *Inquirer*, I started in on *The New York Times*, turning first to the book page. The novel under review today was called *Hubba Hubba*, by Neil Rabin. Neil had been a friend of ours during those halcyon days on Perry Street around the time Olivia was pregnant with Michael and I was working on my second novel, and our walk-up was full of Albert King, California wines, small magazines, and arguments about Foucault. Neil was horse faced, curly haired, large, awkward, and angry. He looked as if he had just finished chasing a pickpocket through a crowded street. Back then, he made his living working in a Xerox shop, and his wife, who worked as a dental technician, supplied him with stolen Percodans which Neil dealt on the side. Rabin was not well read—he was barely literate, actually—and he not only relied on clichés when he wrote but often misused them. "It's a doggy dog world" was a Rabinism I particularly remembered.

But now the *Times*'s reviewer was using words like "astonishing" and "riotous" to praise *Hubba Hubba*, which described the lives of a number of writers and would-be writers in Greenwich Village during the years in which Neil and I had been friends. The rivalries, love affairs, delusions of grandeur, and moneymaking schemes were all presented, in the reviewer's phrase, "as if *La Bohème* had been rethought by

William S. Burroughs, Robin Williams, and Tim Burton." I sat there wondering if I was "the brooding novelist whose small but early promise collapses beneath an onslaught of babies and bad reviews." Or was I "the hack who shuffles off to Buffalo after being fired as a gag writer for a homosexual pill-popping stand-up comedian?" Yes, perhaps changing my sweet son into an avalanche of babies and my generally favorable notices into an avalanche of pans, or metamorphosing my work as a writer for hire into some Maalox-encrusted tour of the Catskills, was evidence of Rabin's newfound astonishing riotousness.

"Were you listening to the radio before we left?" Heather asked, as I closed the paper and shoved it into the seat pocket before me.

"Absolutely not," I said, with emphasis. My jealousy was making me inappropriately vivid.

"I usually watch TV when I'm alone," she said. "I love TV. The stupider the better. Talk shows, the Home Shopping Network—yummy. But anyhow, I was listening to public radio up in the room. You kind of got me into that."

"I did?" I sounded quarrelsome, pedantic; I had the sour enunciation of someone whose lover is leaving him, who feels his last shred of security disintegrating.

Heather frowned ever so briefly, letting me know I was acting badly, boring her.

"Well," she said, "actually, I'm relieved you weren't listening. I wasn't even going to mention it, but you're going to hear about it anyhow."

"Something about Michael?"

"Michael?"

"My son."

A trace of color came into her normally opaque face, little brush burns of feeling. She shook her head. This reference to a painful aspect of my private life seemed like a breach of etiquette; I had shown her the crack in my life, like President Johnson yanking up his shirt to show off his gallbladder scar.

"No," she said, "nothing like that. It was about your book."

"What about it?"

"That guy who interviewed you? Ian Lamb?"

"I thought he liked me."

"Ian said that after he interviewed you, the station was inundated with calls about you and the book. Some of them, you know . . ." Heather shrugged, meaning to indicate that some of these callers were rather skeptical about my theories of extraterrestrial visitations, and some thought I was so full of shit it was a miracle I could breathe. (The awful part was I actually resented these bastards.) "But he said most of them were positive."

"I'm going to remember how these public-radio types waste airtime next time they try to hit me up with one of their fund-raising appeals."

"No, he wanted to talk about the weird ones."

"The Weird Ones? Is this like the Men in Black?"

"No, come on, cut it out."

Ah: so my jests already exhausted her. Somehow, while trying to comfort each other through a night, we had managed to go through twenty-five years of unhappy marriage. I was doomed.

"Sorry," I said. "Clearly you meant to indicate weird calls. So sorry."

"It was more of that predicting-and-prophecy stuff. One guy from Winston-Salem said he was reading your book, the part about the Plains of Nazca—"

"Have you read the book?"

"Yes, of course."

"You said you hadn't."

"I never said that, Sam."

I rolled my eyes. She had definitely said that, no doubt about it.

"The Plains of Nazca," she said. "Massive configurations in the Peruvian desert, made by space explorers in the year 1500. Okay? Do I pass the test?"

I shrugged.

"Well, just as he was reading about it, a low-flying plane went over his house and the sonic boom shook his bookshelves, and guess what fell out?"

"Tell me."

"A travel book about South America."

"Wow."

"Well, come on, it's strange, you've got to admit that. But it gets weirder."

"Things generally do."

"The book fell open, and when he picked it up it had opened itself to the section about Peru, and then he read the page and sure enough it mentioned the Plains of Nazca."

"Probably word for word as it appeared in *Visitors*. I remember pinching from a travel book or two—maybe for the Nazca part, or the Yucatán section. I can't remember."

"Then Ian said that someone from the Monterey UFO Network called. This time they played a tape. He had a real low, echoing voice, as if he was calling from inside an oil drum. He said that there have been like ten recent sightings and that MUFON—"

"MUFON?"

"Monterey U—"

"Right, right. Go on."

"MUFON has pictures of them, which they are sending to John Retcliffe, who they believe to be a great man. And they also sent you a personal message, over the air."

"This isn't happening."

"They said you should be careful."

"Of who? The Men in Black?"

"Yes. The Men in Black. Come on, I think it's very nice of them. It's *sweet*. They've made you an official member of the Committee for the Open Investigation of Fringe Science and the Paranormal."

"What are the dues?"

"I'm serious, Sam. Do you realize how good this is for your book?"

"Ian Lamb was talking about all this stuff because he thinks it's all a big joke."

Heather looked disappointed for a moment, but then she brightened; she found a way to solve the issue and put me in my place all at once. "Just make the best of it, Sam," she said. "Success is what we all struggle for. Yet when we have success, we always feel as if people don't truly see us as we are. But don't you understand? Everybody feels completely misunderstood. Most people just don't have the success to empower them to *complain* about it. Just go along and don't take it too seriously, like we did last night."

"Empower?"

"Screw you, Sam. I mean it."

We parted for good at Penn Station, amid the throngs weaving in and out of the homeless people who lived along the edges of the terminal. The stench of donuts was in the air. Heather got in a cab going uptown to her apartment, and I went to Wilkes and Green, where one of Ezra's assistants hovered amiably over me, after telling me that Ezra himself was at the dentist, having spent a brutal night tormented by an abscess.

"I guess his heart will have grown fonder, then," I said.

The assistant, a rangy kid about twenty-four, pointed a long finger at me. "I get it. Abscess makes the heart—"

"No, no, I'm sorry I said it. I will take that coffee you offered, though."

"Cream, sugar, Sweet'n Low?"

"Just coffee. Do you have any idea when he'll be back?"

"It should be any minute. He left an hour ago. Say, Mr.—"
He groped for a moment and I let him. "—Holland," he
decided. "Do you mind if I ask you a question?"

"Not at all." I heard my own voice, rich as a fruitcake
with its own satisfactions; maybe I *was* becoming successful.

"You say in your book that gravity distorts time and
space, right? That it would be like dropping a bowling ball on
a waterbed. So does that mean if you were in a space-travel
machine, a disc or a saucer or even a rocket, then you'd be
creating your own gravitational field and could actually warp
both space and time?"

"Sounds okay to me," I said after a moment.

He nodded, relieved. A pet theory had just received
the benediction of an expert, apparently. "What about
abductees?" he asked.

"Abductees?"

"People taken prisoner by aliens. I was wondering why
there wasn't more about them in your book."

"Yes, well, it's a large subject. Maybe next time."

I had no idea why I was saying this. Was pandering a
reflex now? I had been taken aback by the kid's not being in
on the con: I thought everyone in the office knew I was a novelist and that *Visitors* was a scam. Before publication, when
the book was in galley form, no one believed more than a few
paragraphs. Now, however, it wore the vestments of green
money, and the people in the office were willing themselves
into a kind of Dark Ages, forgetting what they once knew.

"Next time," said Ezra's assistant, nodding sagely. He
looked like what he was: a perpetrator and a victim of the
same lie. "Well, that answers my other question." He stood
up, ready now to get my coffee.

"What question is that?" I asked.

"Whether or not you're planning a second volume,

a sequel or something. God, everyone here really wants you to."

What was I? Their Christmas bonus? Monogrammed T-shirts for their softball team?

While I was alone, I helped myself to the telephone on Ezra's desk and tried to call Olivia again. And again I heard my voice on the answering machine. The machine had a remote code by which I could change the greeting on my machine. Was it star 2 or double 3?

I took out my wallet, where I had once put the small card that listed the machine's remote functions. But where was it? I had a Mobil credit card, a revoked Visa—fuck you, Chem Bank, I'm rich now and I'll be waltzing my dough over to Morgan. I emptied the contents of my wallet onto Ezra's desk—old library cards, receipts from the Xerox shop next door to International Image, Inc., a lapsed membership to the Authors Guild and another one to PEN.

Then I chanced upon a piece of paper, which clearly wasn't the code for my answering machine. It was written in Olivia's powerful, feminine hand, and these are the words she wrote: "Dear Sam, Drive carefully and bring yourself home to me. I miss you already." Not exactly the balcony speech, but I remembered finding it in my shaving kit when I was off with an Australian shepherd borrowed from a friend to do research for *Traveling with Your Pet*. That Olivia had written this to me and that my own hunger for good memories was so keen that I had saved it and carried it with me, and that there had been no note whatsoever skipped into my kit this time, and that there might never be again—all of this created in me a sadness so vast and alive that I could feel it within me like an ocean.

It was then, naturally, that Ezra returned from the dentist, nicely buzzed from painkillers, but still with a pronounced swelling in his lower jaw.

"Sam! What are you doing?"

I quickly looked up at him.

He noticed the credit and membership cards spread over his desk. "Identity crisis?" he inquired.

I gathered the cards, stuffed them into my wallet. "How's that abscess treating you?" I said.

"Lenin said that a bourgeois's idea of suffering was a trip to the dentist."

"Lenin? You surprise me, Ezra."

"I'm a book guy—I quote, therefore I am." He touched the side of his face, winced. "Have you seen the latest figures?"

He came around to my side of the desk, stood there for a moment, waiting for me to realize he wanted his chair back, and then he opened the top drawer of his desk and pulled out a computer readout.

"We're selling three thousand copies a day. At this rate, we'll be at a quarter-million in ten weeks! Viva Las Vegas, motherfucker!"

He let out a startling, piercing whoop, just as his assistant appeared with my coffee. The kid's hands shook, but he managed to keep his composure and he didn't spill a drop.

"Come on, Sam," Ezra said. "Let's talk about our next John Retcliffe project. Something really *wonderful* this time."

A half-hour later, I was standing in the lobby of International Image, Inc. I had become accustomed in the course of my tour to arrivals at places where I would rather not be and to coming in with not only a spring in my step but a smile on my face, and a false persona to boot. This life of lies had surely frayed that little thin scarf of character we call the Soul, but there was still enough of Me left to feel sick with dread at the prospect of facing Nadia under these circumstances.

I rode alone in the elevator, heading up to the seventh floor. Last time I had ridden in this elevator I was mad to see her, mad to touch her, to feel her body next to mine, to feel her desire for me, her acceptance of me, to receive the benediction of her fierce and undivided attention. She used to touch me while I talked because she wanted to feel the skin of someone who said such interesting things. I fell in love with her. I repeated her name under my breath as I went through my day. I wrote her name on scrap paper, like a schoolboy, with a towering N and the rest of the letters of her name huddled humbly in its shadow.

But that Nadia was gone. Now I was coming to see the new Nadia, the furious Nadia, Nadia the wounded, the vengeful, and I had nothing to offer her but five grand's worth of hush money, which Ezra had said I should disguise in the form of a consultancy fee.

Up in the III offices, light streamed through the huge, high windows while archivists knelt reverentially before long gray drawers filled with images from the past. Near the elevators, a young Asian woman sat at her desk. Her hair was pulled back tightly; she wore dark lipstick, a black sweater, pearls. She looked up from her book as the elevator doors closed behind me.

"May I help you?" At the end of her desk was a stack of brown envelopes, awaiting the messenger service.

"I'm here to see Nadia Tannenbaum."

"Who may I say is calling?"

Not this again. Not having a stable identity was like having a sunburned back that suddenly everyone wants to slap.

"Sam Holland," I said, finally. Easy as pie.

She picked up her phone, punched two numbers on the keypad. "Nadia? Mr. Holland for you?"

There were a couple of leather-and-chrome chairs and issues of *New York* magazine and *Aperture* and I busied myself with them while I waited for Nadia. Though the center of III was one vast open loft, there was a fringe of glass-enclosed cubbies on the north side. I couldn't recall which of these was Nadia's, and then, at last, I saw her emerge from one.

She moved with great confidence and a lovely grace. Her hair was short, in a sort of Louise Brooks–ish fashion. She wore a brown suede jacket, a yellow skirt, boots. She seemed fuller breasted than I remembered her. There was a glow of good health in her skin, beaming out of her like a flashlight under a silk scarf.

I threw the magazine aside and started to get up, but somehow remained seated. I watched as she made her way toward me; if she had looked up she would have seen me, but she did not look up. She stopped to talk to a young, overweight kid crouched in front of an open drawer filled with photos, and when she was finished with him she stopped to say something to an elderly guy in a maroon beret who was inspecting a photograph, holding it in a quivering spoke of sunlight and peering at it through a magnifying glass.

The last time I had come to this office was to make love to Nadia, and somehow the drastic change of circumstance hadn't yet reached the Iron Age hinterlands of my nervous system, and I sat there with sexual excitement spreading through me, like roses blooming in a battlefield.

And now she was standing before me. I stood up, offered her my hand.

She took it, briefly, coolly.

"Where are we going?" she asked.

"There's that coffee shop next door."

She shook her head no. I wasn't sure why, and I was in no position to ask. Somehow, despite her horrible behavior, she was still the injured party.

"Any place you'd like to go?" I asked, managing to omit the word "special" at the last moment.

"How about a bar so we can get totally drunk?" I must have looked confused, because she laughed, happy for the moment. "I'm not serious, Sam." She pressed the call button for the elevator and the doors immediately opened.

The elevator descended. We stood close to each other. I felt sick with nervousness, and simply became John Retcliffe for the ride. I thought of interviews coming up, questions to anticipate, things I might say. I did not think of the nights I had spent in Nadia's arms, the slightly yeasty taste of her sleepy kisses. I did not think of Olivia, and I did not think of my son.

When we were in the lobby I said, "Now where?" and Nadia said she was hungry for lunch and there was a new Japanese restaurant around the corner.

It had a Grand Opening sign in the window and little plastic pennants flapping in the breeze, as if what they were offering were used cars rather than tempura. Inside, the place was so ordinary it looked as if it had been taken out of a box, ready-made: little Formica tables, carnations stuck in saki decanters, posters of Mount Fuji.

The waitress was dressed in a kimono, but that was as traditional as she went. She had a Queens accent, and when she unceremoniously placed our tea on the table the sleeve of her kimono rode up, revealing an antismoking patch on her forearm.

I could somehow tell by the way Nadia ordered her meal that I was in trouble. Her tone was harsh, authoritative; she ordered more than she could possibly eat. When our little lacquer bowls of miso came, we ate in silence, until I tried to break, or at least bend, the silence.

"You're looking well," I said.

"Oh, fuck you."

I rolled my eyes, as if I were used to this sort of verbal abuse, as if it barely fazed me.

"Can I ask you a question?" I said.

"No!" She took another spoonful of miso and then changed her mind. "What?"

"Why do you want to make all this trouble? You've been talking to my publisher—I mean, I don't get it. I've never had a book sell in—"

"Don't talk to me about that book, Sam. I mean it."

"What are you talking about? That's why we're here, to talk about the book."

"Maybe that's why you're here, Sam. But not me."

"What do you want, Nadia?"

"I want you to face what you did to me. Okay? I want you to squirm. I want you to come to my office and pick me up for lunch."

"Well, then you should be very happy, all of your dreams have come true."

"To me, you look very comfortable."

"I do? Well, that's just amazing. Because I'm not. In fact, things could hardly be worse." Hearing I was feeling bad made me feel worse. The stone fell into the well of self-pity, raising a wave of the stuff. I dropped my mock-ivory spoon into the miso and covered my eyes with my hand.

"I called your wife, Sam, the precious Olivia."

"You did? When?"

"This morning. Before you called. Before I even knew I was going to see you."

"I don't believe you."

She shrugged, and a surge of wild energy went through me. It felt like madness. The world, its conventions, propriety, a sense of consequence—all of it began to fade. I felt as if I might literally die of anger.

"That was a terrible thing to do, Nadia."

"I can call whoever I want," she said. She placed her spoon in the bowl and nodded agreeably at the waitress as she cleared the table.

"No, you *cannot* do whatever you want," I said. "There are people involved here, Nadia."

"That's a good one, coming from you."

I gestured my lack of comprehension.

"Since when did you become a big carer about people?" she asked, and then she folded her hands in her lap and smiled happily as a new waitress appeared with our lunches—we both ordered chicken teriyaki, if it matters.

"That psycho letter you sent to me?" I said, while the waitress served us. "In which you so delicately said I used your cunt as a toilet?"

Nadia gestured toward the waitress and then made a shushing sound.

"Well, Michael got his hands on it."

"Oh."

"And you know what else? He was so fucked up by it, he disappeared."

"What do you mean?"

"Disappeared. He's so bent out of shape by what you said, he can't face me and he can't face his mother, either, knowing as he does a great deal more about what a shit heel her husband is than she does. Or—I don't know, I usually think about this at night, when I'm alone—maybe he ran away because he wanted to create some emergency that would bring me and Olivia together."

"Are you and Olivia apart? Or is this just more of your song and dance?"

I stared at her. I had no idea what I might do next. The line that tethered me to civilized behavior was gone; I felt only the ghostly pressure of where it had once secured me to the shore.

"Are Olivia and I apart? Why are you asking that?"

It wasn't as if I was trying to make my voice sound violent; it was only the lack of effort to make it sound reasonable. Nadia visibly drew back from me; I could sense her struggle to maintain a certain impassivity in her stare.

"I seem to recall your saying something about a divorce."

"That is completely untrue. That was happening in your

own mind, and in fact it's probably something you made up afterwards. It was never fucking mentioned."

"Look, Sam, I didn't come here to be verbally abused. And do you think you could manage to keep your voice down? You're terrifying the waitresses."

"I am not terrifying the waitresses. I'm looking right at one of them and she couldn't care less. Now listen, Nadia. I don't want you calling my house."

"I'm sure there are a great many things you don't want me to do."

"There are. And I think we'd better discuss all of them."

"Sam."

She was trying to alter the chaotic mood of the moment by merely modulating her voice, by putting a little burr of appeal in it. And it worked.

"What?"

"When you told me you loved me . . . when we had sex and you held me and you were so patient with me . . . when you fell asleep with your hand on my breast and your leg thrown over mine . . . what, if anything, did that mean to you?"

"It meant a great deal to me."

"Did it?"

"Yes, of course it did. I was crazy about you."

"You were crazy about me. But did you love me?"

"Yes, as a matter of fact I did." Did I? In fact, I couldn't remember with any great accuracy. I recalled the heavy perfume of her, the sludginess of the sheets on the hotel bed. I remembered the meals we ate, I remembered the passion, I remembered the sudden vast openness of her, I remembered walking the back acres at the Leyden house whispering "Nadia, Nadia" to myself, enlarged, engorged by the secret of her. But did I love her; had I ever? Yes. No. Suddenly, I could not recall. I could remember the urge toward her, the rationalizations I constructed to excuse my behavior; but the soul of the matter was beyond my reach, its truth sailed off in the moments in which it existed, carried out on the vessel of time as it made its way into the darkness.

"Then what happened?"

"Look, Nadia, did you really call Olivia? Or are you just trying to drive me crazy? Because if you are, if that's what you're doing, I think you should know that this isn't a very good time—"

I stopped myself. Nadia looked as if I'd just slapped her across the face. In fact, I had been vaguely considering doing just that, though I'd never raised my hand against a woman.

"Is that all you care about?" she asked. "Do you realize how much I'd have to be suffering to make a call like that?"

"Did you actually make that call?"

"Yes. God damn you. Yes. God, you are such an asshole."

"What did you say to her?"

She stood up. She held the edge of the table as if to fight back a sudden pain. "I have to go to the bathroom," she said.

I considered insisting that she tell me what she said to Olivia *before* she went to the bathroom, but as unhinged and irrational as I felt, my own madness was modulated by some vague sense of fair play, and so I said nothing. I watched her make her way across the restaurant; she knew my eyes were on her. "You have to at least try the sushi, my pet," an older gent was saying to his émigré companion—I figured her for a Ukrainian, partly because I had a couple of nights before read an article about the influx of Ukrainian women in New York, looking for husbands.

One of the waitresses came to the table and refilled our cups with clear green tea. I kept my eyes averted; in the little respite of sanity occasioned by Nadia's exit, I fully realized what a scene we had been making. Our angry, disappointed voices must have filled the place like pneumatic drills.

I thought of Nadia calling Olivia and the terror of my life being altered beyond any recognition made me want to cry out. I found some quarters in my pocket and asked the sushi chef if there was a pay phone. His eyes were very dark beneath his white paper hat; he wore opaque white plastic gloves. He pointed his pudgy white finger at a phone in the back of the restaurant, near a couple of cool, unused hibachi tables.

I dialed my number, dropped in a buck and a half, and then let the phone ring once and hung up. As I waited for the phone to return my coins, I wondered if I would have done better not to use the signal. If Nadia had spoken to Olivia, then my chances of getting through might have been improved by her not knowing it was me who was calling. Then, to make matters immeasurably worse—sometimes all it takes is a small thing to fuck up to drive you over the edge—the phone failed to return my quarters, and I had to go to the cash register, where a wizened old woman stared at me with fear and defiance, as if I might be Death Himself, and counted out change for a couple of dollars for me, while I popped an anise-flavored peppermint into my mouth. Then I called Olivia again, and either I let too much time pass between the signal and the second call, or she was out, or she was simply (!) not taking my calls, because between the second and third rings my slurring, uncertain voice came onto the answer machine.

"Olivia? Are you there?" I said, just as Nadia was coming out of the bathroom.

She took one look at me and disappeared behind the ballerina-embossed door once again.

"Nadia!" I called, but she didn't want to hear me. I stood there for a moment and then it seemed okay to just follow her in. Surely there would be no other women in there, no shouts, no eeks—and as to the staff of this place, well, they could hardly think worse of us than they already did.

Walking into the women's bathroom, I was struck by an old, buried memory: my mother taking me into the ladies' room with her at Macy's when we were shopping for a winter coat for me. She needed to use the toilet, and leaving me unattended in that vast store was out of the question. I was only five or six years old, and she told me to wait by the sinks while she went into a stall. "Hey, what's he doing in here?" said a woman in a pillbox hat, a woman with orange lipstick, stout legs. "Oh, he's just a little boy," my mother said from her stall. "You're getting carried away over nothing." The woman looked startled, she didn't know exactly where my mother's voice was coming from; then she looked at me, shook her head, and turned away.

"Nadia," I called, though I was looking right at her. Unlike the one at Macy's, this bathroom was apartment tiny: just one stall, a sink, an electric hot-air machine to dry your hands. Nadia was leaning over the sink, fanning water into her face.

"What did you say to her, Nadia? I just called and there's no one home."

She turned to me. Tusks of saliva hung from her mouth; her hair was plastered to her sweating forehead.

"Let me alone," she said, pleadingly. She wiped her mouth with the back of her hand.

"You have to tell me what you said to her. Did you say we were lovers?"

"I didn't say anything. I asked her if you were home. I love you, Sam. I wouldn't do anything to hurt you, or make you hate me. But . . ." She put her hand on her belly. Her eyes were desperate and I knew what she was going to say. "I'm pregnant."

My heart beat wildly, my blood raced; yet still I lived, which seemed to imply that the drama and dignity of sudden death would be denied me. A kind of hyperawareness came over me. I looked away from Nadia's hurt, dangerous face and glanced at the tiles on the walls, the sloppiness of the workmanship, the grouting between the white and the aqua squares. I could sense the movement of the earth, our orbit around the sun, the millstone grind of day into night. Of course, I was noticing too much, madness often being a matter of something stripping the threads off of the spigot that controls how much information gushes into you. I felt sensation soaking through the soles of my shoes, and a few heartbeats later I was up to my chin in it—the smells of raw fish and seaweed, the pungent corkscrew aroma of the wasabi, the beep of the chef's Casio watch, the chop of his long knife, the rumble of the traffic outside, the flap of the fabric ribbons near the cool air vents, the slightly askew center part of Nadia's hair, which looked like a zigzag of lightning, the subzero blue of her eyes, her teardrop-shaped nostrils, her small, square teeth. . . .

"Don't look at me like that," she said. She covered her abdomen with her hands, protecting the life within her from the corrosiveness of my stare. Yet then her gaze met mine, and even in my near-derangement I recognized in her eyes that mixture of stubbornness, sexuality, and a slightly depersonalized desire to be noticed and loved that had drawn me to her in the first place.

"And, yes, it's yours," she said.

"But I thought you were—"

"Don't you dare start questioning me about birth control, Sam, or I swear to God I'll start screaming."

She was right; I was going to say she'd told me that she was taking birth control pills. (In fact, I had given her a little paternal talking-to on the subject, relating some of the dangers of the pill—the high blood pressure, the phlebitis fears.)

"Are you going to have this baby?"

"What do you think I should do?"

"How should I know? I'm just now hearing about it. Do you want some off-the-cuff answer?"

"Yes, I would. I think that would be a lot more honest than something you've thought about for a long time."

"Okay, then. No."

"You want me to kill our baby?"

"I want? When was the last time my life was about what I wanted?"

"You've changed, Sam."

"Look, Nadia," I said, quickly shifting gears, though not so gracefully as I would have wanted, "fatherhood has never been a talent of mine. I haven't done very well with my own children—"

"What do you mean, your *own* children? Who do you think put this life inside me? One of your bullshit space visitors?"

"I'm not disputing this, Nadia. Anyhow, there are scientific ways of determining—"

"You are really incredible, Sam."

"What do you want me to do? Just accept everything you say? The reason I'm here in the first place is you've been threatening my publisher—"

"Publishers should not feel threatened, not by the truth. And neither should writers."

"You've been practicing for this meeting, haven't you? Everything I've said so far, you've run in through your head and have figured out what you would say in reply."

She shrugged. I didn't know if she was conceding the point or deeming it irrelevant.

"Why are you doing this to me?" I asked. But before she could answer—if, in fact, she ever intended to answer—I said, "No, forget it. I don't care. Why would I want to know the fucking *reason* you're calling my publisher and my *wife?*"

"You're doing bad things, Sam—someone has to stop you, you're out of control."

"What did I do? I kissed you, I wrote a book to feed my family. What?"

"You're making people believe things that aren't true."

Just then, the bathroom door flew open, and the young Ukrainian woman staggered in, her bejeweled hand over her mouth. Her eyes widened as she saw me, but she could do little more to register her shock over seeing a man in the ladies' room. She shouldered her way into the toilet stall, closing the door behind her with her ample, tweedy hip. Soft Russian sounds of revulsion and distress preceded her retching, and for some reason I found myself staring in the mirror. How had my life led me to this spot? Where had I turned; what wind had blown me: what would the line look like connecting the place in time when I had decided to give my life to Art and this moment, here, now, in this chemically reodorized room, facing one woman who wanted to reveal my various forgeries while another regurgitated sushi?

I bolted out of the bathroom, with Nadia following behind. I didn't even want to look at her. I dropped some money on the table, grabbed my coat, and fled the restaurant. Taxi!

The taxi took me to Penn Station, where, a few minutes later, I boarded a train to Leyden. It was two o'clock; the train would get me there by three-forty-five, at which point I'd get in one of the Chariots of Fire, which the local cab company called the green-and-brown junkers loitering around the train station. I'd be home by four; Mandy's bus came a few minutes after that; Olivia would certainly be home. It would have been better if I could have time alone with Olivia, to dispel whatever Nadia had said, to explain it, or, more likely, deny it, to, at any rate, somehow make it go away. Who knew? Perhaps I would throw myself on her mercy. Was Olivia's mercy a large enough target to hit? Would it cushion my fall like those immense trampolines firefighters hold for those who must leap from burning buildings?

The train made its way along the Hudson. I didn't have anything to read. The Amtrak magazine lasted me for five minutes; the river looked gray and nervous. The train, bound eventually to Niagara Falls, was only half-full. Often, in the past, I had run into Leydenites on the train from New York. I hoped with a fervency that approached the boundaries of prayer that I would not see anyone I knew today. I wanted to be alone with my thoughts—not that I was having any thoughts, but I assumed a notion or two would be forthcoming. I didn't want to have to make small talk. I didn't want to have to account for one thing about my life—how my kids were, how my wife was, what I was up to. My life had been irradiated; my tolerance for small talk had been burned out of me.

Sitting across the aisle from me was a guy my age, at least two hundred and fifty pounds, dressed in outpatient chic: torn trousers, a leather vest, a leather World War I pilot's cap, goggles, a beard to the third button of his flannel shirt. Despite all that, he was affluent enough to be wearing a gold Rolex and carrying a cellular phone in his backpack. He took it out, unfolded it, took off his tinted goggles and put on a pair of half-frame reading glasses, and dialed a number.

"Hi, honey, it's me," he said. "I just remembered I forgot to tell you how much I love you." He listened to whatever Honey was saying and then he laughed happily. "That's right, built for comfort, not for speed." He listened and squirmed happily in his seat. "I know, I know, it was for me, too. Hey, what do you say? Is Antoine still there? Put him the hell on, will ya?" And then, with Antoine on the line, he began speaking rapid French, this time in a tone that suggested an employer speaking to a subordinate.

"Would it be too much of an imposition for me to make a call on that?" I asked him, when he was folding his phone back up. "I would of course pay for my call."

"You're not worried about these things giving you brain cancer?" he said.

"I really couldn't care less," I said.

I thought I was going to phone Ezra, but I found myself

dialing Olivia, first hearing my voice and the machine and then calling her again, letting it ring once, hanging up, and calling again. I then indicated to the man across the aisle, using a mixture of shrugs and smiles, that I was going to make one more call, and this time I phoned Ezra.

"Where are you?" he practically screamed, once his assistant put me through.

"On the train."

"Train? What train?"

"I'm going to Leyden."

"Leyden?"

"It's where I live, Ezra. When I'm not you-know-who."

"You-know-who? What are you talking about, Sam? This is serious. We've got you booked on an eight o'clock flight out of Kennedy—it'll get you in to Los Angeles at ten, L.A. time, and then a car will take you to the studio. You're going on 'The Nash Benton Show.' You have no idea what it took to get you on."

"Yeah? What'll it take to get me off?"

A silence. Then: "Nash himself is reading your book, as we speak, Sam, as we speak."

"I'm on a train, going in the opposite direction."

"Then get off of the train, Sam. What happened with that woman? Did you fix things?"

"I can't get off the train. It's moving. As angry as you are right now, I still won't jump off a moving train."

"Then when the train does stop, Sam, you have to turn around, right away. If there's not another train, then hire a car. This thing, thirty minutes on 'Nash Benton,' Sam, it can be worth fifty thousand dollars, in your pocket, Sam. You only have to be in L.A. for one day, Sam. Okay? Sam?"

Was it just my imagination, or was Ezra overusing my name, sort of slapping me across the face with it, to bring me to my senses?

"I'll do my best."

"You have to be there. I don't want to say this—"

"Then don't."

"—but you're—"

"Contractually obligated?"

"That's right, Sam."

We went back and forth a few more times, and at the end, naturally, I promised I'd be at the airport by seven. It would give me a half an hour to see Olivia. I handed the phone back to the man across the aisle, along with a twenty-dollar bill, which I thought might be too much for the use of his phone, but which he accepted, keeping his eyes averted, stuffing the twenty into his backpack and then turning away from me and looking out the window.

A wave of exhaustion washed over me; I felt as if I had just been injected with flu virus. I rested my head against the cool window and immediately fell asleep. When I awoke, I was filled with fear. A light rain was falling, and the train was just pulling in to the station in Leyden.

I bounded off the train. I took the slippery, rusting steps from the platform up to the station two at a time, huffing and puffing; this author's tour and all that room service had taken its toll. The river fell away from me, the train whistle howled, and steam from the engine rose up like a ghost, blending with the rain.

One of the trusty Chariots of Fire was waiting in the upper-level parking lot, a battered old Chrysler dappled with rust, and when I got in I was surprised to see that my driver was Greg Pitcher.

"Greg!" I said. "What are you doing here?"

"I'm working, Mr. Holland." His voice was thick; there was the smell of booze in the car.

"You dropped out of school?"

"No, after school. Two-thirty to nine-thirty. You're my first fare." His blond hair was dirty, unevenly cut. His normally cheerful expression now looked tentative, short-changed. Greg had always been such a handsome, self-possessed kid, but today he seemed on the skids, dissolute, windswept; it made me feel as if I'd been away for a long, long while.

"You remember where I live, don't you?"

"Um . . . not really."

"You lived with us for a week, Greg. Red Schoolhouse Road."

He nodded, shrugged. He turned on the ignition; the engine blew a plume of black smoke out of the tailpipe. Sniffling, clearing his throat, Greg put the car into gear and steered out of the parking lot.

"Mike hasn't made it back to school yet, huh," said Greg, glancing at me for a moment in the rearview mirror. All I could see then were the tops of his light brown eyes, but I sensed in them a dull, double-thinking glimmer of guilt. Had he some news of Michael that he was withholding? Was he somehow responsible for Michael's disappearance? Or was it just adolescent guilt, the kind connected to a sexuality so omnivorous that you end up feeling guilty about everything?

"I'm afraid not, Greg. He's called a couple of times, so we know he's all right. But still . . . any ideas about where he could be?"

"Around here? I don't know, Mr. Holland. I've lost six friends in the past two years. Soon as I can, I'm getting out of here."

"And going where?"

"I don't know. Someplace safe."

We were on the outskirts of town, passing the Leyden Antiques Barn, a ramshackle wooden structure with a bronze weathervane on the roof; behind that, in the distance, Holsteins grazed on the new grass—they looked like bloated black-and-white saddle shoes scattered over a carpet. Was this the danger from which Greg dreamed of escaping?

We drove in silence. We were in town now, driving on Broadway, past all the symbols of Michael's discontent—the rinky-dink stores, the hi-how-are-you old-timers, the seething rural hoods jammed into Pepperoni Pete's Pizza Parlor. Except for searching for Michael, I hadn't been in town since my son disappeared from Pennyman's office; I had barely been Sam Holland since that day, and as we rolled through town and out toward Red Schoolhouse Road, with the rain beading on the windshield, and the alcohol in Greg's breath mixing with the gassy fumes coming from the car's shot exhaust system, and the sound of the tires hissing over the blacktop, I stretched my legs out and breathed as deeply as I could, and for a moment the nervous nature of my mission and my utter indecision over what I would say to Olivia, how I would make things better—all of it receded, and I reveled in the simple animal pleasure of just being alive, myself.

"Wait here," I said to Greg when we finally reached my house. The sky was sinking under its own weight. I knew in a glance there was no one home. The windows were dark; there was no car in the driveway.

"Hello?" I cried, like countless fools before me, into the empty darkness of the house. "Hello?" I closed the door behind me and breathed the familiar air of home, looking now at the old tavern table in the foyer to see if there was a note, or perhaps some interesting mail, and then at the diminutive chandelier, which Olivia said looked like an Edwardian earring, and which now shined a bleak, irregular light because two of its four Ping-Pong-ball-sized bulbs were dead. And then I saw the parlor walls.

At first I thought I was hallucinating. I switched on a lamp and stared at the walls, feeling sick, stranded.

Scrawled onto the walls were the gloomy, lost rantings of a soul in prison, a spirit catching the whiff of its own decay. At first I thought we'd been attacked by vandals, but then I recognized Olivia's writing—the demure U in "FUCK," the T with its hat blowing off in the wind in "NOTHING," the E's shaped like pitchforks in "HELP ME."

Some attempt had been made to clean away the damage. On the western wall, where the mahogany grandfather's clock stood and the nineteenth-century silhouettes of waterbirds hung in their barn-board frames, the explosion of scribbles and X's had been sponged to a smear, but the task had been abandoned.

I walked with real fear in my step. I heard the furnace straining in the cellar. The house was boiling hot and I turned the thermostat down from ninety to sixty-five. Somewhere within me, I realized that most of the life I had been living a month ago was now completely over, gone. My sense of myself as a man with some basic core of decency was evaporating; my son was missing, my wife had gone mad. . . .

I walked through the house. In the kitchen, I found a note from Olivia.

Dear Windsor Cleaning Service,

Do whatever is necessary to take care of the mess. We'll be gone for a couple of days, but I'll call your office this evening to see how things are going. Good luck!

Olivia Wexler

She was alive. I went upstairs and wrote her a note—"Where are you?"—and placed it on the pillows of our unmade bed, and, fighting back tears, got back into the Chariot of Fire. I offered Greg two hundred dollars to drive me to the airport. It was time to be John Retcliffe again, and I realized as we pulled away that after a day as Sam Holland, I was relieved to make the change.

chapter thirteen

n Columbus, Ohio, a nurse who was working in the West Side Women's Health Collective was bludgeoned to death by a young Elvis-haired "pro-life" activist who called himself Mr. Baby. He murdered her in the clinic's parking lot, got into his Nissan, and drove home, where he was arrested a few hours later. The cops found him in bed, dozing, and at his side was a copy of *Visitors from Above*, a detail that was repeated in nearly all the newspaper accounts of the crime. In Albuquerque, New Mexico, fifteen-year-old twin sisters leaped from the roof of their low-rise, adobe-style apartment building, wearing red dresses, holding in their long, skinny arms Boston terriers and copies of my book. Both survived the fall, and when they were interviewed they insisted, "We knew we wouldn't die." On the ABC nightly news, there was a thirty-second story headlined "Visitor Mania," in which the out-of-nowhere provenance of the book was commented upon, the lack of author photo, the possibility that John Retcliffe might be, for all we knew, a Man in Black. "To some, it is a book of prophecy, a guide to the upcoming apocalypse. As the second millennium draws to a close, we are likely to see more and more of this sort of thing," said the news reader. "And in the meanwhile, now as never before, it is Buyer Beware, as a whole new breed of charlatans prepares to take advantage of our cosmic jitters as we approach the year 2000."

After a one-day trip to L.A., I was back on the East Coast, going from mall to mall, radio station to radio station, moving south through Washington, Baltimore, and on down—Richmond, Norfolk, Greensboro, Charlotte. It was a tour out of the annals of the Benny Goodman Orchestra. The spring days went from mild to sultry; flowers I saw in full bloom one day would be decayed the next, two hundred miles south.

Heather was no longer on the case. I didn't know if she had herself transferred off because of some weariness with me or if, as her replacement, Phil Baz, said, she had a long-standing commitment to work on another account. Phil Baz was a stocky young kid with a moist, frantic face. He wore an Oscar Wilde suit, parted his hair in the middle; he smelled of Tic Tacs and garlic. He ran my tour as if we were a football team trying to mount a comeback in the final quarter: we were always racing for a plane, an interview; he sweated in traffic, tapped his feet frantically in elevators, thrust his fist up in the air and said "Yes!" whenever we arrived on time. I took to having most of my meals in my hotel room, to avoid having to eat with him, and at night, after trying to call Olivia, watching a little TV, trying to call Olivia again, and raiding the minibar, I often fell asleep obsessing pointlessly over how much I disliked him.

Even with trying to find my family, and being constantly on the move and having to go to book signings, press interviews, and radio programs as John Retcliffe, I found myself hitting air pockets of empty time that would send my spirits plummeting. I called the Leyden Police looking for news of my family. I called the Windsor Cleaning Service. I called Michael's school; I called Russ; circumspect to a fault, I called the Wexlers; I called Allen, Connie; I called, over and over, my own home. Cursing the unanswered phone and slamming the receiver down was better than the vortex of nothingness I experienced sitting alone in my room for the fifteen minutes before the car came to take me to the Crossgates Mall.

I needed to be doing something. I needed to eat, or watch TV. If there was a gymnasium at the hotel, I used it. If we were not stuck on some beltway, I walked. I went to movies, bars, nightclubs. I struck up conversations with strangers, something I'd never been able to do before, but now—behind my Retcliffian mask?—no problem. In fiercely air-conditioned southeastern bars, I held court, as voluble in my new incarnation as I had been reticent in my former life. I was insatiably curious about the lives of the shifty, middle-class drinkers around me. So what does your lawyer say? Maybe you need to see an orthopedist? So why don't you hang on to it until real-estate prices come back to their '88 level? Hey, this one's on me: what are you drinking?

Adding to what I will charitably call my loquaciousness was that law of emotional economy: Adversity Loosens the Tongue.

"I've got troubles at home," I told Ken, or Kip, or Kit.

"You and me both," K. said. He raised his stout eyebrows, as black as electrical tape.

"I had an affair. In fact, for a while, I fell in love—whatever the fuck that means. You know what I mean?"

"Tell me about it," K. said, in that way that means, When it comes to this particular subject, I've forgotten more than you'll ever know.

"My wife son daughter house life guilt anger fear."

"What are you drinking, John?"

"Too much."

"Tell me about it."

Now we were far from New York, and my publisher and Phil Baz convinced me it would be perfectly safe for me to make local TV appearances. We zigged west to Knoxville and I went onto a local show called "Tennessee Temptations," which was a half-hour things-to-do show hosted by a jovial woman in a Hawaiian shirt named Abby Carter. I no longer cared very much about showing my face on TV. My picture had already appeared in several newspapers. There was no way to control this any longer. And as for John Retcliffe somehow getting in the way if I wanted to do promotion for one of my own books—I realized I would never write a book under *my* name that became as successful as *Visitors*, and that I would never, ever want to.

I was on with a restaurant "critic," the new U. Tenn basketball coach, and another author, a handsome, unstable guy named Ed Bathrick, who had written a book of advice for people coping with an addiction to gambling. In the greenroom before going on—it was nine in the morning and we were live—I chatted with Bathrick.

"Dostoevsky was crazy about gambling," I said.

"I believe so," said Bathrick, rather noncommittally.

"The way he crawled across the floor and kissed his wife's feet until she gave him two more rubles for the roulette table. God, the poor man."

"The poor man?" asked Bathrick. "What about her?"

On the show, I heard Bathrick tell Abby Carter that in many marriages it was a battle between the better half and the bettor half. "John here," he said, jerking his thumb in my direction, practically putting my eye out, "tells me that the famous Count Leo Tolstoy and his lovely wife, um, Betty, I believe, had absolutely *horrendous* fights over his gambling addiction."

After the show, I used a phone in the greenroom; there was, as usual, no human answering at my house. I was really getting sick of that. Panic and guilt had fused and now were changing into hatred. I tried to think of someone else I could call who might know where Olivia and Amanda were, but there was no one: our old friends in New York were no longer really a part of our lives; our lives had gone north and crazy and down the drain without them.

Out of sheer obstinacy, I dialed Olivia again, first with the "It's me!" signal and then without it, and this time when my voice came on the answering machine I didn't hang up.

"Hey, it's me. Where are you? I'm worried. I'm in Knoxville and tonight I'll be in—in, oh shit, I don't know. Athens. At the Athena. Call me, okay? As soon as you get this message."

I hung up for a moment and then dialed Nadia's number. I had no idea why I was doing this or what I would say to her. But her answering machine came on and I hung up.

Then I did something I hadn't done in quite a while: I spontaneously called my father.

He answered halfway through the first ring. "Hello?" he said, through a knot of phlegm.

"Hi, Dad."

A silence, while he adjusted to the fact of me. Then: "Oh, Sam, it's you."

"Nice of you to say so."

More silence. I heard him sitting up in his bed, picking up the clock on his night table and checking the time—knowing the time had always made him think he had a handle on things, like knowing the name of the maître d'. Once, I would have rushed to fill the silence—said anything, asked anything, joked, informed, declared—but no more. It was one of the nice things about getting older: you got less cooperative.

"You're lucky you didn't take the John Retcliffe job," I said, finally. "It's grueling. It's just a fucking nightmare, really."

There was a silence on the other end—not a distracted one, but a wounded silence. To my vast annoyance, I felt something clutch within me and I wanted to ask the old man if he was all right.

"I'm all alone here," said Gil, after a few more moments. "I don't feel comfortable."

"Where . . . ?"

"Out. Out. She has an unquenchable thirst for social life. She goes to the theater three times a week. Breakfast seminars on investing. She swims. Back and forth, back and forth. Who knows who's been in that pool?"

"Well, then she'll come home and you won't be alone."

"Where are you now, Sam? Nearby?"

"Knoxville. Hey, Dad, I don't suppose you've heard from Olivia?" As I said this, I heard a click on his end of the line, signaling that he had another call coming in.

"Who? Wait, can you hold for a second?" he said.

There was something about being put on hold by my father that just didn't work for me, and when he went from my line to the other I hung up. I walked down the corridor, past the closed doors to the editing rooms, the sound stages, the utility closets, stepping over thick cables, hearing from somewhere a man singing along with a record of Ray Charles doing "Georgia on My Mind."

And before I knew it, I was in the actual Georgia, staying at a nice downtown hotel. It was filled with great-looking women and dumpy, loudmouthed men, but somehow the women didn't mind. Once my eyes adjusted to the gray-purple light of the cocktail lounge, I realized the women weren't so great-looking after all. I asked for a Scotch and water, took a handful of Pepperidge Farm Parmesan-flavored Goldfish, and had the strange but somehow compelling idea that I would like to get into a fistfight and spend a couple hours in the emergency room.

My room had a fabulous view of a wall, but it was a full suite, which was, God help me, flattering. There was a basket of peaches; the bathroom had white towels of every known size. There were telephone messages for me, though none from Olivia. One was from Graham Davis, who for the first time left his home number, and the other was from Ezra, who also honored me with his intimate residential digits. I called Graham first.

"I'm having a dinner for you, when you get back," he announced. "I've been meaning to for a long time. There's a hell of a lot of people I want you to meet—writers, publishers. . . . If you want, I can invite some of those girls who pose for the Calvin Klein panty adverts."

"I trust that means they've gone back to press on *Visitors*."

"For another hundred thousand copies. These grisly events are fueling visitor mania, especially those twins leaping off the roof."

"This dinner party, Graham—"

"Three weeks from tonight. After your western swing."

"My western swing?"

"California, Oregon, Washington. You know. Out there."

"Your party—"

"I'm going to do all the cooking myself."

"Will I be there as Sam Holland?"

A long silence, during which I imagined Graham regretting he had given me his home number, and calculating how much it would cost him to have it changed.

"Why don't we both think about that very interesting question?" Graham said.

"Actually, what would be the point? It's John Retcliffe who people are interested in meeting, right?"

"Don't get sulky, Sam. You don't get to make a fortune and sulk about it. Do you know how many authors I have who would kill their mothers for one-tenth of the sales you're enjoying? And I'm not talking about little nobodies from nowhere. I mean name authors, with reputations, prizes, the works."

"I'm curious, Graham. As you conceive of the party, do I stay in the Retcliffe mode throughout, or do I just call myself Retcliffe and act like Holland, or do I call myself Retcliffe and act like Retcliffe except, say, over dessert and coffee, at which point I reveal that I'm really Sam?"

"Let me simplify this for you, Sam. Why don't you and Olivia come over for dinner? I'll have Ezra and whoever Ezra is with these days and it'll just be cozy and you won't have to be plagued by these concerns."

I suppose I was meant to feel chastened, but all I felt was annoyance. I said goodbye, Graham offered his congratulations again, I said goodbye again, Graham wished me luck on my tour, and I said goodbye a third time and hung up.

Next, I called home again, got my machine, slammed the phone down. Not reaching Olivia on the telephone was now our sole means of communication.

Then I called Ezra. I was becoming one of those men in a hotel room, dialing numbers, hoping for someone to talk to.

I expected Ezra's apartment to be a place of tumult, but it was hushed in the room where he spoke to me, and his voice was soft, contemplative. Ezra was perhaps more of a rake during business hours than at home.

"I've got good news, Sam," he said, in a voice somewhere between a late-night disc jockey's and an unmedicated depressive's.

"I know, Graham told me."

"About the woman?"

"The woman?"

"Your friend. Natalie."

"Nadia."

"She's withdrawing her claim. Whatever you said to her, it did the trick."

"There was no trick. I'm all tricked out, Ezra."

"How much money did you offer her?"

"Money? None. We didn't even get that far."

"I'd feel better if she'd taken a payoff. Not that she deserved it or anything. Don't get me wrong. But it would just seem cleaner that way."

"Would it?"

"Oh, come on, Sam. Don't get self-righteous. You're the one who said we should have her killed."

It was around this time I began thinking of my mother. It started when I got to Florida.

In Miami, around ten in the morning, with a little free time before a noontime appearance at a bookstore in Coconut Grove, which would be followed by a radio broadcast from downtown Miami, I noticed something very disappointing: my hand, when it opened the door to my hotel room, did not seem attached to my body, did not seem to belong to me in any way.

I walked out of the hotel and along a beachside promenade, past the cafés and the beautifully coiffed coffee drinkers tan as wallets, who dressed to go with the decor of the art deco hotels in that part of town. The ocean was bright turquoise, the sky was pink and white; my heart seemed to be pounding downward, as if to excavate an escape route through my chest cavity and into my bowels.

There was so much wrong in my life, even the laws of triage could not help me decide what to attend to first—the disappearance of my son, the destruction of my marriage, the dissolution of my identity, Nadia, *Visitors*. Everything was an emergency.

Yet the odd thing was that it was my mother's timid, cringing, rather beautiful face that came into my consciousness, like a body long submerged in icy waters breaking the surface and floating into view. The lack of her, the loss of her, the feeling that I had failed to rescue her, had betrayed her, had through my silence, my ignorance and selfishness, contributed to the thanklessness of her life, made me realize that selfishness *is* ignorance, because if we knew how much people needed us and how much we needed to be needed, then we would not act for ourselves alone. It made me also realize that thanklessness is a torment as great as physical pain, and all of it, the speculation, the revelation, the grief, all of it made me wonder if everything of any emotional importance that would ever happen to me had already happened. "Mother," I whispered to myself. "Mama. Mama. I am so sorry."

But I could barely remember her. All I could really remember was my failing her. I could not remember the exact shade of brown in her eyes, the lines in her face. I could not remember the sound of her voice—I could more easily summon up the timbre and pronunciation of Phil Baz, or the hotel doorman who wished me a good day when I stumbled out into the bright Florida morning. My mother was denied me now in memory because I had denied her in life. I was without her; I was without my brother, Allen, whom I barely knew; I was without my sister; I could neither forgive nor tolerate my father; and so I had no first family to whom to return now that my second family was falling apart. My life was a long suicide.

Shaking, I went back to my hotel. There was a message to call Ezra, and after making my ritual call to Olivia I called him at work. He was in a meeting, but his assistant said, "He wanted me to give you this message. I don't really understand it—I wrote it down. Okay? 'Nadia called to say the baby is dead.' "

I wept in my bed until I fell asleep, and then, at noon, Phil took me to the bookstore in Coconut Grove, which was in an upscale mall with an immense, fancily filigreed cage in its center, inside of which screeched a thousand multicolored parrots.

We were met outside by the store manager, a seething, squared-off woman in khaki shorts and a Marlins T-shirt, and by a Wilkes and Green salesman who covered the South. After Phil introduced me, the salesman embraced me with wild enthusiasm, pressing his humid bulk against me and whispering into my ear, "I made my yearly nut on your book. You're the greatest."

Inside the store, there was a large crowd, mostly of the sort of people I was coming to expect—not for me the girls in their summer dresses, the sultry women in their black leotards, the grad students with pulsating eyes, the latter-day bohos in berets. No, my readers had casts on their feet, Ace bandages on their ankles, patches on their eyes; they received radio signals through the fillings in their teeth; they needed to lose weight, gargle; they had lost their meager inheritances in pyramid schemes; they wouldn't mind selling you mail-order shoes or Amway kitchen cleansers; they rattled around the country on secondary roads where the gas and food were cheaper; they tested their cellars for radon; they called the Culligan Man; they watched the Christian Broadcasting System; they looked for stores that still sold eight-track tapes; they lived near electric-power-line towers the size of the Washington Monument; they had guns.

I sat at a table and signed their books, listened to their stories. "Sign it 'To Buster' and say 'See you on the other side,' " one demanded, and "Do you worry about assassination?" asked another, his mustache twitching, his teeth flashing.

A line of at least fifty people snaked through the store. Some had come to view me totemistically and to see all the money I had made, which I would represent in their eyes. Those who did not come to be near the money wanted to share their visions of apocalypse, of the interstellar goings-on, cosmic hijinks, conspiracies of silence that went to the very highest reaches of the Senate, the Air Force, the Pentagon, the Trilateral Commission. And some came to further decode my book, to devise textual analyses that were rather more alarming than my own tabloid assertions: predictions of planes tumbling from the heavens, which they garnered by reading every other vowel on every fifth page, or visions of the Last Days, which they discovered by reading the book backwards in some serpentine fashion I could never follow—something about finding the first repeated word and reading the word to its immediate left.

I was seated in the middle of the store, with the cookbooks on one side of me and the diet books on the other. I had been provided with a pitcher of water, a University of Florida beer stein, and three black felt-tipped pens. The doors to the book shop remained open; somewhere from the mall's center court came the sound of a grammar-school band—snare drums, trumpets, and trombones—playing "Chim Chim Cheree" so slowly that it sounded like a Sicilian funeral march.

Yet stranger still was this: every few minutes my spirits would unaccountably lift and the act of selling and signing all these books would make me practically laugh with happiness. Olivia once told me about a lover she had in college, a boy named Ted, who, when he came, giggled—"like a little boy who's just gotten away with something," said Olivia. I don't suppose my laughter had much more dignity than Ted's, but for a moment the relentless, ridiculous realities of my life would fall away and I would be filled with a kind of nasty, larcenous pleasure at being away from everything, having a false name, and making a lot of money. But when this pleasure subsided, usually after a minute or so, I would find myself even more lost than before, as if grief were my only anchor and to cut it away for even a moment allowed me to drift still further out into the fog and treachery of the open seas.

"Hello there," said a woman, placing her book in front of me. Her hands were well tanned; she wore a large ruby ring.

I looked up and saw Olivia. I stared at her. And then I realized it was not Olivia but her older sister, Elizabeth. I hadn't seen her in two years; she had been living with a much older man, a professor of classics at Duke University, and then the professor fell in love with a young student and Elizabeth went to Greece, where she visited the sites she and Professor Swann had so vividly discussed during their love affair. Now, she stood before me, in a brightly striped shirt, a wheat-colored skirt, a look of wounded self-possession on her face. She had become melancholy, as only a failed romantic can be; she was going through the paces of life, expecting little but bound to the rituals by some vague hope—she was living the way a lapsed Catholic prays.

"Elizabeth! What are you doing in Florida?"

"Hello . . . John," she said.

"We *are* in Florida, aren't we?"

"I made a friend when I was in Crete and she lives with her children in Key Biscayne. They're going to take me swimming with the dolphins."

Over the years, Olivia had made so much of the fact that she and I had met through Elizabeth and that Elizabeth and I had been well suited for each other that, by now, I had almost come to remember that Elizabeth and I had once been lovers.

"This is great," I said. "Can you wait around? Maybe we can have a drink or something?"

"A drink?"

"Coffee."

She looked at her watch, a Cartier with diamonds around its oval face. I had no idea where she got her money. No university job could have given her enough money to pay for that watch.

"How long will you be?" she asked. "I'm supposed to meet Ricey."

"Ricey?"

"My new friend, from Crete." She laughed, a merry but absentminded laugh. There were lines around her eyes. She'd been getting a lot of sun.

I looked to see how much was left of the line. There were just a few more people, ten at the most.

"Have you heard from Olivia lately?" I asked her, hoping to sound casual.

"No. Is everything okay?"

"Ten minutes," I said. "I have to go to a radio interview, but I have time for a coffee—if you do."

"This is so exciting, isn't it? I'm really very happy for you."

"Well, that's nice of you. Can you wait?"

"If you sign my book."

I opened it to the title page and crossed out the "Retcliffe" and encircled the "John," drawing an arrow to what I then wrote: "In the beginning was the Word and the Word was God."

She accepted the book without reading my inscription. "I'll be in the nature section looking for a book about dolphins," she said.

I went through the rest of my readers quickly, until I came to a Man in Black. He was tall, aged from thirty to fifty, so pale it was hard to believe there was blood in his veins. His large eyes fixed on me but gave no flicker of attentiveness. His hands were as large as my feet. He hadn't bought a book.

"You must be careful," he said. He pressed himself against the folding table at which I sat; he seemed to be deliberately making genital–card table contact.

"Careful?" I asked. "How so?"

"You have been warned," he said. And then slowly he raised his right hand and held it before me, as if I were meant to inspect it, to see if it exceeded regulation size.

I found Elizabeth in the nature section; time was short, so we went to a Burger King in the mall. We ordered the coffee but dared not drink it. We sat in a booth; the table was damp and stank of disinfectant. Phil Baz, who did not let me out of his sight, sat by himself at a table, near an immense old woman in a sundress who wore a button that suggested, ASK ME ABOUT MY GRANDSON! She tried to engage Phil in conversation and quickly succeeded.

"I can't believe I'm meeting you down here," said Elizabeth. "This is just so weird."

"You look wonderful, Elizabeth."

"I do?"

"Yes. Ravishing. In fact—I want you."

She smiled uncertainly; my little jest hadn't worked very effectively.

"Sorry," I said. "I'm losing track of what I can and can't say. So. How'd you know I was down here?"

"It was in the *Miami Herald*."

"But how'd you know it was—"

"Mommy told me." She smiled; it embarrassed her to call her mother Mommy, but she could not break the habit.

"Mommy knows?" I said in mock horror.

Elizabeth laughed. "Yes, and Daddy knows, too."

"They must be thoroughly disgusted."

"Why do you say that?"

"They're academicians, for Christ's sake. They sat at Max Schachtman's bedside while he died and told stories of the great Teamsters strike in Minneapolis. They're principled and rational—and now their son-in-law is traveling around the country pretending to be someone else, flogging a book about flying saucers."

"First of all, they both have open minds—"

"Elizabeth! Nothing in my book is true!" I looked around and then lowered my voice. "Nothing."

"It's just a job, Sam."

"And this name I've taken for myself. It's the same name the guy used who wrote the *Protocols of the Elders of Zion*."

She looked at me blankly; I wasn't sure she knew what I was talking about.

"He just wrote it for money," I whispered. I sounded awfully fucked up, even to myself. "He got paid by the page, you know. Half the time, he just wrote whatever popped into his head. And then look what happened!"

"What happened?" Elizabeth had always been aggressively uninterested in anything political, and the only history she liked was ancient—if it didn't involve myths, chalices, and togas, it wasn't for her.

"The Holocaust."

"Do you think your book can—"

"Did *he*?"

"Who?" She leaned back, as if my breath was bad. (In fact, there was a kind of heavy metal taste at the back of my throat.)

"John Retcliffe. He meant no harm. From what we know of his life, he bore the Jews no particular grudge. He was just a Polish postal worker. He probably didn't know any Jews, he probably never laid eyes on one. Like me and creatures from deep space. The Men in Black."

"The Men in Black don't exist, do they?"

"But the Jews did."

"I know, Sam. That's what I'm saying."

"But that's what I'm saying, too. It's all so fucked up. I wrote something that wasn't true and now it's out there. And people are paying attention to it."

"You can't blame yourself for that."

"Really? Who should I blame? You?"

"Maybe no one needs to be blamed. Maybe the whole idea of blame doesn't really make sense."

"Yeah, maybe."

"I mean it, Sam. You don't look well."

"I hate to interrupt . . ." said Phil, who had drifted over to our table without my seeing him. He tapped his wristwatch.

"Just a few more minutes, Phil. By the way, this is my sister-in-law, Elizabeth Wexler. Phil's keeping me company while I flog my book hither and yon."

"I work for the firm in charge of his publisher's publicity," Phil said, apparently wishing to correct any possible impression that he and I were friends. I heard the edge of disdain in his voice. Really, it was like stepping on a rake: I just hadn't stopped to consider the possibility that Phil might dislike *me*.

I watched him as he left and then turned back to Elizabeth, with greatly renewed urgency.

"Are you sure you haven't heard from Olivia?" I asked her, reaching across the table, touching her hand.

"Not since coming back. She wrote to me in Greece. Why? Is everything okay?"

I shook my head no.

"What's wrong?" Elizabeth asked. "Did she get into trouble with that antiques business of hers?"

"We're having relationship problems."

Elizabeth let out her breath, as if relieved. Were all the Wexlers expecting Olivia to run afoul of the law because of her fast dealings with pack-rat country widows?

"I'm sorry to hear that, Sam."

"I've been trying to get in touch with her."

"Where is she?"

"That's the thing. I don't know. I went to the house and she wasn't there. There were signs of a lot of commotion. I know she's okay. She left a note. But she and Amanda are gone."

"What kind of commotion?"

"Writing on the wall."

"Like the saying?"

"No. Real writing on a real wall."

"What was written?"

"I don't know. It had been mostly washed off."

She looked at me. I could feel her leg jiggling under the table.

"Where are the children?" said Elizabeth.

"Amanda's with her. I know they're safe. It's not about that."

"Sam—"

"You don't understand. I'm very worried. She's not taking my calls. And that's not the half of it."

"You two should never have left New York. I knew it, when you moved to that little town. What business do either of you have in a place like that?"

"I couldn't afford to stay in New York."

"Well, now you can."

"Except I don't have anyone to move there with. Olivia isn't speaking to me. And Michael has disappeared." I didn't give her a chance to say anything about it. "Look, Elizabeth, my life has fallen to pieces."

"*Your* life? What about Olivia's? What about Michael's? Where is he? What kind of trouble is he in?"

"I don't know. It's all worked in to the problems between Olivia and me. We know he's alive and all that. He calls in from time to time. We just don't know where he is." My face was scalding; I felt the pressure of tears against my eyes.

Elizabeth remained silent. She touched the surface of her coffee with her fingertip. She bowed her head. Vigorous strands of gray hair ran alongside her center part. She studied the spermlike squiggles on the Formica table. When she lifted her head again to face me, her eyes were stark.

"You know, Sam, when Olivia married you, we all felt you would take such good care of her."

"Oh, give me a fucking break. Who am I? King Arthur?"

"You just gave the impression of being aware of what was best."

"Being aware is one thing, being able to do it is another."

"Are you having an affair, is that it? This 'commotion,' these 'relationship problems'?"

I had already passed by my chances to tell Olivia the truth, but perhaps I could confess by proxy if I leveled with Elizabeth. Yet I could not say the words. The words themselves could not be uttered.

"No," I said. "That's *not* it. It's . . . very complicated." In the beginning was the Word and the Word was Bullshit.

At last, Baz could no longer contain himself. I was about to miss my interview, and this could not be permitted—this would affect *him*, his sense of well-being, his job, the next installment in the incredible saga that was his life. "You're going to miss your interview!" he said, his voice rising.

"I sort of like what Samuel Beckett said to Plimpton," I said leisurely, "when George was trying to cajole him into giving a *Paris Review* interview. Beckett said, 'I have no views I wish to inter.' "

"That's very funny," said Baz. "Maybe on the way to the radio station you can tell me who Samuel Beckett is. But I'll tell you one thing right now—I feel very sorry for his publicist."

I said goodbye to Elizabeth—"Tell Olivia I love her!" I shouted back at her as Baz gave me the bum's rush out of Burger King.

In San Antonio, my book was selling more than all other hardcover books combined. It was particularly popular with the men and women in the nearby Air Force base, many of whom had been appearing on radio and TV before we arrived, telling of their own experiences with unexplained heavenly phenomena. (What I would like them to explain is why, when they roam around San Antonio's demure, rather poky downtown area, the whites walk on one side of the street and the blacks on the other. They're fooling around with too much expensive equipment to behave like that.) After San Antonio, I went to Austin, Houston, and then Dallas. The money was pouring in, but there was no one to spend it; the home phone was ringing, but there was no one to pick it up.

In the beginning was the Word and the Word was Madness.

chapter fourteen

We flew up from Dallas to Chicago, where, at the Four Seasons, a half-hour before leaving for the WGN studios, where I was going to be on something called "Chicagoland Confidential," I called Olivia, and to my immense surprise Michael answered the phone.

He picked it up right after the second ring; the answering machine came on, too. "Wait," he said, shouting over the sound of my recorded voice. "Wait."

In the beginning was the Word and the Word was Wait.

"Michael?" I shouted, gripping the phone with one hand, grabbing my hair with the other. I was standing at the window, looking down at Michigan Avenue. Rain lashed the streets; the sidewalks were empty except for one figure dressed in black, walking with his shoulder to the wind.

"I've got it!" I heard him calling, his mouth away from the phone. I heard Olivia's voice in the background, sounding displeased. "Well, I picked it up," he said to her. "Hello?" he said, to me.

"Michael, it's me."

"Dad!" I could hear, feel the distress in his voice. The first D was high, piping; the vowel wavered unstably; and then the word ended in a hoarse, strangulated sound.

"How are you?" I asked.

"Well, I'm back, if that's what you mean."

I closed my eyes, sat on the edge of the bed. So then it was true; it had all happened.

"When did you come back? Are you all right? God, Michael . . ."

"Oh, Dad. Dad."

"What happened?"

"I've got to get to the hospital. Mom won't even take me."

"What happened to you?"

"We got caught trying to rob the Connelly house."

" 'We'?"

"Walter Fraleigh, this guy who used to work for Mr. Connelly. He lives in the woods."

"He lives in the woods? What woods?"

"Not anymore. I don't know where he is. He's gone, he ran away. He's really an asshole, Dad."

A silence. I tried to put together what was being said to me. Michael took a deep breath; I realized he was crying.

"Are you hurt?" I asked. "Tell me what happened. Please."

"My girlfriend got shot."

"Your girlfriend? Is that why you ran away?"

"Don't you know anything?"

"I guess not."

"Didn't you talk to Mom?"

"Not for a while."

"She didn't call you?"

"No." Then, worrying that I was contradicting a lie she had told him, I amended it to "I don't think so. Maybe she left a message I didn't get. I've just been going from place to place."

"Her name is Carmen," he said. "Mr. Connelly shot her. And then he just stood there, staring at us and shaking all over. Johnnie and I got her out of there and put her into the car. I sat with her in the back. She looked at me the whole way and I was screaming like crazy for Fraleigh to drive faster, I could see the life going out of her eyes—"

"Michael—"

"He drove us to the hospital. Fraleigh stopped by the emergency room entrance and I pulled Carmen out of the car. 'You and that nigger can forget you ever saw me,' he said, and then he and Johnnie took off and left us there."

"Oh God, Michael. I'm so sorry."

He had been waiting to hear it, and to hear it from me. The spur in my voice was all the permission he needed, and a moment later his sobs rushed into my ear. It was intolerable that I could not touch him, hold him to me.

"Are you coming home, Dad?"

"Of course I am. Soon—as soon as I can. Right away."

Then I heard a break in the line. "Michael?" It was Olivia, sounding stressed, sour.

"I'm on the phone, Mom," he said.

"Lunch is ready."

"It's me," I said. "I'm in Chicago."

Olivia did not respond. She was recovering from the fact of me. I heard the click of one of the extensions hanging up.

"Hello?" I said, hoping not to sound too frantic.

"Hello," she said.

"Where have you been?" I said.

"Where have *I* been?"

"I've been calling. Every day, for I don't know how long. I went to the house, there was nobody home."

"I wasn't here."

"Okay. Where have you been?"

"Poughkeepsie."

"Poughkeepsie? What were you doing there?"

"Lunch is ready, Sam. I have to go. Maybe we can talk later."

"Olivia, I miss you so much. My soul cries out for you."

"Give me a break," she said, but I could tell she was pleased—or at least unrepelled.

"How's Amanda?"

"She's in a play. She wrote a play with her friend Elektra and the school is putting it on next month."

"You're kidding me."

"It takes place in Barcelona; it's about thieves."

"Barcelona. I didn't even know she knew where Barcelona was."

"She said, 'If Daddy can write about outer space, I can write about Spain.'"

"Olivia," I said.

She did not answer. And for the first time in a long while I did not flail at the silence. The silence was what I wanted her to say.

"Are you ever coming back here?" she said, finally. "Your children miss you."

"Is Michael okay?"

"Physically, yes."

"Where did you find him? Was it the detective?"

Outside, the rain poured down as if from high-pressure hoses. I turned away, sat on the bed.

"No. He came back on his own."

"This girlfriend thing—"

"We can't talk about it now."

"He's nearby?"

"Yes."

"Listening to every word?"

"That's right."

I closed my eyes. I could see them there.

"I am astonished that Mandy wrote a play. Maybe she'll be a writer, a real writer."

"Like her father."

"I wish."

"It's time to come home, Sam."

Baz managed to get me to the WGN studios, not far from the hotel. Since convincing me to go on TV in Knoxville, Baz had gotten me into several television appearances. In the elevator going up to the studios, Baz told me that tapes of my local appearances had gotten into the hands of the networks and now there was no reason why I shouldn't agree to go on national shows.

"This is it for me," I told Baz. "I'm going back home after this show."

"You can't do that," said Baz.

"We'll see about that, Phil."

Makeup and then into the greenroom, where I joined Robert Redford, who was on tour promoting a new scholarship fund for minority filmmakers. He was reading *Eleven Kinds of Loneliness*, a book of stories by Richard Yates; his blue eyes looked strained and weary behind his donnish half-frames. He glanced at Baz and me as we came in, to see if he knew us, and then returned to his book. He frowned as he read. His skin was rough; his face was a Wells Fargo pouch filled with his contracts and reviews, his citations, divorce papers, honorary degrees. There was something blessed and enchanted about him; a man-boy in his pastel sweater, his thick, coppery arm hair curling over the leather band of his watch. His hands were sun-spotted; as he turned the page, he sniffed back a bit of postnasal drip.

I sat on the other side of the room, even though he was near the mineral water, Brie and crackers, and seedless ruby grapes that suddenly looked so appealing. I didn't want him to think I was snacking as a way of being close to him. He recrossed his legs as he read; there were little grape stems on the floor near him, looking like bitten-off nerve endings.

I watched Redford read. He looked at his watch, turned

the page. There was a purity to him, a sense of the great American hopefulness. I wondered what it would be like to know him. If he was reading Richard Yates, he was wandering rather far from standard reading. I wondered, could not help but do so, if he had ever looked at anything I had written. And then, before I could censor myself, I heard myself saying, "Excuse me."

He looked up, smiled.

"How's the book?"

He looked at the book and then back at me. "Amazing," he said.

"I read it, a long time ago."

"I'm reading the story called 'A Glutton for Punishment,' " he said.

"You want to know something? I know I read the book, but, unfortunately, I can't remember a thing about it." I laughed. I had somehow stumbled upon the idea that when famous media figures met, they liked to share their shortcomings.

"Are you a speed reader?" Redford asked.

"No, just forgetful. Tell me, have you ever read Sam Holland?"

Redford squinted up at the ceiling. It was clear he had never heard of me, but he seemed a little defensive about it; being a sex symbol might have made him a little touchy about his education.

"Fiction or nonfiction?"

"Oh, fiction," I said.

He seemed truly distressed. What did he expect—to have memorized the Library of Congress catalog?

"He's not very well known," I said, hoping to comfort him. "His books aren't even in print."

Just then the door opened, and one of the "Chicagoland Confidential" production assistants poked his prematurely bald, round-as-a-cue-ball head in. "You'll be going on in a few moments, Mr. Redford." Then: "Just sit tight, Mr. Retcliffe, okay? You'll be going on right after Mr. Redford."

Redford put his book down in his linen lap. "Retcliffe? John Retcliffe? The author?"

"I don't really think of myself as an author," I said.

"Well, you'll get no argument from me on that one," he said.

"Look—"

"One of my ranch hands is reading your book about the Men in Black. He's circling the key words and drawing arrows all over the pages. And in the meanwhile, I just lost one of my best barrel horses because this clown is up all night quaking under his army blanket, waiting for some creature with three heads to fly into his cabin."

"I don't think you can blame my book for that. I'm sorry about the horse, though."

"You guys. Ever hear of working for a living?"

"I *am* working for a living, *Bob*. And if you don't like what I do, then too bad. I wasn't exactly transported by what you did to *The Great Gatsby*."

Knock, knock. The door opened. Bald-headed assistant, this time with "Chicagoland" host Irwin Carr, a tall, sleek fellow with an underslung jaw, long nose, piercing eyes; he looked like a guy with a finger in a lot of pies—a string of rib joints, a Cadillac dealership in the ghetto.

"Mr. Redford!" he said, heartily, as if just having sold him a parcel of Florida swamp land. "Do me the honor of allowing me to escort you to my humble set!"

Redford followed Carr out of the room, and I moved to where he had been sitting, where I feasted on cheese and grapes. In Miami, there was crabmeat in the greenroom; in Houston they had chicken wings and a blue-cheese dip. Here, the Brie was cool and tasteless and the grapes were warm, soft, as if Redford had roughed up the ones he hadn't eaten.

There was madness in the carpet. I dug the toe of my shoe into the rug's gray weave and wrote my real name—I was writing it large, and in order to finish my last name I had to stretch my leg so far I practically slid out of my chair.

The door opened and in walked Ed Bathrick, hot on my heels in his promotional tour for the book he had written about compulsive gamblers. He wore a T-shirt that showed a man on one side and a woman on the other; the letters said, THE BETTER HALF VERSUS THE BETTOR HALF. He looked at me sprawled in my chair and tried to remember where he had seen me before.

"Hello there," I said, not bothering to sit up.

Eventually, I was escorted to the set, with its cushy orange chairs, the skyline painted on hinged panels behind Carr's desk. The main camera was being run by a woman in shorts and combat boots. The audience sat in folding chairs; they seemed an unusually raucous group—whistlers, booers, cat-callers, many of them with tough faces, hard faces, strongly scented hair gel. Redford had already hightailed it out of there; the seat he had used was still wrinkled and warm.

"So level with me, John," said Carr, holding my book and moving it up and down, as if he was trying to guess how much it weighed. "What does *Visitors from Above* have to do with Chicago?"

Was it then, or significantly before, that I took final leave of my senses? Was it then that the laws of cause and effect seemed antique, outmoded, and that I began to "think" that if I were to fall off my chair and curl into a fetal position on the carpet that it would be no big deal? Was it then that my heart became a frightened animal and my tongue first felt cold, sour, and metallic, like a soup spoon?

"Chicago?" I said, according to the videotape.

"I've often wondered," said Carr, "why is it that the people who see flying saucers and things always live in Armpit, Arkansas? How come no smart Jewish surgeons on the Gold Coast?"

"What's so smart about surgeons on the Gold Coast?"

"Do you have to believe in these things in order to be contacted? Is that the deal?"

"I don't think so."

"You don't *think* so?" He looked out at the camera, made a droll face.

It was then that I noticed Carr was dressed in black.

"Are you trying to discredit me?" I asked him. "Because if you are—let me make it easy for you. My book is a piece of shit. Okay? I wish people would stop buying it, stop referring to it, stop, stop, I just want the whole thing to stop."

"Now look here, John—"

"Don't call me that! Please."

"Okay. What would you prefer? Mr. Retcliffe?"

"Fuck." I closed my eyes. Lowered myself into the bat cave of self. I felt calm. It seemed my body temperature had dropped twenty degrees, pleasantly so. And then I noticed that not only was I cooler but the studio had gotten darker. I looked up. All of the bright lights had been turned off and the camera operator was standing near her camera, with her arms folded over her chest, looking at me and shaking her head. Irwin Carr was standing behind his desk; stagehands were milling around; the audience was talking among themselves; Phil Baz was approaching me from the wings. It was all too silly, too much. I closed my eyes again.

And then, the very next thing I was aware of was O'Hare Airport, where I was alongside an elderly airport security guard watching my carry-on bag through the screen of the X-ray machine. I saw the greenish skeleton of what I owned. Hundreds of flights had been canceled because of the bad weather—a late-spring storm had flapped north from the Gulf of Mexico. Only one runway was working; I was told if I ran I could catch the plane to New York, which left from Gate 6 in a few minutes. I ran, with my suitcase, which I had somehow managed to pack, in one hand, and my ticket, which I had managed to buy, in the other.

The plane was sold out. Half the passengers were from other canceled flights; all were willing to brave the high winds and turbulence. The stewardesses walked quickly up and down the aisle, paying more attention than usual to our seat belts. We took off into gusts of headwinds; we bumped over successive currents of wind. The engines were straining. The stewardesses were double-strapped into their pull-down seats, their faces blank, rigid as mummies. You had the feeling at least one of them was deciding on a career change.

"Good afternoon, ladies and gentlemen . . ." someone in the cockpit said. I, of course, felt perfectly calm. Airline safety was not on my mind.

I fell asleep while we were still climbing. The jet fought gravity and nosed its way upward through surging clouds, and I dreamed I was kissing Olivia while the phone was ringing. I woke for a moment, feeling exhausted, unstable, unclean. I felt my jacket for my wallet, poked my foot beneath the seat in front of me to make sure my bag was still there. And then I fell asleep again, for over an hour. I seemed to be speaking to myself as I slept, a dream of soliloquy. I told myself I was going home. I said, "The first thing you must do is hold the children." I was dimly aware of shifting in my seat, banging into the people who sat on either side of me. But nevertheless I slept, and would have slept even longer had not the man sitting to my left—a florid, high-school coach of a guy in a sky-blue nylon windbreaker, the kind who carefully shaves in the airport bathroom and then has a couple quick beers before the flight, one of those hard-living, not quite well-meaning men who go up and over the hill too fast for their own good—grabbed my arm and shook me awake.

"We're starting to crash," he said, his blue eyes wild with panic.

"Where are we?" I asked him.

"I don't know," he said in his Mel Torme whisper. "But the pilot's trying to land and we can't get down through the storm."

Where had he gotten his voice? Is this what he came up with after a few people told him he was speaking too gruffly, that he was shouting in people's faces?

I rubbed my eyes, tried to wake up. I was aware that he had just told me we were going to crash, but the information was taking time sinking in.

I tried to look out the window, which was to my right. Sitting on that side of me was a long-faced, ectoplasmic guy dressed in an old-fashioned black suit. He was wispy bearded, hollow eyed; he looked like an Amish junkie. He kept his bony hands folded in his lap; though his hands were as smooth as ivory, his bony wrists were darkly furred. A Man in Black! Had I run so far only to come to this place? He did not look at me. His mouth was a straight, unexpressive line. If this plane was going down, it did not so much as make him blink.

"Would you mind if I asked you a question?" I said to him.

What did I need to know? Was I going to ask him if he had deliberately sat next to me on this flight, or if he had followed me? Was I going to ask if he was a part of a (nascent) disinformation campaign trying to discredit my book? Or if he was in fact a visitor from another planet, another galaxy—what the hell, another dimension (why be a piker in these matters?)? Are you by any chance from a parallel universe?

But in fact I asked him none of these questions; I asked him nothing. He did not respond to my initial request, and a moment later the plane hit a pocket of air that seemed as intransigent as cement. The plane jerked up and to the left and suddenly the oxygen masks came dancing down like marionettes.

No one told us what to do; I looked up and down the aisle and saw only a few passengers putting on their masks. I held mine to my nose and sniffed at it. It smelled of plastic and cold chemicals.

Finally, a voice came over the public address system. It told us to ignore the oxygen masks. "Please stay in your seats with your seat belts securely fastened until we get out of this choppy air."

" 'Choppy air'?" said the florid fellow to my left. "We've been circling for the past fifteen minutes." He showed me his digital watch. The numbers were a blur.

Then another voice came on, this time the pilot's. "Ahhh, we're waiting for clearance to land at Buffalo Airport," he said, and even over the PA I could sense the frightened boy that existed at the core of his Right Stuff voice. "In the meanwhile, we'll just have to sit tight."

All I could see through the window was surging gray waves of cloud; it was as if we were flying under water.

No one cried out, no one spoke. I heard the sound of thick cold air running over the top of the plane. Pebbles of sleet scratched at the steel. There was an odd sense of lightness at the bottom of us. It felt as if a hole had opened up for us to fall through. The once-neat cabin was suddenly disheveled. Newspapers were strewn in the aisles, pillows on the floor. The light was weak, green, and gloomy. The sharp chemical smell of the toilets was in the air.

My eyes, sharpened by dread, now noticed how cheap and tasteless, how makeshift and bottom-line-obsessed everything about this plane was—the tacky carpeting, the welfare-office wall coverings, the cut-price chairs, the flimsy plastic ceilings. Why weren't they thinking about us when they made this plane? But why wasn't I thinking about my family when I made love to Nadia? Why wasn't I thinking about the power of lies when I wrote that book?

I wrote it for money, just as they had built this plane for money, and flown it during a storm. Yet the people who owned the airline were big-time capitalists. They cornered markets, they kissed and then kicked OPEC's ass. All I wanted to do was pay for my kid's shrink appointments; I wanted to plant some tea roses around the house; I wanted to be able to order a nice bottle of wine with dinner without anxiety ruining the whole meal. Was that such a crime?

Evidently.

Beyond the windows, the jet engines struggled mightily. I heard them groaning in agony. It brought back my father's voice to me, when he was in a small production of *King Lear* and night after night he rehearsed the dying Gloucester, pressing his notion that death on stage must be as horrifyingly real as real death, full of gasps and gruesome animal noise.

Braving the turbulence, several passengers staggered rubber-leggedly to the front of the cabin to use the GTE Air Phones to say goodbye to loved ones.

The nearness of death had a clarifying effect on me. I was not nearly so insane as I had been when I first boarded this jet. Still, I could not help but speculate as to why I, who had made such a tidy sum speculating about strange skyward occurrences, would be meeting my end in the sky. And why would it have to happen sitting next to this waxy man in black?

Had we been pulled into the force field of some UFO squadron? Was I dreaming?

I reached for my carry-on bag. The plane shuddered; I hit my head against the seat in front of me. I opened and poked through my bag and finally pulled out my copy of *Visitors*. I didn't know what I was doing; I could neither meditate nor premeditate. I simply opened the book and poked my finger onto the page. "Hidden." I blindly opened to another page and pointed randomly again. "Travelers." Ah: hidden travelers. It seemed to want to mean something. I repeated the process and came up with "flood." Next was "Palenque." What the hell was Palenque? Oh yes, that Aztec ruin in the Yucatán, with the carving of what could be construed as an interplanetary commuter at the controls of a spacecraft. Well, that probably didn't mean anything. Drop "Palenque" and go on to the next word. Flutter through the pages, jab onto— "vast." Again: "flash." Again: "in." Fuck the prepositions. Again: "aloneness." All right. "Hidden travelers flood vast flash"—okay, use the preposition—"in aloneness."

I felt my spirits soar. My soul had wings, and it was content to glide within my body like a hawk riding the thermals. We were going to be okay. I felt warm with relief, a human cup of herbal tea. Life! It would continue, and I'd be right there in it! I closed the book, looked at the cover, and then put it into the seat pocket in front of me, along with the in-flight magazine, the safety instructions, and the air-sickness bag.

"Don't worry," I said to the jock at my left, "we're going to be all right."

He looked at me as if I were mad, but he was glad to hear it as well. I patted his arm. He looked at my hand as it touched him, and then his eyes met mine and we smiled.

"I'm really scared," he said. "I think I'm going to blow my lunch."

"Don't worry. We're in good hands."

I felt so magnanimous, I even turned to the man in black. "You okay?" I asked.

He stared straight ahead, silent. At last, he nodded: yes.

. . .

I arrived in Leyden near midnight. With the limo waiting at the bottom of my driveway, I stood on my porch, wondering how to get in, until I realized I had the key.

I opened the door, turned, waved goodbye to the driver, Jake, with whom I had been talking for the past eight hours—he'd driven me all the way from Buffalo.

Inside, I breathed the aromas of home—butter, paint, carpet, wood. Popcorn. I put my bag down and walked into the living room. A clear glass bowl of popcorn, half-full, was on the coffee table, along with three tall glasses with a little soda in each. Olivia and the kids had been watching a movie together.

I poured myself a drink, waited for someone to awaken and find me there. But my family slept deeply.

I opened the refrigerator. The remains of a roasted chicken was on a platter. I broke off a wing, ate it. Home.

I stepped on the pedal and opened the trash can, dropped the chicken bone in with my family's garbage.

The kitchen window was open. The night air was warm, filled with the yearning peeps of the tree frogs. In the beginning was the Word and the Word was Peep Peep Peep.

I went to my study off the kitchen. A huge stack of mail was piled on my writing table. I picked up pieces at random—subscription notices, Save the Children, Guatemala Watch, Authors Guild. I let them fall from my hands. I turned on my typewriter; it was silent for a long moment and then came to with a rasping hum. I quickly shut it off.

I sat on the sofa in the living room and finished the popcorn, drank the dregs of each of their sodas.

Finally, I gathered the courage to go upstairs. I took off my shoes, walked as quietly as I could. The floorboards creaked and I stopped, gripped the banister, listened.

The bedroom doors were all shut. I touched the walls. Home. The word filled me like a second beating heart.

I opened Michael's door, looked in. The moon shined in

the mirror above his dresser. He slept on his stomach, his feet poking out from beneath his blanket. I didn't dare walk in. He looked safe. I stood there, watching him sleep.

Next, I looked in at Amanda. As usual, she was on her back, her hands resting on the satiny border of her blanket, her lips parted.

Finally, I opened my bedroom door. The reading light on Olivia's side was on, and she was propped up in bed, looking directly at me.

"Oh," I said.

"Oh," she said, imitating me.

I didn't know if I should move toward her. I stood in the doorway. I was returned to where I most belonged in the world, yet I could no sooner put my arms around Olivia than I could embrace a stranger, a woman in another country.

"I was trying to be quiet downstairs."

"This house carries sound."

"Sorry."

"The phone's been ringing all night. Are you all right?"

"Yes." I closed the door behind me.

"Ezra called . . . this . . . Bill Baz."

"Phil."

"Everyone wants to know where you are."

"I'm right here. Is that okay?"

"What happened in Chicago?"

"I quit."

"Why?"

I shrugged. "I wanted to come home."

"They were talking nervous breakdown."

"No."

"They're very worried."

"Don't worry."

She reached over and switched off the lamp. I heard her sliding down in the bed, arranging the pillows.

"It's so late."

" 'Midway in our life's journey, I went astray from the straight road and awoke to find myself in a dark wood,' " I said.

"Sam. Please. It's late. And I'm exhausted. Michael was in tears all day."

"Why?"

"Carmen."

By now, my eyes had adjusted to the darkness. I saw Olivia flat in the bed beneath the diamond-patterned summer quilt, the slight rise of her breasts, the hollow where her legs were parted. She slept in the center of the bed.

"My plane landed in Buffalo," I said.

"I know. We've been following you every inch of the way. All of us."

I breathed deeply; the breath caught in my throat, snapped like a frozen twig. They'd been up there with me. It was enough for tonight.

"That was very kind of you," I whispered. I backed out of the room, her room, and closed the door quietly behind me.

I finally dropped off to sleep around five in the morning, only to be awakened at nine by Michael, who shook my arm until I awakened. The day was already hot. Heat hung from the trees like laundry.

"Michael!" I said, sitting up on the sofa, reaching for him.

He didn't ask what I was doing sleeping downstairs. He fell into my embrace. I felt his warm breath against my chest; I stroked his long silky hair. I realized that I had almost given up on ever touching him again.

Finally, he stepped back. There was a gauntness to him, a glint of fierce manhood in his eyes. He had not been destroyed; he was stronger.

"Can you drive me to Newburgh?" he asked.

"How badly is she hurt?"

"She'll be all right. She can go home in a few days."

"But she was shot."

"In the side."

"Oh God, Michael. I feel so sorry for you."

"For me?"

"It must have scared you."

He didn't answer. But he seemed grateful that I knew.

"Is this okay with Mom?" I asked.

"She doesn't want to drive me. She's really angry about me running away."

"I am, too, Michael."

He just looked at me.

"Mom says if you want to make the drive, it's okay with her. Carmen's in the hospital there and I have to see her."

"Is Mom awake yet?" I was sitting on the edge of the sofa. I rubbed my hands over my face. I felt alert but exhausted. I looked down at my feet on the carpet. Home.

"All the females are sleeping," said Michael. He put his hand out to me, pulled me up off the sofa.

"Okay," I said. "I'll take you."

"They've got these very tiny visiting hours. We have to hurry."

The sun was bright, though it could not burn through the haze; it was a lemon in a jar of olive oil. We drove south, crossed over the river on a suspension bridge. Below us, the water rushed, bright, new, and blue.

Michael fiddled with the air-conditioner controls and then held his hand up to the vents, shook his head.

"The air conditioning doesn't really work," I said.

"It's okay." He looked out the window; the streets of Newburgh looked desolate, blasted: empty storefronts, boarded-up churches. "I guess I'm in a lot of trouble, aren't I?" he said.

"We'll all have to sit down and talk it over," I said.

"I'm going to need to talk to a lawyer, Mom says."

"You are?"

"I was with him when he was robbing those houses. Going to the Connellys was my idea. I've already had to tell the police everything. I had to snitch."

He had lived in the woods; he had regressed to some elemental state of being, a life of cunning, an animal's existence. He had broken into houses, grabbed what he wanted. What could I tell him? I had longed for this moment, when he was returned to me, without fully realizing that the boy who came back would not be the boy who had disappeared.

"We'll work it out. We'll get a lawyer. And don't worry about snitching. It doesn't sound like you owe that guy Fraleigh very much."

"So what's going to happen to me? And Carmen's in trouble, too. It's not just me. The cops came right into her hospital room and asked her all these questions, and she doesn't have anyone to look after her. Her mom's broke."

"I don't know, Michael. We'll have to sort through it. You shouldn't have run away. Whatever happens, you shouldn't do that, you shouldn't run."

"I'm glad I ran away. I'm glad I met Fraleigh and lived in the woods. I guess it was the best thing that ever happened to me."

"Really? I wonder."

"I did things I never thought I could do. I lived on my own, I took care of myself, I wasn't afraid—I wasn't even that uncomfortable, you know? And I met her. I never would have, otherwise. I would have never even known she existed."

"You must have hated us to do something so mean. We didn't know if you were dead or alive."

"Dad, let's not go into that, okay? We've been through it. I said I was sorry."

"You're sorry? Do you think that's enough?"

"Yes. Anyhow, what else is there?"

There was nothing I could say to that. I felt myself being lowered into a vast silence. It was the silence that is usually just out of our reach, and I longed to be a part of it, the silence of understanding, the silence of acceptance, trust.

"What are they going to do to Mr. Connelly?" Michael asked me.

"I don't know."

"How come he's not in jail?"

"They don't judge harshly when someone shoots during a robbery," I said.

He looked away. He would have liked swift and certain justice, but now he was no longer a child, and justice would never be swift or certain again. It would all be ambiguous from here on in.

"I've been really pissed at Mom," he said, as we pulled into the hospital parking lot. "For not bringing me here."

"That's what they call a lot of nerve."

"I wanted to see Carmen. She's my girlfriend."

"Well, now you're here."

"I knew you'd bring me, Dad."

"You did? Well, you were right."

"You always come through for me. That's the thing. You're always there for me. No matter what." He turned to face me; his eyes were electric with feeling.

"I want to be there for you, Michael. It's what I want most."

"Well, you are. You always are."

I found a parking space, turned off the engine. The heat of the day began immediately to seep into the car.

"Do you want me to come in with you?"

He looked relieved.

"I'll just be a few minutes." He looked at his watch. "It's almost ten-thirty. Morning visiting hours end at eleven."

"I'll wait in the waiting room," I said.

We walked across the parking lot. The sunlight bounced off the roofs of the cars. The hospital was small, Catholic, rundown. On the lawn, daffodils past their bloom decayed

around a steel cross. An elderly nun was gently throwing a
ball back and forth with a little girl with braces on her legs.

While Michael found out Carmen's room number from
patient information, I settled in a green vinyl chair in the
waiting room. The gift shop was directly across, selling fuzzy
stuffed animals, boxes of chocolates, last week's magazines.

"She's in 303," Michael said. He noticed the gift shop. "I
should have brought flowers."

"Do you want to get some? There must be a place
nearby."

"No, it's okay."

"Next time."

He did not reply, but put his hand on my shoulder. I gathered him into my arms and held him close.

"I really want you to meet her," Michael was saying, as
we made our way back to Leyden. "And she wants to meet
you, too."

"I thought you said her mother was probably going to
take her back to the Bronx."

"Yeah, well, maybe she won't." He smiled. "I won't *let*
her. Are you hungry?"

We stopped at a roadside shack called the Hi-Way Diner,
with a large, deteriorating neon rendition of an Algonquin
Indian presiding over its blacktopped parking lot.

"I don't know why the hell I'm so hungry," Michael said,
as we slid into a stiff red booth. The vinyl was patched up
with electrical tape.

"The body has its own mysteries," I said.

"God, it was so great seeing Carmen. You should have
seen her face when I walked in."

I ordered a coffee; Michael asked for a hamburger deluxe,
well done, fries, a Coke. The waitress who took our order was

a tough-looking girl—cracking gum, inky eyeliner, a jutting right hip. Michael watched her ass as she walked away. That was new.

"So Michael," I said. I cleared my throat. "You're back."

"So are you."

"I know. Are you pretty far behind in school?"

"I'll take care of it," he said.

"I think about what it's like to be young now," I said.

"I thought you considered yourself young."

"Me? No. Not at all."

"Well, that's a relief. I thought you did."

"It's hard to be young now, isn't it?"

"I don't know."

"I think it is."

"But you always write about how hard your own childhood and stuff was."

"Gil was difficult. There were mistakes, failures. But the time, it was a good time. The schools were good, the public schools. The teachers worked hard, and it was safe to be there. Most people had jobs. It was just easier. Then the sixties. The party continued. Pot, free love. I was doing some John Retcliffe shit in Detroit and they were playing all those old Motown songs. They're so happy, deliriously happy. Party music, romantic, cheerful. There was never a time to be young like then, never before and never since."

"Can I ask you a question?"

"Sure."

The waitress came with our beverages. Michael smiled at her as she placed them before us.

"There's a free refill on the Coke," she informed him.

When she was out of earshot, he said, "Are you sure you won't get angry?"

"What do you want to know?"

"When are you going to tell Mom about you being with

that woman you met at the photo place, the one you brought home and made us go bike riding with?"

I had been waiting for this, but it didn't make it easier.

"Have you already told her?" I said.

"I was going to. But I can't."

"Do you want to?"

"Do I *want* to? No. Of course not."

"Then don't."

There. My offer was on the table.

"But I *know*. If I don't say, then I'm being on your side."

"I'll tell her myself, Michael. I'm sorry I put you in this position. I can't begin to tell you how bad that makes me feel. But it's over now. I'm going to take care of it."

"She'll divorce you."

"I hope not."

"She will."

"I don't think so. I really don't. Our relationship is too big and too complicated to end over one thing."

"It'll never be the same, though."

"That's true."

"It'll be worse, is what I mean."

"Maybe it'll be better. Are you worse for what happened to you?"

"It's not the same."

"Not entirely."

He took a bite of his hamburger and chewed it slowly.

"I guess we'd better not talk about it anymore."

When we arrived home, Olivia and Amanda were out. Michael went to his room, he said to do homework, but I noticed his book bag was still in the foyer. The message light was blinking on the answering machine, but I didn't listen to it. I sat in my study for a while. I ran my hand over my desk, feeling the grain. I looked out the window. The grass was so vividly green, it seemed to pulsate in the sunlight.

I watched basketball on TV and fell asleep on the sofa and dreamed of my last plane flight and finally awoke to the sound of Olivia and Amanda coming in the front door. I had placed a small gray blanket over me—the kids kept it on the sofa to bundle up in while watching the VCR late at night—and now I cowered under it, too tired to move, but full of alarm: the dream, the sound of their footsteps, their voices.

Amanda came in, dressed in mauve Danskins, sweaty and excited from her movement class. She saw me on the sofa.

"Are you sick?"

"In the head," I said. Big joke.

She sat on the sofa, picked my hair up in little clumps, rubbed it between her fingers like a savvy textiles buyer, let it fall. She smelled of chicken soup and baby powder.

"When are you leaving?" she asked.

"What makes you think I am?"

"Well, are you?"

"I have no plans."

"Oh, there you are," said Olivia, to Amanda. She stood at the edge of the room, holding a large bag of groceries. She looked overheated, distracted. There was a slight downturn at the corners of her mouth, but it didn't seem a product of unhappiness so much as determination. "I thought the deal was you were going to help put everything away."

"I am. I'm just fixing Daddy's head, he's sick in it."

"Go on," I said, "help your mother."

I heard Michael's footsteps upstairs. He must be crossing his room, opening the door, listening, trying to figure what the hell was going on.

I got up, folded the blanket carefully, placed it on the back of the sofa, and walked quickly into the kitchen, where Olivia and Amanda had interrupted their chore of putting the groceries away and sat now at the table, eating those organic instant soups in a recycled cup Olivia favored.

"I'd like a chance to talk to you," I said to Olivia, standing behind her, putting my hands lightly on her shoulders. Palpitations. Music. The whole bit.

"Does that mean I have to talk to you?" she said, managing to make her voice sound merely curious.

"Yes," I said. "It does."

She took another spoonful of her healthy soup. She stuck the spoon in the middle of the cup; the gelatinous goo inside made it stand straight up.

"We'll be right back," she said to Amanda.

"In a while," I said. I linked my arm through Olivia's and whooshed her toward the back door. There was the scent of flowers in the air. My car was in the driveway; the keys were in the ignition.

"Where are you taking me?"

"We'll just take a spin."

"I don't want to take a spin. It reminds me."

"Of looking for Michael?"

"Sam, let me make this easy for you."

"Great. Now you're talking my language."

Despite herself, she smiled. She wanted to touch me, was wondering what it would feel like.

"You're here for a while," she said, reciting it, "you don't know how long you can stay, you have to be back on the road, you need a little rest. . . ."

"No. That's not it at all. Come on, let's at least take a walk."

"I don't want to take a fucking walk."

I gestured as if to say "Fine with me." The heat in her voice silenced me, but I knew I would not be going back in the house without saying what I needed to.

"You know what the worst thing about my childhood was?" I began.

"No. Yes. What? Just tell me."

"I was a part of a conspiracy." I moved away from her. If we would not take a drive, or a walk, I at least wanted to put a little distance between us and our windows. I held my hand out to her and she took it.

"My father—"

"I know, Sam. I know all this."

"My father invited us to join him in his campaign against our mother. And we did it, we just went along."

"That *is* the worst thing."

"And now I've put Michael in the same position." There. The thing was said. The words had been formed, heard; it was really happening—nothing could stop or erase it.

"How?" Her voice lost its clarity; currents of feeling scraped against it, like the wind against the plane when we were falling.

"I slept with Nadia Tannenbaum. She sent me a letter, an angry letter, and Michael found it. He hasn't known what to do about it. It's why he didn't come home after his appointment with Pennyman. His loyalty to me . . . his loyalty to you. It's been a nightmare."

"How often?"

"How often?" I waited for an explanation, but she just stared at me. The color had drained from her face, leaving her eyes pulsating. "How often did I sleep with her? I don't know. A few times."

"How few?" She looked back toward the house, like a swimmer seeing how far she is from the shore.

"Not few enough. Olivia, I'm sorry. I don't want to lose you."

"Oh, please. How many other Nadias have there been?"

"None."

"How long did it go on?"

"Six months."

"Six months. And you made love to her 'a few times' in six months? Give me some credit, okay?"

"I don't know how many times we were together. It was more than a few times."

"Where did you find the time?"

"There was time."

"I'll bet there was. Was I washing your clothes while you were with her? Did Mandy have a cold and was I giving her Tylenol? Where was I?"

"With your back to me."

"Oh, poor you."

"We've been drifting, Olivia."

"We've been *married*. We've been getting older. What were we supposed to do?"

"Olivia, if there was something I could do, anything, to make it so it hadn't happened . . ."

"But there isn't, is there? That's the thing. She called here, you know."

"I'm sorry."

"Oh, I'm sure I deserved this all. I'm sure I deserve every possible humiliation."

"She wants to hurt me."

"So do I."

"Yes. I do, too."

"No. No, you don't get to do that. Are you in love with her?"

"No."

"No?"

I put my hand on her arm and she jerked it away. She was not even making a point; it was sheer instinct.

"Who are you, Sam?"

"I don't know. I've been this creature going around the

country answering questions. I can't bear the sound of my own voice. And I love you."

"Is it my turn now?" she asked.

"For what? Yes."

"You know where I was staying after I left here?"

"Yes. In Poughkeepsie. You told me."

"That's right. But there's more. Come on, let's get into the car."

"All right."

I followed her into her Subaru. The backseat was full of lamps needing to be rewired.

"So," I said. "Poughkeepsie."

"I was there for a few days. I couldn't stay here."

"What were you doing in Poughkeepsie?"

"Staying there."

"Was Amanda with you?"

"Yes."

"Do you just want to tell me what happened, or do you want me to ask you questions?"

"I was with Jack Phillips."

"Who's Jack Phillips?" Though the name was familiar.

"He was helping to look for Michael. The private detective. The dick."

What right to jealousy did I have? Yet there it was, dragging its filthy tail through me. The ashtray in Olivia's car was full of squashed-out Marlboros; I supposed they were his.

"Was this a sojourn romantic in nature?"

"Romantic?"

"You know what I mean. Are you in love with him?" I breathed deeply; I could smell him.

"I was thinking I'd better get tested. I might be pregnant or have some disease. He wouldn't practice safe sex. I'd tell him to put on a condom and he'd pretend to put one on, but half the time he wouldn't. I was furious with him."

The intimacy. It rained down on me like glass.

"Is that all?" I asked.

"You know every man wants a big penis?" she said.

"Is this necessary?"

"But it's as much a pain as it is a pleasure. He kept hitting the tip of my cervix. I don't think I like that very much."

"I don't want to hear one more word," I said.

She shrugged, looked at me for another brief moment, and then let herself out of the car. I sat there, watching her as she walked into the house.

I sat there. I climbed over the gearshift, and now I was in the driver's seat. I gripped the steering wheel. I wanted to go inside, but I didn't know how to. Maybe I needed to drive around a little. I turned on the engine. The radio came on. There was a talk show from somewhere; Ed Bathrick was talking about the Bettor Half. I turned it off. I needed silence. The car motor chugged away. I turned that off, too.

"Let's go out to eat," I announced, walking into the kitchen.

Amanda was helping Olivia cook. Michael was setting the table. He had folded the napkins into complicated shapes.

"We're cooking!" said Amanda.

"What were you doing out there?" asked Michael.

"Just getting used to being here," I said. "And being thankful that I am."

"Yeah," said Michael. "Me, too."

"How do you get used to being in your own house?" said Amanda, as if it was the stupidest thing she'd ever heard.

The night passed. Dinner, not very much conversation. I went to the video store and rented *What About Bob?* and *Groundhog Day.* "A Bill Murray festival," I said.

The phone rang several times. No one made a move to answer it. We let the machine pick it up and didn't listen to the messages. Then Amanda fell asleep on the sofa and I carried her to her bed, tucked her in. She never stirred. When I came down again, the television was off and Olivia had gone to bed.

"Mom's in bed?" I said to Michael.

"I guess."

"I told her, Michael. You don't have to worry about that letter anymore."

"So what did she say?"

"Not an awful lot. We'll work it through."

He was quiet for a few moments.

"I know that I put you through a lot," I said. "And if it seemed as if I was pressuring you to keep my secrets, then I'm sorry, really sorry. Everything was just completely out of control."

"Do I have to keep on seeing Pennyman?"

"You never had to. It was always up to you."

"Are we going to move back to the city?"

"I don't know."

"We've got the money."

"I don't know, Michael. I don't know what's going to happen next. Is that what you want to do?"

He shrugged. "I'm tired," he said. "I'll see you in the morning."

"See you then," I said, trying to keep the excess of emotion out of my voice.

I sat on the sofa, listened to him going up the stairs. His footsteps disappeared down the corridor and then I was alone.

The furnace kicked on, but just for a moment, and then it was silent again.

I stretched out on the sofa and closed my eyes. The house made its noises. Insects ticked against the screens. I fell asleep for a few moments and then put my arm out quickly because I thought I was falling.

I wanted to sleep upstairs, in my own room, and since Olivia had not asked me not to . . .

I slipped into bed next to her. As soon as I did, she rolled onto her back, her eyes wide open.

"Jack Phillips—"

"No," I said. "Not now. No more about him. Please."

"Jack put me into contact with a good lawyer. Michael's in a lot of trouble. He was involved in a lot of bad stuff. Even Russ Connelly might press charges."

"What does the lawyer say?" I could smell her next to me, the warmth coming off her skin.

"You know what I was just thinking?" she said.

"Tell me." I could hear the radio playing in Michael's room, the throb of the bass.

"It's going to cost a fortune."

"Well, for once we've got money."

"And now it's gone."

"I made quite a bit."

"It's going to cost quite a bit." She lifted herself up on one elbow and looked at me.

"I guess that's funny," I said.

I got out of bed to get a glass of water. The floor felt soft, strange beneath my feet. I was still arriving at this place, still somewhere out there trying to get back home. I kept the light off in the bathroom, not wanting to see what I looked like. I leaned against the sink and drank slowly. I sat on the edge of the tub, waiting.

At last, I got back into our bed. Olivia was on her side, breathing softly into her pillow. I was still. I tried to breathe as infrequently as possible. It was good not to be talking. I did not know what to say, and it was too dangerous, putting more words out into the world. I put my hand on her hip, lightly, afraid to disturb her, but needing to feel her. Her flesh, her bones, this woman, next to me at last. The radio went off in Michael's room. The house was quiet now. I moved closer to her, gathered her body in, pressed myself against her. I listened to her breathing, the faint hiss of the sheets as she unconsciously moved toward the simple human warmth of me. This silence I realized was paradise.

A NOTE ON THE TYPE

The text of this book was set in Sabon, a typeface designed by Jan Tschichold (1902–1974), the well-known German typographer. Based loosely on the original designs by Claude Garamond (c. 1480–1561), Sabon is unique in that it was explicitly designed for hot-metal composition on both the Monotype and Linotype machines, as well as for filmsetting. Designed in 1966 in Frankfurt, Sabon was named for the famous Lyons punch cutter Jacques Sabon, who is thought to have brought some of Garamond's matrices to Frankfurt.

Composed by Creative Graphics,
Allentown, Pennsylvania
Printed and bound by The Haddon Craftsmen,
Scranton, Pennsylvania
Designed by Virginia Tan